All Change at

Francesca Capaldi has enjoyed writing since she was a child, largely influenced by a Welsh mother who was good at improvised story telling. She is a member of the RNA and the Society of Women Writers and Journalists. Francesca currently lives in Kent with her family and a cat called Lando Calrissian.

Also by Francesca Capaldi

Wartime in the Valleys

Heartbreak in the Valleys
War in the Valleys
Hope in the Valleys
Trouble in the Valleys

The Beach Hotel Series

A New Start at the Beach Hotel
All Change at the Beach Hotel

All Change
at the
Beach Hotel

Francesca Capaldi

hera

First published in the United Kingdom in 2023 by

Hera Books
Unit 9 (Canelo), 5th Floor
Cargo Works, 1-2 Hatfields
London SE1 9PG
United Kingdom

A CIP catalogue record for this book is available from the British Library.

Print ISBN 978 1 80436 135 1
Ebook ISBN 978 1 80436 134 4

Look for more great books at www.herabooks.com

Printed and bound in Great Britain by Clays Ltd, Elcograf S.p.A.

Dedicated to Mum and Dad, Maureen and Giuseppe (Joe) Capaldi.

Wishing so much that they were here to see the publication of this series.

Prologue

'I'm a grown-up now, for pity's sake. You can't tell me what to do, Carys.'

Liliwen Probert tugged the last piece of clothing from the washing line and dropped it in the straw basket. She looked past the back garden, up the slope of the steep hill that overlooked Dorcalon, to the terrace further up.

'I'm the oldest in the family, look you, and I know better than you do what's good for you, see. And since when has nineteen been *grown up*?'

Lili picked up the basket and started walking down the long garden, calling behind, 'You're not the oldest. Mam's the oldest and she approves of me going, so there.'

Carys followed on, shuffling sideways to talk to her sister. 'Listen to yourself. You even sound like a child. And we all know Mam's not been herself since Da passed.'

'No, *you* say she's not herself.' She stopped suddenly. 'She seems perfectly fine to me.'

Carys grabbed her arm. 'Morys, Wyn and Dilys agree with me, and they're all older than you. And who'll look after Mam if you go away?'

So that was it, was it? She had to forever be her mother's carer, while the rest of them got to be married and have homes of their own?

Moving on once more, Lili shrugged her sister's arm away. 'If I married, I might move away, so what would be the difference? And you're all nearby.'

'But you wouldn't if you married a nice boy from the village. A nice Welsh boy. Like Aneirin Pendry. Or Bryn Lloyd. I'm sure he likes you.'

Lili emitted a groan. Bryn was the farmer's son and the last thing she could imagine was being a farmer's wife. There were so many things she wanted to do, to see. Marrying a boy from the village was the best way she could think of to guarantee that she *never* got to do anything exciting with her life. 'They're all right, I suppose, but not very interesting.'

'Interesting? They're not supposed to be interesting! You're too fussy, that's your problem. What about Henry Austin? He's a nice-looking lad.'

That was true enough, but he still wasn't the one for her.

'And how is working as a chambermaid in a hotel any different to working as a maid up at the Big House? It's still drudgery. And living in, you'll be at their beck and call.'

'Because… because… it just is different!' She looked into the distance, imagining what it would be like. 'The hotel is in a town, not a village, with lots more shops. And there's the beach, right there, behind it, and lots of fancy people to serve, constantly changing, instead of just the mine manager and his family, who aren't really *that* posh.'

'Of course they are!'

'There's a big staff, not just a cook and a washer woman, so lots of people to make friends with, probably from different places theirselves. And the food will be much fancier than what we get for tea breaks and dinner, or lunch as they call it, up at the Big House.'

'But *you* won't get the fancy food. And why do you have to go so far? I mean, Sussex, on the English south coast. If it's by the sea you want to be, why not go to Barry, or even Swansea? They're not so far on the train.'

Yes, why so far? She looked around at the gardens, the long terraces of houses, then sideways to the green slopes of the mountains beyond. They'd moved here when she was nine, and

2

she'd had a good late childhood in this house and a happy youth. They'd never had much money and their house was plain and practical, not like the Big House, where she'd worked the last year as a maid. But she'd been lucky in other ways. Until Da had died of emphysema last year.

She poked her fingers through her black curls to scratch her head, willing herself not to cry. No, that wouldn't do, not in front of her bossy big sister.

Now she simply needed a… change. A chance to see somewhere else.

She dropped the basket and leant against the wall of the outside lavatory.

'I dunno, Carys. It'll only be for a few years, then I'll be back. Who knows, I might bring a nice English husband with me.'

'Well, I *won't* be speaking in English all the time just so he can understand.'

Lili shook her head, gazing into her sister's dark brown eyes, which reflected her own.

There was a click. She looked towards the back gate as it opened. 'Oh no, what are *they* doing here?' She pointed to her older brothers, Morys and Wyn, and her older sister, Dilys. 'Did you send for the cavalry?'

'No. Well. Maybe. If I can't talk some sense into you, maybe they can.'

Lili groaned once more. She'd been planning on doing some gardening for Mam while she was out with Auntie Megan, especially on such a warm day, but it looked like she'd be putting on the kettle and listening to the evidence for the prosecution.

She let them go in ahead of her, stopping briefly in the yard to pull a hand-tinted postcard from her pocket. It was the one that Mrs Bygrove had sent her when she'd been informed that she had the job. The picture was of a large hotel. It looked almost gothic, with its selection of smaller and larger gables with pointed roofs, long chimneys and numerous windows.

Let her siblings have their say. She was going to her new job at the splendid Beach Hotel in Littlehampton, whatever they said.

Chapter One

Liliwen Probert stood at the dark oak desk in the foyer of the Beach Hotel, peeking through the double doors to the sunny exterior. She could have sat on the stool provided, since there was no one around, but she chose not to, feeling important in her latest, temporary role as desk clerk. She looked around the elegant room, with its cream walls, marble floor and crystal chandelier, sighing with satisfaction.

Normally, she served meals in the dining room or drinks in the conservatory for morning coffee and afternoon tea. Even that had only been a recent development, since so many men at the hotel had enlisted in the army. Originally, she'd been a chambermaid and had expected to be so for the rest of her days. Or, at least, until she got married.

Norman. She sighed long and noisily. The possibility of marriage seemed much closer now than when she'd lived in Wales, or when she'd first arrived at the hotel. Or had done. He had enlisted in the army back in February and had been sent to the Western Front a month ago. That nagging worry overwhelmed her once more.

'Whassup with you?' Gertie Green stopped in front of her at the desk, her fingers lodged down the raised collar of the portress's jacket that frequently made her neck itch. She, likewise, was replacing the enlisted men. 'Got a face on you.'

Not wanting to admit she was thinking about her sweetheart, she said, 'Just getting a bit bored, standing doing nothing,' even though she'd been enjoying it. 'It's so quiet this morning.'

Gertie lifted her circular portress's hat by its peak and rearranged it, tucking some of her wayward auburn hair inside. 'Not even many in for morning coffee today, considering it's still August and a sunny day. I'd make the most of it if I was you. We've got quite a few guests coming tomorrow and Saturday, so I'll no doubt be lugging cases up to the rooms.' She blew air out through pouting lips and looked heavenward.

'That's your job, it is. You won't be on your own anyways; either Stanley or Leslie will be on a shift too. And it's better than being a chambermaid, surely. I certainly prefer waiting to cleaning.'

'But you're not doing neither now, are you? You're standing still behind a desk and chattin' to folk.'

'Only for this morning, isn't it, while Mrs Bygrove and Edie are visiting a supplier in town and the other desk clerks have time off.'

'So, where's Mr Bygrove?'

Lili hadn't seen the manager all morning. 'No idea. Probably chatting to the morning coffee guests.'

'Hm. Don't s'pose he's doing anything more useful, that's for sure.'

It wasn't unusual for Gertie to be in such a dour mood, especially since the incident a few months ago when, while working as a chambermaid, she'd been assaulted by a guest as she was cleaning his room. At least she's learned to cheer up when dealing with the clients – even if it was for better tips. But she suspected that, underneath the façade, she was still worried about it happening again. Lili knew that she would have been.

Gertie leant in. 'Oh gawd, here's Major Disaster.'

'Gertie, Major Thomas is a nice old stick. Don't be so mean.'

'Morning, ladies.'

The major, a permanent resident at the hotel, strolled over, twiddling his gingery-grey handlebar moustache, a newspaper under his arm, as was so often the case. As he neared, he pulled the newspaper out and held it aloft. 'Says in here that Italy has declared war on Turkey.'

6

'At least there'll be someone else to fight the Ottomans,' said Lili.

'The war could go on forever at this rate, every country declaring war against half the other countries.'

Lili didn't want to think like this; she wanted to believe that Norman would come home in one piece, and soon.

'I'm off for my daily constitutional. See you later, ladies.' He raised his hand with the newspaper as he made his way to the door.

Lili pointed her finger towards his retreating back and widened her eyes at Gertie. The portress looked confused to begin with, then realised what Lili was getting at. She ran ahead of the major and opened the door for him.

'Much obliged, Gertrude, though it's not necessary.'

When she returned, she leant on the desk. 'See what I mean? More talk of the war. Major Disaster.'

Lili's reply was stalled by the manager, Douglas Bygrove, entering the foyer from the staff corridor in a check suit and cap. He was struggling to get a bag of golf clubs onto his shoulder.

'There he is,' Gertie whispered, creasing her brow. 'He's not going out too, is he?'

'I'm off to the club,' he called over.

Then the answer was yes. Lili shouldn't have been surprised, but something occurred to her.

'Mr Bygrove,' she called. 'Who's in charge?'

'My wife, of course, you silly girl.'

Lili bit back the resentment his insult caused. 'But she's gone to visit some suppliers.'

'She's what?'

Lili and Gertie exchanged brief glances.

'Oh, hm, yes. I vaguely remember her mentioning it. But she knows Wednesday is my morning off.'

She resisted retorting that every other morning seemed to be his morning off. 'Either way, she isn't here.'

'She'll be back soon, no doubt. How long can it take?'

Getting ready to head off once again, he was halted by Lili: 'But who's in charge while neither of you is here?'

He thought for a moment. 'It's not busy and everything is running smoothly, so there's no need to have anyone in charge.' He lifted the clubs once more and carried on, calling, 'Cheery bye'.

'Cheery bye?' Gertie mocked when he'd left. 'I don't care that he's gone, but there should be someone in charge. Since you're standing at the desk, I guess it's you.'

With that, and on spotting a guest leaving, Gertie headed off.

Lili supposed she had sort of been left in charge. She felt important in that moment, deciding to tell her mother about it when she wrote to her next. Even if it wasn't strictly true and she was only *sort of* in charge.

In charge.

Yes, she liked that idea.

The telephone on the desk rang, and Lili lifted the receiver and spoke the words she'd been taught. 'The Beach Hotel. How may I help you?'

Gertie headed back towards the desk and was about to speak, so Lili pointed to the telephone receiver, saying: 'Hello Mrs Bygrove... Oh I see... I'm afraid Mr Bygrove has... yes, that's right.' She pulled a face, hearing the impatience in the manager's wife's voice at guessing her husband had gone out. 'I could, yes... All right.' She wrote down the telephone number of the greengrocer on Beach Road. 'We'll be as quick as we can.' She placed the receiver back down.

'What was all that about?'

'Mrs Bygrove left an important list behind. She did a tour of downstairs this morning, before breakfast, and reckons she left it in one of the rooms. I wonder if you could have a... oh, here's Colonel and Mrs Bradley. Edie did say they'd already paid and had a motor taxi arriving at ten thirty this morning. You'll need to fetch their cases.'

'I'll look for the list when I get back.'

'No, Mrs Bygrove needs it as soon as possible. I'll just have to go myself and hope no one needs attention.'

Gertie pulled her usual face, before turning and striding off to inform the couple she was fetching their luggage.

Lili came out from behind the desk, deciding to check the unoccupied rooms first.

She headed across to the private dining room, its door not far from the entrance. She walked around the six tables in there, envious of the pastel-green walls and wooden panels that stopped halfway up. She wished her room here, up in the staff quarters on the second floor, was decorated in this elegant way. As she headed towards the long windows, she admired the dining chairs, with their inlaid mahogany and rosewood frames and green brocade padded seats. There were heavy curtains in this room, a dark green, tied back with gold tasselled ropes. The room looked out on to the righthand side of the hotel, over the kitchen garden. There was no sign of a list in here.

Back in the foyer once more, she was relieved to see that nobody was awaiting her attention. She moved on to the dining room, turning right into the ballroom. This overlooked the side and back gardens, with their lawns, shrubs and flower beds awash with colour. She walked a little faster, scanning the parquet flooring, with its oak hexagons and walnut stars. She looked under the chairs that sat in lines by various parts of the walls. No, not there either.

She checked the desk in the foyer once more before heading back to the dining room. It had a view of the back lawns, the part nearest the garden being under a glass roof. There were no guests in here currently, only Simon Lane, one of the young waiters, laying the tables ready for luncheon.

'Are you looking for something?' he said.

'A list that Mrs Bygrove left behind this morning.'

'I haven't seen nothing like that.'

She checked underneath the tables anyway, before heading for the conservatory, which was only about a third full. The outside doors weren't open today, like they had been the past few days. Despite being south facing, it was gloomy in here. Phoebe, who'd been commandeered from the stillroom when the men had started enlisting, came over to her.

'I thought you were on the desk this morning.'

'I am.' She explained about the list again.

'Ah, I found it earlier.' She went over to the chest of drawers where they kept cutlery, crockery and glassware, and retrieved it.

'There you go.'

'Thank you so much. Better go and telephone her.'

Returning to the front desk, she was relieved to see that no one was waiting. She felt even more important as she sat on her stool and picked up the telephone receiver to ring Mrs Bygrove.

—

The front entrance opened and Lili looked over to see Gertie struggling in with two cases, in a plume of smoke. She was trying not to cough, judging by the expression on her face.

Behind her was a woman who looked to be in her early thirties, dressed in a burgundy high-waisted linen dress with elbow-length sleeves and turnback cuffs. The skirt had a long, loose hanging tunic, divided in front, which was embroidered. How Lili would love such a dress. The woman's dark-brown wavy hair was gathered in a coil at the back and around her head was a silk band with pink flowers. A cigarette, in a holder, was held elegantly between her fore and middle fingers.

Mrs Lolita Carmichael, if she wasn't mistaken. She'd stayed for a month a couple of years back with her parents, though she'd been Miss Foster then. Mrs Bygrove had mentioned that she'd booked a stay, though Lili hadn't realised she'd be turning up while she was on the desk.

'Come along, girl. Either move more quickly or get out of the way.' She knocked into Gertie as she passed her, causing the portress to stumble a little.

At the desk, the woman stubbed out her cigarette in the ashtray and placed the end in it. She took another from her handbag to replace it in the holder.

'Damn it, I seem to have misplaced my lighter. You, girl—' She pointed at Gertie. 'Retrace our steps and find it. I hope I didn't drop it in the horse bus.'

'Yes, Mrs Carmichael,' Gertie replied politely, though Lili could tell she was annoyed. She left the cases by the desk and hurried outside.

Lili didn't blame her for being irritated. As Stanley, who was a porter along with his twin, had put it, last time she'd stayed she'd been a bit of a pain in the... *neck* came to mind, though it wasn't what Stanley had said. He'd got a right telling off from the housekeeper, Mrs Leggett, for saying it in front of the female staff at supper a few evenings back.

'Good morning. I'm Mrs Lolita Carmichael,' she said with a flourish, as if the name was immensely significant. 'Since neither the usual desk clerks nor the manager appear to be here, I suppose *you* will have to accommodate me. I hope you're up to it. I need to be reminded of the mealtimes and any other information I need to know.' She peered at Lili more closely. 'Good gracious, weren't you a *chambermaid* when I was here last?'

She was amazed Mrs Carmichael remembered her at all, though not pleased with the implication that such a person was beneath her contempt. 'Yes, madam. There's a war on and most of the men have enlisted. I'm afraid the usual desk clerks are off duty and Mr and Mrs Bygrove are... out.' She didn't need to know where they were.

The woman pointed and looked down at Lili. 'I beg your pardon? I can't understand a word you're saying. Where on *earth* are you from?'

'Wales, madam. The Rhymney Valley.'

'Wales, was that? Well, no wonder. I don't know why people can't all speak the King's English, instead of all these silly accents.'

Had Lili not spoken to her when she was here last? Possibly not, since she'd only been cleaning the rooms. *And* she'd put on her more 'proper' accent, as Mrs Leggett referred to it. They all had to when serving the public. Lili felt the indignation growing. It wasn't the first time she'd encountered such prejudice against her accent and place of birth, but for now she'd have to swallow the irritation and get on with the job.

She opened the register in front of her. 'Here we are. Room 208 on the second floor. Lovely view of the sea. If you'd like to take a seat, Gertrude will take you there when she returns.'

'What's that?' Mrs Carmichael put a hand up to her ear. 'Speak more clearly, will you?'

'I said,' she started more slowly, 'if… you'd… like… to—'

'No, it's no good. You'll have to get someone else to attend me. One of the usual receptionists.'

'Neither are here.'

'Or the manager, or his wife.'

'As I said, they're not here either.'

'Well then, whomever is in charge, you insolent girl.'

She understood that then. Lili couldn't see what was insolent about her replies, but if she didn't get out of Mrs Carmichael's presence soon, she'd be severely tempted to give her a piece of her— *Gertie!* Thank goodness she'd returned.

'I found your lighter, madam. It was on—'

The woman snatched the offered item. 'About time.'

'Gertrude, would you fetch Mrs Leggett please?' Mrs Carmichael surely couldn't object to the housekeeper's middle-class accent.

'Why?'

Lili widened her eyes in appeal. 'Please.'

Gertie nodded and headed off.

'One moment, madam.'

'I'd better not be kept waiting.' She sauntered elegantly over to one of the Sheraton chairs by the wall, lighting her cigarette and crossing her legs once she'd sat down.

It was strange how Mrs Carmichael seemed to understand her when it suited. More likely she was enjoying having something to be superior about. Edie, a fellow waitress who was often on the desk because of her background, would have known how to handle this awkward customer.

After a couple of minutes, Gertie returned, not with Imogen Leggett but with Bridget Turnbull, the storekeeper.

'What's the problem, pet?' she said in her Tyneside accent.

'Where's Mrs Leggett?'

'She said she were busy and sent me.'

By this time, Mrs Carmichael had stood up and was walking back to the desk. Lili, guessing what was coming, felt like laughing. It wasn't really funny, but by the time she related it to Edie, hopefully it would be.

'Perhaps *you* can tell me the relevant information in an accent I can understand.'

Mrs Turnbull looked a little shocked initially, but soon rallied. 'Why hinny, of course I can. Now what is it you'd like to know, pet, before we get yoursel' settled in.'

Lili pressed her lips together. If anything, Mrs Turnbull had made her accent even stronger.

Mrs Carmichael looked aghast before she announced: 'That's even worse. I've never understood Scottish accents.'

'I'm a Geordie, pet, though it is true my mother was from over the border.'

'What? What? This is Sussex, for pity's sake. Is there not anyone local here?'

Gertie put up her hand meekly. 'Me?'

'Oh, you're an imbecile. I don't suppose you can string two sentences together?'

Gertie's mouth opened in shock. Although Mrs Carmichael had been difficult before, Lili couldn't recall her being this rude to the staff. She had no doubt that she'd have been less than polite in return had Major Thomas not entered the building at that moment.

'Hello again, ladies. Good day… Miss Foster, if I recall correctly.'

'Mrs Carmichael now,' she corrected.

'Major Thomas,' said Lili. 'Perhaps *you* can help out here with… interpreting, if nothing else.'

He strolled over. 'Interpreting what? I speak a smattering of French and a little German, that's all.'

Mrs Carmichael explained the situation in her plummiest voice yet, pointing accusingly at each of them.

When she'd finished, Major Thomas said: 'All I can say, *young woman*, is that you are being extremely impolite.'

'What? But I—'

'Yes, impolite. I have never had any problem understanding Miss Probert, although I have never had the privilege of speaking with this young lady here,' he said, pointing to the storekeeper, who blushed.

'Bridget, that is, Mrs Turnbull. I don't normally come out and meet the guests.'

'Pleased to meet you. I served with a Newcastle man in the regiment. Captain Routledge. Good chap, he was. Not at all difficult to understand, if you make the effort.'

'That's *your* opinion,' said Mrs Carmichael. 'I'm sorely tempted to walk out and find somewhere else. I never had this much trouble last time. But since it's the most luxurious hotel in the area—'

'It sounds to me like *you* are the one causing the trouble,' said the major.

'How dare you!'

An argument broke out, leaving the staff present speechless. This was not going to go down well with Mr and Mrs Bygrove when they heard about it.

So much for being in charge, thought Lili.

Chapter Two

'I'm glad we're back before the lunch period,' said Helen, as they approached the hotel from the opposite side of the road.

It never ceased to amaze her that she owned this magnificent edifice. That is, her husband owned it, even if it had been bought with her mother's inheritance. It looked striking, with its red brickwork, its terrace and the balcony that curved all the way around the building. As soon as she and Douglas had seen it, they'd known it was the place they'd wanted to buy. The extensive gardens had clinched it. How excited they'd been. In the other hotels and guesthouses they'd viewed, the grounds had been minimal. The public house on the side, with its short clock tower, had been their one misgiving and they'd considered converting it into a function room of some sort. But it had proved to be an asset with its professional, middle-class clientele, not a gathering place for drunkenness and trouble as they'd feared.

'I'm sure Lili will have coped admirably with the front desk,' said Edie, rousing Helen from her thoughts. 'She seems a firm favourite in the restaurant, with her sunny nature and proficiency. Even among those sceptical about women taking over from the waiters.'

No sooner had they stepped in, Helen was wishing they had taken a little longer. At the desk stood Lili, Mrs Turnbull, Gertie – *and the major* – being shouted at by Mrs Carmichael. She remembered her being a slightly difficult guest when she was here a couple of years ago.

'What on earth…?' she whispered.

'Oh heavens, I think I know that woman.' Edie sounded alarmed. It must be someone from her past life before she came to Littlehampton.

'I'd better sort this out. I didn't think she'd arrive this early.' Helen strode over, performing the wide smile she'd long practised for difficult guests. 'Mrs Carmichael, how nice to see you back. Is there something I can help you with?'

She noticed Edie hang back.

Mrs Carmichael turned, clutching her cigarette holder aloft, her lips in a stiff line. 'Yes, I should say there is. I'm trying to get to my room and find out a few details, and I cannot comprehend a word your... your *regional* staff are saying.'

'Regional?'

'Yes, yes, regional.' She took three determined steps away, then returned. 'I do not recall so many staff from outside the county when I was last here. Or chambermaids in the place of porters and desk clerks.' She pointed at Gertie and Lili as she spoke.

'That, young lady, is unnecessary,' the major barked, as if talking to someone in his long-ago battalion. 'These young women have done very well, stepping into the breach.'

'I only came here because my dear husband has enlisted, being the hero he is, and I wanted a distraction from my sorrow.' Mrs Carmichael closed her eyes and tipped her head back, wearing an expression of grief.

'Mrs Turnbull, what are you doing out here?' Helen asked.

Before the woman had a chance to speak, Lili replied, 'I asked Gertie to fetch Mrs Leggett, but she was busy.'

While Bridget seemed amused by the exchange, Helen could tell that Lili was upset. Afraid this might turn into an even bigger argument, she decided to take over. However, Edie now swept forward.

'Maybe *I* could assist you.'

'Oh, that's better. Another voice I can... Good gracious, is that you, Miss Moreland?'

'It certainly is, Miss Foster. Or Mrs Carmichael, as I gather you now are.' She went through the counter and stood next to Lili.

'That's right. I'm married now.' She showed Edie the two rings on the third finger of her left hand. 'But what on earth are *you* doing, working in a hotel?'

'It's a long story and I do not have time to share it currently. And I'm known as Miss Moore here. Or Edie.' Even though the staff and management now knew of her background and the reason for her name change, she didn't feel inclined to keep explaining it to others. 'Now, let us get you signed in, your questions answered and safely deliver you to your room.'

Helen smiled. Mrs Carmichael was the daughter of a rich, though untitled, Sussex businessman, but Edie's presence seemed to have confounded the woman's attempts at condescension.

A couple came through the door, bringing Helen back to the job in hand. 'Lili, you see to Mr and Mrs Aldous.' They didn't seem to have any problem with Lili's accent.

'Yes, Mrs Bygrove.'

'Major Thomas, is there anything I can help you with?'

'No, no, I was just helping Miss Probert out. I'm heading out for another walk and will be back for luncheon.'

'Mrs Turnbull, you may return to your duties.'

'And right grateful I am for that,' she muttered, before pottering towards the staff door.

'If that answers all your questions,' Edie said to Mrs Carmichael, 'then Gertrude will show you to your room.'

Gertie pursed her lips, making Helen afraid there would be more trouble. At that moment, the staff door opened once more and Leslie entered the foyer. He must have come to take over from her.

'Mr Morris is on duty now, so he'll show Mrs Carmichael up.' Helen gestured to him to hurry over. Gertie didn't wait for him to catch up but headed off straight away.

'That's a *much* better idea,' said Mrs Carmichael, eyeing the young porter up and down appreciatively.

He picked up her suitcases and led her to the lift. Once there, she made it clear that *she* would take the lift, but he could take the cases up the stairs.

By the time he'd reached the first step, Lili had finished with the other guests' request for information on the local entertainment.

'I'm sorry about that, Mrs Bygrove,' she said, 'but Mrs Carmichael was terribly rude, she was. I'm sure she could understand us. I was speaking as Mrs Leggett instructed. It's not like I was speaking Welsh now, is it?'

'Don't worry about it, Lili,' said Helen. 'You'll always get people like her. Mr Watkins has certainly dealt with a few in his time. It's just a matter of learning how to handle them.'

'Perhaps we should pretend not to understand her rather put-on posh accent?' Edie chuckled. 'I am jesting, of course.'

'It would be tempting,' said Helen.

Lili looked forlorn. 'I feel I've let you down.'

'Not at all. It's a shame my husband wasn't here. So, did he say where he was going?'

'To play golf. It was shortly after you left.'

Helen willed her face to show no emotion. She had specific-ally told Douglas yesterday that she'd be out this morning. Did he genuinely not remember, or had he not bothered listening in the first place?

'I see.' She smiled. 'You need to go on your lunch break now. You're on an early one, I believe.'

'Yes, but Mr Watkins isn't here yet, to take over.'

'Don't worry. I'll fill in until he arrives.'

Lili scampered off to the staff door.

'So, you know Mrs Carmichael, then?' said Helen.

Edie nodded. 'She moved in the same circles as me when I was still at home, something of a social butterfly. Her father had business dealings with my father now and again.'

'Are you not worried that she recognised you?'

'No, not now everyone here knows. And my parents know I'm here. It's funny though, isn't it? All that time I could have been spotted, and only my brother's friend, Dan, and the governess, Mrs Harrison, found out my secret. I'm glad Lolita didn't come to stay before, for she is known to be a tittle-tattler.'

'What if she spreads it around that you're here?'

'Let her. I really don't care. And there's nothing to be ashamed about, working here.' She placed her hand on Helen's arm and smiled warmly.

'Go on now, I believe you're on an early lunch break too, aren't you?'

'That's right. I wonder where Mr Watkins—'

She hadn't finished when he came rushing through the staff door. 'Sorry for my tardiness, Mrs Bygrove. The train from Lancing was late. Thank you for holding the fort.'

Helen followed Edie to the staff area. 'I think I'll collect the children's lunches from Mrs Norris now and eat with them and Vera. Then I'll be ready for any staff shortfalls that might occur over luncheon.'

Unlike Douglas, who might well be out until mid-afternoon. As was becoming increasingly usual.

'Mumm-eeee,' cried five-year-old Arthur, as he came careering down the corridor towards Helen. Seven-year-old Dorothy came skipping after him, grinning broadly.

It was lovely having them home on weekdays during the summer holidays, but she felt sad she couldn't spend more time with them. If only Douglas pulled his weight a little more, as he used to, then maybe she could.

'Children, Mummy's busy,' called their young nursemaid, Vera.

'It's all right, Vera. I was planning on having lunch with them now anyway.'

'Very well, madam. I'll fetch the meals from the kitchen.'

'Pass the milk over, Fanny.' Lili held her hand out, ready to take the jug from the chambermaid.

'Can't you reach it yourself?'

'No, otherwise I would.'

Fanny Bullen took a sip of her tea, before complying with the request.

Young Jack Sinden, the sous chef since various others had enlisted, scurried into the staff dining room, keeping hold of the door.

'You lot, come 'ere and listen to this.'

Fanny was the first to rise, followed by Annie Twine and her sister Alice, two of the scullery maids.

'What on earth?' Mrs Leggett barked.

Fanny was soon back. 'There's a right to-do going on upstairs. Sounds like Mrs B is giving Bygrove hell.'

'Sit down at once.'

The maid left, ignoring the housekeeper, prompting a couple more staff members to go to the hall.

'I give up.' Mrs Leggett raised her hands in frustration.

Lili couldn't resist any more and lifted her legs over the bench seat to get out. She noticed Edie stay put.

In the corridor, Jack had the door to the back stairs open and the staff there were gathered around it. As Lili joined them, she could make out voices. They weren't as loud as she'd expected, but it certainly sounded like an argument.

'As I was coming down,' Jack whispered, 'I 'eard Mrs Bygrove give 'er 'usband a right earful for going out when 'e knew she was off to visit suppliers this morning.'

'Quite right too,' said Lili.

Annie tutted. 'Like he'd take any notice.'

The door upstairs clicked open and, as one, they stepped back, as a louder voice announced: 'Let me remind you, Helen, that *I* am manager here and you are simply my wife.'

'Lazy clod, more like,' Lili murmured.

'Now, I'm going down to do my job and I suggest you do yours.'

Jack pushed the door closed quietly and they all scarpered back to the dining room.

'Bygrove's coming,' Fanny announced in an undertone. 'And he's in a right mood.'

Lili half expected Mrs Leggett to say, *That's* Mr *Bygrove to you*, as she once would have done. But since the incident with Lord Fernsby assaulting Gertie, and Bygrove's consequent support of the vile noble, the housekeeper seemed to have lost any respect she'd had for the manager.

The room went silent as they heard the back stairs door open and close. The manager's footsteps faded into the distance.

Lili sighed with relief and noticed several others do the same. It wasn't long before the murmur of chatter started up again.

Shortly after, the door to the dining room opened and several of them jumped. But it was only Mrs Bygrove.

'Lili, Edie, would you come and see me in the kitchen after you've finished. I'd like to talk to you and Mrs Norris about the final arrangements for Monday's event.'

'Yes, Mrs Bygrove,' the two women replied in unison.

When she left, Fanny piped up: 'What's all that about then? Are you two teacher's pets again?'

Lili was about to retort sharply, but Edie got in first, more calmly. 'It's the event for the wounded soldiers in local hospitals. And it's raising money for the Red Cross hospital at Belgrave House at the same time.'

'Oh, that. Didn't want to be involved with that anyway, seeing men with missing limbs and wounds. Ugh.'

Mrs Leggett scraped her chair out and stood. 'Miss Bullen, those men have been injured fighting for their country, and certainly don't need your disgust to add to their troubles.'

Lili and Edie glanced at each other, surprised at the intervention.

'I know they have, but, well, I've seen some walking along the streets and being wheeled like babies with 'alf a leg. Not nice, it's not. They should be kept inside.'

'What an appalling view. How would you like it if it was your brother, or father, or uncle and someone said that?'

'I ain't got no brother, or… or… uncle.'

'That's not the point.' Mrs Leggett picked up her teacup and placed it on the tray with the used cups. 'I do wonder about your upbringing, Miss Bullen, to have such bitter opinions.'

Fanny pursed her lips and hung her head, then fiddled with her thick tawny hair, which was sprouting out of its bun.

'Well, I'm looking forward to bringing some cheer to those young men,' said Lili. 'I know how I'd feel if it were one of my brothers.'

'Good for you, Miss Probert.' The housekeeper rose and walked away.

Lili and Edie gave each other a *well fancy that!* look, before draining their cups and rising for their meeting with Mrs Bygrove.

–

It had felt like a very long day to Lili, by the time afternoon tea had finished. With a little free time until early supper, she and Edie had decided to take a walk on the promenade. The gloom had cleared a little during late afternoon and the sun was peeping out from behind the clouds.

'I'm looking forward to blowing a few cobwebs away,' said Lili, as they walked over the wide grassy common between the hotel and the beach.

'It hasn't been an easy day, that's for certain, what with Mrs Carmichael and Mr Bygrove, and that minor spat at afternoon tea. What on earth was it all about?'

'Oh, just one table of guests overhearing something about the war from another, and then having a disagreement with them about it. Lucky, it was, that Mrs Bygrove was on hand to sort it out, and that the guests were willing to apologise and calm down. Dunno where Bygrove was.'

'Shut away in his office, I believe. Feelings do often seem to be running high with the guests at the moment. I suppose it's the war.'

'Talking of which, I had a letter from Norman earlier.'

'What does he say?'

'I haven't read it yet. I'm saving it for this evening.' Lili smiled, imagining holding the letter against her heart, as she had when Mrs Leggett had handed it to her.

'It must be coming up to a year that you've been sweethearts now,' said Edie. 'It was September last year you started walking out, wasn't it?'

'You're right, it was. The tenth of September. And it's just over a year ago since we met, that time I was taking a walk with you. Rather like we are now!'

She recalled his brilliant chirpy smile. It's what had first attracted her to him. And when they shook hands, his was so soft and warm. She got a little thrill in her tummy, thinking about it. Then, when she'd bumped into him again, by the Oyster Pond, it was like it was meant to be.

'You were interested in him the first time you met him, weren't you?'

'I was. He seemed so... *nice*.' She giggled.

'I still can't believe I didn't know you two were walking out until nearly Christmas, when Charlie and I saw you in town.'

They'd been shopping for presents, having just had some lunch out. They'd spent such a lovely day together.

'I'm sorry I kept it from you. I know it sounds silly, but I felt like if I told someone, it would all end.'

'Well, nearly a year on, and you're still together.' Edie tipped her head sideways. 'Albeit, at a distance, sadly.'

'Yes. Like you and Charlie.'

They both became quiet as they strolled. Lili took in the scene before her. Streetlights graced the length of the prom, along with occasional benches and shelters. There were striped beach huts every few yards, some with groups of people gathered around them on chairs. A couple of long, slim wooden boats were being pushed into the water on a tide that was part way out. A Punch and Judy show, set up on a flat piece of sand near a groyne, was entertaining a group of children. A couple of nannies were walking along the prom with perambulators, chatting.

Lili looked back at the beach to see a group of children making sandcastles: girls in short summer dresses and sunhats, boys in sailor suits.

Children. One day, God willing, she would bring her own children here. She pictured herself walking along the prom with Norman and their children. She wondered how many they would have. Two girls and two boys would be nice. Would they be dark like her, with her black curls and deep-brown eyes, or fairer, like Norman, with his mid-brown hair and blue eyes? Maybe a combination.

She was thinking about the names she'd like to give them when she was roused from her daydream by a bicycle bell behind. Edie jumped at the sound, before the two of them stepped to one side to let it pass.

'Oh dear, I can see him getting into trouble before he gets to the end of the promenade.' Edie pointed to the sign ahead: *No cycles allowed on the Parade.*

The interruption brought the daydream about Norman to an end. It was probably better not to ponder such things. It could be a while before the war ended.

'Are you all right?' said Lili. 'You've gone a little pale.'

'As much as I love walking on the promenade, I'm always a little nervous that someone will jump out on me.'

'Well, it's only been, what, nine days since Gordon Hadley attacked you on here, so it's bound to affect you for a while.'

Lili thought back to that terrible day, when someone Edie had known, Pamela Brownlow, had been killed by the same man.

'It could so easily have been me lying in the mortuary, alongside Pamela.'

'Are you all right, Edie? It was such a relief that it was all over, that we've not given much thought to how it might still be affecting you. Selfish of us, that was.'

'Helen did ask if I wanted time off to stay with my sister-in-law, Lucia, but, to be honest, I'd rather work, and keep cheerful, so that I have little time to think about it.'

'As long as you're sure. Do talk to me if you have any worries, won't you?'

Edie smiled at Lili and took her hands. 'I will. Thank you, for being concerned.'

'Of course I'm concerned. Any news yet as to when they're planning to release Pamela's body for burial?' Lili shivered a little, saying those words, since she hadn't long lost her sister-in-law, Jane, to the consumption.

'I've no idea. Inspector Davis said he'd let me know.' Edie checked her wristwatch. 'Let's forget that for a while. We should be able to make it to the river and back before early dinner. Or would you rather sit and read your letter?'

'I haven't brought it with me. Like I said, I'm saving it for after my last shift. I 'ope there are no more dramas. I shall be glad when this day's ended.'

'So will I,' Edie agreed.

With that, they linked arms and carried on.

Chapter Three

The last of the ham and tomato canapés had gone from the salver Lili was holding. The canapés they were serving tonight were not fancy and expensive like the usual ones provided here. There were no Canapés à l'Amirals, topped with prawns and caviar, for the wounded men from the local hospitals, like there'd been at the wedding reception they'd held here last Saturday. She passed Mr Bygrove, talking to an officer with an arm in a sling, explaining how the event had been all his idea. She pursed her lips.

'It is indeed a splendid place to hold such an event,' said the officer in a plummy voice. 'The best in the area, by a long chalk, what what?'

Bygrove lifted his chin and put on that pompous grin he so often displayed these days. 'Indeed it is, sir, indeed it is.'

At least the event was being held in the elegant white ball-room, with its arched mirrors, fancy embossed walls with pillars and intricate crystal chandeliers. It was nice that these men could experience a little bit of luxury, after all they'd been through.

As she neared the door to the dining room, she grinned, imagining she heard a voice from the Valleys. She stopped. Could it be? Looking towards a group of four men, she noticed one regaling the others with a tale of some misdemeanour in his youth. Her breath hitched. He was handsome, oh my he was, with his thick black hair and large brown eyes, the colour of conkers. He had a long straight nose, full lips and a dimple in his chin. He was leaning on a walking stick.

She shook herself and carried on. What a wanton piece she was. Poor Norman was away on the Western Front and here she was eyeing up another man. But there was nothing in it, just an appreciation of an attractive face, like she would have had at the picture house, watching Rudolph Valentino on the screen. However, the weird, squirmy feeling – she could think of no other description for it – lasted until she got into the kitchen.

Lili placed the empty salver on the table. 'Could I have another one with the ham and tomato, please, Mr Fletcher?'

'Right you are, love. Could you manage a tray of cheese and chutney ones too?'

'Of course.' They really were just cheddar and ordinary onion chutney today. For the guests it would have been a nice French camembert with fig conserve.

Returning to the ballroom with the two trays, she found that the Pierrots had started singing. Tonight, rather than their usual baggy costumes with pompoms, they were in evening dress, though she suspected their repertoire would be the same since the current song was *Where Did You Get That Hat?* The chatter had decreased, but not stopped.

She passed the group of men where the Welsh voice had been, not looking over at Mr Handsome, as she seemed to have nicknamed him.

'Hey there, hold on a moment!'

It was his voice, she was sure. It was tempting to walk on, pretend she hadn't heard, but that wouldn't be very welcoming now, would it?

She turned and smiled.

'Hello sir. After some canapés are you? These are both very nice.'

His eyes widened in surprise and a smile formed. 'Good gracious, is that a Valleys voice I'm hearing?'

'It is indeed. The Rhymney Valley, to be precise.'

'It almost feels like I'm 'ome.'

His grin widened, lighting up his face, making her stomach do that wobbly thing again.

'I'm from Aber Valley, originally,' he said.

'Well, I never. It's good to hear a Welsh voice.' She was supposed to be serving, not chatting, but then, she was only being friendly, as they'd been instructed.

She held up the salver and he took a ham and tomato canapé, as did the three men he'd been talking to. One had a partially amputated arm in a sling, one was on crutches with a foot missing, while the other had a bandage over his eye. She should have moved away by now, offered the canapés to others, but she couldn't resist staying to chat awhile.

'Are you all from Belgrave House Hospital?'

'That's right,' said the Welsh soldier, a corporal by the look of the two chevrons on the arm of his jacket. 'And we're all from the 7th Battalion, Royal Sussex Regiment.'

'These are good,' said the one with the sling. He was blond with a floppy fringe and a middle-class accent. 'The hospital food's not bad, but, well, the food here is marvellous. And it's the corporal's birthday today. It's a good way to celebrate.'

'Happy birthday, Corporal,' said Lili. 'Here, try one of these.' She lifted the salver of cheese and chutney canapés towards them.

'Thank you.'

The other three embarked on a discussion of their food experiences during the war. The corporal turned towards her.

'I'm Corporal Morgan, by the way. Rhodri Morgan.' He held out his free hand.

She placed one tray down on the table beside her to shake it, glancing around quickly to make sure neither the manager nor his wife were close by. 'Liliwen Probert. Lili. I work here, as a waitress. And sometimes on the desk.' Only once, but it sounded good.

'Nice to meet you, Lili.'

'Likewise. Have you been at the hospital long?'

'A few weeks. Took a bullet to the thigh. But I'm being discharged soon.'

'So, you'll be going back to the war?' She felt an over-whelming sadness at this prospect, as she did at the thought of any of the more able-bodied of these men returning to the Front.

He lifted his walking stick. 'I still have a limp, so it seems unlikely. Think I'm destined for a desk job.'

She wanted to reply, *every cloud has a silver lining*, but didn't know how he would take that. Instead, she said: 'I see.'

'Miss Probert, what have you been told about chatting to guests?'

She turned sharply to find the manager standing behind her. Just her luck.

'My apologies,' said Corporal Morgan. 'It's my fault, sir. I engaged the young lady in conversation when I heard her Welsh accent, see. Like a taste of 'ome, it were.'

'Well, yes, of course, Corporal. We're happy to, er, cheer people up. She does need to hand out the canapés though.'

'Of course.' The corporal gave a quick bow of his head.

Lili picked up the salver from the table and walked away, sorry to be doing so. She noticed Edie raise her eyes at her as she passed by, no doubt a comment on Bygrove's intervention. Her first destination was a pair of men in wheelchairs, being attended by a nurse. The Pierrots had finished their song and a comedian had come to the front of the room. The audience became quieter to listen to his jokes. Lili moved among the crowd of wounded soldiers and some paying guests, the elite of the town, who'd been willing to make a contribution to the fundraising. There was laughter at the jokes, which she found funny too.

About four o'clock, the crowd began to thin out. Lili was heading for the door with yet another empty tray when Corporal Morgan waylaid her.

'I'd just like to say thank you for the lovely afternoon. I've wondered several times, as I've passed by this hotel, what it was like inside. And now I know. It's even more luxurious than I'd imagined.'

'I'm glad you enjoyed it. And I 'ope you're completely well soon, Corporal.'

'Thank you. And I 'ope we bump into each other again.'

She simply smiled, not knowing how else to reply to that, apart from: 'Cheerio then.'

'Bye bye. For now.'

He limped off to the door, where the blond friend and the one with the bandaged eye were waiting for him. He turned to give her one last glance.

'He seemed interested in you.'

Lili jumped. 'Oh, don't creep up on a body like that. Thought you were Bygrove first off.'

Edie laughed. 'Do I sound like Bygrove?'

'No. What do you mean, anyway?'

'The corporal. You two seemed to be having a nice chat earlier. Then I noticed his eyes, following you around the room.' She raised her eyebrows twice and displayed a cheeky grin.

'Oh Edie, of course they weren't. It was just nice having a chat with someone from 'ome. He's from down the road, in Aber Valley.'

'You still think of the Valleys as home then?'

'I'm not sure, really.'

Edie nudged her. 'Look out, here comes Bygrove.'

They headed off in different directions.

–

Rhodri Morgan exited the hotel to blue skies and a warm breeze, feeling a lot jollier than when he'd entered it.

'You've cheered up,' said his pal, Chris, scratching at his arm stump in its sling, even though it was bandaged.

'It were a good do. It were nice of such a premier hotel to put on an entertainment for us.'

'You seemed quite taken by the pretty little waitress too,' teased his other friend, Mike. 'Reckon she was the main entertainment for you, mate.'

'It were nice to hear an accent from 'ome, that's all.'

'You keep telling yourself that, mate.'

'Come on, Mike, leave the poor lovesick boy alone.' Chris put on a bad Welsh accent to add: 'Found his soulmate from the Valleys, 'asn't he, *bach*?'

Rhodri looked heavenward. 'Can't even have a bit of a chat with a waitress without you two seeing too much in it. A coupla days back you were accusing me of 'aving a fancy for Nurse Caffyn.'

'We're only teasing,' said Chris. 'You've not got wives like us two. Reckon it's time you got yourself a nice girl.'

He thought it was too, but she had to be the *right* girl. He'd felt an instant attraction to Lili when she'd appeared in that room. Such a fancy room, but she'd outshone it. It didn't mean she was the right one for him though.

'Love at first sight, was it, *boyo*?' said Mike, putting on his own version of the accent.

Rhodri shook his head. 'Don't believe in such a thing, I don't. It's illogical.'

'Love ain't logical, mate.' He tapped Rhodri on the shoulder twice with his hand.

Either way, was he ever likely to bump into her again? He didn't want to stalk the poor girl. And he might be gone from here soon.

'We've got that concert on the Common to go to next Tuesday,' said Chris. 'You'll likely find a nice girl there.'

'Who knows?'

Maybe it would be better to forget Miss Lili Probert, with her silky black curly hair, eyes as dark as plain chocolate and her pretty lips.

'Come on, you're dawdling,' said Chris.

'Yes, yes, I'm coming.'

–

'Good morning, Mr Janus,' said Lili, as she approached the owner of the local Kursaal. He'd looked a little down but perked up when she greeted him.

'Good day to you, Lili. Fancied breakfast out this morning.'

'Thank you for donating the services of some of your entertainers on Friday. They were much appreciated by the soldiers at the do.'

'Poor young men. It was the least I could do. Can't serve myself, being a bit long in the tooth. Some of them have certainly suffered with their missing limbs and whatnot.' He tutted three times and shook his head.

'Thank goodness for our wonderful 'ospitals, treating them for free.'

'For now, while there's a war,' Mr Janus said, with a sigh. 'Not sure what'll happen to them afterwards. Sorry to be so gloomy, but yet another one of my troupe enlisted yesterday. That's five now. I daresay they'll all be gone soon. The men anyway. I admire them but worry for them too. They're like family.'

'I can understand that. The live-in men who've enlisted from here were like family too.'

'I can imagine, with you all living under one roof. Now it seems, I'm also going to have to change the name of The Kursaal.'

'Why is that?'

'Too many complaints about it sounding Germanic. I've resisted it until now, but I'm going to have to bow to pressure.'

'What will it be called instead?'

'The Casino Theatre. Doesn't have the same ring.'

Lili had spotted Edie walk into the dining room to speak to various guests. Mrs Bygrove must have sent her to make sure everything was all right.

'I suppose it's better than losing trade,' Lili replied to Mr Janus.

'Indeed. Now two of the girls in my troupe are unwell and I'm short of acts for the charity event I'm involved in on

Tuesday, to raise money for the Duchess of Norfolk's home for disabled soldiers and sailors on South Terrace.'

Edie must have overheard, as she headed over to say: 'You're short of singers, Mr Janus?'

'Why yes, I am, Miss Moore. I don't suppose you have a decent voice, do you?'

'Only for singing in a crowd in church. But Lili here has a beautiful voice.'

Lili reddened. 'Oh, I wouldn't say—'

'She used to sing in her chapel choir and performed many solos.'

Mr Janus looked up at her hopefully. 'You did?'

'Well, yes. But only hymns, of course.'

'I've heard you sing plenty of popular songs while you were cleaning the rooms.'

'Um, yes. I…' She wasn't sure what to say. The choir master had declared that she had the best voice in the village, along with Anwen Rhys, but she didn't want to go blowing her own trumpet. She'd only told Edie about it.

'Miss Moore.' They all looked around to see Mrs Bygrove coming towards them. 'The artists are asking to speak to you in reception as they value your local knowledge of galleries and theatres.'

'Mr Janus was just saying he's short of singers for Tuesday's charity show on the Common and I was telling him what a beautiful voice Lili has. Do you think we could spare her?'

'Oh, I dunno about—' Lili started.

'I would be eternally grateful if you could.' Mr Janus held two fists to his chest and put on an appealing expression.

'Of course we could,' said Helen. 'Lili is part of the team collecting money that afternoon anyway.'

'But I've never sung in a concert.'

'What about those… what were they called?' said Edie. 'Gamanver somethings.'

'*Gymanfa ganus...* singing competitions,' Lili added, when the other two looked confused.

'And didn't you win a few prizes?'

'Um. Yes.' She could hardly lie about it.

'That's settled then,' said Mr Janus. 'Would you be able to come to see me when you've got a break between shifts, to tell me what you'd like to sing? I haven't much of a band left but—'

'I won't need a band, if that helps.'

'Yes, it does. But I do have a pianist. That's the least I can do. Come to talk to me and I'll give you a rundown of the programme so you can choose what you'll sing. I'll add you to the end.'

'You can go this afternoon, about three o'clock,' said Helen.

'Come to the Kursaal... Casino Theatre. I'll make sure the pianist is there.'

Mrs Bygrove directed Edie back to the foyer.

'Right, Mr Janus. Have you decided on breakfast?'

'It'll be the prunes, then the fresh herrings for me. Followed by a... sultana scone and some marmalade, please. And a lovely pot of your Darjeeling.'

'Very well, sir.'

Lili took the menu from him and headed for the kitchen. Her heart was racing due to the rising panic. Singing in front of an audience, yes, she'd done that before, but in a village she'd grown up in, where she knew almost everyone. And she hadn't sung properly for, well, *years.*

It was for a good cause. But if she sounded dreadful, people wouldn't give any money. They might even boo her.

Really, Liliwen Probert!

She was genuinely petrified though. Perhaps she could find somewhere to practise. Or try out some songs on her fellow workmates this evening.

'Whassup with you?' Nelly Norris asked as Lili entered the kitchen. 'Looks like you've lost a half crown and found a penny.'

'Nothing much. Mr Janus wants prunes, then fresh herrings, followed by a scone and marmalade.'

'Righty-ho. And here's the lamb collops and grilled ham for table six.'

'Lovely. I'll just give Mr Janus's tea order to the still room.'

She was soon back to pick up the two plates, then headed to the dining room, wondering what she should sing.

–

What on earth had Edie got her into?

Lili didn't know whether to be excited or terrified as she walked along High Street in Littlehampton on Monday, on her afternoon off.

Terriified was winning so far.

She'd decided that, to perk herself up, she'd buy a new blouse to wear tomorrow, during her 'debut', as she joked to herself it was. She had enough money for it – if it wasn't too expensive.

She looked in a shop window, halfway down the street. She'd been here before. They had a nice selection and weren't too expensive. While debating with herself whether she really needed a new blouse, she heard a voice call.

'Hello there. It is you, Lili. I thought it was.'

'Yes, it's me. Hello Flo.'

Florence Stubbs, Norman's sister, stood shyly, twiddling her fingers. She was a slim girl, even more slender than Lili. A little underweight really and her clothes always looked slightly large on her, like a little girl waiting to grow into hand-me-downs. She knew what that was like.

'How are you, Lili? Haven't seen you for a while.'

They'd only met twice: Christmas Day last year and just before Norman enlisted in February. Lili had been tempted to ask her to have tea in town on a day off, but she hadn't been quite sure whether Florence liked her or not, or whether it was just her shyness that made her reluctant to say much to her.

'I'm fine. On an afternoon off. How about you?'

'Me?' Florence pointed to herself. 'I'm all right. Just doing some shopping for Mum, on my way back from the chemist.'

Lili recalled that she worked part-time at Smarts the chemist, on the corner of High Street and East Street.

'We did have some bad news a month or so back though. My grandma, Mum's mum, she had a stroke.'

'I'm so sorry, Flo. Is she…?'

'Still alive? She is. It was only a mild one, thank the Lord. She seems all right now. Even getting out and about a bit, though she's a bit wobbly. Granddad's there to look after her, luckily. We didn't tell Norman. Mum didn't want him having anything else to worry about. So don't mention it when you write, please.'

'Don't worry, I won't. I presume you've had a letter from Norman recently? I had one last week and, from what he says, he does seem to get them over and done with at the same time.'

Florence chuckled, relaxing the strained atmosphere. 'Yes, he's never been a keen letter writer, has Norman.'

Lili laughed too. 'At least he enjoys our efforts to him.'

'That he does… So, I gather you're still at the Beach Hotel. Norman told us you've been promoted to the dining room.'

She made it sound so much grander than *made a waitress*. 'That's right. Needs must with so many of the male staff enlisting. We've got female porters now too. Portresses.' She did hate the word, which was so cumbersome. But Mr Bygrove had insisted on it.

'It's the same at the chemist. The owner's afraid there'll be only him left with any expertise. He didn't appreciate me suggesting he could train a girl up.'

'I bet.' Lili leant forward. 'Our manager's not keen either. But you're not to tell anyone I said that. I don't want to get into no trouble.'

Florence touched the side of her nose to indicate she'd keep it a secret. 'I understand.'

'Do you know about the charity concert tomorrow, on the Common, at two o'clock?'

'I did see a poster somewhere.'

'It's for the home that the Duchess of Norfolk has established for disabled soldiers and sailors. And, well...' she didn't want to sound like she was showing off. 'See, they're short of entertainers – the war again – so, I've, um, volunteered to sing. That is, *been* volunteered, more like it.' She giggled.

Florence raised two fists and banged them together in excitement. 'I shall definitely come then. Norman said you had a *lovely* singing voice.'

Lili felt herself well up. Her lovely Norman. She'd sung *Calon Lân* to him one time, and he'd told her that her voice was as beautiful as she was.

'And I do love your accent,' Florence continued. 'It's so... lilting and lyrical. Bet it sounds lovely in song.'

'Florence Stubbs, I could hug you!'

'That's nice.' Florence looked unsure, making Lili hope she hadn't been too familiar. 'But it's true. I'm not just being kind.'

Lili told her about Mrs Carmichael claiming she couldn't understand her and Mrs Turnbull.

'How rude of her. Sounds like she was in a bad mood and wanted to take it out on someone. I wouldn't take no notice.'

'Thank you, Flo.' Lili did now lean forward and give her a quick hug. 'Edie said much the same thing.'

'I'm so glad I've seen you, but I'd better get on with this shopping before Mum wonders where I am.'

'And I have a blouse to buy myself for tomorrow, so I'll 'opefully see you there.'

'You'll *definitely* see me there. *Hwyl*... What was that Welsh farewell you taught us?'

'*Hwyl fawr.*'

'*Hwyl... fawr.* Awful pronunciation, sorry.'

'At least you tried. And I 'ope your grandma's completely well soon.'

Florence nodded and walked away, a spring in her step. Lili felt similarly heartened and entered the shop with determination.

Chapter Four

'There they go again,' Lili whispered as she and Edie headed down the staff stairs, past the first floor, where the Bygroves lived.

They stopped a while to listen. The voices were coming from an open door, by the sound of it, and loud enough for them to gather they were discussing the staff going to help at the charity do this afternoon. Or arguing, in Bygrove's case.

'We've already agreed to provide four people to collect money and I've rearranged the rota accordingly, so there's enough staff for afternoon tea,' said Helen. 'A couple of the part-timers are coming in to fill any gaps.'

'Which I will have to pay for!' Bygrove roared.

'*We* will have to pay for. It's our contribution to the collection, Douglas. I'm sure you can appreciate the publicity value of that. And it's something else you can take credit for.'

Lili clasped her hand to her mouth in an effort not to giggle, nudging her friend at the same time.

'She's not wrong,' Edie whispered. 'Come on, we're supposed to be meeting in the corridor in a couple of minutes.'

'If Mrs Bygrove ever gets away from *dear Douglas*.' She giggled again. She admired Helen's ability to speak calmly to her difficult husband.

Exiting the stair door on the ground floor, they saw that Fanny was already waiting in the corridor, leaning against a wall, her hands clasped around her waist. Lili had been surprised when Mrs Bygrove had asked her to help, considering all the trouble she'd caused in the past year. But maybe that was the reason: to try to get her a little more involved. The chambermaids working with her had been given other jobs, all of which had seemed like promotions. Only Fanny and a couple of existing live-outs were still cleaning the rooms, while new chambermaids had been taken on. It was maybe no wonder she was a little peeved.

Fanny pushed herself away from the wall. 'Where's Mrs Bygrove?'

Edie and Lili glanced at each other before Edie said: 'I'm sure she'll be down in a minute.'

The door opened at this moment and Helen stepped out, all smiles.

'Come along ladies, we don't want to be late. Especially as Lili has a spot in the entertainments.'

Fanny humphed. 'As long as she doesn't embarrass us.'

'Fanny, behave,' Mrs Bygrove chastised gently.

Lili, who'd managed to keep her nerves at bay for the past hour, felt anew the terror of performing for the crowds.

-

They left by the staff door and were soon at the venue, between the hotel and the promenade. They headed for the side of the makeshift stage, where Mr Janus was standing.

'Ladies.' He stepped forward, holding out his hands in welcome. 'I'm so grateful to you for coming to help. Especially Miss Probert here, who showed me what a fine voice she has when she came to see me yesterday. I'm sure she'll prove popular.'

Lili felt herself redden, but experienced pleasure at the compliment, nonetheless.

They were handed a metal bucket each and, with five minutes to go before the entertainments began, headed to their allotted areas.

Lili went to stand near the fountain. Part of the audience had gathered here as all the seats were full. She was concentrating on breathing slowly, reminding herself she *was* a good singer and had never let herself down yet. Except as a ten-year-old, at the singing festival in the chapel. Oh, why had she remembered that? But she'd only been a child. She'd croaked her way through the first verse of a song and had been mortified. Especially when a boy at the front of the audience had laughed. It had been her first *gymanfa ganu*. She had recovered, going on to give a 'sterling performance', as Da had put it.

'Miss Probert. How delightful to see you here.'

Lili came to, confused at first. 'Corporal Morgan. Fancy seeing you here.' She had difficulty keeping her voice level. He was a welcome sight.

But that meant he'd be here when she sang. Her confidence dropped a little more.

'They're collecting money...' He noticed her bucket. '*You're* collecting money, for our fellow soldiers. It only seemed right to support them.'

'Of course.'

Fanny approached, a smirk on her face. 'Well, what do we have here? I promise not to tell Norman you've been talking to a handsome soldier.'

'What are you doing over here, Fanny?' Lili could have crowned the girl. Trust her to interfere.

'Mr Janus suggested I came over to help you as there were already two collectors where I was.'

'Oh, good,' said Lili, flatly.

'Norman?' Corporal Morgan asked.

'Her fiancé,' Fanny replied delightedly, before Lili could get a word in.

'No, we're not betrothed, we were... walking out.' She felt the heat in her face as she reddened. She'd been going to say *sweethearts*, but had thought better of expressing such feelings to someone she barely knew.

'I see.'

Was he disappointed? It seemed to Lili he was.

'Corporal Morgan was at the fundraiser we had at the hotel last week,' Lili explained.

'I wouldn't know, would I? I was busy cleaning up after people.'

Lili was losing her patience, but she wasn't going to show this in front of the corporal.

'And a lovely do it was, too,' he said.

Fanny was distracted at this point by someone asking her about the afternoon's entertainments.

'Sorry about her,' Lili whispered. 'A right miserable piece she can be.'

'Don't worry. I know a few like her.' He chuckled.

His smile lit up his face, like it had the first time she'd met him, making him even more... handsome? Attractive? Beautiful? *Don't be daft*, she told herself. If she hadn't already had a sweetheart, she would have been interested though, she was sure. No. It was terrible, to think like that. But she was only human. *Tut, tut, turned by a pretty face.* She almost fancied Auntie Megan was speaking to her.

The corporal looked at his wristwatch. 'I'd better take my seat soon. It's being saved for me. Look... I'm leaving 'ospital next week.'

'That's... good,' she said, thinking the opposite.

'It is, but because I'm still limping, I have a clerical role at the training base at Shoreham-by-Sea.'

He'd be nearby, but still far enough away for her never to see him again. He was a connection to Wales, to home. That's what she was thinking. And no doubt he'd return there after the war.

'However, since my family are here in Littlehampton, I'll be visiting regularly on days off.'

'Your family are here? I assumed they were in Aber Valley.'

'We moved two years ago next January. To get away from the mines, wasn't it.'

'I've known a few who've done that.'

41

'Maybe we'll bump into each other again, Miss Probert.'

'Lili,' her mouth said before her brain had a chance to intervene. It was rather informal. She'd been the same with Norman when they'd first met.

'Then you must call me Rhodri.'

She loved the way he rolled his Rs, after all the flat 'r' pronunciations of those around here.

'All right.'

Fanny had finished talking to the person who'd made the enquiry and was concentrating on the pair again, so Lili said, 'See you around then, Rhodri,' in Welsh, so she wouldn't understand, hoping that he did, in fact, speak Welsh. Not everyone in the Valleys did. She kept her face neutral, so that Fanny couldn't deduce anything from her expression.

He replied in kind, saluting and lifting a hand in farewell before limping away with his stick.

'Wassat mean then, what you said?' Fanny asked, looking cross.

'Just *cheerio*,' she half-fibbed, not wanting to explain about Rhodri's new post.

'Huh, sounds silly to me.'

'I'm not going to dignify that with a reply, Fanny Bullen.'

'You just did.' Fanny grinned. 'Looks like the show's starting.'

Lili hadn't mentioned her performance to Rhodri, not wanting him to have any expectations. She closed her eyes, lifting her thoughts to the heavens. *Let my slot be over quickly and go well.*

—

'What's up with you, mate?' said Mike, sporting only a patch over his eye today. 'You've a bit of a crease to your brow there.'

Rhodri sat next to his pal, his heart heavy. 'What's that? Oh, nothing, *boyo*. Just my natural expression, isn't it. Miserable old git, I am.' He humphed briefly.

'No, you're normally cheerful. That's why I like your company, mate.'

'There's nothing wrong. Leg just itching a bit, isn't it.'

Chris leant past Mike to say: 'At least it's a real itch. It's weird having an arm itching when it's not even there.'

'That's your mind telling you your arm's still there, ain't it?' said Mike.

Chris shrugged. 'I suppose.'

Mr Janus came on stage to introduce the first act, but Rhodri couldn't take his mind away from his disappointment; Lili had a sweetheart, even if she did seem to be playing it down. Perhaps she was embarrassed. Or hadn't wanted to admit too much in front of her colleague.

Either way, she was off-limits, which made him more down-hearted than he'd expected. He'd felt a connection between them and not only because they were both from the Valleys. With any luck, he'd get a chance to have a last word with her before he left this afternoon. He'd have to be content with that.

-

The show had gone well so far, Lili considered, with rapturous applause from the audience after each act. Although this was good and might encourage people to throw more money in the buckets, it also meant she had a high standard to live up to.

She hadn't noticed Florence Stubbs anywhere, but the crowd was large so she could be lost in it. She liked the idea of Flo writing to Norman to tell him how well she'd performed – always supposing she did – and him being impressed with her. She could write to tell him herself, but that wouldn't be the same and would just sound like she was boasting.

Alternatively, if her act went badly wrong... oh dear, the humiliation. Hopefully, if that happened, Florence would be kind enough not to mention it.

A band came on to play *Alexander's Ragtime Band*. This was the cue Mr Janus had given her to go backstage, such as it was, to get ready. Her heart was pounding. That wasn't unusual, happening as it did every time she performed. Mam had said it was good to be nervous, that it made you try harder, but she'd always hated the stomach-churning sensation.

She handed the bucket to Fanny, who took it without complaint, and made her way around the audience to her destination. She looked out for Rhodri on the way, spotting him next to his friend at one end of a row.

Please let it go well.

Reaching the back of the stage, she encountered Mr Janus, smiling.

'Nice and early for your cue. That's what I like to see. Don't look so scared, m'dear. If you sing like you did for me, the audience'll love you.'

'Thank you for those kind words, sir.'

'They're not just kind words. You'll do just fine.'

Lili breathed in and out slowly, attempting to still her nerves.

The band on stage had finished their tune, provoking what seemed even louder applause than the previous acts.

Oh Lord! She tried to picture herself in the chapel at home, singing in the choir for people she'd known many years. It didn't work. She was outside, in the sunshine, on the south coast of England, nowhere near her chapel.

The applause died down as the band left the stage. Mr Janus went up three steps and through the backdrop to announce the next act.

'And now, ladies and gentlemen, we have a young lady, all the way from Wales, via the Beach Hotel, to entertain and delight you with three songs.'

'Go on, your turn,' said one of the women in the Pierrot troupe, holding out a hand to indicate that the stage was hers.

Here goes.

She went up the steps, entering the stage via the backdrop. Some people were already smiling expectantly. Most didn't look so sure, maybe because they were regulars, and she was unfamiliar to the crowds outside the hotel. The clapping was polite but subdued.

Don't look at the audience, look at the wall. Imagine it's an empty room. It was her mam's voice. There was no wall to look at though, just the hotel. She'd concentrate on that.

After the muted applause died down, Lili glanced at the lady playing the piano, who nodded at her and began the introduction to *I Do Like To Be Beside The Seaside*.

This was it.

She sang the first words.

> *'Everyone delights to spend their summer's holiday, down beside the side of the silvery sea...'*

But it didn't sound right. She was that ten-year-old again, croaking on stage. Oh no, this was terrible. What should she do?

Coming to a halt at the end of the first line, she coughed and looked over at the pianist, who must have realised something was up and stopped playing.

'Sorry, excuse me,' said Lili. 'I seem to have a little frog in my throat. Must be being near the river, see.'

She wasn't sure where that had come from, but the audience laughed, and she relaxed. When she looked back over at the pianist, she was grinning at her. 'If we could start that again, please?'

The pianist nodded and began the introduction once more. She started the song again: this time her voice was smooth and the notes correct. It was such a relief that her spirits rose and she felt herself being swept away by the catchy beat of the song as people swayed along to it. On the last chorus, the audience joined in. When she'd finished, she received enthusiastic applause.

So far, so good. *Calon Lân* was what she had planned next, despite being afraid they wouldn't appreciate it being in a different language. Mr Janus had seemed to think it would be just fine. Nevertheless, she explained its meaning, adding: 'See, it means a lot to me as I don't wish for the world's wealth, just to have a happy heart, an honest heart and a pure heart, like it says in the song.'

A member of the audience whistled their agreement, while several nodded and a couple held their hands up to clap.

As she sang, she dared to look briefly at Rhodri, who she was surprised to see miming the words along with her as he smiled.

Much to her amazement, she held the audience's attention, receiving a nice round of applause at the end.

'For my last song today, I'm going to sing a favourite of mine: *Let Me Call You Sweetheart.*'

A cheer went up: it was clearly a favourite of a few here. As she sang, she noticed Florence join the audience, standing at one side. She was a little disappointed that she might not have heard the rest of her performance, though it was possible she was just moving position.

The song finished and the applause was instant. Edie and Mrs Bygrove, standing together near the front of the crowd, held their hands high as they clapped. Her attention was alerted to someone in the seated audience standing. It was Rhodri. Following his lead, several others did the same, and soon half the audience was on its feet. She tried to see if Florence was clapping, but she was hidden by the now-standing members of the audience.

Curtsy. She should curtsy, to thank them.

As she did so, Mr Janus came up beside her. 'Thank you, Miss Probert, for a marvellous debut on our stage.'

Lili took another bow, to more applause, before beating a hasty retreat, leaving Mr Janus to speak. She headed to join Fanny and hopefully find Florence along the way.

'I do hope you enjoyed the splendid entertainments this afternoon,' he said. 'Please, do give what you can. It's for the Duchess of Norfolk's home for disabled soldiers and sailors.'

Lili reached Fanny, not having seen Norman's sister. Never mind, when the crowds cleared a little, she might spot her.

'Here's ya bucket,' said Fanny, almost chucking it at her. 'Well done, by the way,' she added, almost reluctantly. 'Ya sing good.'

'Why, thank you.'

They'd only just started collecting money when a figure rushed towards them. 'Lili! Oh, Lili.'

Here was Florence, at last. Her opening words were hopeful, except… when Lili saw her worried expression, she couldn't figure out what she might have done wrong.

Florence grasped her free hand and it was then her eyes welled up with tears.

What could have happened? Even as the words went through Lili's head, an icy dread coursed through her.

'We had a telegram… this morning.' Florence was struggling to speak.

'What… what is it?'

'Norman. He… he's missing.'

She didn't add 'presumed dead', but Lili had heard about these telegrams. A friend of Mam's had had one. The noise of the crowd seemed to fade and all Lili could hear was the voice in her head screaming: *Missing, presumed dead*. She dropped the bucket.

'I… I thought you should know as soon as possible, as they won't write to tell you.'

'But missing could mean just that,' said Lili, despite what she'd just told herself. She had to keep her hopes up. And Florence's.

'We know what it means.'

Lili sprung forward to hug the distraught Florence. It must have taken a lot for her to come to this event to tell her, after only hearing this morning.

'Lili!' Edie came running towards her. 'Fanny's just told me.' The maid was coming up behind her. 'I'm so sorry. And for you. Florence, isn't it?'

Florence moved away from Lili, hanging her head. 'That's right. I'd better get back to our mum. She's in shock. We all are.'

'Of course.' Lili took her hand and gave it a squeeze.

Florence lunged forward to give her another hug. 'Perhaps we could meet up, on one of your days off.'

'Yes, yes. And keep me informed.'

'Of course.' Florence let her go and hurried away towards South Terrace.

Fanny picked up Lili's bucket, taking it with her own to collect money from a crowd who were slow to move off.

Edie held Lili's arm. 'You know, missing might mean just that.'

'I already said that to Florence and she was as unconvinced as me. Oh Edie, I do hope it's the case, but... I fear not.' She expected the tears to come at last, but it was as if they were stuck behind her eyes.

'Lili! What a wonderful performance. We were so impressed, weren't we, Mike?'

'Yes, it was—'

Seeing Rhodri there, with the guilt she'd felt at finding him attractive, did the trick. The tears burst from her eyes and she ran. She hadn't run this fast since taking part in the village sports day as a young girl.

Relieved to get into the staff door in the scullery, she ignored Annie Twine's 'What on earth?', and kept running, through the stillroom and into the kitchen.

There was worse to come. Standing close to the kitchen door was Mr Bygrove, berating Mrs Turnbull over something.

'Here you, gal. I need someone to—'

She didn't stop to hear the rest of it. Instead, she flung the door to the stairs open and clambered up the steep back steps.

Blast Bygrove and his orders. She didn't care if she did get into trouble. Let him rant and rave. She reached the second floor and the small bedroom she shared with Edie, shutting the door after her with an accidental bang.

Collapsing on the bed, she gave full rein to her tears.

Was this her fault? Was she being punished by the Almighty for just looking at another man? It was an attempt to make sense of what had happened, even if it made no sense.

'Oh Norman. Norman,' she sobbed. She recalled their first meeting, walking by the River Arun with Edie. Being a porter at Littlehampton station, he'd been the first person Edie had met when she'd arrived and he had been very kind to her. Later, when he'd spotted her on Pier Road, he came to talk to her to find out how she was getting on. Lili had been immediately attracted to him, with his happy face, lively blue eyes and cheeky smile.

Oh, this war, this *damned* war. She hit her pillow several times. What could she do? She felt helpless. If he was gone, he was gone. That was it.

She pressed her face into the pillow and let out a long moan, before going limp. And exhaustion assailed her. If she could just sleep and sleep…

She'd half nodded off when there was a knock at the door, causing her to take a noisy in-breath.

'Who is it?'

'Only me, pet,' said Mrs Turnbull. 'There's a letter come for you. And Mr Bygrove wants you to come and do some work.'

Lili staggered out of bed and pulled open the door a crack. She took the letter.

'I'm sorry, but I've just heard that I've… I've lost my sweetheart in… in the war.'

Mrs Turnbull's hands went to her mouth. 'Oh lass, you poor thing. Is there anything I can do for you?'

'Could you tell Mr Bygrove that I won't be down until my shift later this afternoon. I need some time.'

'Of course you do. Yes, I'll tell him.' She turned away and Lili shut the door.

She looked at the writing on the envelope. Her mother's neat hand. It wasn't something she could face just now. She placed the letter on the chest of drawers and slumped back down on the bed.

She lay on her back, staring at the ceiling, remembering her times with Norman. She doubted she'd sleep now.

–

Rhodri felt like an idiot and he didn't even know why. He watched as Lili bolted through the crowds, crying.

'What, what did I say? She *was* very good.'

'I'm afraid she's just heard that her sweetheart, Norman, is missing in action,' said her friend, Miss Moore.

He felt an even bigger idiot, but at least he now knew why. 'I am so very sorry to hear that. What a terrible thing.'

'Missing in action? That usually means they've copped one,' said Mike, scratching at the corner of his eye.

'Mike!'

'Sorry, but it's the truth of it.'

'I fear you are right,' said Miss Moore.

'Please, if you wouldn't mind passing on my condolences to Miss Probert.'

'Of course, Corporal.'

'I'm being discharged from 'ospital this week and will be moving to the camp in Shoreham-by-Sea, to do clerical work, so I might not see her to tell her in person.' Despite what he'd said to Lili before the show, it didn't seem quite proper to 'bump into her' now. It would feel like taking advantage of her loss.

'Good luck, Corporal.'

'Thank you.' He saluted her, then led his friend away.

It was just as well he was off to Shoreham.

–

Edie watched Corporal Morgan walk away, then turned to find Helen beside her, lugging a half-full bucket of coins.

'How's the collection going, Edie?'

'Sorry, I've barely done any. Norman's sister just came to tell Lili that he's missing.'

Helen closed her eyes. 'Oh no. Where is she?' She looked around.

'She ran back to the hotel.'

'Go and make sure she's all right. Give me your bucket. Where's Lili's?'

Edie looked around the area. 'Fanny has it.'

The chambermaid was wielding both buckets, encouraging people either side of them to donate to the fund, which they were.

'Come on now, ladies and gents. It was a great show, so give generously. And think of the worthy cause it's going to.'

'Gosh, who knew Fanny could be so persuasive?' said Helen. 'When it suits her.'

'You get back to the hotel and look out for Lili. What a terrible thing to happen.'

Edie rushed as fast as she could without running, across the Common to the hotel. *Oh, bother being ladylike!* She broke into a run, eliciting looks of disapproval from some.

In the stillroom, Edie could hear Bygrove holding forth in the kitchen as she reached the door. There was no chance of being able to slip up the stairs without him noticing.

'Miss Moore?'

Bygrove came marching up to her as she entered the kitchen, his face puce. 'Miss Probert *might* have good reason to skive off to her room but, now you're back, I assume the charity event is over. In which case, where is my wife and the maid?'

'It's not over, sir. Hel— Mrs Bygrove sent me to check on Lili. She and Fanny are still collecting money.'

He glanced at his watch, lips pinched. 'I am due to meet the cricket club committee in twenty minutes and I don't want to leave some nincompoop in charge. Being who you are, you would be a much better choice.'

Yet *another* activity for him to run away to? And to which 'nincompoop' was he referring, exactly?

'I'm sorry sir, but I really need to check on Lili.'

'Then I'll just have to put Phoebe in charge, since she is on reception.' He started to move off. Raising his arms and regarding her once more, he stopped to add: 'Don't be long consoling Miss Probert. As soon as you've checked that she's all right, *you* will be in charge.'

'Very well, sir.' There was no point in arguing, and even less in voicing the opinion that he could just stay put for a change.

—

In their bedroom, Lili was lying on her back on top of the blankets. She quickly brought her legs to the floorboards when Edie entered.

'Edie, you didn't have to—'

'Yes, I did. And, anyway, Helen told me to.'

She sat next to Lili on the bed. 'I'm so very sorry, Lili. I know it doesn't help to say they might find him, but they might.'

Lili's head flopped onto Edie's shoulder. 'I have to hold on to that hope.'

'Of course.' At least until they knew one way or the other. But what if they never found him? The possibility seemed worse to Edie than knowing for sure he was gone. Charlie's face came into her mind and she brushed it away. She didn't ever want to entertain the idea of anything happening to him.

'Corporal Morgan asked me to pass on his condolences.'

'That was kind of him,' she said, flatly.

Another idea flitted through Edie's mind: if Norman really was lost, the corporal might be a new love for her friend, sometime in the future. But she would not say this to Lili. Not for a while. She knew how she'd feel if someone said the same about her dear Charlie.

She spotted the envelope on the drawers. 'Is that yours?'

'Yes. From Mam. I suppose I should open it. No point putting it off. It'll be about what everyone at home's doing and any local gossip, so it'll all seem pointless. But I'd better write and tell Mam what's happened.'

Lili rose slightly to grab the letter. She ran her finger through the back of the envelope and quickly pulled out the single page.

'That's not like Mam. Normally writes about four sheets, back and front, she does. Oh Lord, I hope she's not going to say that either Morys or Wyn have enlisted. Or both.'

Edie placed her arm through Lili's, but looked away as she read so as not to pry, even though she knew it would be written in Welsh.

The sudden jerk from Lili and the cry of 'Oh no!' made Edie jump.

'What is it?'

'Oh no. Oh no.' Lili lowered her head to her knees for some seconds. Edie rubbed her back, much as Nanny Street would have done to her when she was upset as a child.

Eventually, Lili straightened herself. 'M… Morys's baby daughter, Emily… she… she's died! She's not even a month old. And Morys's wife… Jane's only been gone, what, three weeks?'

Edie could barely believe the timing of this tragedy. Poor, poor Lili.

'Her funeral's tomorrow, so I can't even go. Oh Morys! He must be so broken. And little Ffion, losing her mam and her sister. I… I need to write him a letter. Right now. I can't leave it.'

Lili rose and went to the bottom drawer, pulling out a paper bag, which held a pad of paper and some envelopes. She took a fountain pen from her handbag on the chair.

'I've run out of ink.'

'You can have some of mine.'

'Thank you.' Lili collapsed onto the bed once more and cried.

'Here it is,' Edie whispered, placing the bottle on top of the drawers. 'You write the letter when you feel up to it. I'm so sorry, but I'd better get back down. I'll be up later to see how you are.'

Lili nodded, then grabbed Edie's arm as she was about to walk away. 'Thank you… for being such a good friend.'

Edie patted her shoulder, not really knowing what she'd done in particular, but glad she could be of some help to her distraught friend.

Chapter Five

Edie Moore and Helen Bygrove stood solemnly by the graveside as the coffin was lowered into a large opening in the far end of the cemetery in Littlehampton.

It was now the middle of September; it had taken the authorities nearly four weeks to bury her erstwhile fellow boarder. Edie shook her head. 'It seems wrong that there isn't even a minister to say a few words for Pamela.'

'Sometimes there is, sometimes there ain't, at the paupers' funerals,' commented the gnarled and weathered old man who seemed to be in charge of the two men lowering the simple coffin. 'Depends if the vicar knew 'em. Don't suppose he 'ad much truck with this one. I'm told she was that woman found in the alley behind Pier Road, what was a strumpet.'

He considered them with narrowed eyes, as if to enquire how they would know such a woman. It was best to ignore the comment, Edie decided.

It didn't seem right that Pamela should be worth a pauper's funeral. Whatever her occupation. Wasn't it enough that she'd been murdered by that ruffian, Gordon Hadley, who had tried to see *her* off too? But Pamela had clearly had no money of her own and who else was there to pay for it?

She could hardly believe that this had all taken place just under a month ago, yet in some ways it still haunted her as if it were yesterday. It was the same with the death of Gordon Hadley's estranged wife. She'd owned the guest house on South Terrace where she and Pamela Brownlow had been staying, before Edie had got the job at the Beach Hotel. That had happened fourteen months ago, but she could still picture Mrs Hadley's body in her sitting room, then Gordon Hadley appearing at the doorway, before he once again ran away.

'Good morning, Edie. Mrs Bygrove.'

Edie found Julia Nye next to her, who'd been another fellow boarder at Mrs Hadley's and was now a firm friend. Just behind her was Detective Inspector Davis.

'Ladies.' He lifted his homburg briefly.

'We thought it only right to pay our respects,' said Julia, who had begun walking out with the Inspector after he'd closed the original murder inquiry, following Mrs Hadley's killing.

Edie had known her friend would come, but not the inspector. She supposed he was here to support Julia, the same way Helen had come to support her.

Helen cleared her throat. 'Since there's no minister, I'll say a few words.'

The four of them stood and looked into the open grave, which clearly contained other coffins. Edie shuddered at the stark reality of mortality.

Helen began to recite Psalm Twenty-three: 'The Lord is my shepherd…'

Even the workmen standing there pulled off their caps, despite the old man's slur on Pamela's character.

Helen finished with: 'Lord, we commit Pamela's body to the ground, earth to earth, ashes to ashes, dust to dust…'. She ran out of words and simply bent to pick up some soil that had been dug out, throwing it in. The other three did likewise.

'Will she be covered over now?' Edie asked the old man.

'Nah. Got another one to go in later.'

'And there'll be no stone or plaque?'

He shook his head. 'Never is with no paupers' graves.'

Edie felt that familiar rising emotion in her chest. She breathed in to stem it.

'We'll leave ya to yer mourning,' said the old man, and the three of them left.

'It's hard to think that a month ago Pamela was still alive,' said Edie. 'And I had no idea that the Kursaal thief I encountered, my first week in Littlehampton, was not only Mrs Hadley's killer, but also her husband.'

'At least he's locked away now, with no bail and unlikely to see the light of day for many years. If ever,' said Davis.

'Why has it taken so long to get her buried?' Edie asked.

'I suppose the pathologist wanted to get evidence from her, um, body. But other than that, I have no idea.'

'Perhaps they forgot about her, because she's unimportant. And was poor.'

'It does seem terribly disrespectful,' said Julia.

The inspector nodded.

Edie's stomach squirmed as she remembered that the trial was likely to be held in the autumn, maybe even next month. Inspector Davis had already informed her that she would have to give evidence being, not only a witness to Hadley's presence in his wife's home, but herself the victim of an attempted murder.

Edie's mind was thrown back once more to that day on the promenade, feeling the knife pressed against her back as Hadley had pushed her towards the shelter. A cold dread slithered through her, even though she was now safe. She was sure she'd have been yet another casualty had her sweetheart, Charlie, not turned up and given the brute what for. She felt the tears prick at her eyes.

'I'm sorry, Miss Moore, if the memory of what happened is upsetting you.'

'It's not your fault, Inspector. I think it will be a while before I can put the memory behind me.'

Helen took her arm. 'Hopefully, when the trial is done, you'll be able to close that particular door.'

'I may well have to give evidence as well,' said Julia.

'I will be grateful for your presence... Now, Helen and I should be getting back to the hotel.'

'We'll walk with you to Norfolk Road.'

Edie nodded, hoping they would find some other subject to discuss along the way.

–

It had been two weeks since Lili had heard about Norman going missing and about her baby niece's death. She pondered this as she sat down for staff supper, watching as the roast mutton, gravy and potatoes were placed on the table and people started to help themselves.

Norman going missing. She wouldn't entertain the idea that he was... gone. If that had been the case, she'd have felt it in... what? The Heavens? Her heart? She had no idea, only that she wouldn't – couldn't – believe he was gone.

Consequently, she felt sadder about baby Emily than about Norman. Then she felt guilty about that. Then numb. Her emotions changed with the nearby tide.

Was Norman's disappearance maybe a sign that she should go home? Her family must be going through hell, with Jane's, then baby Emily's deaths? What could she do though? It wasn't like she could bring them back. She could help, somehow. Perhaps. What if Norman was only missing? Then she could come back.

But if she ever went back home, she feared she'd never return.

She wanted to forget it for the moment. It was hard to talk to anyone about it, even Edie, which left her feeling utterly alone.

She'd avoided engaging with the staff, but that was more because of the way they tiptoed around her, talking in low tones. Some of them, anyway. Others were overly bright and breezy, as if to lift her out of her gloom. As if they could.

Only Gertie and Fanny had been the same as usual and – whether it was an attempt to be normal, or because they didn't care – she appreciated this.

'You all right, hinny?' Mrs Turnbull touched Lili's arm from her place opposite.

'Yes. Why shouldn't I be?'

'You're so quiet, and, well, have every right to be, of course.'

'No, like I said…' She took a deep breath for courage. 'You know what? I'm fed up I am, of people treating me like a… an invalid. Yes. An invalid. Like one of them soldiers in Belgrave House Hospital, what's shot or missing a limb. I know you're all being sympathetic like, and I appreciate it, I do. But I don't believe Norman's gone, see, and I want to get on with things and be normal. I know my brother's babby has just died too, and his wife Jane with the consumption not long before, and sorry to my heart I am about it. But I can't do nothin' about it, see. I've got a job to do here, at this hotel, and I just need to get on with it.'

She looked around at the silent staff, all regarding her. Had she sounded too cold-hearted?

'That's probably for the best, me duck,' said Mrs Norris, standing at one end of the table, next to Mrs Leggett, her arms crossed under her abundant bosom. 'I was the same when me 'usband died. And now I keep busy to stop me thinking about the danger my poor Joseph might be in. Eat up now, before it gets cold.' She strode back to the kitchen.

Mrs Leggett stood and fetched an envelope out of her pocket. 'That reminds me. A letter came for you in the late post, Miss Probert.'

She passed the envelope along the row to Lili, via several members of staff, including Gertie and Fanny.

'Thank you, Mrs Leggett,' she said, while wondering why the woman couldn't just leave personal letters on the table for people to pick up when they came in. At least if the house-keeper was ever tempted to open one, she wouldn't understand a word.

It was another one from Wales but had Morys's obvious scrawl this time. She placed it in her skirt pocket. It was unusual for him to write letters and he'd never sent one while she'd been here. If it was more bad news, it would have to wait.

'Does anyone know how Mrs Bygrove and Edie got on at the funeral today?' said Mrs Turnbull. 'Right worried, I've been, for poor Edie, havin' to relive that day.'

'She's been on different meals to me today,' said Lili, 'but I saw her briefly earlier. She were relieved it were over, I think, but she did say that the court case probably won't be until next month.'

'Hopefully that scoundrel, Gordon 'adley, will get what's comin' to him.'

'Yes, probably… I was reading about this Derby Scheme of the government's in the newspaper today,' said Lili, to change the subject.

'I don't suppose Mr Bygrove'll be keen to sign up for it.' Fanny said, in a low rumble. 'More's the pity.'

'That's not an appropriate thought to share.' Mrs Leggett raised her eyebrows, though she wasn't as censorious as she once would have been about such a statement.

'What *is* the Derby Scheme exactly?' Gertie asked, helping herself to another potato.

'They're hoping more men will come forward to register their willingness to join the forces, should they be needed,' said Mrs Leggett.

'Aye. They're hopin' that it'll prevent the need to introduce conscription,' Mrs Turnbull added.

Gertie's brow creased and she looked down forlornly at her meal.

'There's no need to worry, lass. They're not goin' to press women to join.'

'No. Just thinking about my three brothers. If they introduce conscription, they'll have to go.'

Lili was surprised to hear this. 'You've never mentioned them before.'

'S'pose not.'

'Where do they work, then?'

'Up in Wick. On a farm. Where I was brought up.'

That was the most Gertie had ever volunteered about her past. She and Fanny had never been that chatty with staff other than themselves. Even now, she wasn't sure whether Fanny's mother was alive or dead, as Fanny had claimed both at different times.

'Hopefully the war'll be over soon,' said Mrs Turnbull. 'Then we won't have to worry about the menfolk no more.'

'What, over by Christmas, like last year?' Fanny clucked her tongue.

Mrs Leggett pointed at the maid. 'No need to be cheeky. It doesn't hurt to hope.'

'Anyway, won't farmin' be considered vital work?' said Mrs Turnbull.

'I hope so,' said Gertie.

Fanny crossed her arms. 'Women could do that work just as well, so it probably won't be.'

Gertie knocked her friend's arm. 'Don't say that.'

'Why shouldn't they be sent to war, same as any other man?'

'I'm not saying they shouldn't,' Gertie snapped back. 'I don't want no one to go to war. It's cruel!'

'Well, neither do I!' Fanny's face crumpled. She struggled to get off the bench, shoving Gertie out of the way on one side and Hetty, the maid in charge of the stillroom, on the other.

'Hey!' complained Hetty.

Having got herself off the bench, Fanny ran off, crying.

'What on *earth* is wrong with her now?' said Mrs Leggett. 'It's not like she's got much to cry about, with a nice secure job and a place to live.'

'I think…' Gertie began, not looking sure of herself.

'Spit it out, Miss Green.'

'I think Fanny might have a sweetheart. She's been going off a lot in her spare time, not spending it with me, like she used to. Perhaps she's worried he'll get called up.'

Lili felt her anger well up, which burst out as: 'Perhaps all the men should go to fight, then maybe we'd win the war quickly and not so many would be killed.'

'Don't you start, Miss Probert,' said the housekeeper.

'Sorry, Mrs Leggett,' she said, although she wasn't.

'It's understandable, hinny.' Mrs Turnbull leant over the table to pat her hands.

She didn't want the sympathy; she was angry, not upset. All right, she was upset too, but the anger was winning.

'I'm fine. Thank you.'

The meal proceeded with bits and pieces of chitchat about current guests, especially the difficult Mrs Carmichael, and about the way it had been warm and sunny earlier but now the rain had set in. Lili half-listened, the letter in her pocket weighing heavily on her mind. She finished the meal quickly, then fished it out. If it was more bad news, there was no point in putting it off.

She needn't have worried: it was Morys simply thanking her for the letter she'd sent him, his regret at her finding out too late to attend the funeral, and saying how sorry he was that her sweetheart had gone missing. It had taken him two weeks, but she appreciated it all the same.

But, as she read on, she realised there was another motive for him writing. Was it possible, he asked, that she might leave Littlehampton and come home for good? Especially now Norman was unlikely to return. How strange, that she'd been thinking about this only minutes before.

Now she'd seen the request in writing, her stomach plummeted at the thought. It wasn't that she didn't like Dorcalon and the people in it – though there were some she had not missed. It was only that… there were more opportunities here for her. Especially now. Maybe back home they wouldn't see being made a waitress as an opportunity. But this was a prestigious hotel. And sometimes she was even put on the desk as receptionist. Yes, it was because the men were at war, but what would she do at home? Sort coal at the pit? Serve in a shop? Go back to being a maid at the Big House? Or was Morys wanting someone to look after little Ffion, while he worked?

And what freedom would she have, being the youngest of five, with her older sisters and brothers always bossing her around? Especially Carys, the oldest of her siblings.

'Miss Green, Miss Probert, please remove the plates to the scullery so we can have pudding,' said Mrs Leggett.

Mrs Turnbull rubbed her hands together. 'Indeed. It's apricot puddin' today. I'll go and fetch it.'

Gertie and Lili rose. Writing to Morys would be her job this evening, when she didn't have a shift. She'd hoped to read the book she'd borrowed from the library, but it would have to wait. The quicker she dispelled any ideas that she was coming home, the better.

–

A day later, on Lili's afternoon off, she decided to take a stroll on the prom. It was much quieter than it had been a few weeks back, now it was nearly autumn, even if the weather was still warm.

Before she set off walking, she turned to survey the hotel. It looked so imposing from here, from anywhere on the prom really, or even on South Terrace, come to that. She experienced a wave of pride that she was part of this prestigious institution. Occasionally, when she was out and about, and someone had cause to ask her where she worked, they always looked most impressed with her reply. It was almost as if she had the standing of the clients who came to the hotel.

With that positive thought coursing through her, she carried on.

When she reached the pier, she came to a standstill. She looked down the length of the pathway on the river's edge, to the coastguards' cottages, the Casino Theatre, tearoom and windmill on the right. She looked further, past the Oyster Pond, the Nelson public house, and down to the fisherman's cottages on Pier Road. She hadn't walked down here since she'd heard about Norman being… missing. A seagull keened a mournful song, gliding in the air above the river, before it swooped down to the water.

After staring at the area for a few seconds, she took a deep breath. There was no point in avoiding it forever. And she'd stroll down here with him again. She just knew she would.

Walking briskly, she recalled her and Norman's very first meeting here, near the drinks stand. It was closed currently. When she reached it, she stopped, the sudden urge to cry washing over her.

Don't be daft, she heard her sister Carys's voice say, a common phrase of hers. Then her mother's more sympathetic, *It'll be all right, cariad, I promise.* Of course, it wasn't always 'all right', and she wished people wouldn't say such a thing so often when they didn't know if it would be.

Wasn't that what she was doing now? Promising herself that Norman was all right?

She stared at the drinks stand, picturing that first meeting, Norman buying her and Edie bottles of ginger beer, even though he'd only just met her. Kind like that, he was, Norman.

'Lili, I am so glad I've seen you.'

She almost fancied it was Norman talking, but she knew, by the Valleys inflection, that it was Rhodri Morgan.

Turning, she said: 'Corporal. Hello. I thought you'd gone to Shoreham-by-Sea by now.'

He was in uniform, standing to attention. 'I have, but it's a day's leave I'm on, to visit my family.'

She looked around, as if expecting to see them.

'No, they're not here,' he huffed the beginning of a laugh, but then seemed to think better of it. 'After dinner, I wanted a walk out, but Auntie Charlotte didn't fancy it. And Uncle Islwyn's at work still.'

'Where do they live?'

'River Road.'

'By the water. That's nice.'

'Their house is opposite the warehouses, so they can't see the river.'

'Of course.'

It was a much stiffer exchange than the first two times they'd met, but that was probably just as well.

'I presume Miss Moore passed on my condolences, but I'm grateful to be able to tell you in person how sorry I am.'

'Thank you, but I've not given up hope.'

'Nor should you. I've seen a lot of losses on the battlefield, but sometimes you do find people alive and well who you thought... gone.'

He had a haunted look in his eyes. She wondered how many friends he'd lost.

'That's what I'm holding on to, that possibility.'

He nodded. 'I was heading down to the pier, if you're walking that way...'

'Yes, yes, of course,' she said, even though she'd been walking in the opposite direction.

'Were you hoping the stand would be open for a drink?'

'No. It only opens at weekends in September. I was... I was just remembering that this was where I met Norman. He already knew Edie.'

'I see.' He looked down.

'Let's walk and you can tell me how your clerical job is going.'

They headed off in the direction Lili had come, Rhodri limping and using the stick to aid him. It was still quite pronounced, though he could move at a reasonable rate.

'It's going fine, the job. I did clerical work before the war, see, so I already had an idea of what to do and how to do it.'

'That's something... Where did you work before the war then?' She wasn't sure how interested she really was, but it filled a gap.

'In the office of Duke and Ockenden's, the well engineers. Dando, it's known as.'

'That's a big company.'

'It is.'

There was more silence, before he said: 'What did you used to do, back in Rhymney?'

'Dorcalon it actually was, the village next door. When I first left school, at fourteen, I were a sorter at the mine, you know, sorting the coal from the rock.'

'Yes, I know.'

'I did that for a coupla years, but it were awful: too hot in the summer and bloomin' cold in the winter.' She performed a small shudder. 'Mam got me a job as maid up at the Big House, where the mine manager lives. Then a girl I knew moved to Worthing and wrote to my friend about how much she liked living by the sea and how many jobs there were for young women. My da died. I needed a change. So, I thought I'd give it a go.'

She'd made it sound simple because she didn't want to go into all the dramas involving her siblings, in their bid to stop her leaving. Both her Mam and Auntie Megan had said they understood and would have relished the chance to do such a thing at her age.

'You said you'd lived here going on two years?' she said.

'We moved here in January 1914, from Senghenydd.'

'Oh, that was where that mine was, what had the terrible disaster in 1913.'

He studied his feet, frowning. 'That's right.'

'Mam had cousins there and a couple of them died.'

He shook his head forlornly. 'Terrible business. Auntie Charlotte and Uncle Islwyn decided they wanted a better life for me and my brother, Glyn.'

He'd only spoken of his aunt and uncle, not his parents, but it seemed too personal a question to ask why.

'My brother's still out in France,' he said. 'With the 11th South Downs Battalion.'

They'd reached the pier and walked onto it, heading for the end.

'That's the one some of the men at the hotel joined. My brothers are still hewing coal in Dorcalon. I know it's selfish of me, but I'm glad they haven't enlisted.'

'Mining's a necessary job. We need coal for the ships.'

'That "good steam coal", as my brother Morys puts it.'

Rhodri chuckled. 'Aye, that's the stuff.'

When they reached the end of the pier, Rhodri looked at his wristwatch. 'Time for a cuppa tea, I reckon. We could go to that cafe next to the Kursaal, if you'd let me treat you.'

'It's called the Casino Theatre now, the Kursaal.'

'Is it? I 'adn't noticed. Shall we?' He stretched his hand towards the suggested cafe.

Lili considered this for a few moments. 'It's very kind of you to offer, but I was hoping to head into Beach Town to get a few bits and bobs from the shops there.'

She hadn't been really, but it didn't seem quite proper to have tea with him, what with Norman not long missing.

'Very well,' he said. 'I'll go back to have tea with Auntie. I'll be in town again, likely once a month, maybe more. Perhaps I could treat you another time. As a friend from the old country, like.'

'All right.' No point in being rude and saying no.

'I could write to you at the hotel, if that's acceptable, and let you know when I'm coming, and you could write back and let me know if you've got a day off. Do you normally have Thursdays off?'

'At the moment. Thursday afternoons, anyway. And I can always request a certain day.' If she asked Mrs Bygrove and not her husband. She added: 'Probably,' not wanting him to think she was being eager. But it would be nice to have some company on her time off. And he clearly thought so too.

Of course, Florence had asked to meet up, but she'd not been in contact with her yet, dreading an afternoon of sadness where the only subject would be Norman. But she must do it.

'I'll see you soon hopefully then.' He turned, lifting a hand to wave, and limped off.

67

As he left the pier, heading down past the river, she decided she might as well move off herself, to look at the shops on Norfolk Road she'd claimed she wanted to visit. She'd just spotted Rhodri ahead, passing the theatre, when a woman, a nurse in uniform, caught up with him. The woman took his arm and walked beside him. Lili recognised her from the charity event at the hotel; she recalled that she was called Nurse Caffyn.

So, he *was* just being friendly. He was clearly already courting. What would she have thought of him, having tea with another woman? A little bit of her felt disappointed. What a good job she hadn't been free and interested.

She slowed down now, not wanting to catch them up before she reached Empress Maud Road. Loneliness descended on her like a thick blanket. If Norman really was gone, maybe, just maybe, it was time for another change.

–

Arriving back at the hotel, Lili headed to the staff dining room for late afternoon tea. She'd thought of visiting somewhere in town, but it would be free here, which would give her a bit more spending money on her next afternoon off.

Only Edie was there when she entered. 'I didn't expect you back this early. Do you feel refreshed after your walk?'

'I dunno about refreshed. It were nice to get out of the hotel, certainly. I... um... met Corporal Morgan on Pier Road.'

'Met?'

'I don't mean we arranged it.' She didn't want Edie to think badly of her. 'I should have said, came across him. He was having a day's leave from his new clerical position and had been visiting his family in River Road. His aunt and uncle. But he fancied a walk, and his aunt didn't want to go.'

Now she was over-explaining, which would make her look equally guilty.

Edie nodded. 'I remember him saying about the clerical job. It's nice he's got one so close to home, not on the other side of the country.'

'Yes, nice for him and his family,' Lili added, in case Edie thought it was nice for her. 'He, um, asked to buy me tea, but I didn't think it were appropriate.'

'He was likely only being friendly, Lili. Perhaps he's lonely.'

'In a camp full of men?' It seemed unlikely.

'It's amazing how you can be surrounded by people and feel lonely. I used to feel like that, back in Downland House, before I came here.'

Lili sat down as Edie poured her a cup of tea. 'I suppose I did too, sometimes, in Dorcalon, after all my siblings and friends got married. Even though I sang in the choir and helped in the chapel, and with flag days and the like, sometimes there was no one my age to talk to. They were all too busy... Anyway, I believe Corporal Morgan is walking out with Nurse Caffyn.'

'There you go then. He was just being friendly and you needn't have worried. I met up with my brother's friend, Daniel, a couple of times, but it didn't mean anything. Not to me, anyway, though I suppose it did to him.' She sighed. 'To me, he was simply someone to socialise with, an old friend, albeit of Freddie's.'

'But it did get you into bother with Charlie.'

'Yes, true. I should have been more upfront with him. I had a letter from him today, by the way.'

'How's he doing?'

'You know Charlie. He always finds plenty to joke about with the training and the rather stern sergeant major. But I think he's dreading going overseas.' Edie cast her eyes down and locked her fingers together on the table. 'He doesn't want to have to kill anyone. Even a supposed enemy.'

'I don't blame him. They haven't a date for goin' overseas yet?'

'Not that he mentioned. When Charlie goes, Freddie will be going too, since they're in the same battalion... Sorry, we were talking about Corporal Morgan, not me and Charlie.'

'You know...' Lili didn't go any further, wondering if she should voice her thoughts.

'What is it? You're frowning.'

'It's just... when I meet Rhodri – Corporal Morgan – and hear him speak, I do miss the Valleys.'

'Do you speak Welsh together.'

'Only once, strangely, when Fanny was listening in. I suppose we've got used to speaking English all the time.'

'Homesickness is inevitable. Well, mostly.'

'You don't feel it?'

'No. Is that terrible of me? I miss Freddie, that's all. You know I hated that privileged life, the endless rounds of social-ising and meeting "suitable" young men. But I can tell from how you speak about your family that you had a loving upbringing, in a close community.'

'Things weren't perfect, Edie. We were all quite poor. Even if the miners get more than some labourers, it's still a pittance. And diseases like consumption are rife there. And there's so much infant death, like my poor tiny niece, Emily. And some women were beaten and no one did much about it. But yes, I was lucky with my family. Even if they have been annoying, treating me like the baby still.' She sighed.

'I suppose they're looking out for you.'

'I know. And what I was thinking was, that, well, wondering if, maybe, I should go back to Dorcalon. It's been nearly two weeks since Norman went missing. If they were going to find him alive, they would have done by now. Being here, it constantly reminds me of him. I could go home, find a... a nice Welsh boy.'

As she said the last three words, the tears began to fall, despite her attempt to sniff them back.

'Oh Lili.'

Edie removed a clean handkerchief from her skirt pocket and handed it to her friend. Lili took it and wiped her eyes, then blew her nose.

From the corridor, they heard Mr Bygrove shouting into the kitchen at Mrs Norris about something on the menu.

'At least you wouldn't have to put up with that,' said Edie. 'You're getting on well here though, a waitress in a first-class restaurant, sometimes on the desk. I wouldn't be too hasty. And two weeks isn't that long for someone to be missing. Have a think first.'

'I will. But let's face it, when the war ends and the men return, I'll probably be back cleaning the rooms.'

Gertie and Fanny entered, having what seemed to be a disagreement. Lili shoved the handkerchief into her pocket.

Edie cleared her throat. 'I also had a letter from the court today, about giving evidence in Gordon Hadley's trial in Lewes.'

That got Fanny and Gertie's attention, and they hurried to sit down.

'When's that then?' Lili asked.

'Eighteenth of October the trial starts.'

Lili was glad of the change in subject and even the distraction of the other two women. She'd put her woes to one side for a while.

Chapter Six

Lili was laying the staff dining room table ready for early supper, wondering how Edie was getting on at the trial, and whether she'd be back soon. Major Thomas and Mr Janus had also been due to go in, having witnessed Hadley's assault of Edie.

Her mind wandered to Rhodri Morgan, thinking about how she hadn't heard from him yet, though it had been just over a month since she'd seen him. Part of her hoped he never wrote, so she wouldn't feel guilty about the friendship, even though he appeared to have a sweetheart. A bigger part, though, looked forward to his company, as a friend who knew what it had been like to come from a mining town. But if he never wrote, what could she do?

The door opened and Edie entered. 'Hello Lili.' She went to the fire and to warm her hands.

'How did it go?'

Edie gave a laboured sigh as she sat heavily on the edge of the bench. 'Since Julia isn't going until tomorrow, I got the train back with Mr Janus and Major Thomas, as Detective Inspector Davis was staying overnight. When we changed at Brighton, I so wished I could walk into the town and down to the beach, just to forget it all. I haven't been there in a while.'

'I've only been the once. But it was the trial I was meaning, more than the journey.'

Edie looked up at her. 'Of course.' She stretched and yawned. 'Gordon Hadley's barrister tried to make out I was mistaken about seeing him at Mrs Hadley's the night she was murdered.'

'What a cheek. I suppose he thinks your poor, weak female memory had let you down.'

'He was just doing his job.'

'As if that scoundrel needs defending after trying to strangle you. He can't deny that, given he was caught red-handed. And he *told* you it were him what killed Mrs Hadley. And Pamela Brownlow.'

'But that was only my word against his. He's denied telling me any of that. And the barrister claimed I could have imagined him saying that, as he was strangling me at the time.'

'What about Mr Janus? He identified him as the thief at the Kursaal didn't he? And as the man he caught attacking you? And Major Thomas saw him attacking you too.'

'Yes. But that doesn't prove that Hadley killed his wife.'

'Was Charlie called to give evidence?'

'No, he had to send a statement though, about catching Hadley strangling me, which was read out in court. Anyway, DI Davis reckoned I had done well, so that's something. Hopefully he'll let me know when a verdict's reached.'

'Get yourself settled. Supper'll be served in five minutes.'

'Good, I'm starving. I only had a cup of tea and biscuits for lunch.'

'Then you'll appreciate the macaroni and tomato omelette.'

'I think I'd appreciate anything at the moment.'

'There you are, Miss Moore,' said Mrs Leggett, coming through the door with Mrs Turnbull. 'How did it go?'

Edie's eyes darted in Lili's direction, her expression implying she didn't want to go through it again. 'I gave my evidence. But it's not over yet.'

Others trickled in, chatting, greeting Edie with similar questions as Lili finished laying up. Poor thing. At least when the hearing was over, Edie might feel some peace. There was no way that brute Hadley wouldn't get at least some years in gaol.

'Settle down now and let's say grace.' Mrs Leggett uttered her usual words, to which they all replied: 'Amen.'

73

'I've just seen in the paper about that poor nurse, Miss Edith Cavell.' Mrs Turnbull shook her head.

'What's happened?' Gertie asked.

'Been shot, she has, by the Germans. Few days ago now.'

There were varying reactions of shock, even from the usually self-absorbed Fanny.

'It's terrible,' said Mrs Turnbull. 'For she were nursin' soldiers on *both* sides.'

'And Britain's now declared war on Bulgaria,' said Mrs Leggett.

Lili served herself some potatoes. 'As if we need anyone else to be at war with.'

'Huh, we've got enough war going on here,' said Fanny.

Mrs Turnbull leant forward. 'How's that, lass?'

'Heard Mr and Mrs Bygrove having yet *another* barney this morning, when I was cleaning the back stairs, about him going to a golf club lunch today.'

Mrs Leggett laid down the ladle in the green beans noisily. 'Miss Bullen, that is *none* of your business. You have enough to be getting on with in this hotel without poking your nose into our employers' business. If you need something else to occupy you, there's plenty of other cleaning to do.'

'I'm only saying what everyone else does.'

'Even *I'm* having to do some cleaning because of maids being taken off to do waiting or to *sit* on reception.' Mrs Leggett sent a brief, disapproving glance in Edie and Lili's direction.

'That doesn't include me, 'cos I'm still stuck with cleaning.' Fanny looked resentful.

'That's enough of your cheek. Now, unless you can say something civil, I suggest you keep quiet.'

Fanny stuck her bottom lip out and speared a bean with her fork.

Poor Fanny. Lili felt a little sorry for her, despite what she was like. And she was right: she was only saying what others had said plenty of times.

'Maybe you'd like to hear a little more about the trial?' Edie suggested, despite her earlier reticence. She was maybe trying to change the subject.

There was an eager reaction, even from Mrs Leggett. They all leant in as Edie began.

Towards the end of her account, Mrs Bygrove stuck her head around the door, then came in. 'The second post has arrived. There's one for you, Mrs Turnbull, and another for you, Lili.'

Mrs Leggett stood up, her mouth pinched in. 'I will distribute them, Mrs Bygrove.'

She took the letters from Helen and gave them out. As usual, it seemed unnecessary to Lili, but she knew the housekeeper considered it her job.

Seeing the Shoreham-by-Sea postmark, Lili was about to let out an exclamation, but stopped herself in time. She made her expression neutral and placed the letter in her pocket.

For once, she couldn't wait for supper to be over. She made the excuse of needing to get something from her bedroom before her shift in the dining room and sprinted up the stairs. In her room, she opened the letter and read it quickly. Rhodri was to be in town, on a day's leave, next Thursday, and was it possible, he asked, to have tea with her that afternoon?

She wondered whether Nurse Caffyn would join them, or maybe he'd picked that time because she'd be working. Did she know he was planning to meet her? Lili imagined a conversation between Rhodri and the nurse, about how lonely Lili must be now Norman was missing, then pictured her telling him he should meet with her to make sure she was all right.

Whatever their situation, it was none of her concern. She'd write a letter to him after her shift, before she went to bed, and get it posted tomorrow morning during her morning break. She could suggest a time and a place to meet.

Then at least she'd have something to look forward to.

–

Lili removed her apron as she made her way to the staff area. That had been a busy luncheon for a Wednesday in October. It was as if the sunshine had encouraged everyone out, for who knew how many more mild days there'd be? The guests had all been pleasant enough, even Mrs Carmichael. Still, she was looking forward to a sit down and it would be the early staff afternoon tea soon.

'Lili, good.' Mrs Bygrove came out of the kitchen. 'Would you join us for a quick meeting about some Christmas charity events?'

She was tired, but Lili was always pleased to be included in these. It made her feel useful, beyond her paid job, as if she had something valuable to contribute. She wondered what they might be collecting funds for this time. The year had certainly become filled with such events since the war started, not just at the hotel. Thinking about helping others was what she needed to take her mind off Norman.

Dear Norman.

'We're in the dining room,' said Mrs Bygrove.

Lili followed her and found a few people there already. 'What will we be collecting money for this time?' said Fanny, half-dismissively.

'Christmas boxes for the troops abroad,' said Edie, leaning against the table.

'S'pose that's a good thing.' Fanny took a seat and the others followed suit.

Mrs Bygrove opened her mouth to speak, when the door was flung open and her husband entered. He was standing tall, with that haughty expression he liked to display, looking down on all of them as if they were dirt on his shoes.

'Ah, here you are. Having your little women's meeting about charity dos, are you? Well, while you've been doing this, *I've* been left to make the serious decisions, as usual.'

Even Fanny raised her eyes heavenward, while Mrs Leggett pinched her lips together.

'Leslie and Stanley, those witless twins, have enrolled in the Derby Scheme, so no doubt will be off to the army soon.'

'Not necessarily, dear,' said his wife. 'It could be months. Or longer.'

'I'm not going to be left in the lurch again so I'm off to put an advertisement in the *Littlehampton Gazette* for more male staff. We might even get some more porters and waiters, and the women can then go back to the jobs they're capable of.'

There were several offended intakes of breath from the women, but only Mrs Bygrove spoke.

'That is very unfair, Douglas. The women have done an exemplary job, all of them who've replaced the men.'

'We'll have to beg to differ on that one. And those twins, they've only gone and got those silky khaki brassards to sew on their jackets, so everyone can see they've enrolled. I warned them, they're not to sew them on their porters' jackets.'

'At least they're willing to do something for their country.' Helen smiled benignly.

'Huh! All the good they'll be, out at the Front. There's nothing to them. They'll be blown away by the first explosion they encounter.'

'Oh, that's not nice, Mr Bygrove,' Gertie piped up, her eyes wide with shock.

'Enough of your lip, Miss Green. Anyway, after I've been to the *Gazette*, I'm off to have afternoon tea with some councillors to see if I can't summon up more trade for the hotel. I really don't know what we'd do without my connections.'

He was about to leave when Mrs Leggett said: 'I think you're forgetting, Mr Bygrove, that The Defence of the Realm Act states that you are not able to employ men between eighteen and sixty for non-essential work.'

'Pff. There's bound to be a few who can't enlist for some reason or other. I hear flat feet's one of the categories. Doesn't stop them walking around a restaurant or the foyer.'

'I think you're missing the—' the housekeeper started.

But he marched back through the open door, not bothering to shut it.

Mrs Bygrove said nothing for a few seconds. Eventually she looked around at them all. 'Now, where were we?'

'The event for the soldiers' Christmas gifts,' said Mrs Turnbull.

'Of course. Mr Janus admitted to me the other day that he started his entertainment career as a comic and a singer, and because so many men in his troupe have enlisted, he has decided to come out of retirement in that respect.'

'I remember him doing that, now you mention it,' said Mrs Leggett. 'He was very talented, as I recall.'

'We'll hold this event on the twenty-second of November. The money's going to Miss Sophia Perryman, who runs the Arun Children's Aid project and is now also in charge of organising the Christmas boxes from this area.'

'Is it going to be similar to the do we put on for the injured soldiers from the hospital?' said Lili, her hand up as if she were at school.

'No. I want to hold more of a concert this time, a sit down event, with the public buying tickets.'

'They won't be wanting extra singers will they?' she asked reluctantly.

'I'm not sure. Would you like to sing again, Lili? I could ask Mr Janus.'

'Oh, no. What I mean is, I'd rather not. Not after what...' She didn't want to say the words, *after what happened last time I sang.* It was like her singing was a bad portent. That was nonsense, of course, but she felt it all the same.

'Of course. I'm sure Mr Janus has got it all in hand.'

There were some moments of silence before Edie said: 'And talking of the *Littlehampton Gazette*, as Mr Bygrove was, we could advertise it there, though we'd have to be quick.'

Helen nodded.

Phoebe, the stillroom maid who'd been promoted to waiting in the dining room along with Lili, appeared at the door.

78

'Excuse me, Mrs Bygrove, but Miss Julia Nye is here to see Edie about the court case. It's now finished.'

'Please, invite her in. She can have some tea and biscuits with us, as I believe it's time. We'll have another meeting in the week about the event. I've already made some enquiries, as has Mr Janus, so I might know a little more by then.'

'Come on Gertie, pet, let's fetch the tea things in,' said Mrs Turnbull.

Gertie rose enthusiastically, smiling, in contrast to her usual grumpy stance when asked to do anything. Come to think of it, she'd been a whole lot brighter recently.

Phoebe fetched Julia in, and she sat between Edie and Helen.

'Thank you for inviting me in for tea, Mrs Bygrove. I hope you didn't mind me coming to the staff entrance, but I thought Edie would want to know the verdict.'

'We all would,' said Helen.

Mrs Turnbull and Gertie returned with the tea and plates of biscuits, made by Mrs Norris's fair hands, as she always put it. As cups and plates were passed around, Stanley joined them.

'Miss Nye's going to tell us the result of Gordon Hadley's trial,' Fanny called.

'Ooh, right.' Stanley sat quickly.

'You'll be glad to hear that he's been committed for all crimes,' said Julia. 'The murders of his wife and of Pamela Brownlow, the attempted murder of Edie and the attack on the Kursaal.'

Edie leant back, closing her eyes and letting out a lengthy sigh. 'Thank goodness.'

'Then it's the death sentence for him?' Fanny rubbed her hands together with some glee.

'Indeed,' said Julia.

Edie took the offered teapot and poured some milk in. 'I'd rather he just spent the rest of his days in gaol, for I have severe reservations about capital punishment, but at least justice has been done.'

'Course he deserves to die,' said Fanny. 'Why should the country pay for his food and keep.'

'I'm not sure putting prisoners to death makes us any better than them. And there are still cases of miscarriages of justice.'

'But—'

'I don't think this is the time to start a debate on capital punishment,' said Helen.

Fanny picked up a biscuit, looking glum once more.

'What about this associate of his, the one known as Jim?' asked Helen.

Julia shrugged. 'He must have done a moonlight flit and who could blame him. Philip says there's no evidence to say he was involved in the murders, only with the... oh, how shall I put this politely?' She glanced around the room, looking unsure.

'The soliciting of young women?' Edie suggested. 'Of whom I believe Pamela was one.'

'Yes, that. No one knows who the rest of the women were, or how many of them there were.'

'Who on earth is Philip?' Gertie asked.

Julia chuckled. 'Sorry, I should have said Detective Inspector Davis.'

'Oh, him.'

'At least it's one evil bas— I mean, brigand, off the streets,' said Stanley.

Mrs Leggett pointed at him. 'We hear you've been up to no good, Mr Morris.'

'What, me? Oh, ya mean the enrolling in the Derby Scheme?' He looked down at his chest, where his khaki brassard was displayed.

'Didn't Mr Bygrove tell you not to sew it on your porter's jacket?' Helen looked at him with pursed lips, though didn't look too serious.

'It ain't sewn, see. It's just pinned.'

'All right, Stanley. I'm not cross. Well done to you and Leslie for caring about your country. Even if you are too young.'

'We're eighteen, madam. The legal age to sign up.'

'Still too young in my opinion.'

There was a rumble of agreement.

'Now, you're the closest to the pot, Lili. Pour yourself one and pass it around.'

'Righty-ho, madam.'

–

She knew it was daft, given the circumstances, but Lili was excited as she left for her afternoon off the following Thursday.

It was still mild for the time of year and, though it was cloudy today, there was a brightness to part of the sky that suggested the sun might get a look in at some point. She put on her grey striped woollen dress to keep her warm. It was a little old-fashioned now, but it was a good-quality dress she'd acquired cheaply second-hand. She thought the winter coat might be a little too warm, so she opted for her jacket instead. It didn't match, like Edie's skirts and jacket did, but the colours went together.

After changing, she considered herself in the mirror against the wall on the landing. She'd swept her hair up into a coil at the back; simple but tidy. She knew that some of the ladies who visited the hotel wore hair pieces or padding, but she didn't need it with her thick curly hair, even though the curls themselves could be a problem in styling. On top, she neatly pinned a straw hat. It had been plain when she'd bought it, but she'd since added a lilac ribbon and a small posy of lilac fabric flowers. She opted for her sturdy boots rather than her Oxford shoes, in case it rained. But if it rained, she'd need a coat. Going back to the bedroom, she hung the jacket back up in the wardrobe and took her old coat out.

What did it matter? She wasn't trying to impress Rhodri.

She attempted to pass through the scullery quickly. Annie Twine was there, washing up.

'Your day off, is it?'

'That's right.'

'Where you off to?'

Lili had only told Edie about meeting Rhodri, as she wouldn't judge her. If she told Annie, she knew she'd tell everyone else and the assumption would be that she'd found a new love. But she didn't want to lie either.

'Fancied some posh afternoon tea so I'm going to the Harbour Tea Rooms.'

'Very nice.'

'See you later.' Lili rushed through the door before Annie had a chance to ask her anything further.

She turned left out of the hotel and walked more leisurely down South Terrace and on to Empress Maud Road. She had plenty of time and she didn't want to get overly warm from hurrying, nor look overkeen if Rhodri spotted her before she got there. Not that she was keen, well, only for some company. She'd had a bad night, barely sleeping, feeling alternately guilty and eager about the day ahead. Surely Norman wouldn't have minded her having friends, doing things to try to keep her mind off what had happened. Yet seeing Rhodri always brought Norman's fate into her mind.

But she'd said she'd meet him now, and she couldn't not turn up.

Reaching the brick edifice of the Nelson public house on the corner of Pier Road, her nerves got the better of her and she had to stop at one point. Would she get around the corner and find him there already? Would she have to wait? Maybe he'd thought better of the meeting too and wouldn't turn up.

No point just standing here. Just walk around the corner!

She did as she instructed herself, taking the corner briskly, so there was no chance she'd turn around and go back. There was no one waiting outside the single-storey Harbour Tea Rooms. The disappointment was overwhelming. She stopped at the side of the public house. The river was at high tide and rushing along as it always did. Across the road from her, on the rocky bank of the riverside, was a pile of lobster pots, then a line of rowing boats. A few yards down there was a sign announcing 'Fishing boats for hire'. The briny tang of fish was more noticeable here than closer to the beach.

Might Rhodri already have gone into the tearoom? They did say they'd meet outside. A couple, well-to-do, passed her on the pavement, looking down their noses at her. She was standing in front of the entrance to the Nelson, so it maybe looked like she was about to go in. No wonder they looked so disapproving. She walked on to the next building, a single-storey dwelling, still not knowing what to do.

It was then she spotted a figure in uniform, limping along the pavement, past the Drill Hall. Relief flooded her. *Thank goodness.* She went forward to meet him, passing the disapproving couple, more than anything to show she wasn't some fallen drunkard of a woman, as they might have assumed.

'Lili, hello. You must have been even earlier than me,' he called.

So, she was early. That's why he hadn't arrived. She waved and called: 'Hello'.

When she reached him, she walked beside him, smiling at the other couple as they passed, wishing them 'good afternoon.'

They returned the greeting, looking more favourably upon her now.

'How are you today, Lili?'

'You know, glad to be out for a while. It were busy this morning. And how are you?'

'I'm fine thank you. I've just left Auntie Charlotte, who's very well, and I'll see Uncle Islwyn when I get back.'

'Good, good.'

Was this going to be the limit of their conversation again? She hoped they would find more things to talk about.

'Here we are. I don't think I've ever been in here.' He stopped outside.

It was tempting to say *not even with Nurse Caffyn?* 'Really? It's not far from your family home.'

'True, but neither were you far away before I enlisted and we never met. Or we didn't notice each other because we didn't hear each other's accents.'

So, without their Welsh connection, she'd have been just another girl and he'd never have noticed her? She felt a little disappointed but did as she always did and berated herself for such a sentiment.

'Are we going in then?' she said.

'Of course.' He stepped forward to open the door, keeping it open to let her in.

There was a hum of chatter among the customers, and the distant hiss of the boiler that made the tea and coffee in the stillroom. A swarthy gentleman in his forties, sporting a white apron tied around his middle and a black jacket, came forward to greet them. It was Mr Crolla, the proprietor.

'Good afternoon,' he said in an Italian accent, performing a small bow. 'A table for two?' He showed them to one by the double window. 'Carlotta will be over shortly to give you menus.' He stepped backwards, performing another small bow, before walking away.

Lili loved the stylishly decorated room, with its small square tables, white lace cloths and slat back chairs. The dark parquet floor had blocks and triangles of wood in a repeating pattern. The bottom half of the wall was made up of dark wooden boards, while the top half was cream, with flowers painted as if growing out of the wood. There was a counter at the back, taking up half the width of the room, with a tall glass display case next to it, exhibiting various scones and cakes.

The tables were already adorned with cups, saucers and side plates. On top of the white linen napkins sat a knife and pastry fork. In the centre were small pots of greenery.

Rhodri leant back and surveyed the room. 'Very nice it looks.'

'Edie – Miss Moore – brought me here once, when we had an afternoon off at the same time. I've been meaning to come back ever since.'

'Not too expensive neither.'

'Nowhere near as dear as the hotel.' She giggled. 'But don't tell anyone I said that. Anyway, I'm paying my bit today.'

His brow creased as he narrowed his eyes. 'No, you're not. I said when I first suggested going for afternoon tea that I'd pay.'

'But it's not like we're, you know... and it don't seem right, especially when you probably don't earn no more than I do, not as a soldier.' He leant forward, opening his mouth to protest, but she put her hand up. 'There's no argument I'm having about this. And if I'm paying for myself, I won't feel guilty about what I order.'

He slumped back. 'All right. I don't want to argue.'

A waitress came over, handing each of them a menu. Her uniform was a little different to those worn by the waitresses at the hotel. She had on a grey skirt with a white blouse, with what looked like a small lace shawl draped over it. At the hotel, they wore a grey dress with a lacy neck. The white, half-apron she was wearing had two pockets, whereas the apron Lili wore had a bib as well, with a broderie anglaise trim. The waitress's ebony hair was in two plaits, on top of which sat a cap, covering more of her head than the ones at the hotel did.

The pair of them decided on cheddar and tomato chutney sandwiches, and a fruit scone with strawberry preserve and clotted cream.

'I'm sorry about the choice of only two cakes today,' said the waitress. 'I'm afraid the war is rather interfering with obtaining ingredients.'

Lili chose the vanilla éclair while Rhodri opted for the fruit cake.

'That's a shame,' said Lili, once the waitress had departed. 'I was rather fancying a piece of lemon cake today.'

'Are you suffering these shortages at the hotel?'

'To some degree. Mrs Norris, the head cook, is certainly complaining a lot about it these days. But she and the other cooks and chefs make the best of what they have, and the choices are still rather splendid.'

'There might come a time when they're not,' said Rhodri, looking serious.

'I'm sure you're right. I wonder how we'll attract the top-notch clientele if that happens.'

'All the premier hotels will be in the same boat, so to speak.' He chuckled. 'Sorry, that's not really funny, but it's the lack of boats importing goods that's the problem.'

'So I understand.'

While they waited, they discussed how Rhodri was finding his clerical job at the Shoreham-by-Sea camp. It was all very polite.

The waitress brought the tea first, placing the pot down on the table, along with a pot of water, a milk jug and a small bowl of sugar cubes.

'Shall I be mother?' said Lili, immediately regretting that it might sound like they were a family, with him as a father.

He didn't seem fazed. 'You're the expert. I'd probably spill it.'

'It largely depends on the teapot. We do pour for guests sometimes. But often they like to pour for theirselves.' She lifted the pot.

'Aren't you going to put the milk in first?'

'Gosh no, you can't put the milk in first. They'd have our guts for garters if we did that at the hotel. It's tea first, then the milk. And you shouldn't stir in a circular way, always back and forth, and don't touch the sides.'

He looked confused. 'What difference does that make?'

'Mr Smithson, the head waiter, explained it to us. If you stir in a circular movement, the tea can spill over the sides. If the spoon touches the sides, it makes a tinkling noise, which isn't acceptable.'

Rhodri seemed amused by this. 'I see.'

'I know it's silly really, but we've got to do it for the guests, many of whom are very genteel.' Though not all, she thought to herself.

86

'I suppose they're paying for the top treatment.'

'Exactly. It's very nice here though, despite being a lot cheaper.'

The waitress brought the cake stand along, with the sandwiches in the bottom layer, a scone each with jam and cream in the middle, and the cakes on the top.

As they ate the sandwiches, the conversation ceased. There'd been something she'd been wondering for a while and when she finished her first triangle of sandwich, she decided to risk broaching it while he was sipping at his tea.

'Do you mind me asking, Rhodri, about your parents? You've only mentioned your brother, and aunt and uncle.'

His lips left the side of the cup and he paused for a moment, staring at the cake stand. Oh dear, had she put her foot in it? What a clumsy piece she was. It was his business, so why had she thought it was hers?

'I'm sorry, I didn't mean to intrude.'

'No, it's all right. I should have explained before, when I mentioned that we lived in Senghenydd. I'd like to tell you. My mother died in childbirth, when she had my brother, Glyn. I was two. Auntie Charlotte, my mother's sister, took over, helping to bring us up while my father worked. He were a hewer in the mine.'

He paused here and she kept quiet, wanting him to tell his story at his own pace.

'In October 1913, when there was the disaster, he were one of the men killed.'

She took a sharp inbreath. Rhodri had said that they'd moved in January 1914; it should have occurred to her there was a connection.

'I'm so, so, sorry. That must have been terrible.'

He looked into her eyes. 'You'd understand what it's like, to lose your da.'

'Yes. It wasn't in an accident, but he did have lung trouble, emphysema, which was because of hewing coal. Did you work in the mine?'

87

'Yes. I had been a hewer, but management discovered I were good at arithmetic after I questioned some payment decisions and they put me in the office. Probably to keep me quiet. But it may well have saved me. As for Glyn, he was an ostler's assistant and was taking a pony to the field at the time.'

'So, you went to live with your aunt and uncle?'

'That's right. Glyn and I suggested we rent a room together at a neighbour's, who had a couple of other miners living there, but Auntie Charlotte insisted we live with her. The accident persuaded her and Uncle Islwyn that we should get out of the mining area altogether.'

'Why Sussex?'

'A similar reason to you. A cousin of Auntie Charlotte's lives in Rustington and wrote that there was jobs in the brickworks here. Uncle Islwyn works in a brick field in Wick. It's not as well paid, but it's a lot less dangerous. And he's outside in the fresh air instead of underground getting a lungful of coaldust. Auntie takes in washing, just like she did back in Wales. Come on, let's get this eaten up.'

They continued with the tea, talking of their old villages, about aspects of their lives that had been similar, and of their families.

Finally, when that conversation stalled, Lili moved onto the tales of Gertie and Fanny, thinking they might be amusing. She ended with how they'd picked on Edie when she'd first arrived at the hotel.

'Gertie's a bit put out, see, because she thinks her best friend's got a young man, but Fanny 'asn't said nothing, so we don't really know.'

Rhodri picked up his fruit cake from the top of the stand. 'They sound a right pair. I'm surprised management didn't get rid of them long since. Especially that bit about them trying to get Edie into trouble for something she didn't do.'

'They have improved. And they're good workers. We're short of those since the war started.'

'I suppose everywhere is.'

They went quiet once more and Lili racked her brain to think of something else, but Rhodri spoke before she'd settled on anything.

'Have you had any more of your charity events at the hotel?'

'Not since the do for Belgrave House Hospital. But we're holding a concert on the twenty-second of November for anyone to come to. The proceeds are going towards Christmas boxes for the Sussex battalions abroad.'

'What a wonderful idea. I'll be sure to tell... Who's that at the window peering in at us? Is she a friend of yours?'

Lili, who'd been concentrating on Rhodri, twisted around to look out. There, looking cross, was Florence Stubbs.

Oh no, what must she think?

'It's Norman's sister. Hold on a moment, I'll just go and have a word.'

She was bound to be thinking something was going on that wasn't.

Out of the door, she said, 'Hello Flo. Fancy seeing you here.'

'Didn't take you long to forget Norman, did it? He's only been gone two months.'

'What? You mean Rhodri? No no, he's just someone who comes from where I used to live. We're only friends who've met up to have a chat about the old country.'

'Looked very cosy, you did.'

'It's not like that, Flo. And besides, Rhodri has a sweetheart: a nurse from the Belgrave, where he recovered.' The usual vague sense of disappointment hung around her as she said this, even though she wasn't sure of the situation.

'I can't imagine she's very impressed with him meeting—'

'Is everything all right,' said Rhodri, peering around the door.

'This is Florence Stubbs, Norman's sister.'

Rhodri stepped out and put his hand forward. 'Pleased to meet you. I'm Corporal Rhodri Morgan. I was sorry to hear of your brother's... disappearance.'

Florence didn't take the offered hand. 'And why are you here and not abroad, Corporal?' She narrowed her eyes.

He slapped his leg twice. 'Took a bullet to the leg, I did, and still have a limp. Not conducive to running across a battlefield, I'm afraid.'

'Corporal Morgan is based in Shoreham-by-Sea, in a clerical role.'

'I see.'

'We must meet up, Flo, for a cup of tea,' said Lili.

'I'm busy at the moment. I've got to get going. Goodbye.' She headed off, not waiting for a reply.

The pair went back into the tearoom and sat down.

'Oh dear, did I say something wrong?' asked Rhodri.

'I'm afraid she was cross about me keeping company with another man. She thinks I've replaced Norman already. I explained we were only friends and that you also—'

The waitress walked over to them. 'Is everything all right?'

'Yes, yes,' Rhodri reassured her. 'We were just greeting an acquaintance.'

The waitress walked away.

Rhodri considered Lili. 'You were saying?'

'I've forgotten where I was. I hope I haven't upset Flo.'

'What you do is not really any of her business. Especially not now.'

'I know, but I don't want her thinking I'm a flibbertigibbet who flits from one sweetheart to another.'

He smiled sympathetically, but said nothing.

She lifted the lid of the pot and poured some of the hot water into it. 'Would you like some more tea?'

He pushed his cup towards her. They were silent again, awkward, like they'd been at the start of the day.

As Lili picked up her éclair from the stand, they remained quiet. He stared out at the river, where people were gathered by the boats. A steam tug passed by. She turned her attention to the interior, watching their waitress as she chatted to Mr Crolla, who Lili knew to be her father. She wondered about their past lives, what it had been like for them in their home country of Italy, why they had come to England. Maybe it wasn't so very different to why she had come here.

'I'm sorry if I've made it awkward with your friend,' said Rhodri, laying his fork down on the plate.

'You haven't. And I only know her because she's Norman's sister. I doubt we would have been friends if it hadn't been for her brother. Regretful it is, that she took our meeting the wrong way.'

'Would it be unwise then, after we've finished, to take a walk on the prom. It seems a shame not to take advantage of the sun.' He looked worried, as if maybe he shouldn't have suggested such a thing.

Lili looked out of the window, to find that the sun had, at last, found its way through the clouds and there was a gleam of light on the river.

'Florence went in the opposite direction, if that's what you're worried about.'

'Is that a yes?'

She thought a moment. 'It is. No point in wasting the reasonable weather, for who knows how many such days we'll have now.'

The creases on his forehead cleared and a smile formed. 'I do love walking by the sea. It's not like I was living here long before I enlisted.'

'And you enlisted in September 1914, you said?'

'That's right. Five weeks after the war began. I'd only been living here about nine months.'

'Well, I'm done, so whenever you're ready, we'll get the bill and have a walk.'

–

It wasn't often now that Lili was asked to do bedroom cleaning since she'd been promoted to waitress. She understood that they were short-staffed due to illness, but she did resent the job more now.

Her mam would have said that she should think herself lucky she didn't have to do it that often. She and her sisters had to do it for hours every day: scrub steps; blacklead fireplaces; cook; wash clothes and dishes; dust; wipe; over and over and over, from early in the morning until late at night. That was the lot of the housewife in a mining village. And most other working-class housewives, no doubt. But worse in a mining area, with the ever-present black soot.

And here she was, resentful of doing a couple of rooms, with good cleaning products and a view of the sea. The room she was in presently had a four-poster bed, an elegant, tiled fireplace and was decorated and furnished in the fashionable arts and crafts style, with William Morris upholstered armchairs. She'd never be able to afford to stay here as a guest, so working here, even if it meant sleeping up in the cramped staff quarters, was the next best thing.

But what would happen when she married, if she ever did now? She doubted she'd be able to keep her job here, earning her own wage, not if she wanted babbies. If she went home to Wales, as she had been considering, her mam could look after them, like she had Carys's at one time. But that was when her sister still only had two children, and Da was still alive, before he died and Mam had to get a part-time job. And they'd both still had to do all the housework. Morys didn't have Jane any more, but Jane's mother looked after his other daughter, Ffion.

Do stop moaning. At least you're still alive. She thought of her deceased sister-in-law, who'd been her friend too. Inevitably, Norman came to mind. She squeezed her eyes tight shut to prevent the tears spilling over. That wouldn't get the job done.

She turned her mind to the day before, the tea and walk with Rhodri. During the stroll on the prom, the incident with Norman's sister had been constantly at the back of her mind, detracting from her enjoyment of the walk. When they'd reached the end of the prom, where the coast road leading to Rustington turned down to join Norfolk Road, Rhodri had examined his wristwatch, declaring it to be a quarter to five. She'd looked at the sun, beginning to set beyond the coastguard cottages and river. He'd announced that he'd better get back to see his aunt, as his uncle would be in shortly. And so, they'd parted company.

Blast the autumn, with its increasingly earlier sunsets, she'd thought. But would he have stayed any longer, had it been summer? He'd still have needed to get back to Shoreham and would have wanted to see his uncle before he'd gone.

He hadn't mentioned organising anything for November, and she wondered whether that was it, whether the ghost of Norman and the indignation of his sister had put paid to the friendship. Maybe he felt guilty about Nurse Caffyn. Or did he just find her boring and no longer wanted her as a friend?

Wiping the coving was the last thing she needed to do in the room. Then she could go to early-morning break, before her stint at morning coffee in the conservatory.

Taking the wooden cleaning box and leaving the room, she encountered Gertie in the corridor, clattering her box to the ground and looking cross.

'You all right, Gertie?'

'Dunno why it's the women what have to do the cleaning when we're short-staffed. Stanley and Leslie could do it.'

'Except they've had no experience and we have.'

'I can't get no tips up here.'

'At least you've got this afternoon off.'

'Huh. I was supposed to be spending it with Fanny, but now she's got other plans. Again.'

'This so-called sweetheart you thought she might have?'

'Guess so, otherwise why not say what she's doing?'

'I wonder why she'd want to keep it a secret?'

Gertie shrugged.

'Come on, it's breaktime. Want to make the most of it, I do, before I have to serve morning coffee.'

'Whereas I 'ave to come back 'ere.'

Lili led the way, wondering whether Gertie worried about being attacked by a guest again. She couldn't blame her for being cautious.

Lili and Gertie placed their boxes away in the scullery. Entering the staff corridor once more, they heard a clear argument. It was the manager and Mrs Norris in the kitchen.

'Not again,' said Gertie. 'I swear that man could start a fight with a nun.'

Lili grinned. That was the nearest to a joke Gertie had made in ages. But she was right. 'Let's leave them to it. It's parched, I am.'

In the staff dining room, Edie was pouring herself a coffee.

Mrs Turnbull sat nearby, stirring her tea. 'They're at it again, are they?'

Lili left the door open. 'They certainly are.' She and Gertie sat, and they all listened.

'I've been through all this with my wife,' came Bygrove's strident voice. 'And I'm telling you that my friends are coming here for dinner and I intend to impress them.'

'I can't just change the menu on a whim,' barked Mrs Norris. 'The food's already been delivered. What am I supposed to do with the chicken, marrows and sirloin? And how do I order what's on your list at this late time?'

'You can still do the salmon with the mousseline sauce and the filet mignon for first course, and the roast duckling and venison for second, but I expect some oysters in the first course, and fillet of sole Veronique in the second. And add asparagus to the vegetables.'

'Asparagus is out of season, Mr Bygrove.'

'Well, some creamed carrots then! And for dessert, take the rhubarb tartlets off the menu and add Charlotte Russe.'

'I ain't got time to get the ingredients for that, let alone prepare it.'

'Send staff out to fetch what else is needed from the shops.'

'We're short-staffed, if you 'aven't noticed. And that'll take a while.' Mrs Norris was getting more rattled by the sentence. 'We're dealing with dainties for morning coffee at the moment, then there's lunch and afternoon tea to prepare. And the menu me and Mrs Bygrove decided on is a good one, quite impressive enough for your friends, what with the sauté of chicken Lyonnaise and the sirloin of beef, not to mention the marrow farci. And there's a nice consommé.'

'But I want—'

'I can't do it in the time! And there'd be a lot of wastage and the country's starting to get short of food and...'

Mrs Norris raged on. Lili knocked Edie's arm with her elbow and pulled a face. 'Good for Mrs Norris for speaking up, though I'm not sure how she dares be quite so bold.'

'Because he's hardly goin' to sack her,' Mrs Turnbull muttered, looking up from her knitting. 'She's too good and experienced staff are hard to come by now.'

'Well, *that's* what I want on the dinner menu and there's an end to it.' There was a tip-tapping of Bygrove's shoes as he marched away. Mrs Norris was soon clomping into the room.

''Ere Gertie, are you free now, to go to the shops?'

'No. I've got more cleaning after the break.'

'Lili? Edie?'

Both shook their heads.

'I'm on morning coffee,' said Lili.

'And I'm on the desk,' said Edie.

Mrs Turnbull stood. 'I'll go, pet. Don't fret now. I've got a store cupboard to take stock of, but I can do that anytime today. Come on, you tell me what you want.'

She took Mrs Norris's arm and led her away.

'You're a life-saver, Bridget. That Bygrove. He gets worse and worse.'

'I know pet, I know.'

Chapter Seven

Lili had looked forward to the show tonight and was now showing people to seats in the ballroom. The hotel had only served early dinner to the resident guests this Saturday, allowing more staff to help in the ballroom to set up the chairs and the stage area that Mr Janus had organised.

Despite the short notice, Mrs Bygrove and Mr Janus had managed to summon up several singers and musicians. There were also to be a couple of elocutionists reciting from literary works and, in contrast, Mr Janus providing some humour. There seemed to be something for everyone, which was just as well given the variety of people who'd turned up.

Mr Bygrove had decided, after all the organisation and hard work had been done by others, to come and greet the guests. Lili had overheard him taking credit for the event from at least two parties of people and not correcting them in their mistaken assumption. Poor Mrs Bygrove. Would she ever get recognition for her dedication to these causes?

Having just shown the major to the single seat left on the front row, she turned back to see who she could help next, only to get a huge surprise. Coming through the door was Rhodri, in uniform, with two older men. She hurried to be the one to help them before any other staff members got to them.

'Corporal Morgan,' she greeted him. 'How nice that you could make it.' She tried to sound friendly without making her pleasure at seeing him obvious.

'After you told me about the concert last month, I mentioned it to the captain, as I fancied coming. This is Captain

96

Deeprose and Lieutenant Hatter.' He gestured to the officers with him.

'I'm so glad you could make it, gentlemen.'

'Yes, we thought it was a spiffing idea,' said the captain. 'Raising money for Christmas boxes for the men in our local battalions abroad. And since Morgan here was keen to come, I got him to book tickets for us too. I've passed the hotel a couple of times in the motorcar in the past and wondered what it was like. I've heard excellent things about it.'

'I'll see how close to the front I can get you gentlemen,' Lili said, leading the way. She found them three seats in the fourth row, which she was pleased about, given how quickly it was filling up.

'I hope you enjoy the evening, gentlemen.'

Rhodri gave her a warm smile, which disconcerted her a little. 'I'm sure we will.'

On the way back, she was so distracted she almost bumped into Gertie, who was showing a couple of soldiers to seats. Judging by their slings, they'd probably come from Belgrave House Hospital. Gertie had been exceptionally pleased to have been made one of the ushers this evening and was doing a good job of it, chatting cheerfully to them.

Lili was a few steps in front of her when Bygrove loomed into sight, looking cross.

'Miss Green, I do not expect you to flirt with the guests. This is a respectful hotel.'

Lili stopped to see where this was going.

'I wasn't, sir. I was just talking to 'em, telling 'em it should be a good evening.'

'If I see you bothering guests again, I shall remove you from this duty. And it's "them" not "'em". How many times have you been told to talk properly when you're engaging with guests?'

'What's wrong,' said Helen, approaching.

'I was reprimanding Miss Green here for flirting with the guests.'

'But I wasn't flirting with 'em. Them.'

Lili took the few steps back to join them. 'I heard her, sir, madam, and she was just being friendly.'

'Well, *I* heard otherwise, and I'm the manager. And I'll have both of you out of here if you argue with me.'

'Douglas, I'll deal with this,' said Helen.

'Make sure you do… ah, Mr Rotherham, how nice to see you here.' Bygrove, his ingratiating smile in place, followed one of the local councillors as he was shown to a seat by Edie.

'I'm sorry, madam.' Gertie looked forlorn.

'I'm sure there's nothing to apologise for. Carry on.'

Gertie scurried away, looking less sure of herself.

'I wish…' Helen began, but seemed to think better of saying more. 'You carry on too.'

Lili nodded and went to find some more guests to guide to seats, wondering what Helen had been about to say. Probably nothing complimentary about her husband.

When all were seated, the concert started. Mr Janus was compere. Lili was delighted the staff were allowed to stay and watch, albeit standing at the back of the room.

In the first half, a soprano and a tenor performed a couple of songs each, one from an opera, and one popular. Next, a retired string quartet performed some classical pieces. The first half of the concert was finished off with a pianist playing Beethoven's *Für Elise*, which Lili recognised from a couple of concerts she'd attended at the Workman's Institute at home in Dorcalon.

As Mr Janus announced the end of the first half of the concert, the staff at the back opened the doors and made ready to guide the audience towards the dining room, where refreshments were being served.

'Will you be in the dining room?' Rhodri asked her as he left the ballroom.

'I'm not sure yet,' she replied, before heading off to the staff area.

In the kitchen, she called, 'Is there anything else to be taken out,' to Jack, the sous chef.

'Just this last salver of cheese and chutney canapés here.'

She whisked it up and headed to the dining room, where the tables had been rearranged around the edges of the room, with some seats around them for patrons who wished to sit down. The tables with the snacks and refreshments were laid out in a line to one side of the door into the staff area. The audience had already gathered in groups, chatting. As she placed the canapés on the table, Helen approached her.

'Would you help serve the refreshments, Lili?'

'Of course.' She was glad of the opportunity to chat to the audience as she served them.

On the refreshment table were several jugs of squashes, juices and cordials. Lili stood next to Phoebe, who seemed quite animated as she served guests. The head waiter, John Smithson, was serving on the next table.

'A glass of the quinine and orange cordial, please.'

It was Mrs Carmichael, not looking at her but around at the guests. 'Mr Bloomfield,' she declared, beaming. 'I didn't expect to see you here tonight.'

Bloomfield was the council leader, a so-called friend of Bygrove's and a pompous piece as far as Lili was concerned, demanding this and that when he came into the hotel for an occasional meal. He and Mrs Carmichael often exchanged pleasantries and the last time he'd come in for afternoon tea, he'd invited her to join him. Lili wondered what her husband, away at the war, would have thought. But then, was it any different to her having a friendship with Rhodri?

'Mrs Carmichael. How delightful.' Despite his words, he looked worried. 'Excuse me, I must take this back to my wife.' He held up a glass of lemon squash.

So, his wife was with him on this occasion. Perhaps he was afraid she'd take the friendship the wrong way. Like Florence had with her and Rhodri.

'I'm glad to have seen you tonight,' came another voice.

'Rhod… Corporal Morgan,' she amended, seeing him to one side of the table. 'Would you like some refreshment?'

'I've been sent to collect lime juices for Captain Deeprose and Lieutenant Hatter. I think they'd rather have had beer, but you're obviously not offering any.'

'No, not for a charity do like this.' She poured the limes and pushed them towards Rhodri. 'Nothing for yourself?'

'I'll deliver these and come back for mine.'

'Righty-ho.'

He took the drinks away.

'Is that the corporal who was at the do back in August?' Phoebe asked, looking curiously at him.

'Yes. He's stationed at Shoreham base now.'

'Because of his limp, I suppose. That's nice for you though, as he seems to have taken a shine to you.' Phoebe nudged her arm gently.

'It's nothing like that! Norman's not been gone three months yet.'

'I'm sorry, it was rather thoughtless of me.' Phoebe looked regretful.

'It's all right. We get on because he's from near where I come from, see.'

Phoebe was distracted by a guest and turned to serve them. Lili was similarly kept busy, looking over every now and again to see if Rhodri was about to return, even though she tried not to.

'Looks like we're running out of the quinine and orange,' said Phoebe.

'I'll go to the stillroom and see if Hetty's got any more made up.'

She strode towards the door into the staff area, hoping Rhodri didn't come back while she was gone. Why had she volunteered to do this?

About to enter the stillroom, near the end of the corridor next to the kitchen, a voice called her name.

'Lili. Wait a moment.'

'Rhodri, you shouldn't be back here.'

'I thought you might not return and wanted to speak to you.'

'I'm only going to get some more refreshments.'

'Oh, I see. How are you, though? I'm sorry I haven't written the last month. We've been busy at the camp and only got a few hours off, so I haven't had time to come to Littlehampton. I could only come tonight because the captain offered to drive me here.'

'You could have written and told me that. I'm all right, though.'

'Yes, sorry, I should have done. Any news of Norman?'

'No, I've heard nothing. And now...' She was loath to voice her thoughts, afraid that to do so would seal Norman's fate forever. As if she had any influence with the Almighty, or destiny. 'Now I doubt I ever will. I must accept that he's... gone.' She sighed and slumped a little, the inevitability of it weighing her down.

'Oh Lili, I'm so sorry.' He sprang forward, extending his arms, as if he were about to hug her.

She pulled away. 'Whatever are you doing?'

'I... I'm sorry. You looked sad. I was only trying to offer some comfort.'

'That would be all right if you were one of my woman friends, but otherwise it's inappropriate.' Even as she berated him, she regretted that she had to do so. But then she remembered Nurse Caffyn. 'And what about—'

'Excuse me,' said Annie Twine, causing them to move as she rushed past with an empty tray.

'I apologise,' said Rhodri. 'You are right, of course. I don't know what I was thinking. I didn't mean to offend you. I had better collect my drink and re-join my companions.'

He walked away. Lili watched him as he went, guilt-ridden. Really, she would have welcomed a hug from him. It would have been like being cuddled by one of her brothers when she was younger and had fallen over.

Lili found two more jugs of quinine and orange cordial in the stillroom and returned to the dining room. She spotted

Rhodri near the door into the foyer, with the officers, nodding to something the captain was saying. Should she write to him, apologise for overreacting? It would be sad not to see him again because he'd thought he'd offended her. Perhaps it would be better to wait for him to write. After all, he might get the wrong idea.

She stared at him for a few seconds, before her attention was taken by another customer.

—

'What was all that about, Corporal?' said the lieutenant, when Rhodri returned with his drink.

'What was all what, sir?'

'Don't play the innocent, Corporal.' The captain smirked at him. 'You followed that waitress out of that door. Lili, did you say her name was? I'm guessing it's the kitchen and whatnot behind there.'

'It is, sir. I was only checking how she was, see. Remember I said she'd lost a sweetheart in France?'

'Of course, of course. And didn't you say that she's from Wales, near where you came from?'

'That's right, sir.'

The officers were soon distracted by other subjects, leaving Rhodri to sip his cordial and listen, trying to forget what had just happened.

A gong was struck and a voice announced that the second half of the concert would commence in five minutes. The audience filtered back into the elegant ballroom and Rhodri took his seat next to the lieutenant once more.

The next half of the concert consisted of several elocutionary items, both prose and poetry.

Rhodri's mind wandered. What a clumsy dolt he was. What had made him lunge at Lili like that? No wonder she'd been annoyed with him. But he had to admit to himself, as reluctant as he was to do so, he had become fond of her. She was always so kind, so considerate. She listened to him when he spoke, not always trying to interrupt with her own interests, like his one-time sweetheart in Senghenydd had. A silly gossip she'd turned out to be, only interested in clothes and hairstyles.

Lili wasn't like that. And now he'd gone and spoiled their friendship. If he'd ever hoped to make more of it, that likelihood was gone. He should have given her more time.

Mr Janus took the stage once more, performing a humorous routine. Rhodri started to take an interest as people laughed. He was surprised to find that the owner of the local entertainments was a talented comedian. Who would have thought it? He finished his act with a funny song about the Kaiser, causing the whole audience to fall about laughing.

By the end of the concert, Rhodri's spirits had lifted – until he remembered his faux pas with Lili. His mood dipped once more. He had no idea what to do about the situation. If he approached her again, she might think he was harassing her.

Nevertheless, he'd have a word with her, if he could, at the end, and decide then what to do.

–

The concert was finished and the audience was filing out. Lili and the other staff involved had lined up in various places along the foyer to wish them good night. There had been many positive comments about the evening's entertainment and several requests that the event might be repeated in the future.

Lili's breath hitched when Rhodri came into view, talking to Stanley and smiling. He was only a few feet away, so she'd be sure to catch him, to apologise. He finished speaking to Stanley and edged closer, glancing over at her briefly. Any moment now…

'Miss Probert, see Mrs Carmichael to her room.' It was Bygrove, sounding pretentious as usual, with the guest in question standing nearby, a pained expression on her face.

'I'm nearly finished sir. I'll take her in a mo—'

'Now, Miss Probert! Mrs Carmichael is feeling faint, and I want you to ensure she doesn't pass out on the way up.'

'Very well sir.' Lili followed it with a long breath out, which she kept to herself. As she turned to join Mrs Carmichael, Rhodri walked past, gazing at her briefly with a frown, but not stopping until he reached the outer doors. Then he was gone. Her heart sank.

Mrs Carmichael was rubbing her temples and closing her eyes. 'Thank you, Lili. I'm not myself tonight. It must be all the noise and bustle.'

Lili resisted rolling her eyes. What an actress she was, for she had no doubt that the woman felt perfectly fine but was looking for attention, as usual.

'You're welcome, madam. Let us take the lift rather than the stairs.' Lili led the way.

When she came back downstairs ten minutes later, some of the staff were carrying chairs back to the dining room. In there, the twin porters, Leslie and Stanley, along with John Smithson, were rearranging the tables with Mrs Bygrove. The housemaids had moved in to clean and sweep. Mr Bygrove was nowhere to be seen.

Lili went to fetch one of the stylish mahogany Chippendale dining chairs that she so admired, with their claw feet and padded leather seats, to return it to a table.

'That was a good evening,' said Phoebe, placing the chair she'd collected next to Lili's.

'It certainly was.' Lili put on a smile, all the while thinking that it *would* have been a good evening had she not been so sharp with Rhodri.

Mrs Bygrove came over to them. 'Lili, could I speak to you, please, in the foyer?'

'Of course, madam.'

When Helen also beckoned John Smithson over, Lili became anxious. Had he reported her for talking to Rhodri in the staff area? Serving drinks at the next table, he may well have spotted him following her. Maybe he'd even peeped around the door without her noticing and had seen Rhodri try to hug her.

Why hadn't he reprimanded her at the time? That's what he'd normally have done, not gone tittle-tattling to management. She feared the inappropriateness of engaging with a customer in such a way could only spell doom for her time as a waitress. Could she bear to be a maid again, for the rest of her days?

Helen came to a standstill by the desk, manned now by Stuart Coulter, one of the regular desk clerks, who lived out. Lili stopped a few feet away, while Mr Smithson stood next to the manageress.

'Miss Probert...'

Here it comes, thought Lili.

'I'm told by Mr Smithson here that you've been an exemplary waitress in the dining room and the conservatory.'

'Oh. Oh.'

'Don't sound so surprised,' said the head waiter.

'You have also proved more than efficient on the desk on the few occasions you've stepped in, dealing with enquiries competently.'

Despite what happened with Mrs Carmichael, thought Lili.

'Mr Smithson, here, is retiring after Christmas.'

'For the second time,' he chuckled.

'And he has recommended that you take on the role as head waitress.'

Her eyes opened wide in surprise. 'Me?'

'Yes, you,' said Smithson. 'I'll train you up in whatever else you need to know while I'm still here. Won't take much time as you're pretty well informed already.'

'I... I don't know what to say.' It was literally the last thing she expected.

'Hopefully just yes,' said Helen. 'And it would mean a pay rise.'

'Then, yes!'

'Wonderful! Now, I'd better go and see how close everyone is to finishing.' Helen wandered off.

'Thank you so much, Mr Smithson, for recommending me.'

'It's well deserved, Miss Probert.'

'Do you have any plans for your retirement?'

'Going to join the Volunteer Training Corps, defending the homeland. So, I won't be doing nothing all day. Don't think I could. But it's not till after Christmas, so I've a few weeks left yet.'

Helen reappeared, announcing: 'We're all cleared up for the evening. I suggest you leave the housemaids to their work and head off for a drink before you retire or go home.'

Mr Smithson took a few steps away, turning back to ask: 'Are you coming, Miss Probert?'

'I think I'll head straight off to bed. I'm worn out.'

'Good night then.'

She waited a few seconds while the rest of the staff disappeared, trying to take in what had just happened. A promotion – to head waitress!

She couldn't wait to write to Mam and tell her. She tried to picture the look on her siblings' faces when she passed on the news. Especially that of Carys, who'd always reckoned she wouldn't make anything of herself in England.

That would have to wait until tomorrow. Tonight, she needed to sleep and forget the unfortunate scene with Rhodri.

Chapter Eight

Helen was on the desk when Douglas marched through the foyer door on the first Saturday afternoon in December, his golf clubs slung over one shoulder. He was whistling a merry tune.

Helen looked at the grandfather clock: two thirty-five. She did not feel so merry, dealing as she had done at lunch time with her children's tears.

He strolled over to the desk.

'I thought you didn't like staff entering by the front entrance,' she said.

'I'm not staff. I'm the manager. And the owner. And I could easily be taken for one of our prestigious guests with my spiffing outfit.' He looked down at his golfing attire, with its knickerbockers, jumper and tweed jacket. 'Don't spoil the splendid day I've had.'

She moved a little closer to him, lowering her voice. 'Spoil *your* day? You were not so considerate with your children, seeing as you were supposed to be taking them out in the motorcar to Worthing today for lunch. And, more importantly, for a look at the toy shops to choose what they'd like for Christmas.'

His face displayed only momentary surprise. 'Was that today?'

'Yes, Douglas, it was. The children were very upset at lunch-time. I had to leave poor Vera to deal with them.'

He glanced at his wristwatch. 'I suppose it's too late now.'

'Of course it is! How could you forget your own children?'

'I was offered lunch by someone. They're... um... a good customer here, so I could hardly refuse.'

'And *that* was more important than keeping your children happy?'

He flicked his hand as if belittling the matter. 'There'll be plenty of opportunities to take them.'

'Perhaps you'd like to tell them that yourself. Here's Edie to take over from me... Edie, do you know where the children are?'

'They're in the staff dining room with Vera. She thought having others around might distract them from their...' She glanced at Helen, before finishing with, '...tears.'

Douglas raised his eyebrows. 'All this fuss about nothing.'

'You're not a child, Douglas, and you clearly don't remember being one.'

In the dining room, the children jumped up and ran to their father as he and Helen entered. Lili, Mrs Turnbull, Phoebe and Mrs Norris were in the room too.

'Daddy, can we go now?' said Arthur, clinging onto his father's leg, his blond hair dishevelled.

'Please, Daddy, please,' Dorothy echoed.

'Not today. Come on now, no pulling at my clothes. They're Daddy's best.' He pushed them both away, gently but decidedly. 'We'll go on Monday.'

'But we have school on Monday,' said Dorothy, before her face crumpled and she started crying. This set Arthur off.

'You can go next Saturday,' said Helen.

'No, I've got something on.'

'Then *I'll* take them,' said Helen, aware that her tone was becoming strained, which she'd rather not display with both the children and staff present. She'd already spotted Lili and Phoebe glancing at each other when Douglas had made a fuss about his clothes.

'But if I'm out, you'll have to be acting manager.'

'Let *me* take care of that. I will, of course, need the motorcar.'

Douglas bit his lip before saying: 'Very well. I'm only going to be local anyway. I'm going to change.' He left, despite the children still being in tears.

Even Helen's own father, drunkard that he'd been, had displayed more affection for his children. Her heart went out to her babies, and she stepped forward to give them both a cuddle.

'Come on, me ducks,' said Mrs Norris. 'I'll make you a nice cup of cocoa each. And I'm sure there are a few leftover biscuits what won't pass muster for afternoon tea.'

Vera guided them towards the kitchen. When they'd gone, Helen slumped onto the bench. 'I'm sorry to have disturbed your tea break like this.'

'It's not your fault the bairns were upset,' said Mrs Turnbull.

Helen knew the unspoken implication was that Douglas was to blame. Which he was. Serves him right if the staff lost respect for him. Guiltily, she realised that she herself was a long way down that path. He was her husband, after all.

An idea occurred to Helen. 'Lili, when is your day off this week?'

'Thursday, madam.'

'Have you anything planned?'

Lili let out a long sigh. 'Not this week, no. I did write to Florence, Norman's sister, but had no reply.'

Helen had suspected that Lili was still missing Norman a great deal and wondered if she could help cheer her up.

'Do you fancy swapping Thursday for Saturday and taking a trip to Worthing with us, in the motorcar? You could have lunch with us, then you could look around the stores while I take the children to the toy shops.'

'That… that's very kind. Are you sure? What about the staff rota?'

'I'll rearrange it, don't worry about that. At least it would be a change of scenery for you.'

'Yes, yes, it would. Thank you, I would love to come.'

Lili's beaming smile convinced Helen that she'd at least achieved something in this whole debacle. Poor Lili. She really hoped the trip would lift her spirits.

–

Saturday arrived and Lili's last shift before she was due to leave for Worthing was morning coffee. But even before she'd had a chance to get ready for the trip out, a snag occurred.

Lili was enjoying a quick glass of lime cordial in the stillroom, before heading to her bedroom, when Mrs Bygrove entered. Her face was pale and expressionless.

'There you are, Lili. Good. I'm afraid we've a slight problem with the trip to Worthing today.'

Lili's heart sank. She really needed this day out. What would she do otherwise? Drag herself, yet again, around the town, seeing the same old shops. It wasn't a day for walking on the beach, with the odd spit of rain that had fallen in between vague glimpses of sunshine. And it was a little breezy.

'We're not going then?' said Lili, trying not to sound too disappointed.

'We're still going, as I couldn't let the children down again. They're so looking forward to spending time in the toy shops there. But we'll have to walk to the railway station and get the train. It appears my husband has taken the motorcar after all.'

Mrs Leggett, who'd been giving Annie and Alice Twine instructions, looked over. 'Did you not both agree that you could have it today?'

'We did. He must have forgotten.'

The look on the housekeeper's face said what Lili was thinking. More likely he'd just sneaked off with it, despite the arrangement.

'That's all right,' said Lili. 'I like going on trains.' While that was true, she'd so looked forward to riding in the motorcar. She'd never been in one before.

'If you could get ready straight away, we'll try to catch the quarter-past-twelve train. That should get us there in time for some lunch.'

'Very well, madam.'

Lili finished the cordial quickly and rushed to her room. It was a good job her hair was already neat and tidy. She pulled off her uniform impatiently – putting the white apron and cap to one side for the laundry – and put on the warm clothes she'd worn when she'd last spent the afternoon with Rhodri.

She still hadn't decided whether to write to him, to apologise for her shortness. He'd been kind, ensuring she was all right at the concert, and she'd told him off for it.

Never mind that now: they had a train to catch. She picked up her handbag, which had seen better days, with its peeling leather and dull metal chain. She'd already prepared it with what she needed, along with a sack bag for any purchases. She ran down the stairs, ready for her adventure.

–

Mrs Bygrove treated Lili to a tasty lunch of grilled mackerel, which had, claimed the menu, been caught on the coast at Worthing. She felt quite full-up by the time they vacated the dining room on Montague Street, one of the main shopping thoroughfares, parallel with the promenade road.

'It's ten past two now,' said Helen, regarding her watch. 'Shall we meet by Hubbard's on South Street at half past four?'

'Yes. Except, I don't have a wristwatch, so I'll have to find a clock to check.'

'No need to worry.' Helen undid her wristwatch, which Lili was sure had a silver strap.

'Oh no, I can't take yours. What will you do for the time?'

'I've got Granddaddy's fob watch,' said Arthur, fishing it out of his coat pocket and displaying it proudly.

'It was my father's,' said Helen. 'I let Arthur take it out on special occasions.'

'How lovely,' said Lili, leaning down to take a closer look. 'You look very handsome with it, Arthur.' It was a fine piece, so it was a wonder that Bygrove hadn't claimed it for himself.

Helen lifted Lili's coat sleeve to clip the watch onto her wrist.

'Thank you, Mrs Bygrove. And I'll see you at half past four.'

They headed in opposite directions, Lili making her way towards South Street.

She wondered about buying a couple of Christmas presents while she was here, but the shops were all a little overwhelming for her. Walking from the station, there'd been so much choice: clothes shops, drapers, milliners, butchers, grocers, greengrocers, fruiterers and florists, fishmongers, confectioners, refreshment rooms, boot and shoe sellers. The windows were maybe not as full as they'd been before the war, but it still made her hanker after things she would never be able to afford. A new pair of boots would have been nice. She'd also passed a couple of hairdressers. How she would love to sit in one of the seats and have someone else cut her hair or put it up in the latest style for her. When she wanted to trim her long hair, she always did it herself. Back in Wales, her mother had always done it.

Some of the shops were beginning to look a little festive with holly and ivy, and a sprinkling of baubles.

She reached a small side street called Bath Place and decided to head down it, towards Marine Parade. Half-way down was the Theatre Royal. How she longed to step inside to see a play or an operetta. She'd enjoyed the ones that had come to the Workmen's Institute in Dorcalon every now and again. But this was a proper theatre.

Lili pictured herself here, all done up like the mine manager's wife or daughter, holding someone's arm. It was meant to be Norman, but her imagination conjured up Rhodri.

Wouldn't it be strange if she saw him here today? She wondered again about writing to him. No, that would be unwise. The way he'd glanced at her when leaving the do at the hotel had shown her that he clearly didn't want to talk to her any more.

She shook the image from her mind. A visit to the theatre with either him or Norman was never going to happen.

At the end of the street, she turned left and crossed over the promenade road, waiting first for a motorcar, a horse and carriage, and several bicycles to pass by. The sun had appeared from behind the clouds once more, so now might be a good time to walk along the pier. There wouldn't be any entertainments this time of the year, but she'd enjoy the view.

She wondered where the girl from Dorcalon lived, the friend of a girl she'd known called Polly, whose adventure to Worthing had encouraged her to look for a job on the coast here. Perhaps this town would have been a better choice for her too, being bigger and having a larger range of shops, though she preferred the beach in Littlehampton and loved the river.

She was nearing the end of the pier now. The sky had cleared a little more, giving her a good view of both sides of the coastline stretching out into the distance. It was a little breezier here, but she didn't mind its freshness against her face. How far up and down the coast could she see? Looking eastwards, she wondered if Shoreham was visible. It was only two towns away, so it could well be. Perhaps she could even spy Rhodri's camp, though she didn't know if it was by the sea or more inland. She'd have to ask him when – if – she ever saw him again.

She checked Helen's watch. Twenty to three. She'd better wander back if she wanted to go into any of those shops. As she walked towards Marine Parade, a cloud covered the sun and there were more on the horizon. The breeze became a little stronger, causing her to check the safety of her velour hat. Yes, it was well pinned on.

Entering Marine Parade once more, and about to cross over to South Street, she noticed a group of soldiers across the road, outside Maynards Confectioners. For a moment, her heart stalled, as one of them was tall, with dark hair beneath his cap. It was possible Rhodri might come to Worthing, on a day off.

He turned to tap the man next to him on the shoulder. No, it wasn't him. Her disappointment was almost overwhelming.

Enough of that. She'd go and look for a gift for Edie for Christmas, and something to send to her mother.

Heading down South Street, she detected the familiar scent, before reaching the tobacconist. She stood looking in the window at the pipes, the tins of tobacco and boxes of cigars. The aroma always reminded her of her father, of the kitchen at home. How she missed her da. Looking back though, she doubted that his pipe smoking had helped the emphysema, despite what advertisements claimed about the health benefits.

She moved swiftly on, glancing in a jeweller's window at expensive trinkets she'd never own. At Bentall's the drapery store, she did a quick tour inside, looking at the fabrics, imagining what she might make with the ones she liked best.

A couple of shops along was a domestic bazaar. She perused the window, full of crockery and household goods. No, they were too impersonal for gifts and she couldn't send china in the post.

Mrs Bygrove had mentioned a fancy repository she was hoping to visit on Montague Street, further up from the dining room where they'd had lunch. That might be a better bet.

She hurried along to it, taking in the other shops' windows briefly as she passed, deciding to have a more leisurely browse on her return, determined as she was to get the presents first. Then she could relax a little more.

The fancy repository had a fragrance of patchouli, and was filled with costume jewellery, brushes, combs, perfume, leather goods, papier mâché and glass ornaments, headdresses, gloves, and so many more delightful gifts. What might she have bought Rhodri as a Christmas present, had they still been friends? A clothes brush, maybe? No. They hadn't been that well acquainted, so it would have been inappropriate.

Lili gazed around in wonder, but she soon found the perfect gifts: two artificial silk scarves. One was largely teal, a favourite colour of Edie's. The other had a lot of purple, which her mother favoured. But she wanted something extra for Edie, who'd been such a good friend the past few months. Scanning the shop, she spotted an ebony hairbrush. It was a little on the expensive side, but she'd saved a bit for Christmas. Edie had talked of needing a new one and she had a fondness for ebony wood. She paid for the items and put the three parcels, expertly wrapped in tissue and brown paper, into her sack bag.

What a relief. She checked her watch: twenty past three. More than an hour to have a look at the other stores.

She'd only walked a few shops down, stopping to look in a baker's window, when she was surprised to hear her name called. Confused at first, she imagined, once again, that Rhodri had come to Worthing. But it was a woman's voice.

Turning, she saw Norman's mother, Mrs Stubbs, heading eagerly towards her. A little behind, not looking so sure, was Florence. Of all the people she'd have liked to bump into, she wasn't sure that Norman's sister was near the top of her list any more.

'Why, Lili, how lovely to see you here. What are the chances, eh?' said Mrs Stubbs.

Indeed, what were the chances?

'And a much nicer reason for being here than the reason we came.'

'Oh dear.' Lili didn't know what else to say to this. Did it have something to do with Norman?

Florence caught up. 'We've been to visit my grandmother in the hospital here.'

Of course, Mrs Stubbs's mother lived in Worthing. Florence had mentioned her not being well.

'I'm sorry to hear that. Did she have another stroke?'

'They don't think so,' said Florence. 'She fell over and hit her head, probably from still being a bit wobbly after that stroke though. She's still slightly concussed, according to the nurse.'

'She's going home tomorrow,' said Mrs Stubbs. 'Probably too soon, but my father can't afford to have her in there any longer.'

Lili nodded. It made her grateful for the community hospital in Dorcalon, which all the families paid a sub towards so they could have free treatment when they needed it. 'I hope she recovers soon. Especially with Christmas coming up.'

She was about to say it had been nice seeing them, but that she had to get on as she was meeting Mrs Bygrove soon. Before she had the chance, Mrs Stubbs took hold of her arm.

'We were just about to walk down to Perilli's Refreshment House, for a drink and a biscuit. Come and join us, and tell us what you've been up to. I loved hearing about the hotel when you visited before.'

There was a plea in the woman's eyes she couldn't ignore. Lili glanced at Florence, expecting her to look unimpressed with the request, but she was smiling.

'All right.' What else could she say? 'But I will have to leave just before, um, a quarter past four, to meet Mrs Bygrove… my manageress.' It was half past four really, but she wanted to pop into a confectioner before leaving Worthing.

'That gives you the best part of an hour,' said Mrs Stubbs, smiling.

Already the day was coming to a close, not helped by the gathering clouds. Norman's mother told her more about her own mother's accident as they walked. Lili only nodded, adding the odd, 'Oh dear,' and 'Hm mm,' while Florence interrupted with the odd piece of information.

Perilli's was near the other end of Montague Street, where Lili had started off. In the distance, she could hear voices singing *In The Bleak Midwinter*. When they reached the entrance of a broad side street, there was a choir of about a dozen men and women standing with music sheets in their hands. They'd now moved on to *O Come, O Come Emmanuel*.

'What lovely harmonies they have,' said Lili, thinking of her choir back at the Baptist Church in Dorcalon, with much nostalgia. It gave Lili an idea that she could suggest to Mrs Bygrove on the train journey home. Whether she'd like the idea was another matter, but she'd put it forward anyway.

'Bit early for Christmas, if you ask me,' said Mrs Stubbs. 'Shouldn't be here until Christmas Eve.'

As they passed, she noticed the sign. 'They're collecting for wounded soldiers in hospital over Christmas.'

She stopped to fish a couple of coins out of her purse and went forward to toss them into their bucket.

'That's different then,' said Mrs Stubbs stopping to take some money from her bag to add to the collection. Florence did likewise.

A few shops further on they reached Perilli's Refreshment House, with its large glass frontage. In one area of the steamed-up windows, they could just make out the display of bottled drinks, chocolate and pastries.

Inside, there were several rectangular tables, each with four wooden loopback chairs and cream cloths. The counter was next to the window on one side. The room was filled with warmth and chatter.

They were shown to a table in the middle by an older woman, dressed in a light-blue dress and a large white apron tied around her middle. Lili was glad to see that there was a clock on the wall, thus saving her from checking the watch constantly.

'Excuse me, I must go and use the lavatory first.' Mrs Stubbs placed her basket on a chair and headed off.

Lili and Florence sat on the same side, thanking the waitress for the menus.

'While Mum's not here, I must apologise.'

'What for?' said Lili.

'My reaction when I saw you with that corporal. I did believe you, but I suppose it felt like he'd replaced Norman. Of course you should have friends. I imagine knowing someone from your old home could be quite comforting. I'm sure I'd feel like that if I was a long way from Littlehampton.'

Lili felt a little guilty, given what she'd been thinking earlier, about wishing she could bump into Rhodri.

'It were good to have a distraction that day. Having a day off on your own can be a bit lonely. Sometimes I get a day off with Edie, but not often. Corporal Morgan, although based at Shoreham, lived in Littlehampton with his family before he enlisted and was at the hospital there after he were shot in France. We put on a do for the wounded soldiers, and that's how I met him.'

'Your hotel does seem to do some good works for the war effort. It's very well respected in the town.'

'We try.'

Mrs Stubbs returned and sat opposite the girls. 'Now let's see. I think I fancy a nice hot cup of Bovril.'

'Ugh.' Florence pulled a face. 'I've never known how you could stand that stuff.'

'Never been a favourite of yours, I know.'

'I don't mind it,' said Lili, 'but I do fancy a cuppa cocoa.'

'Are you having any cake?' said Mrs Stubbs. 'I'm going to have a fruit tart. It's a shame there ain't as much on the menu as there used to be. It's the war shortage, I suppose. They used to do a couple of Italian pastries, but I don't see them on the menu now.'

'We're starting to feel the shortage at the hotel too. I s'ppose a piece of Genoa cake would be nice.'

'Good, I don't want to be the only one eating.'

'I'm going to have tea and a scone,' said Florence. 'Boring, I know, but it's what I fancy.'

'You have what you like, my love.'

After the waitress had taken their order, Mrs Stubbs said: 'Norman used to like it here, didn't he Florence?'

'He did.' Her face turned a little gloomy.

'In fact, he liked Worthing a lot. Particularly in the summer. Did he ever bring you here?' Mrs Stubbs regarded Lili.

'No, we never came here together.' The furthest they'd ever gone was to Arundel on the omnibus.

'He was particularly fond of the roller-skating rink, at the Dome.' The older woman looked into the distance, half-smiling, as if remembering. 'Especially after the one at the Empire in Littlehampton closed.'

'Was he? I didn't know he liked roller-skating.'

'Do you remember that time we came here, Flo, when he fell over? Flat on the ice he was. Didn't deter him though. He was up and off in a jiffy.'

'I do remember,' said Florence.

The drinks and food came, and still Mrs Stubbs recalled days gone past with Norman. After her initial melancholy, Florence picked up and added to her mother's stories. Lili smiled and listened, asking questions at first. Soon she was barely paying attention. She didn't like to think she was bored by the conversation. It was just that, in her family, when someone had passed, you barely, if ever, mentioned them. That's just the way it was. People kept their thoughts and their sadness to themselves. Mam had always said it was easier to cope with the pain like that.

As she listened, the light got fainter outside, until darkness finally won the day.

'You mustn't get too upset about Norman,' said his mother, bringing Lili out of her partial reverie.

Did she look upset? Maybe it was her boredom showing and it had been misinterpreted as sadness.

'I'm convinced Norman is still around, a prisoner of war maybe, or somehow ended up in another brigade.'

'Mum, it's been over three months now since he went missing. You can't keep saying this. Please.'

'I'm sorry if you find it upsetting, Flo, but I can't help what I believe. There's plenty been taken prisoner by the Hun.'

'Maybe. But we've got to accept the possibility that he's never coming back.'

Mrs Stubbs looked down at her now empty plate, her mouth down at the corners. 'I know. It's just... the thought of him still out there keeps me going.'

'I understand,' said Lili. 'I've felt like that myself. But Florence is right.' The feeling of fullness in her throat grew and it would only go one way, unless she did something. She looked up the clock. Just gone ten past four. 'Goodness, look at the time. I'm so sorry, but I must head off now to meet Mrs Bygrove and the children. She kindly paid for my train ticket and I've got a shift later.' She stood and picked up her bags from the floor.

Mrs Stubbs came around the table to give her a brief hug. 'Bye bye, Lili. I'm so glad we bumped into you.'

'Me too,' said Florence, taking her hand and giving it a little squeeze. 'I do hope we haven't upset you with our talk of Norman.'

'It's fine,' said Lili, putting on her well-practised smile. She used it every day on guests, even when she didn't feel like it. 'Bye bye. A… peaceful Christmas to you, if I don't see you again beforehand.' She'd been going to say 'happy', but it didn't seem appropriate.

'And to you,' both mother and daughter replied.

Relief flooded Lili as she left the refreshment room. It was still busy along the pavements. She hurried back to the end of South Street, to the confectionery shop where she'd spotted the soldiers. Inside, she chose a selection of sweets, each variety placed in a brown paper bag. She'd send some to Wales for her siblings to share, while the rest she'd place on the table in the staff dining room on Christmas Day as a treat.

Now to banish the last hour's conversation from her mind and meet Mrs Bygrove.

Chapter Nine

It had been a long evening the day before – getting the tree up in the foyer and decorating it, after the dinner service was over – but Lili had loved every minute. They'd never had a tree at home, so she always looked forward to the hotel's one going up. It must have been eight-feet tall, and, with the gold bows, the blown glass balls and the dried orange slices on burgundy ribbons, it looked a treat. And this year, she'd been one of the staff members decorating it, along with Edie and Gertie.

The dining room and conservatory had already been decorated a few days before with laurel and berried holly, ivy, yew and mistletoe.

Now it was almost time for her idea to be put into action. After seeing the choir in Worthing, she'd timidly suggested to Mrs Bygrove, on the way home, that it might be nice to have a small group singing carols at the hotel on Christmas Eve. She'd been thinking more of professional singers, of maybe getting Mr Janus involved. However, knowing she could sing, Helen had suggested that Lili and a few other staff members with reasonable voices might like to have a go.

It had taken some persuasion, given what had happened at the concert in the summer, but Lili realised she couldn't keep thinking that singing brought her bad luck. It never had in Dorcalon, so why would it here?

So had been born a hotel choir of sorts, formed of Mrs Turnbull, Annie and Alice Twine, Leslie and Stanley and a live-out housemaid. Lili was the lead singer. They'd all been in church or chapel choirs at some time in their lives. Helen had suggested a carol rendition at half past five in the foyer, and it had been advertised at the hotel for a few days beforehand.

Now here was Lili, at twenty past five, nervously gathering her choir in the staff corridor. They'd had several practices, working around their shifts, and they sounded all right together. They were attired in their Sunday best suits and dresses.

But there was a niggle at the back of Lili's mind. She shook her head briefly, as if to bat it away. This was something to entertain the guests staying over Christmas, to make them feel at home and fill them with seasonal cheer. That was all.

So long as it all went right.

She took a deep breath in, then out. 'It's time we went to the foyer.'

Helen entered the corridor from the stairs with Arthur and Dorothy. 'Good, you're ready. The children are looking forward to this.'

'We're putting our stockings up for Santa Claus later,' said Arthur, his eyes lit up with excitement. 'I hope he comes.'

'I'm sure he will, pet,' said Mrs Turnbull. 'You're very good children.'

They filtered out of the door into the foyer, one at a time, taking up their pre-arranged places around the tree. It was in the furthest corner, near the outside entrance. Already, people had gathered and not only from the hotel. Lili recognised regulars from South Terrace, including the major's best pal.

Helen stood in front of them. 'And now, for the first time, I'd like to present our own hotel choir with some carols for your enjoyment.'

The audience clapped politely. Lili stood slightly in front – lifting her hand to conduct, as her choir master at chapel had done – and they set off with *The First Noel*.

As it came to an end, Lili thought: *One down, five to go.*

The audience's clapping was more enthusiastic after this first carol. Lili looked over at the desk, where Edie was in place. Her friend smiled at her and nodded. The two encouragements combined gave her the confidence she needed. When the clapping stopped, she led the choir into *See Amid The Winter's Snow*. As they sang, Lili could hear the clattering rain against the front window behind them. It was far too mild for snow.

The singers continued with *Once In Royal David's City*, *God Rest Ye Merry Gentlemen* and *Silent Night*. For their last song, they'd decided on the cheerful *Twelve Days Of Christmas*, hoping to send their audience home humming. Better still, before they'd even got halfway through, the audience was joining in, even Mrs Carmichael.

A few moments later, Mr Bygrove came through the front door, his coat and homburg splattered with rain. He looked alarmed at first. Surely his wife had told him about this. Lili looked away from him, not wanting to be distracted.

The rapturous applause began as soon as the last note was over. Lili regarded the audience and beamed. She glanced briefly at Bygrove to find he was grinning and saying something to the guests nearest him. Taking credit again, most likely.

As the applause died down, Lili brought the singers in on cue, as they'd practised, to announce: 'God bless us. Everyone!'

The audience began to disperse – some to their rooms, some out into the pouring rain – as several umbrellas went up. As Major Thomas's friend opened the outside door to leave, a clap of thunder was heard.

'I'd say that's our cue for a nice cuppa tea,' said Mrs Turnbull.

–

'Thank goodness that's over,' said Lili, undoing her apron just after four o'clock.

She and Phoebe had just finished tidying up the dining room after the Christmas luncheon, served only to guests staying at the hotel.

'Looking forward to our meal, I am,' she added.

'It won't be a patch on the guests' lunch,' said Phoebe, rather despondently. 'It'd be nice to have turkey or goose for a change, or lobster. Mrs Carmichael said it was delicious. And I could tell that Lord and Lady Lane were enjoying the oysters for hors d'oeuvres.'

'Can't say I've ever fancied them myself. They always smell a bit… off.'

'Well, the veal consommé then. And they get those fancy-looking piped duchess potatoes while we get plain old roast. And that Charlotte Russe for dessert looked… divine.'

'It did. But our Christmas dinners are always lovely. And we get similar veggies, albeit not as fancily cooked. And we get bread sauce.'

'I suppose. I pity Leslie and Stanley, having to be on standby in the foyer in case anyone wants anything fetching,' said Phoebe.

'They have their Christmas meal in the evening with their family, so they're not missing out.'

'That's something.'

Hetty shuffled through the door with a tray containing jugs of cordial and glasses, while Fanny's tray was filled with mince pies. They would be taking them through to the private dining room for any guests who felt peckish and wanted to come down for refreshments during the afternoon.

In the staff corridor, Lili and Phoebe watched as a tray with a huge roast beef was carried by Gertie to their dining room. Lili caught a whiff of its savoury aroma.

'Mmm. I feel even hungrier now.'

'Then you'd better help bring in the rest of it,' said Mrs Leggett, holding a large bowl of roast potatoes. 'There are parsnips, sprouts, cabbage and carrots still to be fetched from the kitchen.'

Lili and Phoebe raised their eyebrows at each other and smiled, doing as they were bid.

The table was decorated with ivy, laurel and candles, in between the dishes and trays of food. The mantelpiece was similarly decorated. A fire was roaring in the large hearth. Lili looked around at the live-in staff present. Mrs Leggett was seated at the head of the table, nearest the door. Mrs Norris sat on her right, with Mrs Turnbull, Hetty Affleck, Miss Bolton the live-in nurse and Nancy the barmaid down that side. On the other side of the housekeeper sat Jack Sinden, the only other live-in cook. On his side was Gertie, Fanny, Vera Edge the children's nurse, and Phoebe. Lili and Edie sat together at the opposite end to Mrs Leggett. The rest of the staff were either on duty or had gone home to eat. She'd worked with these people for so long now, they at least felt like a family of sorts.

The housekeeper cleared her throat, to indicate they should all be quiet, and said: 'For what we are about to receive, may the Lord make us truly thankful. Amen.'

There was a chorus of 'Amen'. Mrs Leggett kept her eyes closed for some moments after.

'We gonna eat or what?' said Gertie, echoing what Lili was thinking. She was already ravenous, and the fare laid out tantalisingly before them was making it worse.

'Patience, Miss Green,' said the housekeeper. 'Mrs Norris, if you'd do the honours.'

'Of course, me duck.' Picking up the long knife, she sharpened it with the honing rod. She carved the meat and laid slices onto plates to be passed around.

'Why can't we have turkey, like Mr and Mrs Bygrove are 'aving?' said Gertie.

'Because turkey ain't for the likes of us,' said the cook. 'It's posh Christmas food. And what's wrong with my beef, exactly?'

'Nothin', pet, nothin' at all,' declared Mrs Turnbull. 'It's always delicious and so tender. I don't know how you do it.'

'I've got me ways.'

'I bet Edie had turkey when she was a *lady*,' Fanny grumped.

'She weren't a lady, she were an *honourable*,' Lili corrected.

'She was still the daughter of a lord.'

'She were the daughter of a baron, who's title was Lord and—'

'It's all right, Lili.' Edie laid her hand on her friend's arm. 'You're quite right, of course, Fanny. We did have turkey. But, to be honest, I've never been that fussed about it. I'd rather have beef.'

'Either way, Miss Bullen,' said Mrs Leggett. 'You look like you could do with a little less to eat. Put on a bit too much weight around the middle if you ask me. Your shape's all gone.'

Several of the staff looked awkward at the housekeeper's words. Lili had never thought much of Fanny, with her spiteful words and mean actions, but she felt sorry for her, being humiliated in this way.

'Leave the poor lass alone,' said Mrs Turnbull. 'I always put on a bit of fat in the winter, with all the starchy food and not goin' out for a walk so much. Come summer, the lighter food and strolls by the beach sorts it out.'

'The exercise doing the cleaning should sort it out all year round,' declared the housekeeper. 'And she shouldn't be losing her shape at her age.'

Mrs Norris stood to pull the tureen of carrots towards her. 'I think that's enough talk of young ladies' shapes at the dinner table. You've turned poor young Jack here quite red with embarrassment.'

Sure enough, Jack was looking awkward as he shovelled some roast potatoes onto his plate.

'What's for pudding, Mrs Norris?' asked Nancy.

'We do not speak of dessert until the main course is over,' said Mrs Leggett.

'Besides, what do you think's for pudding on Christmas Day?' Mrs Norris chuckled. 'I ain't gonna break with tradition. Besides, it's me favourite dessert of the year.'

'Mine too,' Jack piped up, looking much happier with the change of subject. 'And we worked hard on making them plum puddings a couple of months back.'

'So come on now, we've worked 'ard in that kitchen today and we've still gotta do some dinner for the guests later, so let's get eating.'

People tucked into their meals, some more enthusiastically than others. Edie and Mrs Leggett ate delicately and with manners, as always. Lili looked around this makeshift family, wondering what her mam and siblings were doing in Dorcalon at this moment. Probably sat around the table exactly as they were, enjoying Mam's food, or chatting about the latest gossip. Widowed Auntie Megan would be there, staying a couple of days over Christmas as she always did. Carys would be barking orders at the kiddies, even her nephews and nieces. She'd be bossing Mam and Auntie Megan around too, despite them having done all the work towards producing the Christmas dinner.

After their meal, they'd open the presents, letting the children go first. There were things she missed, such as seeing the kiddies' faces light up, or their joyful laughter when they played games; Mam's look of contentment at having her family around her.

But this year it might be different, with Morys's wife Jane and baby Emily recently gone.

Perhaps she should have been there. And, though she enjoyed the Christmases here, with the staff, it wasn't the same as having her real family around. But if she went back now, for a visit, would she ever leave again?

Norman. If only he hadn't gone off to war, maybe they'd have been married in the next couple of years and she'd have had her own family.

'Are you all right, Lili?'

Dear Edie, always looking out for her, especially since Norman had gone missing.

Missing. She still couldn't quite let go of that hope, despite what she'd said to Mrs Stubbs in Worthing.

'I was just thinking of past family Christmases.'

'You must miss them more than I miss mine. You could have asked for time off. I'm sure Mrs Bygrove would have understood.'

'But Mr Bygrove wouldn't have. And Christmas is a busy time. Besides, I couldn't afford to lose the wages and the train fare is expensive.'

'It's a shame they're so far away.'

'True. But I'm enjoying this, here, with all of you. So I won't dwell on it.'

Edie nodded. 'That's for the best.'

After lunch, the dishes were cleared and washed, and the staff dining-room table wiped down.

Mrs Bygrove came down with her children to give presents of chocolate and dates to everyone. Lili was convinced she did this so that all of the live-ins got something for Christmas, even though there'd never been a year when anyone had received nothing.

'I got a rocking horse from Santa Claus,' said Dorothy, bouncing up and down.

'That's marvellous!' said Mrs Turnbull, hunkering down next to her.

'And I got a train set,' said Arthur, beaming.

'Aw, I wish I could have a go,' said Jack, patting him on the head. 'Choo-choo!'

Arthur giggled. 'We've set it up to go around our tree.'

After the manageress left and the excited chatter of the children faded, the staff exchanged gifts. Edie gave Lili a new handbag. It was black leather, with a pleat at the front. It had a metal frame and a little lock at the top. Inside, it was lined with grey leather.

'It's lovely, but you shouldn't have, Edie.'

'You kept saying you needed a new one and I thought you'd like it.'

'I do. I really do.' She gave her friend a hug. 'Here's your present.' Lili was relieved that she'd splashed out a little on her friend's gift. Yet another handkerchief, even if embroidered by her fair hand, would not have passed muster this year.

'A new hairbrush! I've been meaning to buy one for ages,' said Edie. 'And it's ebony. Wonderful. And the scarf is gorgeous. It matches the gloves that Charlie bought me last Christmas.' She gave Lili a hug in return. 'Dear Charlie. I wish he were here.'

Lili patted her on the shoulder. 'If only the war stopped for Christmas and they all got a week off.'

Edie looked immediately concerned. 'Lili, I am so sorry. How insensitive of me.'

Lili went over what Edie had just said and couldn't figure it out. 'How have you been insensitive?'

'There's me wishing Charlie was here, but at least he's still… with us. I should thank my lucky stars.'

'Oh Edie, you shouldn't think like that. Nothing you say, or don't say, is going to make any difference. I don't resent you still having Charlie, I really don't. If Norman was still out there fighting, I would wish the same as you.'

Edie gave her another hug. As they embraced, Lili noticed Gertie by the fireplace, looking at something in her hands, her lips pushed to one side in consternation. Once Edie had let her go, she'd headed off to help bring in tea and coffee, Lili went over to the portress.

'Everything all right, Gertie?'

'Not really. I gave Fanny a really nice purse for Christmas. We always buy each other something special. But this year I got this.' She opened her hand to display a costume jewellery bracelet that looked rather tacky.

'Maybe she didn't have much money to spend?' said Lili.

'I reckon she's spent it on this, I dunno, sweetheart, or whoever they are.'

'Do you know for sure she has one?'

Gertie shrugged. 'There is someone else. Could be a new friend, I s'pose. She don't seem to have much time for me any more. Guess I'm too boring.' She hung her head.

'Where is she?'

'Said she didn't want to play games, but wanted some fresh air until it's time to turn down the beds. I offered to go with her, but she said she wanted to be alone.'

'It's dark now. Where on earth would she be walking? Nothing'll be open.'

'Exactly. She must be meeting someone or going to their house.'

'Jack said he's going to start a game of charades when the beverages are served. You like games.'

'S'pose.'

Lili was pleased that there was to be no afternoon tea served today, as she enjoyed the games. She wouldn't be working again until dinner, between half past six and half past eight. And then it was only going to be a grand buffet for the guests to help themselves, so the shift wouldn't be so arduous. They should be tidied up by nine fifteen, when their own supper would be served. And then there'd be more games.

But the pleasure of this prospect didn't reach her soul, as it might have done last Christmas. She was missing Norman. Edie was missing Charlie. Gertie was sad that she seemed to have lost her best friend. And how many others were there, celebrating Christmas in a makeshift family, feeling the lack of someone special? It was a strange life really, when she thought about it, living in a hotel.

Then you mustn't think too deeply about it. She'd been doing that with everything recently. She must enjoy what she had. And at least she wasn't in a wet, cold trench in the middle of nowhere.

What was it Mr Evans, a teacher at her school, used to say? Some Latin phrase he'd been fond of using. *Carpe* something. *Diem.* That was it. *Carpe diem.* Seize the day.

That's what she had to do.

‒

The conservatory, still decorated with greenery, had entertained fewer guests than usual for afternoon tea on the Wednesday following Christmas. Some of the guests staying had gone out for the day, while only two tables of guests from outside had partaken of tea.

Lili was thrilled to see the three women artists – Ebony, Hazel and Marigold – who'd booked in yesterday, back for a stay over the new year. They were sitting with Major Thomas, who they had invited to join them when he'd appeared in the room. They were partaking of a conversation regarding the evacuation on the Gallipoli peninsular.

Mrs Carmichael, still at the hotel after all these months, was sitting at a table overlooking the garden, struggling to light a cigarette. She kept looking nervously at the door into the dining room, as if she expected someone to appear.

'Good afternoon, Mrs Carmichael. Are you ready to order?'

Lili stood by the table, her pad and pencil at the ready.

'Good afternoon, Lili,' she replied in a haughty fashion. Even after all this time, she remained aloof, not passing good-humoured pleasantries like the artists or the major usually did.

She took the order of Earl Grey tea, cucumber sandwiches, scones and Swiss roll, writing it as neatly as she could.

'And could you take this ashtray away and bring me a fresh one.'

Lili looked down at the ashtray to see it was already full of ash and had two stubs. The woman hadn't been here much above ten minutes.

She fetched a clean ashtray from the empty table next to them, then picked up the full one, reeking of smoke and ash, and took it with her to the scullery to empty and put by to clean.

Phoebe was already there, placing dirty dishes onto the table near the sink, where Annie and Alice Twine were washing and drying with a live-out scullery maid.

'Mrs Carmichael looks a bit jumpy today,' said Phoebe.

'I thought that too,' Lili agreed.

'I was thinking the other day, it's strange that her husband has never been here on leave, nor has she left the hotel to go home to see him in the past four months. Don't officers get leave every three months or so?'

'Unlike ordinary soldiers, who'd be lucky to get it even once a year,' said Annie, who had three brothers in the army.

'You're right,' said Lili, who had wondered herself why the woman had been here so long. 'And she did say that her husband was a captain.' More than once, to anyone who would listen.

A hand bell in the kitchen was rung twice, sending Lili off to collect her order.

'Fruit scones and the trimmings for table four,' called Hannah, the live-out cook.

Lili picked up the two-tiered fancy silver stand of scones, homemade jam and clotted cream, carrying it carefully to the dining room. As she laid it down in front of Lady Blackmore and her companion, Cecelia, she heard footsteps clip-clopping into the conservatory.

It was Councillor Bloomfield, being shown in by the grovelling Bygrove, who bowed several times as he did so. She felt guilty for hoping he sat on one of Phoebe's or the live-out waitress's tables, for none of them liked his brusque manner and the way he treated them as if they were beneath his contempt.

'Miss Probert.' Bygrove clapped his hands twice quickly, to get her attention.

'Yes sir?'

'Show Mr Bloomfield to our best table.'

Best table? Did they have such a thing in the conservatory? Perhaps one overlooking the gardens? Though they were bare now, being winter, apart from the evergreen shrubs. And it was gloomy outside.

'I will leave you to it.' Bygrove marched away, head high, wishing the guests he passed a 'good afternoon,' in a voice he'd borrowed from the gentry.

Bloomfield looked towards one of the tables as if trying to work something out. 'Is that Mrs Carmichael over there?'

He'd sat with her before, and he'd spoken to her recently at the concert night. Surely, he could tell it was her from here. Unless he was short-sighted.

'It is, sir.'

'Then, if she is agreeable, I will sit with her.'

'Very well, sir.'

She led him over. 'Madam, do you mind if Mr Bloomfield here joins you?'

'Why, of course not. I'd be glad of the company. Do sit.'

Lili left to fetch a menu from the chest of drawers by the staff door where the cutlery and napkins were housed.

When she presented it to him, he said: 'That's all right. I'll have exactly what Lol— Mrs Carmichael has ordered.'

'Very well, sir.'

Had he been about to call her Lolita? That would put them on first-name terms.

How very interesting.

–

The next hour had seen three more tables arrive for afternoon tea. Lili preferred this to hanging around the chest of drawers, hands behind her back, standing to attention, waiting for something to do, as Mr Smithson had taught her.

Mrs Carmichael and Mr Bloomfield were halfway through their separate stands of food, the pair of them conversing as if they barely knew each other. Lili wished she could lipread, wondering whether the discussion was really as dull as it looked. It was in stark contrast to the animated debate the major and the artists were now engaged in.

Mr Bygrove swept into the room, followed by Miss Harvey, yet another condescending piece who occasionally came to afternoon tea here. She owned the large Selborne Road Guest House nearby, and was a bossy and demanding employer who often left her workers alone to pursue her interests, such as golf and tennis. Or so Lili been told by one of the woman's maids, with whom she'd talked a few times at the grocer's in Norfolk Road. Bygrove, it seemed likely, would know her from these activities. No doubt he would claim that she patronised the hotel because of his 'connections'.

He lifted his hand and clicked his fingers a few times to get Lili's attention. What a nincompoop.

'Good afternoon, Miss Harvey,' Lili greeted her, smiling.

Miss Harvey ignored her. 'I want a good seat, Douglas. The window seats overlooking the garden are all taken. Could someone be moved?'

'Miss Probert, could you arrange that?' said Bygrove.

No, I bloomin' couldn't.

'Table four, in the far corner, have just paid, sir, and will be leaving shortly. If Miss Harvey would like to take a seat here,' she pointed to an empty table, 'I will get the table cleared and relaid in a jiffy.'

'It's not the best window seat, but I suppose it will have to do,' said Miss Harvey. 'Be quick about it.'

'Excuse me, Isabella. I had better return to work.'

That'll make a change!

'Very well, Douglas. Will we see you tomorrow, at the golf club?'

'If work is not too busy, I will endeavour to make it.'

Of course he'd make it, whether work was busy or not.

Miss Harvey took the suggested seat and Lili was relieved to see the patrons on table four leaving. The quicker she got it laid up for *madam*, the less likely she was to complain.

Transporting the used crockery to the scullery, she passed Phoebe in the corridor.

'Miss Harvey is sitting on your table ten, but it's only until I've laid up table four for her.'

'Thank the Lord. I've got enough on my plate with Lady Blackmore. She's in a right moany mood today and poor old Cecelia is just sitting there, listening, not saying a word.'

'Don't think there's much to choose between her and Miss Harvey,' Lili chuckled.

‐

Afternoon tea had gone without incident so far, even if some of the most annoying patrons were in the room. Lili was now standing by the chest of drawers, looking from table to table for signs of anyone requiring something. With Mr Smithson off duty until this evening, she was in charge. However, it was only two days now until he retired for good and then she'd be head waitress. She only hoped she lived up to Mrs Bygrove's confidence in her.

There was a clattering sound, which Lili soon discovered was one of the doors from the dining room being opened sharply and slammed against the wall.

What now?

Through the door stormed a blonde woman in a burgundy velvet coat with a large, ostentatious hat. Behind her lumbered Bygrove, trying to talk to her, but she was clearly not listening.

Lili stepped forward to see if she could help the woman, only to be pushed out of the way.

'Mrs Bloomfield, if you'd wait one moment, I'll find you—'

'Oh do shut up, you blathering fool,' she shouted at Bygrove.

Mrs Bloomfield? The room went silent.

'Adrian! So, you are with *her*.' She marched over to Mrs Carmichael's table.

Lili looked over at Phoebe, who widened her eyes briefly and mouthed, 'Ooo dear.'

Mr Bloomfield rose. 'Constance, I am simply having tea and I happened to—'

'You happened to, by coincidence, come across this… this… *hussy*? Don't give me that. You told me you were going to the council offices.'

'I was, but Mr Rotherham telephoned my office and asked to meet me here, but he didn't turn up.'

'I wasn't born yesterday, Adrian!'

'Mrs Bloomfield, I would appreciate if you didn't—' Bygrove started, only to have the woman step back onto his foot with a high Louis heel, albeit accidently. He hopped backwards, crying, 'Ow, ow!'

'Do get out of the way!' she cried.

Bloomfield stood, almost knocking his chair over. 'Constance!'

Mrs Carmichael raised her eyes heavenward, laid her napkin on the table and stood, looking bored. 'Mrs Bloomfield, you are mistaken in your assumption. Now I suggest you do the sensible thing and— *ahh!*'

Before she could say any more, Mrs Bloomfield had delivered a sharp slap to her cheek.

Lili's hand went to her mouth, as did Phoebe's to her own.

'Tut tut, such unbecoming behaviour,' Lady Blackmore called over.

Miss Harvey rushed over to the manager. 'Are you all right, Douglas?'

'Do something,' Bygrove hissed at Lili, his eyes narrowed as he hopped around. His foot must be hurting. Good.

He was the manager and he expected *her* to do something? Well then, he'd better be happy with the way she decided to handle it.

Mrs Carmichael had sat back down, clutching her face, sniffing in distress and fluttering her eyelashes like an injured princess. What an act, as it couldn't have hurt *that* much. But although Lili disliked the woman, she *was* the one who'd been attacked.

'Mrs Bloomfield, it is not acceptable behaviour in this hotel to assault another guest.'

'Who told *you* to interfere? You're just a waitress!' Bloomfield boomed.

Lili imagined herself as Edie, thinking about how she would speak to them. 'Mr Bygrove, asked me to, sir, as he's inconvenienced. If you wish to have an argument, I suggest that it's taken

136

outside of the hotel, as the other guests here are endeavouring to enjoy a quiet afternoon tea. Sir.'

'Hear, hear,' called the major.

'You tell her, Lili!' Marigold added. 'Such appalling conduct.'

Bloomfield's wife pointed at Mrs Carmichael. 'That... that woman has been messing about with my husband and *I* am cast as the villain?'

'But I told you—' Bloomfield began.

'What you told me is a load of lies, Adrian. I found the love notes you tried to hide away in your wardrobe – and the tie, still wrapped in Christmas paper, that *I* certainly didn't give you.'

'You searched my wardrobe? How dare you! And... and you are clearly mistaken. Have you taken your medication today, my dear?'

'What medication? Don't you start that with me, trying to pretend—'

'That is enough,' said Lili, calmly but stridently. 'I am very sorry, but this is not acceptable behaviour in a public area and you are upsetting our guests. Now, Mr Bloomfield, if you would like to pay for your afternoon tea and then accompany your wife—'

'I'm not paying for anything after the shoddy way I've been treated here.'

Bygrove limped over. 'Of course not, of course not, Councillor Bloomfield. I wouldn't expect you to.'

'Bad form,' called the major. Lili could see the three artists nodding in agreement.

Bloomfield rose, taking his wife's arm forcefully and leading her back through the conservatory. The manager limped after them, apologising for any inconvenience and declaring that he'd deal with the waitress forthwith.

That meant her. This could be the shortest promotion ever. She wasn't even properly in the position yet and it might already be gone.

Of all the… If only Mrs Bygrove had been here.

She turned back to Mrs Carmichael, who was dabbing the corner of her dry eyes with a napkin. 'Are you all right, madam? If you'd like to be attended to by our nurse, I could fetch Miss Bolton.'

'No, no, I just need to sit here and recover for a while,' she said in a whimsical voice. 'If only dear Clifford were here, instead of at that beastly war.'

'Let me clear away the stands and plates, madam. Would you like more tea?'

'Oh, yes please. That would be nice.'

As Lili leant forward to pick up the two empty stands, Mrs Carmichael patted her hand. 'Thank you, my dear, for defending me and getting rid of that *awful* woman.'

Lili wasn't sure how to reply to these uncharacteristic words at first. She smiled and said simply: 'You're welcome, madam.'

'Do you have a sweetheart in the war?'

'I did, madam. But… he was killed.' It was the first time she'd said this out loud.

'You poor, *poor* thing.' Mrs Carmichael took her hand and squeezed it.

Walking away towards the staff area, she still felt confused by the woman's reaction. Phoebe caught her up.

'What was all that about? I saw Mrs Carmichael pat your hand.'

'She was thanking me.'

'Good heavens!'

'My thoughts too.'

Lili wondered if there was anything in Mrs Bloomfield's accusation. She certainly had seen the two of them talking before, but it had never seemed particularly intimate. But then it wouldn't, if they were trying to hide it.

Either way, like so many things that went on in this hotel, it had nothing to do with her.

Lili closed the doors on the conservatory and walked across the dining room, undoing her apron. She looked through the glass in the doors between the two rooms, ensuring one more time that all was cleared, neat and tidy.

What an afternoon that had been. Mrs Carmichael had been very withdrawn after the incident with Mrs Bloomfield, sucking nervously on several cigarettes in that ridiculously ornate holder of hers.

She could do with a cup of tea herself now – and a biscuit, which she hoped she could finish before facing the music. Bygrove was bound to come and find her, and give her a good telling-off. She halted by the door into the staff area. Oh well, if that's the way it was going to be…

In the corridor, she could hear a good deal of fuss coming from the dining room. Was Bygrove there already, having an argument with someone? Her heart sank. As she was about to step in, Phoebe appeared at the door, beaming.

'Lili, come and see who's here.' She looked too happy for it to be Bygrove.

Her breath hitched. Could it be…? Was it possible…? Excitement welled up inside her.

She walked through the door and there, by the table, were two men in uniform.

It was Charlie Cobbett, tall and wiry, and Mrs Norris's son, Joseph, even taller but broad. Disappointment engulfed her, then guilt at being mean-spirited.

Edie was beaming and rosy-cheeked, while Mrs Norris was bouncing from foot to foot like a small child.

'Look, Lili, look who's come back on leave,' said the cook.

Lili put a smile in place, despite the effort. It was good to see them, alive and well, but still not what she'd wished for.

'Why, Charlie, Joseph. I didn't know you two were due some leave.'

'It was a bit last minute,' said Charlie, his blue eyes bright with joy.

'Come on, me ducks, sit down, sit down,' said the cook. 'Someone fetch in the tea and coffee. And I've got some nice pastries and little cakes left over from afternoon tea.'

Gertie, who looked pleased to see them, hurried off to the stillroom with Hetty. Even Mrs Leggett was smiling as she laid up the table. Only Fanny showed no emotion either way at the men's arrival, as she leant against the wall and crossed her arms. There'd been some speculation in the past that she'd had a fancy for Charlie and that's why she'd been so mean to Edie in her first few months at the hotel. But if Gertie was right about a new sweetheart, she surely wasn't still resentful.

'You must have only just arrived,' said Lili.

'That's right,' said Joseph, taking a seat on the bench. 'Got on the train at Bexhill late this morning, but there was a bit of a delay at Brighton when we changed.'

Charlie joined him. 'We're due back on the second of January.'

Edie sat next to him taking his arm and leaning her head on his shoulder. It was so touching, Lili wanted to cry.

The dining room door opened and Mrs Bygrove rushed in. 'Charlie! Joseph! Mr Watkins has just told me. How lovely to see you both.' She shook first Charlie's then Joseph's hands enthusiastically. 'I hope you're staying for supper this evening.'

Mrs Norris came in with a tray of leftover goodies as Helen was greeting them, placing it proudly in the middle of the table. 'If that's all right with management.'

'Of course. And Joseph, your old room's still empty, so that'll be perfect for you to stay in.'

'Thank you, Mrs Bygrove. Mrs Cobbett was kind enough to invite me to kip with them, but I was rather hoping I could stay here.'

'I'll be staying with me parents, of course,' said Charlie.

Leslie flew in as Mrs Bygrove left, almost banging the door against the wall in his excitement. 'I 'eard you two had arrived back. It's great ta see ya both.'

Charlie went to him, patting him on the shoulder. 'And what have you and Stanley been up to while ya head porter's been away.' He pointed to himself.

'The usual. There ain't no head porter now though. Never mind what I've been up to, I hear there was a right to-do in the conservatory at afternoon tea.'

'Councillor Bloomfield was having tea with Mrs Carmichael, and his wife came in and a right what-for she gave him,' said Lili. 'She reckons he's having a... fling with her.'

'Wouldn't blame him,' said Leslie, chuckling. 'She's a good-looking woman.'

'Leslie! That wouldn't be right. Anyway, Mrs Bloomfield slapped her face.'

The porter's mouth opened in shock. 'Really? That was a bit unnecessary.'

'I don't know about that,' said Phoebe. 'I'd say Mrs Carmichael deserved it. It's not like she's been the easiest of guests.'

Leslie shrugged. 'She's got a lot better. And, well, she's a jolly good tipper.'

Charlie tutted. 'Is that all you youngsters care about?'

'Eh? You can talk, Charlie Cobbett. You used to like ya tips,' said Leslie.

'True, true.'

Gertie stepped forward, looking sullen. 'She don't tip *me* that well.'

'Let's get the beverages in and all have a sit down,' said Phoebe.

With the tea and coffee brought in, there were plenty of questions for the two men, especially when young Jack joined them. Lili sat and listened, yet felt outside of the situation, looking on, as if they were performing on stage and she was in the audience.

The conversation split into two, with some talking to Charlie and others to Joseph. Lili felt herself withdrawing, wanting to run away, even if just for a moment to pull herself together.

'I'm just going to the lavvy,' she whispered to Phoebe, sitting next to her.

She headed upstairs, going into the bathroom, installed only three years ago, but she didn't use the toilet. She opened the window and stared out for a while, even though it only over-looked the staff courtyard.

After a couple of minutes, she pulled on the long chain and went to wash her hands, in case anyone was around and knew she was in there.

At the top of the winding stairs, she took several deep breaths for courage before heading back down. Opening the door to the staff corridor, she was surprised to find Charlie standing there.

'Lili, I just wanted to say how sorry I am, about Norman.'

'Thank you, Charlie.' How sick she was of people's sympathy, however well intentioned.

'I presume nothing else has been heard.'

'No... Though you'd probably know better than me.'

'I ain't 'eard nothin', I'm afraid. We weren't even in the same regiment.'

'Shall we join the others?' There was nothing else to say about it.

'After you.'

Back in the dining room again, she finished her tea, the smile in place once more. She'd put up with this until the next shift of people came in, when she could remove herself from the situation for a while, without being rude.

–

Lili had just finished her early supper and was making her way to the door to begin preparation for the guests' dinner by the time Bygrove caught up with her. He entered the staff dining room, clearly determined to make an example of her in front of everyone.

'What on earth did you think you were doing in the conservatory today, Miss Probert, talking to the councillor's wife as if you were her equal?'

'Sir, you told me I had to deal with it. Not acceptable it wasn't, her slapping Mrs Carmichael's face like that.'

The room had gone quiet and Lili could see out of the corner of her eye that everyone was looking at them.

'That didn't mean you had to shout at her!'

'I didn't raise my voice at all, sir. I made sure of that.'

'That's not what *I* heard.'

'Sir, I was there too.' Phoebe rose from the bench and stepped over. 'Lili didn't raise her voice, sir, and she was very polite. It was Mrs Bloomfield who was shouting.'

'Are you contradicting me?'

As he said this, Helen came through the door. 'What's going on here?'

'None of your business.'

'But it is my business. And if this is about Lili dealing with the Bloomfields, I heard she did a jolly good job.'

'What, from the other biased waitresses?' He pulled a face. He regarded Lili and Phoebe once more. 'Already gone tittle-tattling to my wife, have you?'

'No, they haven't. It was the major and the artists who spoke to me, when I was on the desk.'

'They're just trying to cause trouble. I'd say this young woman has done herself out of her promotion.'

'We will discuss this privately,' said Helen.

'When I've finished dealing with Miss Probert.'

'There is nothing to deal with, unless you're going to thank her for trying to calm a difficult situation. The Bloomfields were the problem.'

Bygrove's head jerked from side to side, taking in Helen, then the staff, then Lili. 'I've got more important things to be getting on with than… this!' He waved his hand about, indicating them all, as if they were some kind of rabble. 'And you watch yourself, Miss Probert, for I'll certainly be keeping an eye on you.' After twisting around on the soles of his shoes, he marched out, head held high.

Lili went forward once more. 'Thank you, madam. I really did try to calm it down.'

'I know you did. You're on your next shift now, aren't you?'

She nodded. The chatter from the staff started up once more as she walked away. No doubt she'd given them something new to gossip about.

–

The last dinner shift of 1915 was over and the staff's New Year's Eve's supper was well under way, with all the live-in staff in the dining room. Apart from Fanny. Mrs Leggett had asked Gertie if she knew where she was, but she'd shrugged and looked miserable.

John Smithson had joined them for a farewell drink, having finished his last shift ever at the hotel.

'Are ya sure you won't end up coming out of retirement again, John?' Charlie joked. 'You said you was finished for good last time you retired.'

'Definitely for good this time, Charlie. I haven't got the stamina no more. And me and the wife, we've decided now that we'd like to move up to London, to be near the grandchildren.' He took one last swig of his beer. 'Well, it's nearly ten, so that's me done. I'm off to see the new year in with the missus.' He rose. 'Are you seeing in the new year with your parents, Charlie?'

'Nah. They're always in bed long before. They don't see the point in celebrating the new year as they says it'll be just like the old one.'

'They're probably right, but it's an excuse for a bit of a party, isn't it? A happy new year to you all and all the best for the future. Especially to you two lads.' John looked towards Charlie and Joseph, raising an empty glass.

There was a chorus of *good luck* and *write and tell us how you get on*, from the staff as John took his leave. Charlie, Joseph and Mrs Norris went with him to the staff exit. Soon they were back, following a gloomy-looking Fanny, damp from the drizzly weather outside.

'Where have you been on a night like this, pet?' said Mrs Turnbull. 'Gertie didn't seem to know.'

'Why, does she have to know all me business?'

'But I thought, well, it doesn't matter. Do you need some supper?'

'Nah, I ate with a friend.'

'So why aren't you seeing the new year in with this *friend*,' said Gertie, from her place at the other end of the table.

''Cos they had to be elsewhere. With their family. Is there any beer left?'

'Of course.' Mrs Turnbull pushed a bottle across the table towards her, along with a glass and an opener. 'Help yoursel', pet.'

For the next couple of hours, several games were played, including hide-and-seek and Kim's game. Gertie remained silent at her end of the table, while Fanny declined to join in at the other end. Lili had the deep desire to go to bed and sleep. But she knew she wouldn't. The noise of the staff celebrations might travel up to her room and keep her awake. And even if it didn't, she suspected she would simply spend several hours crying. It was better to be down here with people, occupied, her thoughts diverted from Norman and what might have been. *Or from Rhodri and what would never be.* The last thought had come unbidden, filling her with shame.

I'm sorry, Norman.

At five to twelve, more beer was fetched from the stillroom, where, as was traditional now at the hotel, Mrs Bygrove had supplied plenty of bottles for the staff to see in the new year.

Looking at the clock on the mantelpiece as he spoke, Charlie said: 'Well, the war weren't over by last Christmas – nor this Christmas – but with any luck it'll be over by next Christmas, and me and Joseph'll be back here, portering and cooking.'

'I'll drink to that,' said Joseph, clanking his bottle against Charlie's and taking a swig of beer straight from the bottle. 'Doubt it'll be over by March though, when there'll be likely packing us off abroad.'

'Oh Charlie, is that true?' said Edie, her expression pained.

'Why'd ya have to open ya mouth, Joe?' Charlie shook his head. 'We'll have done well over our six months training by then, so I guess we've been lucky in some ways.'

'My boy!' wailed Mrs Norris, throwing her arms around her son.

The clock started to chime the hour.

'Everyone ready?' called Charlie. '*May auld acquaintance be forgot…*'

Everyone joined in, crossing arms and holding hands. Even Mrs Leggett. Lili looked from one to the other. What would the next year hold for them all? The prospect of her new position in the restaurant still left her with a mixture of pride and impending doom, even if Mr Bygrove's threats had come to nothing. He'd hardly been seen in the hotel's public areas, let alone in a place in which he could keep an eye on her.

At the end of the song, Edie and Charlie embraced and kissed, to the hoots and whistles of Jack and Joseph. Watching them, a peculiar sensation crept across Lili's body as she imagined she was the recipient of that kiss, filling her with a surreal pleasure at the prospect. The bestower of the kiss was not Charlie, of course. But nor was it Norman.

It was Rhodri.

It must be tiredness, her brain presenting her with a half-dream, as it often did when she was fatigued.

'Happy New Year, Lili,' said Phoebe, giving her a hug.

'Happy New Year, Phoebe.'

She only hoped it was.

Chapter Ten

Lili consulted the paper calendar pinned to the dining-room wall, to the side of the fireplace: Friday 28 January. She huffed a noisy sigh. It seemed no time since Christmas. The new year was speeding along. She glanced around the empty room. It had been five months since Norman had... been killed. She was tired of *euphemisms*, as Edie called them. *Missing in action*. That was one she'd heard a few times. Dead. He was dead. It was a cold hard fact, but she accepted it now, however sad it made her.

But what was the point in accepting it? It still wasn't allowing her to *carry on*. That's how Mrs Turnbull had put it. It was what she'd had to do when her husband had been killed in the shipyards of Newcastle, twenty years before.

The life she might have had a chance to move on to had gone as well. Rhodri. It had been over two months since she'd last seen him. On her days off, when she'd wandered by the beach or river, or into the town, she'd always looked out for him, hoping to put right what she was sure she had ruined.

But she was forgetting about Nurse Caffyn? Surely he'd have mentioned her if she was significant? Could it have just been a... fling? A brief romance? A friendship? But she'd taken his arm, familiar like.

If only she hadn't been interrupted by Annie in the corridor, at the concert, when she was about to ask him.

She moved closer to the fire, putting her hands towards it, welcoming the warmth it offered. Why not write to him? She'd been over and over this in her head. Her mother would have

147

called that wanton. You let men pursue *you*, not vice versa. Carys, would have called her *desperate*, like she had their sister, Dilys, when she'd chased her Huw. But she'd won him in the end, and they were now married.

'Miss Probert! What on earth are you doing there, daydreaming?' Mrs Leggett was standing in the doorway, her lips as tightly pinched as her hair was in that bun. 'You're meant to be preparing the conservatory for morning coffee and you're standing there, doing nothing.'

'Sorry Mrs Leggett. I was just… just… checking the date.'

'How long does that take? Now hop along and go about your business.'

'Yes, Mrs Leggett.'

Lili hurried along the corridor and was about to open the door into the dining room when Mrs Bygrove opened it from the other side.

'Ah, Lili, there you are.'

Oh dear, not another telling off about her tardiness.

'I'm so sorry about this,' Helen continued, 'but I wonder if I could prevail upon you to do a shift on the desk. Mr Watkins is with his mother and I fear the end is not far off. Mr Coulter has a prior engagement. And, as you know, Edie is off today, visiting her sister-in-law.'

That was Mrs Bygrove all over. She never *told* you to do something, like her husband, or Mrs Leggett. Even though it was an instruction, not a suggestion, she was always polite about it and full of explanation.

'My husband had agreed to do it. However…' Helen sighed and Lili knew without her having to voice it that *Douglas* was off on another trip somewhere. 'I would do it myself, but Mrs Norris and I need to go to speak with the butcher, grocer and greengrocer about our needs, what with some food items starting to be in short supply.'

'I'd be glad to work on the desk, but won't that make us short-handed in the conservatory?'

'Annie popped over to Western Road to see if Simon Lane was free to do a shift.'

The hotel had been fortunate to find a couple of capable fifteen-year-old lads, looking older, who didn't come within the ban of employing men aged between eighteen and sixty.

'Here he is now,' said Helen.

Sure enough, Simon was strolling down the corridor, whistling. He was blond and tall for his age.

''Ello Mrs Bygrove. Always glad to do an extra shift, I am.'

'Thank you, Simon. Go through and Phoebe will allocate your tables.'

'Yes, madam.'

When he'd left, Helen said, 'I'm sorry to take you away from waiting. I know the tips are valuable, but I will pay you a little extra, as usual, to work on the desk.'

'I'll go and change straight away,' said Lili.

'Thank you. My husband is currently on the desk but is keen to leave.'

Frothing at the bit, more like it, thought Lili.

The two women turned to go their separate ways, when Lili stopped. 'Oh, Mrs Bygrove, who will be in charge overall? Last time neither of you was around—'

'There was that trouble when Mrs Carmichael first arrived. Yes. She's not been an easy guest, has she? This time I've ensured that Mrs Leggett will sort out any problems. Nevertheless, I'll be as quick as I can.'

-

Mrs Bygrove had returned in time for Lili to go to the late staff lunch, which she was more than ready for.

In the dining room, the recently appointed chef – a tall, skinny, black-haired man in his early seventies called Will Fletcher – was sitting at the table with a newspaper opened wide in front of him. He'd been a sous chef in his younger days

149

but was happy to muck in and do whatever was needed of him now.

Mrs Leggett was at the head of the table, as usual, with Mrs Turnbull on one side. On her other side was Finn, a new scullery lad of fourteen, his eyes screwed up as he perused *The Boy's Own Paper.*

Will folded the newspaper to reveal a single page, then stabbed his finger at a column. 'Says here that the new conscription law for all single men aged eighteen to forty-one's been passed by the government. Don't suppose it'll be long 'til it's married men. Still, I'm sure Mr Bygrove will get away with it, if they stick to those ages.'

Lili took a seat as far away from the housekeeper as possible. 'I'm sure Mrs Bygrove said he was thirty-nine a while back, so he's probably no more than forty now.'

Mrs Leggett looked up sharply and Lili expected a telling-off, but instead the housekeeper said: 'Yes, that's right. He had his fortieth birthday last month, I believe.'

'That'd be a right shame if he had to enlist,' said Will. 'How would the hotel manage without him?'

Mrs Turnbull emitted a loud, 'Hm!' and pulled herself up straight. '*Mrs* Bygrove would manage very well, for she's perfectly capable of runnin' the hotel hersel', as she often seems to be doin'. In fact, I'd go as far as to say she'd do a better job, without him interferin' the whole while, or takin' credit for her good ideas. She's a right canny lass.'

'I don't think we should be talking out of turn, Bridget,' said Mrs Leggett, though not with much conviction.

'Aye, maybe not, but you know I'm right, Imogen.'

Mrs Leggett nodded vaguely and linked her hands on the table in front of her.

A group of other staff on late lunch came into the room. Mrs Leggett stood up. 'Gertie, Alice, before you sit down, help me fetch the food.'

Gertie raised her eyes but didn't complain as she followed the housekeeper and scullery maid out.

All the dishes had been placed on the table and people had started to help themselves, when Leslie rushed in. 'Hope there's something left for me.'

'Where have you been, Mr Morris?'

The porter took a seat next to Finn. 'Been running an errand for Mrs Carmichael. She wanted something from the fancy repository shop in Norfolk Road.'

'While you are obliged to run certain errands outside of the hotel,' said Mrs Leggett, 'you are not a guest's personal shopper. And you are not obliged to serve the customers beyond your shift time. Someone from the next shift could have done it.'

'I hadn't quite got to the end of the shift when she asked. Anyway, Mr Bygrove says we should be prepared to overrun our shift if we're helping a guest.'

'But the help you've been giving Mrs Carmichael has been above and beyond what a porter should be expected to do. Anyone would think you were her own personal servant.'

Leslie leant over to help himself to a ham sandwich. 'She's giving me extra tips, so it's not all bad.'

'I agree with Mrs Leggett,' said Lili, who'd been concerned for a while about the attention Mrs Carmichael demanded from Leslie. 'She expects far too much and often when there are other guests who need attention.'

Lili had wondered a couple of times whether there was more going on. She thought about Gertie and Lord Fernsby once more. No, maybe not like that. At least, she hoped not. If it were the case, Leslie didn't seem to mind. But that was not the point.

'It's fine.' Leslie flicked his hand to dismiss any worries.

'Make sure it is,' said Mrs Leggett, who perhaps had the same misgivings. 'After that incident at Christmas with Mrs Carmichael and the Bloomfields... well, she is something of a leech.'

'She's just lonely,' said Leslie, before shoving a large piece of his sandwich in his mouth.

'Well, be warned.' Mrs Leggett picked up her sandwich and bit off a dainty corner.

Lili wondered if it would be wise to keep an eye on this situation. She'd have a word with Edie too, so she could do the same. It might be nothing, but she didn't want Leslie getting into trouble, especially as the woman was married. He was a likeable young lad, along with his twin, and that was likely the problem: too nice to decline Mrs Carmichael's unreasonable requests.

Chapter Eleven

'The first of February already. This year is going fast.' Phoebe unfolded the clean white cloth and tossed it in the air above the table in the ballroom. It floated down and landed neatly on the top of it.

Lili laid a cloth on an adjacent table. 'That's just what I was thinking the other day.'

The two of them had reached Stanley and the young waiter, Simon, shifting tables together to lay them out the way Mrs Bygrove had instructed: four tables placed together in a square so that eight people could sit at them and chat easily. This had been repeated six times, to accommodate forty-eight people.

Mrs Turnbull came in with a tray containing small glass vases of pansies, one for each group of tables. She placed them down, while Edie came in behind her with the first of the ornate silver candlesticks, each holding three candles.

'Mrs Bygrove is spot on with this decoration,' said Mrs Turnbull. 'I'm sure Sir William Mowbray will appreciate it for his special dinner this evenin'. What's the occasion again?'

'His fiftieth birthday,' said Lili. 'He has family and friends coming from across the country. I think he'll approve.'

Slowly, the women laid the tables with the silver cutlery and napkins, furled and folded to look like flowers, and placed above the dessert spoon and fork. Four glasses were laid per place. The water glasses were green and engraved with fruit and vines, while the clear wine glasses had several patterns etched upon them. There were also port glasses and champagne coupe glasses.

Helen entered as they were finishing. 'Oh my, I came to help, but I see you've finished already.' She rotated and took in the room, not only the elegant tables but the rest of the ballroom. 'Yes, perfect.' She glanced at her watch. 'Now, you lot get along to the late tea break and we'll sort out any finishing touches afterwards.'

About to turn and leave, she was stalled by her husband marching through the door.

'So, how is it all going?' he asked, hands behind his back.

'It's almost done and—'

'Oh no. No, no, no, no. This will *not* do!'

'What do you mean, Douglas? It's been very well executed.'

'No, no, no. It looks like a *women's* tea party, what with the tables arranged like this.'

He marched to the nearest table. 'And what's all this?' He pulled out some of the flowers and dropped them on a napkin, wetting it. 'They're not little old ladies.'

'But we often have flowers,' said Helen.

'Not this namby-pamby sort. Sir William is an acquaintance with whom *I've* socialised on occasion and the friends who he'll have invited – all important men, I can assure you – will not appreciate this… frippery.' He lifted the napkin on the next setting and flicked it open, before tossing it across the table. 'These should be furled and folded as usual.'

'But the guests are—' Helen started.

'Are you contradicting me again, Helen? I've been in this business longer than you and I know best.'

Helen's shoulders slumped. Lili knew how she felt. All their effort and he was saying it wasn't up to scratch? Glancing around the staff, they all looked similarly deflated.

'Now take all of this off and start again. The tables will be put in one long line, like a banquet, as befitting Sir William and his guests. Remove the flowers and redo the napkins. As for the glassware, something plainer and a little more manly is in order.'

'Douglas, Sir William did say—'

'He said he wanted the best and he'll get the best, not some silly female idea of what a man's man requires at a business dinner.'

'Douglas, it's a—'

'Just *do it*!' He strode away forthwith, not letting his wife finish.

Helen turned slowly to face the staff. 'I am so sorry about this, but we'd better do as he says. I must have been mistaken about it being a birthday party for family and friends.'

'What about our tea?' whined Simon. 'It'll be over by the time we've finished.'

'Don't worry yoursel', lad,' said Mrs Turnbull. 'I'll get us all somethin' when we're done.'

'It's such a shame though.' Phoebe looked at their efforts forlornly. 'It looks so pretty.'

'Maybe he's right then,' said Helen. 'Would Sir William appreciate "pretty" for his birthday?'

'I suppose Mr Bygrove does know him better than we do,' said Phoebe.

'Not really. He's only a vague acquaintance. Never mind, let's get it done.'

Helen sounded determined, but Lili had known her long enough to tell when she was upset. Poor thing. She took a deep breath. *Right, here we go!*

-

The dinner had gone well that evening, with Edie, Lili, Phoebe, a live-out waitress and Mrs Bygrove serving. There had been nine courses in all.

The truffled wild mushroom tartlet hors d'oeuvres had garnered several compliments to the chef. This was followed by a *consommé paysanne*, fillets of brill, an entrée of filet mignon and a cucumber and mint sorbet. The main course of partridge and roasted vegetables had proved most popular. After which came the salad of seasonal greens and French dressing.

The dessert of individual trifles, crafted by one of the recently employed older men, Mr Strong, had attracted the most praise. And well deserved the acclaim had been, Lili considered as they cleared away the dishes. She'd had a tiny taste of Mr Strong's trifle the first time he'd made it and my, had it been delicious with its layers of ratafias and macaroons steeped in white wine, jam-soaked almonds, the rich egg custard and the sherry-infused cream mixed with whipped egg-white top. Mr Strong had been a pastry chef before his former retirement but was able to make all sorts of puddings. She might be unable to pronounce the French names of some of his creations, but he certainly did them justice.

Almost last had come the fruit and cheese. It had all looked very tasty, while the aromas had been heavenly, but Lili still wondered how on earth anyone could eat that much, as she always did at these lavish banquets. She'd have been stuffed after the first three courses.

Furthermore, Mr Bygrove had been wrong about the guests invited and Mrs Bygrove had been correct. In attendance was his wife, adult daughters and husbands, his parents and a host of friends, male and female. How Lili longed to march up to Bygrove and announce, *See, Mrs Bygrove told you so!*

Not that it mattered that they'd changed the table arrangement and setting. Or at least, that was how it had seemed.

They were serving coffee and port when Sir William was returning from the gentlemen's convenience. Lili was delivering a silver coffee service and the hotel's signature white cups and saucers – with their green-and-gold gilt edges and tiny pink roses – when she noticed Sir William stop by the door to speak to Bygrove. The manager had been lingering there for the past five minutes, looking on, that smug expression on his face. He had made several visits to the room and the kitchen that evening, to ensure everything was going to plan. On his first visit, he'd looked worried, but had consequently perked up.

'Ah Bygrove,' said Sir William. 'Jolly good meal. Compliments to the chefs, old chap.'

'I'm so glad you liked it, sir. There, um, does not appear to be any of your usual acquaintances here, from your club and so forth.'

'No, no, a family occasion.'

'I see. And everything else has been to your liking, I hope?'

'Yes, top-notch. Only a couple of things, really. Can't help thinking it was a shame there were no flowers.'

Lili gripped her bottom lip with her teeth to stop herself giggling.

'And the tables, old chap: it might have been cosier if they'd been in groups. Easier to talk to people, what? Having one long table was a bit too much like being at a banquet. Like being at an official function. I get enough of those.'

Oh, this was priceless. Lili, annoyed now, couldn't wait to tell – well – everyone!

'Well… um… yes,' Bygrove spluttered. 'Of course, it was my wife who decided on the presentation. I told her groups of tables would be better. And I suggested flowers. But she always thinks she knows best.'

The lying little toad!

'Never mind, never mind. It was a good meal all the same.' Sir William strolled back to the table.

Her tray emptied, Lili made her way back to the staff area, fuming.

Mrs Turnbull was exiting the kitchen and coming towards her in the staff corridor. 'What's wrong with you, lass? Looks like you've dropped a half crown and picked up a ha'penny.'

'You'll never believe what Mr Bygrove just told Sir William.'

Lili related the conversation to Bridget, whose mouth formed an O as she shook her head.

'Well, the cheek of him. And Phoebe told me that Helen was right about it being family and friends too.'

'She was. If only that man… Oh, I dunno.'

'Would get conscripted?'

'I shouldn't wish that on anyone.'

'I know, pet, but I've wished it too. I think most of us here have. Let's say conscripted, but unharmed, eh? Does that make you feel better?'

'I suppose. Perhaps being involved in something so serious would give him a new perspective on life. And help him appreciate his wife more?'

'Aye, who knows?'

'I'd better fetch the petits fours from the kitchen.'

'And I'll be in the cloakroom soon, givin' out the coats.'

–

Sir William and his guests had departed, the ballroom had been tidied and put back the way it was, and several members of staff were now in their dining room, enjoying cups of cocoa and the petits fours left over from the party.

'It sounds like it was a success,' said Mrs Leggett, at the head of the table as usual. She'd recently acquired a wooden dining chair with arms, and the short bench she'd formerly sat on had been placed to one side of the room.

'The guests certainly seemed to enjoy it,' said Edie. 'And Mrs Bygrove was right: it was a party of family and friends.'

'So I heard.' The housekeeper pinched her lips together but commented no further.

'That's not all,' said Lili, hoping she wouldn't get a ticking off from Mrs Leggett for speaking out of turn. She related the conversation between the manager and Sir William once more, enjoying the opportunity to show Bygrove up for what he was.

There were several expressions of disbelief from those around the table. Even the housekeeper was shaking her head.

'What a nerve!' said Jack, in between episodes of blowing on his cocoa to cool it down.

'How I wish someone would put him in his place,' said Mrs Norris.

Mrs Turnbull put her mug down and leant on the table. 'Well, it just so happens…'

'What's that, Bridget?' said Mrs Norris, next to her.

'It's possible, I might just have let slip, when Sir William collected his overcoat, that Mrs Bygrove *had* organised the tables the way he'd suggested, with the flowers an' all, and that it was *Mr* Bygrove who'd had it rearranged.'

'Oh my, Mrs Turnbull, you didn't, did you?' Phoebe clasped her hands together, grinning.

'What did Sir William have to say about that?' Lili asked.

'He said that he wasn't at all surprised and that, from what he knew of Bygrove, he was a man of little imagination.'

Lili couldn't help herself – she started chuckling. As it grew, she knew it was going to be one of those laughs you couldn't stop, the sort that brought tears to your eyes.

One by one, the rest of the staff were infected by her glee and started to laugh too: first Edie; then Mrs Turnbull; then the rest of them. Only Mrs Leggett's face remained straight. Lili was sure that at any moment the housekeeper would stand up and command them all to be quiet.

But she didn't. Finally, a smile formed, which she tried to prevent by squeezing her lips together. But it didn't work. Slowly, a chuckle built up, until she could keep it in no more and she was laughing as hard as the rest of them.

In the midst of this rumpus, Mrs Bygrove opened the door and stood in the entrance. 'Oh my, you are enjoying yourselves. Sorry to disturb you, but I just wanted to say how well you all did for Sir William's party this evening.'

As the laughter died down, there were various forms of thanks.

'You were right about it being family and friends,' said Mrs Leggett, who was still smiling.

'So it seems. Well, I'll wish you all good night.'

When she'd left, Mrs Norris turned to Bridget. 'Why didn't you tell her what Sir William said?'

'I didn't want her to think we were havin' a laugh at her husband's expense. I'll tell her tomorrow, when we're on our own.'

'Fair enough,' said Mrs Norris.

Lili felt sorry for Mrs Bygrove. She'd been proved right, but her husband had been made to look a fool. The poor woman couldn't win either way.

–

As Lili covered her face in cold cream that night, she noticed that Edie was holding a letter as she sat on the bed.

'Is that from Charlie?'

'No. It's from my brother, Freddie. It's strange, getting letters from three different people in the same battalion. They all have a different way of looking at things, though, of course, Daniel is training to be an officer.'

'Daniel's still writing to you then, despite you telling him about Charlie?'

'Yes. I think he enjoys hearing news from someone his own age. He's an only child, so has no sisters to write to.'

'How is your brother?'

Edie lowered her chin to her chest. 'Oh Lili, he really seems to hate it.' She looked up, her eyes, sad. 'Even pretending to kill someone depresses him immensely.'

'I imagine there's a few what feel like that.'

'I don't know. From what Charlie says, some of them seem to treat it like a Boy Scouts' trip away. Not Charlie, of course. I dare say it won't feel real until they go abroad. But I'm worried about Freddie. I'm afraid it will all be so abhorrent to him that he'll desert. Then who knows what will happen to him. You do hear of deserters being shot.'

Lili sat beside Edie, leaning her arm towards her friend's. 'That's terrible. They're just scared. I can't imagine what it must do to you, killing people like that. I dare say Mr Freud would have something to say about it.'

'I've heard of some men being sent to mental hospitals. But not all. Probably only the officers.'

160

Lili considered this. 'Why did he enlist? I remember you saying he had and that it had caused an upset in the family, but if the idea is so hateful to him...?' She held out her hands in question. 'I know he'd probably have to enlist soon, but he could have been a conscientious objector. Aren't they often taken on as hospital orderlies and the like?'

Edie placed the letter on the other side of her and linked her hands in her lap. 'I... I didn't tell you the whole story before.'

'Something else happened?' Lili had felt at the time that there was maybe more to it.

'Can you keep this to yourself?'

'Of course. You know I'm good with secrets.' Lili wondered what on earth was coming.

'You see... My brother, he's, well, he's a homosexual. You know what I mean, don't you?'

'Um, sort of. There were two men found... together, once, in my village. They were boarders in the next street. They ended up in gaol. But your brother, he's married to Lady Lucia. I don't understand.'

'So are many such men, Lili, for what else are they going to do? They can't live openly with a man. Charlie reckoned that several had stayed in the hotel before.'

'He's obviously a bit more knowledgeable than me about such things.' It did make her wonder if any of the married men she'd known, back in Dorcalon, had been in the same situation.

'Anyway,' Edie continued. 'One of their maids – obviously realising what was going on between Freddie and his friend, Percy – contacted a reporter and was paid for information. He inveigled himself an invitation to the house and then, without any actual evidence, published an article about them in a local paper. The upshot was that both Freddie and Percy were offered a choice: gaol or enlistment. I was there at the time.'

'Good heavens.'

'The paper did print an apology, and the reporter was sacked. It was Detective Inspector Davis who actually dealt with it.'

'In Lewes?'

'They were short of detectives as many had enlisted, so he was called in.'

'Oh my.'

'I don't blame Davis. He had a job to do. He told me he didn't agree with such arrests, but that his hands were tied. Luckily, the local superintendent there thought it a waste of time and resources, arresting Freddie and Percy, and he came up with the compromise.'

'It's sorry I am that your brother hates it so. I remember Charlie saying that he didn't want to kill no one.'

'He still thinks like that. I suppose, if it comes to killing, or being killed, they will defend themselves. Or I hope they will.'

'Edie, what does Lady Lucia think of Freddie's… preference for men? I presume she knows?'

'Oh Lili, that's a whole other story and one for another night.'

'You're right. It's some shut-eye we'd better be getting, else we'll be too tired to work tomorrow.'

Lili put out the lamp and got into bed. But the conversation got her thinking about her brothers. Would Morys be conscripted, now he was a widow? Though he did have a young daughter. And Wyn, if they extended conscription to married men?

Oh Lord, let the war be over soon, she prayed in her head. *And let me get to sleep, please.*

But it was a while before she dropped off.

Chapter Twelve

Fanny was relieved to be out of the hotel today, what with Mrs Leggett giving her those judgemental glares and making comments about her putting on weight. Halfway down High Street, she stopped to look in the hosier's window, but she wasn't looking at the hosiery on display, she was assessing her own reflection. What a sight she was.

She felt the tears well up. She sniffed them back and removed a handkerchief from her worn handbag to blow her nose. Her expanding waistline had meant she'd had to purchase a couple of skirts from a jumble sale. It was a good job she'd swapped to wearing a liberty bodice and didn't bother with a corset any more. But that had been all right when she'd been a skinny thing, as she had been most of her life. Maybe she should buy another, second-hand if she could get one, to pull her body into some kind of shape again.

No. That didn't seem like a good idea, given what she suspected. She wasn't going to think about that. It could still be down to all the guests' leftover biscuits and pastries she was fond of pinching when cleaning their rooms. And her monthlies had never been particularly regular. She shouldn't have said anything to Albert.

And what was the point of having any kind of shape? Her shabby blouse and out-of-date skirts wouldn't look any the better for it. Always second-hand it had been for her. The smartest she'd ever looked was dressed in her maid's uniform.

She gave herself another glance in the window. No wonder Albert had buggered off. Not that she'd been this big when he'd left. He hadn't said it was over as such, just that he'd enlisted and he'd be in touch. But he had never written. That had been the beginning of January, about six weeks ago. He might still write, she supposed. No. He hadn't been very affectionate the past two times she'd seen him. Saying he'd write had probably been his way of letting her down gently. But it still hurt.

A well-dressed woman stood next to her to peruse the window. She glanced at Fanny briefly, her nose screwed up as if she'd encountered a bad smell.

Fanny set off once more, not knowing where she was heading. Nobody liked her, not even Gertie now. But that had been her own fault for being so horrible to her. She'd thought she might escape the hotel, get married. She'd reckoned she didn't need a friend any more. What a silly goose she'd been.

And the way she'd treated everyone else at the hotel: no wonder they detested her so. Still, even if she'd been nice to them, they'd probably still have felt the same. She was *innately unlikeable.* That's how Matron in East Preston had put it. So why should she even try?

She'd just stopped once more to peek into the window of Groom's the grocer's, when she spotted Leslie, a couple of doors along, coming out of the confectioner's. He was smart in a suit. Quite dapper, in fact. It wasn't his usual Sunday best. It was a navy-blue serge suit, up to date. She could tell quality when she saw it, working as long as she had at the hotel.

Not wanting to end up talking to him while looking so shabby, she started to turn back the way she'd come. It was then she noticed the woman coming out of the shop after him. The vision stopped her in her tracks. She tucked herself into the doorway of Groom's, so as not to be noticed.

It was Mrs Carmichael from the hotel and she was taking Leslie's arm. In public! He looked a little embarrassed but was smiling all the same.

What would people think? That she was an aunt or even an older sister? But Fanny knew otherwise.

She crossed over to head back down Surrey Street, even more determined not to be spotted now. Leslie had been warned not to give too much attention to Mrs Carmichael. What on earth was he thinking?

She saw them head in the direction of the station, away from her, and she was relieved. She leant against the wall of the Dolphin hotel. This extra weight certainly wore her out. It had become a problem with her job, as she wasn't as quick as she used to be.

Rousing herself from her thoughts, she noticed a middle-aged man standing close by, grinning to reveal lost and blackened teeth. He was a fisherman by the look – and smell – of him.

'You waiting for someone, gal?'

'No.'

'Perhaps you'd like to come to the quay and keep a man company?'

Cheeky devil. Yet, was it any surprise, the state of her?

She pushed herself away from the wall. Taking a rest here, next to the door of the saloon bar, had clearly been the wrong thing to do.

'I dunno what you think I am, but I'm not, I'm a respectable girl,' she said in her usual aggressive fashion. As an afterthought, she added: 'I work at the Beach Hotel.' That should shut him up, given its top-notch reputation.

'*Tst!* Had to drop its standards in wartime, has it? What d'ya do, clean out the slops?' He looked her up and down with a sneer. 'You're certainly not fit to serve them posh folks, that's for sure.' He walked away, down Surrey Street, swearing under his breath.

He was right though, wasn't he? Neither Mrs Leggett nor Mrs Bygrove had seen fit to promote her to waitressing or desk duty. Instead, she was hidden away, in the bedrooms, cleaning. Even Gertie had been made a portress, with a smart uniform, earning a little more and getting tips.

She'd been right about herself; she wasn't worth a bean.

With that thought, she hurried down Surrey Street, set on heading to the beach. There wouldn't be many there today, even on a sunny February afternoon. She'd brought a *Home Chat* magazine, which a guest had left in the room. At least reading had been something she'd been good at in school. She'd sit on the prom, and read it for a while and escape to somewhere else, if only in her head.

–

Edie had tried to hide it, but Lili had spotted the St Valentine's postcard that she'd half pulled from the envelope. The letter had arrived that afternoon, as they'd sat down for the late tea break. Lili could tell by the handwriting that it was from Charlie.

'It's all right,' said Lili. 'You don't have to hide it for my sake. I won't get upset.'

'I'm sorry, Lili, I should have realised it might have been a card, seeing it was so stiff.'

'No, like I said… Glad I am that Charlie is alive and well, and able to send one. Really, I am.'

Edie picked up the envelope once more and pulled the card out. Edie turned it over and read it, chuckling to herself. Lili looked away, not wanting to nose at something so personal.

'He's even made up his own little rhyme.'

'I can imagine, with Charlie.'

Fanny appeared through the door, removing her straw hat. The headwear was an odd choice for winter, but she didn't seem to own another.

'You back already?' said Lili.

'Yep. It's cheaper to have tea here than at a tearoom. Might go for a walk after.' She didn't sound happy about it.

'No one's making you,' said Lili.

'Didn't say they were.' Fanny removed her jacket and plonked her weight onto the end of the bench.

The rest of the late tea staff filtered in, including Gertie, who sat next to Lili. Annie and Alice, the scullery maids, came in with trays of tea and coffee, and a light rumble of chatter filled the room. Mrs Leggett came in last.

'Where's the biscuits, or other fancies?' Fanny asked.

'Mrs Norris said there was nothing left from afternoon tea,' said Alice. 'And that there aren't enough ingredients to do no biscuits for staff neither.'

'That's what I mainly came back for,' said Fanny.

'It'll do you good to go without, Miss Bullen,' said Mrs Leggett.

Fanny slumped and seemed to shrink into herself, her face more sad than annoyed. It was another of those rare moments when Lili felt sorry for her. It soon passed. Fanny wouldn't have hesitated to have wielded such an insult herself.

Leslie rushed in, all smiles, taking a seat at the opposite end to Mrs Leggett, next to Fanny, already back in his porter's uniform. 'Hope there's enough tea for me.'

'I thought it was your half-day-off too,' said Annie. 'Rather keen you and Fanny are to get back to the hotel. And you don't even live 'ere, Leslie. Damned if I'd be that keen.'

'Language, Miss Twine!' The housekeeper glared at her.

'Mrs Bygrove asked me to get back early to fill a shift. Stanley couldn't do it 'cos he's seeing his girl this evening. Supper with her parents. 'Ere, shift up, Fanny. You don't 'alf take up a lot of the bench these days.' He chuckled.

'Leslie, don't be so rude,' said Lili, compelled to stick up for Fanny this time.

'What? I'm just having a joke, ain't I? Don't mean nothin' by it.'

Lili was surprised that the maid hadn't spoken up for herself. She wasn't normally so backward at coming forward, especially when she was being insulted.

Fanny's face was expressionless. 'That's all right. I can take a joke… So, Leslie, did you enjoy your time off with Mrs Carmichael?'

Everyone in the room turned to her, with varying degrees of surprise in their faces. Leslie's eyes widened and he went red.

'Is this another of your fibs, Miss Bullen,' said Mrs Leggett, peering at her through narrowed eyes.

'No, it ain't. I saw him, I did, on High Street. Mrs Carmichael had hold of his arm. And he had on a dapper new suit that weren't his usual Sunday one, 'cos I've seen him in that one before, but this one was right posh.'

All eyes turned to Leslie. He had the look of a young lad who'd been caught scrumping apples.

'Is that true, Mr Morris?' Mrs Leggett asked.

'I, er... came across her in the town and... and she asked to treat me to lunch, since I'd, um, been such a help to her, in the hotel.'

'Then you should have said, "No thank you," Mr Morris.' The housekeeper thumped her hand down on the table, making Alice, to one side of her, jump. 'We have rules about fraternising with guests, as well you know.'

'I... I do, but, well, I couldn't be rude, could I? And, you know, I think that she's lonely and just wants some company, what with her husband being away and never seeming to come back on leave and...' Leslie ran out of steam.

'I wonder, sometimes, if this so-called husband who's a captain actually exists,' said Phoebe. 'You knew her before, didn't you Edie?'

'I did know her a little, but that was before she married.'

'That is *not* the point,' said Mrs Leggett. 'Leslie, you have already been told off for paying Mrs Carmichael too much attention. If she needs company, she ought to cultivate some friendships with the ladies around and about. There are enough of them, goodness knows.'

'She hasn't tried to compromise you, has she?' Edie asked.

'How d'ya mean?' Leslie looked confused.

Mrs Leggett got in before Edie could reply. 'She means, has she asked you to her room or done anything else she shouldn't have done, somewhere else?'

'What? You don't mean…? No! She's only put her arm through mine and kissed my cheek, just in a kind of grateful way.'

'Ugh!' said Annie. 'She's *years* older than you. Like your mum's age or something.'

Leslie straightened himself now and looked a little less cross. 'She's thirty-one, and, since I'm eighteen, she's hardly old enough to be me mum. Anyway, who wouldn't mind walking around with such a pretty woman. And she pays me extra tips.'

Mrs Leggett pushed her cup out of the way and leant forward. 'That does not sound like tips to me. It sounds more like she's paying you to keep her company. Almost like a… well, never mind.'

'Like a male whore,' said Fanny. 'That's what it sounds like.'

Gertie added: 'She might be holding your arm and kissing your cheek now, but what'll she want next?'

'She's not like Lord Fernsby,' he hollered.

Gertie blanched and lowered her head.

Lili placed her hand on Gertie's shoulder. 'There's no need for that.'

Mrs Leggett stood. 'I'm afraid I agree with Miss Green. I'm going to have a word with Mrs Bygrove, in the office.'

She headed off, leaving Leslie sipping solemnly at his tea, silent, while the rest fell into several muted conversations.

The housekeeper was soon back. 'Mrs Bygrove would like to see you in the office, Mr Morris.'

He slid off the bench. 'Thanks, Fanny, for getting me into trouble.'

'What, can't you take a joke? And you got yourself into trouble,' she retorted.

'It's not like *you've* never been in trouble. You could have kept quiet. I weren't doing nothin' to hurt you. It was just a joke, not like what you did. Just 'cos no man'd look twice at you, the state you've become.'

'And *that* wasn't necessary either!' said Lili. 'And you were doing something to hurt yourself. I reckon she's done you a favour.'

'And you're lucky it's got to Mrs Bygrove before it got to her husband,' Mrs Leggett added.

Leslie stomped out of the room but looked less sure of himself once more.

Chapter Thirteen

Serving morning coffee on the first Saturday of March was a pleasant experience for Lili, with the sun shining into the conservatory. The clientele was being friendly today and there were no awkward customers. Even Mrs Carmichael, though hardly speaking a word, had made neither a fuss nor any awkward requests. She simply sat, smoking one cigarette after another, sipping coffee in between. Lili had heard nothing more about anything untoward between her and Leslie since Mrs Bygrove had given him a talking to.

Through the large windows, Lili spotted camellias, hellebores and daffodils. The spring flowers always gladdened her heart. She placed down the tray of coffee on the table of James Perryman, the owner of several local shipyards, and his wife. They were also the parents of socialite Sophia, who ran various charities. Having done that, Lili returned to stand by the chest of drawers, near the door to the staff area. She watched as Phoebe took the order of regulars Mrs Rhys-Pennington and her daughter, who lived in one of the Georgian houses on South Terrace.

These were the moments she dreaded, standing here, waiting for something to do. It gave her time to think of things she'd rather not. With March here, with its lengthening days and milder weather, she pictured herself out with Norman. It was the kind of weather they'd been having when they first started walking out in September 1914. What lovely times they'd always had together. Looking forward to them had got her through her days. But by the time March had come around last year, he'd already been training for nearly two months. Oh, why had he enlisted? They'd only been walking out four months.

Four months. It had been nearly that since she'd last seen Rhodri. She was unlikely now to see him again. Unless she bumped into him in the town. He'd probably ignore her if they did.

The peaceful atmosphere couldn't last, of course. Although she'd wanted something to do, she'd rather it hadn't been this, for through the door from the dining room came Mr Bygrove. He held his hands behind his back, striding in like the army officers, who were now sitting by the back window, had done. Lili glanced at Phoebe, whose neutral expression told her she was feeling the same way about his arrival, as she passed by on her way to the kitchen.

Spotting the officers, Bygrove went to them first, greeting them effusively. 'We're always happy to serve our brave officers here, what what,' said the manager, making his voice posher than it was. 'Is everything to your liking?'

'Very pleasant, thank you,' said the captain among them. 'Of course, we quite understand that the cakes and whatnot can't be as fancy as they used to be, and—'

'They're not? Then let me put that right.' Bygrove scooped up the plate of miniature tarts and pastries.

'No need for that, old chap.' He stood and relieved the manager of the plate. 'We quite understand that there are shortages.'

'We'd be rather surprised if it were otherwise,' said one of the lieutenants with him. 'I dare say such dainties will become scarcer as time goes on, what with the sugar and other shortages.'

'As you wish.' Bygrove bowed low, as was his habit with guests he deemed to be *important*.

He was about to cross the room, no doubt to speak to the Perrymans, when he was waylaid by Major Thomas calling him over, lifting his newspaper.

'Bygrove, have you seen the latest?'

The manager glanced at the Perrymans before changing direction to the major's table, next to the officers.

'Seen what, exactly, Major?'

'The Military Service Act has come into force. Compulsory conscription for single men in Great Britain and Ireland, aged eighteen to forty-one. They'll be after your young porters, Stanley and Leslie, no doubt. And what about you, Bygrove? What happens if they extend it to married men. You over forty-one yet?'

'No, I'm only forty, Major, but I'm not worried about being called up. I'm sure my important work, keeping up the morale of the important personnel in our country...' He glanced at the officers, '...would be considered valuable and a reserved occupation.'

Phoebe passing by at this point on her way to the kitchen, raised her eyes heavenward.

'I wouldn't be so sure, old chap,' called the captain from the next table. 'Once they set up these local Military Service Tribunals, they'll be loath to exempt anyone if they don't have to. Those considered to have a reserved occupation will probably be along the lines of industrial workers, farmers, teachers, doctors, train drivers and the like.'

'That's the understanding of one of my army chums as well,' said the major. 'There might be some other exemptions considered, but they'd probably be conditional or temporary.'

'That's right,' said the captain. 'Your young porters – and any other men on your staff in that age group – will certainly be called up either now, or later if they're married and they extend the law.'

Lili could tell by his expression that Bygrove's smile was false. He'd probably have loved to have disagreed, but he couldn't win the argument in this company.

'It so happens that our hotel has already donated many of its male staff to the army. Nearly a dozen, I believe. That's why we have so many *females* serving.'

'And a jolly good job they're doing too,' said the captain. 'But businesses won't be judged on what percentage of staff they've contributed. If the job isn't a reserved occupation, or the worker hasn't a condition that precludes them from serving, then they'll be conscripted.'

Lili heard the distant double jingle of the hand bell from the kitchen. That must be the scones for the Perrymans. A shame she wouldn't get to hear Bygrove's reply.

Mrs Carmichael got up as Lili headed for the door into the dining room, still puffing away on her cigarette holder. She sashayed across the empty dining room towards the foyer. Lili headed off to the staff corridor.

On her way to the kitchen, she saw Fanny struggling through the door from the stairs with her cleaning box, rubbing her back. Her maid's uniform was a lot tidier than her own clothes, Mrs Leggett would have seen to that, but her hair was in a messy bun and she looked tired.

'All done then?' said Lili, for something to say.

'No, course not. Just come down for some more linseed oil.' She waddled towards the storeroom, her posture saggy.

When Lili entered the kitchen, Mr Strong, the pastry chef, was having a grumble.

'It isn't my fault if the dainties aren't up to my usual standard. I don't need Mr Bygrove complaining about it. He doesn't seem to realise that, with the shortage of butter and margarine, I'm having to use a bit of lard too.'

'I'm sorry, I shouldn't have mentioned it,' said Phoebe. 'Only, I thought you should be forewarned that Bygrove might come in here, moaning.'

'I think people understand, Mr Strong,' Lili said, as she picked up the plate of scones. 'One of the customers, the captain, said to Mr Bygrove that he understood about the shortages.'

'I'm sure some will, m'dear, but it's a matter of pride for me, see.'

Lili nodded and left. She spied Edie going into the staff dining room, looking down at a letter as she went. She poked her head around the doorway.

'Still fancy that walk this afternoon, do you?' They both had a couple of hours off in between their shifts and had discussed the possibility yesterday.

Edie looked up, her face pale.

'Whatever's the matter?'

'Charlie's off to France tomorrow. So that means Freddie and Daniel will be too. And some others from here.'

Lili took a couple of steps in. 'I'm so sorry. Would you rather miss the walk then?'

'Absolutely not. I need it even more now. And to have someone to talk to without others overhearing. I'll be finished at two o'clock, then I'm back on at five.'

'I'll be finished by three, so we'll go then. I'd better get these scones to the Perrymans.'

Back in the conservatory, she had a new table to serve. It was haughty Miss Harvey, from Selborne Place. She'd been in more regularly recently. So much for all the guests today being pleasant. It was nice while it lasted.

Having taken her order, Lili went back to the kitchen and stillroom to convey it to Mr Strong. On the way back, Leslie rushed past her, looking a little flustered, and went into the staff dining room.

'What's wrong with you?' she heard Edie say.

Being nosey, she poked her head through the door to listen. Fanny, returning from the stores, had the same idea as she squeezed in next to her.

'Mrs Carmichael caught me in the foyer,' said the porter. 'At least I had the excuse that I was going on my break. I added that Mr Bygrove wanted to speak with me, in case she got any ideas about me being free. She wanted me to walk with her to the shops on Norfolk Road. When I told her Stanley could do it, she seemed to change her mind. I've been trying to avoid her.

Been telling her I've got extra errands so can't accompany her to places. It don't make no difference. She's still pestering me. I don't wanna get into trouble with Mrs Bygrove again.'

Edie stood up. 'I'll have another word with her, Leslie, don't worry.'

He looked crestfallen, sinking onto the bench. 'I think she went to her room. It's a shame, as she is a good tipper.'

'It won't matter soon,' said Fanny. 'You'll be sent off to training and she won't be able to bother you any more.'

'Thanks Fanny,' he said grumpily. 'That's *really* helped.'

'Just saying.'

Fanny lumbered off towards the stairs and Lili returned to the conservatory.

–

Although the sun was still shining that afternoon, the air was a little cooler than Lili had anticipated. She wrapped her shawl more tightly around herself as she and Edie walked across the common to the promenade.

The beach was virtually empty, though the prom had a few people walking along its length: couples; women alone; and a few families. A girl ran past pushing a hoop with a stick, as her mother called for her not to go too far. Lili looked out to sea, enjoying the glint of the sun on the water. The rhythmic rumble of the waves washing onto the shore was soothing. She and Edie had talked only of the goings on in the hotel so far and the conversation between Bygrove and the officers.

'I don't suppose you know exactly where Charlie and the others are going,' said Lili.

'No.' Edie looked down at the ground. 'Just France, is what he said.'

'I'm sorry, we don't have to talk about it.'

'No, I need to talk, instead of having it going around and around in my head. I dare say Freddie and Daniel will also write to say they've gone, eventually. Hopefully, Freddie has written to Lucia. I will write to her later to make sure she knows. How are you feeling though, Lili? You don't talk much about… your situation any more.'

'I've started to feel brighter, but then I feel guilty about that. The evenings are getting lighter, which does help though. I've never liked winter.'

'Nor I.'

'Of course I'd like Norman to come back, but I do need to… move forward. Part of that is thanks to Mrs Bygrove having faith in me doing other jobs. So, even if I never meet anyone else, I have work I'm good at and can maybe do even better at.'

'What about Corporal Morgan?'

She hadn't wanted to think about Rhodri again, who was part of why she felt guilty about Norman. 'Sorry I am, that I was short with him before Christmas. I enjoyed meeting up with him. Not that I was hoping for anything romantic from it, mind.'

Who are you kidding! She felt her face become a little warm. Luckily, Edie was looking ahead towards the small Pepperpot lighthouse at the start of the pier.

'Why don't you write to him? It wouldn't hurt.'

'I've thought about it, but would it be proper? And he could have written to me.'

'Mm, I suppose he could have.' There was a pause before Edie said: 'What do you think might be wrong with Fanny? I'm starting to get concerned about her. I thought before that she'd just put weight on – maybe worrying about this supposed sweetheart – but now I'm not so sure. I wonder if she's ill. Maybe she has some condition, like consumption. And if that were the case, we could all get it.'

'No, seen enough people in my village with consumption I have, usually women. She hasn't been coughing or showing any other signs that I can see. And more likely to lose weight, she would be, than put it on. My sister-in-law, Jane, got very thin. I saw her, you know, in her coffin, and was quite shocked.'

'I've never liked doing that, visiting coffins. My mother made us all visit Grandmama when she died, six years back. I'd rather have remembered her as she was when she was alive.'

'I didn't want to do it neither, but everyone else did so I felt I had to. Anyway, I don't think that's what's wrong with Fanny. I think she might just be down because of this supposed sweetheart enlisting, or breaking up with her, if what Gertie reckons is true.'

'Why has she put on weight though? She eats the same as the rest of us.'

'You know what she's like at sneaking cakes and the like out of the kitchen. And she might be finishing leftover food she finds in the guest rooms, for all we know.'

'You could be right. I did see her once eating a biscuit as she came out of one of the bedrooms.'

They'd reached the lighthouse, which had a twin at the other end of the pier.

'Shall we walk on the pier, or by the river down to Pier Road?' Edie asked.

'Let's walk by the river. Oh look, there's one of those navy ships with the dazzle camouflage.' Lili pointed to a large vessel, sailing up the Arun towards the mouth, covered in large geometric shapes in blue, white, grey and black.

'I don't understand those. Won't they stand out to the enemy?'

'Major Thomas told me that it makes it difficult for the enemy to work out the ship's position, course and speed.'

Edie nodded. 'That's clever. The river and harbour haven't been the same since the Admiralty took over though. I'll be glad when it's back to the steamers, yachts and pleasure boats. And maybe some more sailing ships.'

'It's certainly changed the feel of it. I hope it doesn't drive some of the guests and day-trippers away, come the summer.'

'I doubt it. There seems to be a certain amount of fascination with them and pride that Littlehampton is playing its part in the war.'

They wandered down the unmade road past the old gun battery, Casino Theatre and windmill, chatting as they went. Lili was glad of this distraction, but it didn't quite do the job of getting the subject of Rhodri out of her head.

–

'That's all we need!'

Mrs Norris's voice could clearly be heard from the staff dining room as the breakfast things were being cleared up.

'This is getting ridiculous!' This time it was Mrs Leggett.

Edie, Gertie and Lili hurried to the corridor to find the head cook and the housekeeper looking at letters being shown to them by Jack, Leslie and Stanley.

'Are those your conscription papers?' said Edie, speeding up.

'Yep, they sure are,' said Jack, his mouth downturned, taking the letter back off Mrs Norris. 'I reckon Stuart'll have one too.'

'I don't wanna go to no war,' said Leslie.

'We ain't got no choice, mate,' said his brother. 'Anyway, we got training first, so the war might even be over by then.' Stanley shrugged.

'I remember Charlie saying the same when he came at Christmas,' said Fanny, emerging from the kitchen. 'But he's gone now, ain't he?'

'Do shut up, Fanny,' said Stanley.

Mrs Leggett clapped her hands twice. 'That's enough of that rudeness. It's not helping.'

'I was enjoying being sous chef here,' said Jack.

'What are you rabble doing gathered here?' barked the manager, coming from around the corridor that led to the office. 'Get about your work.'

'Excuse me, Mr Bygrove, but we are discussing an important matter.' Mrs Leggett stretched her body to make herself taller than him. 'The porters here and Mr Sinden have received conscription letters. They must report for a medical in a week's time.'

Bygrove's nostrils flared and he balled his hands into fists. 'Well, that can't happen. You lot, you'll have to apply for exemption. How can they expect me to run this hotel with fewer and fewer staff?'

'We've managed to fill a lot of the vacancies so far,' said the housekeeper.

'With *women*!'

'I'm sorry, Mr Bygrove,' said Edie. 'But I just don't think they will get exemptions for the jobs they do.'

'Well, that is *ridiculous*. How do they expect us to keep up our good service for the *important* people in our society, if they keep depriving me of my staff.'

'I think you'll have to take that up with the authorities yourself,' said Mrs Leggett. 'For these young men need to get to their shifts.'

Jack hurried to the kitchen, while the twins spared no time heading to the door to the foyer.

Edie looked at her wristwatch. Time to get to the desk.

Helen was there when she arrived, dealing with a guest who had to leave early that morning. She could see through the window that it was getting light outside but looked gloomy.

A motor taxi driver came through the front door as Edie reached the desk, to let them know he'd arrived. Stanley came and picked up the two suitcases, and the man followed him out.

'Good morning, Edie, how are you today?' Helen asked.

'The early post arrived. Jack has his conscription papers. Leslie and Stanley came in with theirs.'

'Oh no.' Helen shook her head slowly. 'We knew it was coming, but it is still a shock. Does my husband know yet?'

'He came into the corridor as it was being discussed.'

'Was he angry?'

What could she say? 'Somewhat. He suggested applying for exemption, but they have no grounds.'

'I thought he might and you're right. It looks like we'll be advertising for some new staff. We've never had to take on so many new people in such a short time.'

180

'It isn't easy, especially when some need training.'

'Indeed. Now, if you don't mind, I'll leave you to it. I want to help Vera get the children ready for school.'

'Of course.'

A couple of minutes later, Edie spotted Mrs Carmichael heading down the stairs in a check dress with a waistband and full skirt that showed her ankles. It must be new, as it was certainly the latest fashion. If she was coming down for breakfast, she was earlier than usual. The dining room would only just have opened.

Reaching the bottom step, she spotted Leslie by the cloak-room, to one side of the ballroom door, and hurried over to him. Had she *still* not heeded her gentle hints after Fanny had seen them out together in town?

Stanley returned from outside, guiding in guests as he explained what kind of items were available for breakfast. Edie hadn't seen this couple before but was always pleased when new customers arrived.

The smile slipped from Stanley's face when he spotted Mrs Carmichael, speaking with his brother, her face and manner-isms coy.

As he passed her, Stanley said: 'Mrs Carmichael, I'll show you into breakfast at the same time. Being nice and early you should be served even more quickly than normal.'

Mrs Carmichael glanced at Leslie, before accepting Stanley's offer, walking in just behind the new couple.

A minute later, Stanley reappeared, heading straight for his brother. Edie could tell, by his wagging finger, that he wasn't pleased, even though he'd lowered his voice. She had better intervene before someone came down the stairs or out of the lift and spotted them.

When she reached them, she placed her hand on Stanley's shoulder. 'Is everything all right?'

'I'm just telling my silly brother here that he must make it clear to Mrs Carmichael that she can't take up all his time. Didn't you get the opportunity to speak with her?'

'I did, Stanley, and I thought she understood. But to be honest, she was only *talking* to Leslie – that's all, from what I could tell.'

'Yes, she was,' said Leslie. 'Just passing the time of day, she was. Didn't ask me to do nothing.'

'She might have done if I hadn't intervened,' said Stanley, crossing his arms and frowning.

'Although it will be academic soon, with the two of you heading off for training, I will try to have another word with her.'

Lady Blackmore came fussing through the front doors, accompanied, as always, by her companion, Cecelia. Although the porters were normally loath to assist her, Leslie hurried off to welcome her, no doubt seeing it as a way of escaping his brother's annoyance.

'Rather him than me,' said Stanley. 'And thank you, Miss Moore. I appreciate you trying to help.'

Not that she expected it to do any more to help the situation than it had last time, thought Edie as she headed back to the desk.

–

Edie was dealing with a couple wanting to know the times of the trains to Brighton when she spotted Lolita Carmichael emerge from the dining room. Luckily, Leslie was away, taking a message over to South Terrace for Major Thomas.

Lolita looked around the foyer for a few moments before heading for the lift. Edie was keen to speak with her, but the guests were now asking about the aquarium in Brighton and, since she had visited it on a couple of occasions, she felt obliged to tell them a few details.

Stanley, spotting Lolita from his place by the front doors, headed over, making Edie immediately worry about what he might say. It would be rude to ask this couple to wait though, so she couldn't leave the desk.

As Edie picked up the telephone to order a motor taxi for the couple to take them to the station, she saw Lolita clutching her chest and looking forlorn.

'The motor taxi is ordered for you, Mr and Mrs Boddington. If you'd like to take a seat at one of the tables in the foyer, there are magazines to pass the time until your driver arrives.'

The addition of three small coffee tables had been a recent idea of Helen's, one which her husband could, for a change, find no fault with.

When they'd taken a seat, Edie left the desk to join Lolita and Stanley.

'Are you all right, Mrs Carmichael?'

'Edith, Stanley was just telling me how he and Leslie have been conscripted. It doesn't seem right to call upon such *young* men.'

'I quite agree with you,' said Edie.

'And I was telling madam how there'll probably be more women doing the job, like Gertrude,' said Stanley.

'Gertrude is very efficient,' said Lolita and Edie was pleased to hear that she thought so, after her initial comments. 'But it's not the same, women doing the job.'

'There might be some younger men too,' Stanley added.

Edie wasn't sure he'd been wise to mention this, if Lolita had a penchant for such lads. Still, she didn't seem attached to Stanley, so maybe it was something about Leslie. He was the more light-hearted of the two, his twin being more serious. And it wasn't like they were identical. What confusion that would have caused!

'Look, there's Leslie now,' said Lolita. 'I should have a word.'

'He'll be busy bringing back a message for the major,' said Stanley.

'Yes, yes, of course. I will speak to him later.'

She started to climb the curved staircase. Her expression was so pained, Edie would not have been surprised had she placed the back of one hand across her forehead and announced, '*Woe is me!*' She always had been a bit of an actress.

When she was out of earshot, Edie said: 'I'm not sure that was the right thing to do. Maybe it would have been better to let Leslie tell her?'

'He'd never have got around to it, not wanting to hurt her feelings and all. Hopefully, that's the end of that, though I wish it were under different circumstances.'

'So do I, Stanley. So do I.'

—

A week later, Helen was interviewing new staff, not only to replace the enlisted men but to fill some of the shortfall they already had. Nelly Norris sat with her in the office to question the potential kitchen staff and Imogen Leggett sat in for the rest.

After the last of the interviewees had departed, Helen invited both women to her office.

'Then we all agree on the chosen candidates, Imogen, Nelly?' she asked.

The two women nodded.

'I think they have potential, even if some have never done these particular jobs before.'

'Needs must,' said Nelly. 'I can promote a couple of the kitchen maids who've already stepped in from time to time to prepare items. Then the new staff can do the maids' jobs. I'll have to decide who to promote to sous chef, to replace Jack. Right shame it'll be, losing him. He's been here since he were fourteen and he's always been a good little worker.'

Helen checked her wristwatch. 'It shouldn't be too long before they get back from their medicals.'

'Another four men going. It don't seem fair, with Leslie, Stanley and Jack not even twenty yet. And Stuart's not much older.'

'But the world isn't fair,' said Imogen. 'I suppose I'll have to train up some of those who've applied for the cleaning jobs. I'm sure Fanny could do that too. And at least we'll be able to acquire a couple of male porters, even if they are quite young. And a part-time desk clerk, albeit another woman.'

There was a knock on the door.

'Come in,' said Helen.

Gertie put her head around the door. 'They're back from the medicals, Jack and the others. They'd like to speak to you, Mrs Bygrove.'

'Very well. Could you ask them to go to the staff dining room, please? There'll be more room in there.'

Gertie hurried away to carry out the task.

Helen rose. She knew what they'd have to say, but she was still dreading hearing it. It had been the same every time members of her staff had enlisted. 'You two had better come as well.'

In the dining room, the four young men were seated, looking dour. Several staff members were there for an afternoon tea break, but they were all standing around looking equally glum.

'When are you off?' said Helen, wanting to get straight to the point.

'Monday,' said Stuart Coulter. 'Shoreham camp. Well, three of us, anyway.'

'Then who isn't—?' Helen started.

'Me,' said Jack. 'Seems my flat feet are a bit of a problem. Dunno why. I can walk around the kitchen all day.'

'It's not the same as the long miles we might have to walk in the war though,' said Stuart. 'I read somewhere that it can get painful if you've got flat feet.'

'Why're you looking so miserable?' said Stanley. 'You get to stay put.'

'Only 'cos I'm not good enough.' Jack hung his head.

'Well, I'm glad ya staying,' said Nelly. 'Course, I wish you all were. But my kitchen don't need to lose another good cook. And what's all this "not good enough" nonsense?'

'There'll probably be other ways you can serve your country, Jack,' said Helen.

'They said I could join the Volunteer Training Corps, what trains to defend the country in case we're invaded.'

'There you are then. If need be, we'll fit your shifts around any training you have to do.'

'Thanks, Mrs Bygrove.' Jack's expression looked a little brighter.

'I'll be back later for my evening shift,' said Stuart. 'But I'd better go and tell my parents. Dreading it, I am.'

'We are too,' said Leslie.

'Jack, do you want to pop up to Lyminster, to tell your parents now?' said Helen.

'No. I'll go and tell them in the gap in my shifts tomorrow. I'd rather get on in the kitchen now.'

'Very well. The rest of you get on with your afternoon break, before it's over.'

Several of them nodded, but Helen could see that it would be a muted affair, with everyone sad at losing even more valued staff members.

And when Douglas got back from… well, whatever it was he'd gone to this afternoon, she'd have to inform him of this and the new staff recruitment.

She wasn't looking forward to it.

Chapter Fourteen

'I do think, Douglas, that we should do this fundraising at Easter.' Helen was cutting Arthur's sandwiches into fingers as she sat at the small dining table in their living quarters on the first floor. Vera, the children's nursemaid, was on a half-day off, and Helen enjoyed these times with her six-year-old son and seven-year-old daughter.

Dorothy was biting enthusiastically into her sandwich, humming *Goosey Goosey Gander*, and kicking her legs back and forth. She accidently caught her father on the knee.

'Stop that, Dorothy!' he barked. 'And stop that infernal humming. It is *most* annoying.'

Helen's heart went out to her daughter as the girl's mouth dipped down at the corners. Poor little mite. It wasn't often they got to eat together like this, and her father had to be in one of his bad moods. But then, when wasn't he these days?

He hadn't been like this in the early days. She thought back to that first meeting, visiting the keep at Arundel Castle, in 1903. How charming and intelligent he'd seemed in those days. She'd been immediately captivated by him: thoughtful, gentlemanly, opening doors, and putting her needs first. And he'd had humility back then, not always thinking he was right. It hadn't been long before they'd declared their love for each other, and he'd asked her to marry him. How romantic they'd been in those days, holding hands and finding secret spots when on walks so they could kiss.

Working in Arundel back then, he'd been the manager of the smaller Bridge Hotel. He'd always had ambitions to do better and that was something else that had attracted her to him. He'd been sober, sensible, not like her alcoholic father, who'd squandered his family's fortune to the point that he'd had no choice but to sell the manor house and land he'd owned in Rustington. Their home.

'What's all this fundraising nonsense now?' he asked.

'The Littlehampton War Fund committee has asked us if we'll help raise money for the volunteer force at Winterton Lodge.'

'But that's a school!'

'It is. They've now put a room aside where the volunteers make things such as bandages, slings, swabs, pyjamas and all sorts to supply local hospitals. They've heard about our successes in the past and thought we'd be an asset. That's good, isn't it?'

'Of course we're an asset to their little endeavours. We're the Beach Hotel, a premier hotel, no less, attracting prestigious guests. No wonder they want to be associated with us in their campaign.'

'I don't think *us* being associated with *them* will do us any harm either, Douglas.'

'Just remember, we're here to make money for *us*. We're not a charity. But if you want to organise one of your little events, by all means do. But I'm not getting involved. *I'll* concentrate on our guests. And I don't want you using all the staff members on this. We've few enough of them as it is.'

'We have recently employed several more, Douglas, as you know. I've also tried to fill the shortfall we already had.'

'Nearly all live-outs to whom we have to pay extra.' Douglas tutted.

'We can't make people live in.'

'Like I said before, if you want to do some *charity* work, you carry on, but you'll still have to play your part in the hotel.'

'Don't I always?'

'And I don't want our guests bothered about contributing or joining in.'

'Most of them are wealthy enough to give money, so they could be involved in something.'

Douglas clattered his teacup onto the saucer. 'I am *not* having our guests harassed and made to mix with the hoi polloi. They might not come again.'

'They were more than happy to support the concert in November and they mixed with the *hoi polloi* there. I do think a lot of people consider us to be all in this war together, you know.' *Maybe not all*, she thought, picturing the likes of Lady Blackmore, who always thought she was above everything. 'There's a war on and people want to do what they can.'

'Is that it? Or can I eat my sandwich in peace now?' He picked up one quarter.

Where had such disdain for the lower classes come from? She'd been the daughter of a knight of the realm, albeit a disgraced one, but didn't have this contempt for them. Somehow, mixing with the titled and rich had turned him into a… a… the word *bully* came to mind first. That was surely too harsh. He was a conceited snob. But it was almost as if she and the children were also beneath him.

'There is one other thing I'd like to discuss, but do feel free to eat while I'm talking.'

'Oh, what is it now?'

'As you are aware, food is becoming more difficult to get hold of, and that includes fruit and vegetables. We're probably going to have to cut back on our standards a little.'

'*I* will talk to the vendors and use my considerable influence. I'm sure they will see where their bread's buttered.'

'I don't think it will be that easy. But I was thinking—'

'Oh dear, not more of your *thinking*.'

Helen's patience was slipping away. It was good that the children were here, for otherwise she might have said something regretful, even though she disliked arguments and would surely have caused one.

'Well, I wondered, what with the various allotments that have sprung up around Littlehampton, whether it might be an idea to dig up the tennis courts. Just for the—'

'Absolutely not!'

It was the reply she'd expected, but she'd had a small dot of hope.

'They make money for the hotel and it's one of the reasons people choose to stay here.'

'They don't make enough to pay their way. Nor do that many guests from elsewhere take advantage of them. It's mostly people from the area who use the facility.' In particular, Douglas's little tennis group. And he didn't charge them anything.

'Miss Harvey and our friends would be horrified! They play regularly and take part in the tournaments.'

He must have been reading her thoughts.

'Then perhaps Miss Harvey could suggest a way to get hold of more food. It's not as if they're even used in the colder months. Anyway, Miss Harvey is a terrible snob and she's only the proprietress of a guest house on Selborne Place. And she doesn't even pay to use the tennis courts.'

She'd said this calmly, but it felt good to get it off her chest. She really did not like the woman, with that superior air she put on during the occasional times she'd come in for morning coffee or afternoon tea.

'You don't even know her,' was Douglas's dismissive reply.

No, and I don't want to, she thought. 'In that case, what about some of the gardens around the hotel. Mr Hargreaves would be more than happy to do the extra work, he says. He grows vegetables and fruit in his own garden, and now has an allotment. As head gardener, he's sure he could persuade his workforce to do some overtime. And we already have a herb and kitchen garden.'

'That's an even more stupid idea. The gardens are part of the attraction of the hotel.'

'But if there's little food, people won't stay just for the gardens.'

'I've said no and that's that. You seem to forget who the manager and *owner* here is, Helen.'

And you forget whose inheritance allowed us to buy this hotel.

'We *both* worked hard to rebuild the reputation of this hotel when we moved in. We don't want to lose that.'

It had been doing adequately when they'd bought it, back in 1910, but had started to get a little rundown and old-fashioned. They'd redecorated it, while improving the menus and facilities, and had replanted the garden.

'That's enough now.'

So that was the end of that conversation.

The four of them ate in silence, until Dorothy started to chatter about school the day before and how she'd enjoyed drawing a picture of the beach with wax crayons. She was now in Julia Nye's class at East Street School. She liked having her as a teacher.

'Can I get my picture, Daddy, to show you? Miss Nye let us bring them home.'

'Not now. The golf club committee are meeting here this afternoon for tea.' He rose.

Dorothy's little shoulders slumped, and her mouth dipped once more.

'That isn't for another three hours,' said Helen.

'I have things to organise and work out. I'll be in the office.'

'Of course.'

He left without wishing any of the family farewell.

'It wouldn't have taken Daddy a minute to see my picture,' said Dorothy, picking up her glass of lime cordial.

'I know, sweetheart. You can fetch it and show it to me and Arthur.'

'You've both already seen it.'

'But it was so lovely we'd like to see it again.'

Dorothy grinned broadly and jumped off the chair.

'Have you finished, sweetheart?' Helen asked Arthur.

'Yes, Mummy. I can't eat that crust 'cos I'm full up.'

'That's all right. You haven't left much.'

As he slurped at his cordial, Helen gazed around the area. It was a sitting room and dining room combined, plus there were two bedrooms that led off it. The Victorian furnishings were mostly ones that had been in parts of the hotel that had been updated. How she wished for something more modern. And a little more room for their living quarters would have been nice. That was the trouble with residing in a hotel.

Dorothy came rushing back, picture held high.

'My word, I like it even more today!' said Helen. 'That's a lovely blue sky, just like we have now. Perhaps we should go for a walk by the beach after lunch. Would you like that?'

'Yes please!' they both cried.

'Then we will.'

'Mummy,' said Arthur. 'The thing you want to do for Easter, will it be for children too, like at the Children's Project on the beach last summer?'

'I haven't really thought about it yet, sweetheart. But that might be an idea.'

She'd call a meeting with the staff later. It was already the first of April and, although Easter was late this year, they must get cracking on the organisation.

—

'I'm sorry for calling this meeting so late in the day,' said Helen, at ten to eleven that evening, when some of them no doubt wanted to be in bed.

She looked around at Mrs Leggett, Mrs Turnbull, Mrs Norris, Hetty, Fanny, Lili, Edie and Gertie, Miss Bolton the live-in nurse and Nancy the barmaid, all sitting at the table in the staff dining room. Vera the nursemaid and Jack were standing either side of the dimming fire.

'I'm aware that Easter is only three weeks away, but I was approached yesterday by Miss Sophia Perryman, who now runs the Littlehampton War Fund. She wanted to know if we would do something over Easter this year. I know not all of you can be involved on the day, but I'm always open to ideas. I... *We* want to do it on Easter Saturday, which is the twenty-second of April this year, so that it doesn't interfere with the Easter Sunday and Monday meals.' She'd better make it sound like Douglas was involved too.

'The concert you held in November was very successful,' said Miss Bolton. 'How about another one of those?'

'That might be an idea for the future, but we'd like to do something more seasonal and involve the children. Arthur gave me that idea. And we'd like to hold it in the afternoon. We'll offer extra shifts to anyone not due on at that time, so we can have as many staff members available as possible, including the live-out staff, of course.'

'If you're looking for something the children can get involved in, what about a chocolate Easter egg hunt, where you charge an entry fee?' said Edie. 'I read once about how Queen Victoria used to do them for her children and I believe some families do them even now.'

'Huh! Only well-off families,' said Fanny. Helen noticed Lili elbow her and frown. Fanny elbowed her back.

'That... is a jolly good idea,' said Helen, 'As long as we can get hold of enough eggs.'

'Despite the increasing sugar shortage,' said Mrs Norris, 'there doesn't seem to be a chocolate shortage yet. I've got half egg-shaped moulds to make decorations for the Easter desserts we do each year. We could use them to make some nice hollow chocolate eggs. My Joseph used to be good at that, but I'm sure Mr Strong would be proficient.'

'I used to help Mr Norris with those,' said Jack. 'So, I could do some too. Don't mind using some of my hours off if it's for a war charity.'

The staff in the room nodded and agreed, apart from Fanny. She didn't seem keen on anything these days.

'It would be nice to attract a lot of different people to our Easter event, just as we did with the concert,' said Helen, by which she meant *classes* of people, but didn't want to put it like that.

'What if some children can't find any eggs?' said Hetty. 'That wouldn't be fair.'

'How about we use clues to find them instead,' Lili suggested. 'They'd have a clue on a piece of paper, which leads to another clue and so on. At the end, they'd get their prize. Adults could help them, 'specially if they can't read. And it would be easier than hiding eggs.'

Helen smiled. 'That's a brilliant idea.'

'We could have boiled eggs for the children to paint. We used to paint eggs at home in Wales, using dyes my mam made from vegetables.'

'We did that too,' said Mrs Turnbull.

'We already make our own colours in the kitchen,' said Mrs Norris, 'We could do a few more. Hannah's good at that.'

'I'm sure we could make it affordable for everyone and still make some money for the charity,' said Helen. She wasn't sure what Douglas would make of that, nor where exactly they'd hold these events: outside if the weather allowed. But where? In the garden? Would Mr Hargreaves and his gardening staff appreciate that? And where indoors? There was much to think about and not much time to do it.

'Maybe we could have a children's afternoon tea in the ballroom?' Gertie suggested, tentatively. 'They wouldn't have to mix with the hotel guests as they could come in the window door from the garden. I'd have loved that as a child.'

'I wonder if Mr Janus would have an entertainer he could donate for the event, like he did at the concert,' said Vera. 'Dorothy and Arthur love the children's entertainments on the prom, so I'm sure it would make it popular.'

Most of her staff certainly had a lot of enthusiasm for the event. 'These are all wonderful ideas. They might take a bit of extra work, but I think it would be worth it. However, we do also need to think of something we can get our, um, wealthier clients involved in.'

'I have an idea,' said the housekeeper, who up till now had been unusually quiet and unjudgemental.

'Go ahead,' said Helen, dreading what might be coming.

'I do believe that raffles are very popular. We could offer an Easter afternoon tea for the price of a ticket, or tickets, should they wish to purchase more. They could be sold at the desk and mentioned by whoever is on duty. And the waiting staff could mention the raffle to the diners.'

Miss Bolton leant across the table to get the housekeeper's attention. 'What if we get some hoi polloi buying a ticket and winning.'

Helen could have laughed at this apparent reversal. She'd have laid good money on it being Imogen Leggett herself condemning such an idea, not coming up with it!

'If they are sold within the hotel, then there will be no chance of that,' said Mrs Leggett. 'And, having the connections he does, maybe Mr Bygrove could sell some tickets to his friends at the golf club?' She raised her eyebrows, maybe acknowledging that she knew he wasn't keen on such events.

'I can certainly ask him. Thank you, Imogen, I think that can be added to the list.'

'Wouldn't you make more money from a raffle if anyone could enter though?' said Jack.

'I did wonder,' Mrs Norris began, 'whether I could make a box of treats as a raffle prize. I know it's getting harder to get hold of things, but we could still do it proud. A few biscuits, scones, a nice loaf of bread. A couple of Hetty's jars of jam. A box of the premium tea we use. Something like that. We could offer those tickets elsewhere.'

'Yes, a splendid idea, Jack and Mrs Norris. Two raffles wouldn't hurt.' Helen regarded her wristwatch. 'Now, it's getting late and some of you need your beds, so I'll leave it at that for now and speak to you all again tomorrow.' She rose and left the room.

It wasn't worth furnishing Douglas with any details now. Better to wait until it was all worked out. And she'd better do it quickly so that she could get the details to the local newspapers.

Chapter Fifteen

The Easter egg hunt had been a huge success, with a lot of children turning up from the town.

They'd been lucky to have a bit of sun during the actual hunt, which had taken place partly in the gardens and partly on the common just outside, with the fountain being utilised as one of the hiding places. Several members of staff had been stationed at various posts to ensure the children neither ruined the garden, nor got lost on the common.

The boiled-egg painting took place in the private dining room, with lots of old newspaper covering the table and floor beneath. Lili and Edie had taken charge here. The room was noisy, but Lili loved the enthusiasm of the children. She hadn't enjoyed herself like this in a long while. It reminded her of being at school, or in the Sunday School at the Baptist chapel. How she yearned to be young like that again, even if only for a while.

At a quarter to four, the children who were staying for the tea were gathered up and taken into the ballroom, via the garden, to sit at the tables that had been set in one long line. Dorothy and Arthur were among them, being attended by Vera. Most of the children looked around at the striking room – with its mirrors, pillars and crystal chandeliers – with mouths open. The parents and guardians who were not familiar with the hotel seemed similarly impressed.

'Doesn't it look splendid?' Lili said to Edie. 'Young Simon and Dennis have done a great job with the table presentation.'

'Yes. They were lacking in confidence when the hotel took them on. They've come a long way.'

Helen entered the room with a basket containing a few spare eggs from the hunt. 'That went well,' she said, bright-eyed. 'Edie, you must thank Julia from me again when you see her, for passing on the news of this event to her headmistress. We seem to have quite a few from East Street School.'

'I was amazed at how many businesses agreed to put up posters and that some sold tickets for us too,' said Edie. 'Everyone's been very keen to take part in some way, to help the war effort. How has the raffle been going?'

'It was already doing well, but quite a few more have been in today to buy raffle tickets for the afternoon tea,' said Helen. 'I'm not so sure about the Easter treats raffle. Mrs Turnbull is collecting the proceeds and stubs this afternoon from the businesses. Right, everyone's seated. Let's serve the tea.'

The sandwiches, a choice of egg or ham, were brought in first, along with sausage rolls. Several mountains of hot cross buns were placed down next, with butter and Hetty's plum jam. The treats were brought in on silver trays with lace doilies, which seemed to delight the mothers as much as the food did the children. They waited a while before serving up the sweet treats, including ginger nuts, bourbons and almond biscuits. Lili particularly liked the look of the glacé biscuits, with the set icing in pink and yellow, and the little flowers piped onto them. To drink, the children had a choice of orange or lime cordial.

Lili thought about the concert in November, when Rhodri had turned up. He wasn't likely to be here this time, she thought, amused, yet sad at the same time.

The door from the foyer opened and Mrs Carmichael stepped in, remaining close to the wall.

Edie went to talk to her, and Lili overheard her say: 'Mrs Carmichael, this is a children's event.'

'Oh please, Edith, do call me Lolita. And yes, I know it is. I fancied coming to see the children enjoying themselves. It was such a delight to hear their excited voices.'

'They do seem to be having fun.'

'I so wish I had a couple of my own to bring here,' Mrs Carmichael said with a sigh. 'Clifford went to war not long after we got married, you know.'

Lili turned to look at Edie, who glanced back at her with a slight widening of her eyes. Mrs Carmichael didn't notice, looking straight ahead at the children.

'Has anyone heard from Leslie? And Stanley?' she asked.

'Mrs Bygrove has had a letter and they seem to be doing all right with their training.'

'That's good to know.'

Even now, the woman couldn't leave the subject of Leslie alone.

'I'll leave you to watch the festivities,' said Edie. 'I'd better go in case someone needs something. Mr Janus is coming to entertain them soon.'

'The man himself is coming?'

'Yes. He's going to tell some jokes, sing some songs and do some magic tricks, I believe.'

Edie returned to Lili's side and they moved down a little as they watched the children eating.

'That was enlightening,' said Edie.

'Yes, I overheard. I wouldn't have had Mrs Carmichael pegged as someone wanting children. She seems too...'

'Self-absorbed?'

'That's a good way to put it. By the way, I asked Gertie earlier if everything was all right with Fanny.'

'Why, what's happened now?' Edie frowned.

'I just thought it strange, that she hadn't jumped at the chance of helping here today. She normally complains when she's not asked. Gertie said she overheard her telling Mrs Bygrove she didn't want to help and was happy to carry on with any cleaning that needed doing. And Gertie reckons she spends all her half-days off now in their room.'

'That isn't like her. She could still be feeling sad, if she has broken up with someone.'

'Maybe. You'd think she'd be getting better by now though, you know, accepting it more. It's not like he's died. If he exists at all.'

'Not that we know. Though I dare say Fanny would have been more upset if that had been the case. We all deal with these things in different ways.'

Lili knew that comment wasn't aimed specifically at her but wondered if people thought she'd rallied rather quickly after Norman's disappearance. She just hadn't wanted the fuss.

'Here's Mr Janus now,' said Edie, as the man peeped his head around the garden door and waved.

-

Easter Sunday evening Lili sagged onto one of the chairs in the hotel dining room, and sighed long and loudly. There'd only been a buffet for the guests this evening, after the lavish Easter luncheon.

'Thank goodness that's all cleared up,' said Phoebe. 'I'm exhausted. And starving. You look all done in too.'

'See you tomorrow,' called Bert, one of the newer live-out porters, heading to the staff door.

They replied and waved.

'Yes, I am,' said Lili, after he'd gone. 'Yesterday, with the Easter egg hunt and the children's tea, was exhausting. But it was fun all the same.'

'And a great success. Gertie delivered the box of treats to someone on Duke Street.'

'Good. It did actually go to someone from the less well-off part of town. I hear Miss Harvey won the afternoon tea and that she's coming tomorrow.' Lili raised her eyes heavenward.

'How lovely for us all.' Phoebe fluttered her eyelashes and imitated the rather fake posh voice used by Miss Harvey. 'It makes me wonder if Bygrove fiddled the raffle somehow.'

'I know what you mean, but Mrs Bygrove it was what drew the winning ticket.'

Phoebe sat next to Lili and leant in as if imparting a secret. 'Hey, what if Bygrove removed the tickets and replaced them all with ones with Miss Harvey's name on?'

As they giggled over this amusing scenario, Gertie plodded into the room, removing her portress's cap.

'Your shift finished too?' Lili called.

'Yep.' She came up to them. 'Mrs Turnbull just asked me if I'd seen Fanny. I told her there was no point asking me no more. She said she'd gone out, just after turning down the beds, and ain't got back yet. She was supposed to be helping with laying up for supper. She don't normally go out at night. Well, not for a while she ain't.'

'Perhaps she's got a new sweetheart,' said Phoebe. 'Or just a sweetheart, as we don't know for sure that she had one before.'

'It's not very happy she seems, if she does have a sweetheart,' said Lili.

Phoebe stood. 'Could she have gone to visit her family, it being Easter? Maybe that's where she was going before when we thought she was courting.'

'I dunno,' said Gertie. 'When we was friends, she'd never talk about family. I didn't get the impression they was around.'

'Didn't she mention her mother being ill, that time she tried to get Edie into trouble?' said Phoebe.

'Yes, but she'd already told Mrs Bygrove she was dead when she first came for the job.'

'I wonder which is the truth then?' said Lili.

'Probably none of it,' Gertie said dismissively. 'I used to think she was all right, a good laugh. She was to begin with, but I found out she's a right liar about a lot of things. I'm still worried though; in case she's got into some bother. Mrs Turnbull is too. She said she ain't been herself recently and she's right. I don't wanna alert Mrs Leggett to it and get her into trouble though.'

'Well,' said Lili, rising wearily from the chair. 'She is allowed out at night. Could be this possible sweetheart's back in her life, or on leave – or, as you said Phoebe, there's a new one.'

'I have wondered...' Phoebe started. 'Um, sorry to say it, but the state of her these days, with her not caring what she looks like off-duty...'

'Spit it out,' said Lili.

'I wonder if she's at a public house. Drunks often get untidy and careless. Like this woman we had living next to us when I was a girl.'

'They're closed at nine at the latest now though.'

'And she don't smell of it,' said Gertie. 'And I'd know, sharing a room with her. I had an uncle what was a drunk and he stank of it.'

'True,' said Lili. 'I've known a few in our village too and I wouldn't say Fanny were acting like them. Now it's not like we can go out and look for her this time of night, so we'll have to hope for the best.' The grandfather clock in the foyer struck ten. 'Let's get our supper. It'll be ready now and it's late enough as it is.'

–

'Morning Gertie,' Lili called, as the portress entered the staff dining room at five to six the following day.

'Morning.'

'Good morning,' said Edie. 'Lili tells me that you were worried about Fanny. Did she turn up?'

Gertie went to the fire to warm her hands. The three of them were the only people in the room so far.

'Yep, she turned up 'alf-an-hour ago. Woke me up, she did, clatterin' about. She lay down for a while but got up to get ready as I left the room.'

'Any explanation?' Lili asked.

'Nah. She wouldn't tell me now anyway. Hardly says a word to me these days. Wish I had a room to meself. There are several empty now.'

'But on the men's side,' Lili pointed out. 'They're not gonna let you on the other side of that dividing door.'

'There's only Jack there now. Seems a waste. Don't think he's the pestering sort.'

'At least Fanny's back,' said Edie.

'Shhh.' Lili nudged Edie's arm as Mrs Leggett came fussing through the door, her face like thunder.

With her was Mrs Turnbull, who mouthed, 'Is she back?' at Gertie. She got a nod and a smile in reply.

Slowly the staff on the earliest shifts filtered in, and trays of cold tongue, kippers, scrambled eggs and fried potatoes were brought through, along with a pot of porridge and two plates of bread and butter. People started to help themselves, chatting quietly.

At a quarter past six, Fanny appeared, looking pale and tired. Her skirt was tucked up on one side, revealing half a leg of stocking. Some strands of her tawny hair had already come down out of her bun.

'There you are, Miss Bullen,' the housekeeper snapped. 'And look at the state of you.' She stood to yank the skirt down. 'It's hardly any wonder though, is it?'

Fanny stopped by the bench, looking glum.

'I was up at five o'clock,' Mrs Leggett continued, 'and I spied you sneaking in. Where the blazes had you been until that time? Not out soliciting, I hope.'

The glumness became a vague defiance. 'I was up at four, 'cos the sun was rising and a bloody cockerel was making a noise.'

'Language!'

'I went out for a walk.'

Gertie looked over at Lili and Edie, and frowned.

'Are you ailing, pet,' Mrs Turnbull asked. 'You're a little wan.'

'I'm fine.' She sat down, helping herself to a little bit of porridge. Normally, she'd take as much as she was allowed.

'The teapot's empty already,' Fanny complained, trying to help herself to tea.

'Then go to the stillroom and get it filled up, girl,' said Mrs Leggett.

Fanny put the pot down and swivelled around awkwardly on the edge of the bench. She got to her feet, then turned to pick up the teapot, but wobbled. Phoebe's hand went out to steady her. Fanny's eyes closed and she moaned, a second before she fell into a faint. She avoided hitting the ground with any force only because Phoebe caught hold of her, nearly tumbling off the bench herself in the effort.

'What on earth?' Mrs Leggett was the first to her feet, followed by Mrs Turnbull. Both women knelt by Fanny's head, with the storekeeper tapping her face to raise her.

Lili stood and came around the table. 'Oh goodness, there's blood!'

The rest of the table rose and gathered at a distance, apart from Jack, the only male at the table. 'I'll go and get Mrs Bygrove,' he said. He was followed out by Phoebe.

'Fanny? Fanny?' Mrs Turnbull called, still patting her face.

Mrs Leggett was more forceful. 'Miss Bullen! What is wrong?'

Phoebe arrived back with a pillow, handing it to the house-keeper to place under Fanny's head. The maid started to moan, but still couldn't be raised properly.

Helen flew through the door, hunkering down next to Fanny. 'Does she normally have a bad time with her monthlies?' she asked Gertie.

'Not that I'm aware.'

'Maybe she caught a chill, going out in the cold,' said Phoebe.

'No, something isn't right,' said Helen. 'Phoebe, fetch a blanket. Gertie, get Miss Bolton. She was in the kitchen just now. And Edie, would you ring Dr Ferngrove?'

The three of them left immediately to carry out their tasks. Mrs Leggett shuffled the remaining staff out of the room, apart from Lili, Helen and Mrs Turnbull.

'If it isn't her monthlies...' said Lili, having been through something similar with her sister, Carys.

'Yes, I'm wondering the same,' said Helen. 'This happened to me, the first time.'

'A miscarriage?' said Mrs Turnbull. 'Is that what you're thinking?'

'It might explain the weight gain,' said Helen. 'How did we not think of this before? Someone said they thought she had a sweetheart.'

Phoebe returned with two blankets. As they were laid over her, Fanny moaned once more.

'Fanny, can you hear me?' said Helen, but still there was no reply.

An over-excited Gertie returned with the in-house nurse, Miss Bolton.

'What's all this fuss about?' said the nurse. 'Oh my goodness! Has she fallen on something?'

As Miss Bolton lifted her skirt, everyone turned away. 'Has she had a miscarriage?'

'That's what we were wondering,' said Helen.

-

Edie and Gertie left for their desk and porter duties soon after, both asking to be kept informed. Miss Bolton had ordered boiled water from the scullery to clean Fanny up and ascertain what had happened. Lili, Helen, Mrs Leggett and Mrs Turnbull were gathered in the staff corridor when the doctor appeared.

'Our qualified nurse is with her now,' said Helen, opening the dining room door for him.

She left them to it. The four women remained still, not even talking, as they awaited an explanation.

After a few minutes, Dr Ferngrove opened the door and stepped out.

'I'm afraid it's a little more than a miscarriage,' he said. 'I believe it is a postpartum haemorrhage.'

Lili put her hand up as if at school. 'What's one of those, doctor?'

'You mean, she's had a baby?' said Helen, in disbelief.

'That's right.'

Lili couldn't take this all in. Fanny had been that far into a pregnancy? 'Then where is it?'

There was a loud moaning from the dining room, encouraging all five of them to enter the room. Fanny had woken up.

Mrs Leggett hunkered down beside her. 'Fanny, where is the baby? Oh, you silly girl!'

'No,' Fanny replied, sweating and writhing. 'No, they'll take her away.'

'We need to get her to bed,' said the doctor. 'I need to see to her properly, to make sure she doesn't get any sort of infection. May I keep Miss Bolton with me to help.'

'Of course,' said Helen. 'But we do need to know what's happened to the baby.' She knelt down. 'Fanny, is the baby alive?'

Fanny came to, opening her eyes. 'They'll take her away. They'll send us to East Preston and take her away.' She started crying. 'That's what they did to me. They took me away and left me in the workhouse.'

Lili and Mrs Turnbull looked at each other, wide-eyed. So *that's* what happened to her mother. She wasn't ill; she hadn't died. She'd had an illegitimate baby and somehow Fanny had ended up in the workhouse. Lili felt tears prick her eyes. What a sad fate for a child.

'It sounds like the baby is hopefully still alive,' said Dr Ferngrove. 'She will need to be found, or else she might die.' He hunkered back down beside the maid. 'Fanny, please, you *have* to tell us where the baby is.'

'No, you'll take her away.'

'Is she somewhere warm and dry?'

'I want to keep her.'

The doctor looked back at the women. 'She's a little delirious, so I'm afraid we won't get anything from her at the moment. We'll keep trying. In the meantime, would you organise a search, Mrs Bygrove?'

'Of course, Dr Ferngrove. Bridget, help the doctor and Miss Bolton convey Fanny to her bedroom.'

'Breakfast for the guests will be starting soon,' said Lili. 'I should go.'

'I will ask Phoebe to take charge in the dining room. I'll need you to help with the search.'

'Very well, madam.'

–

In the staff corridor, Lili and Mrs Leggett waited for Mrs Bygrove to return. She came from the stillroom with Nancy, the barmaid.

'All right, now we need to make a thorough search,' said Helen. 'Fanny was obviously in labour last night and must have gone somewhere to have the baby. Somewhere sheltered, for it was cold. And Fanny couldn't have walked far in that condition. Mrs Leggett and Lili, you search the gardens. Nancy and I will search indoors. We'll check the empty rooms upstairs first. I know she was seen coming in from outside, but we must consider all possibilities.'

'What if we can't find her?' said the housekeeper, unusually flustered. 'We may need more people to help.'

'We will if we need to. It would be better, initially, to keep this among ourselves, for Fanny's sake mostly, but also the hotel's.'

Mrs Leggett nodded, but looked troubled. 'Understood.'

'We need to be quick and thorough,' said Helen.

'Then let's get going!' Mrs Leggett shooed everyone out of the corridor.

Lili headed into the yard, behind the housekeeper, who rushed ahead.

'Oh my, looks like someone's been sick here, it does,' said Lili, spotting the lumpy yellow liquid on the floor in front of the staff laundry room.

Mrs Leggett's face creased and she looked away. 'I'll get one of the scullery maids to throw some hot water over it when we return.' She led the way out of the staff exit and through the garden gate. 'You search the shed and that side of the garden. I'll do this side.'

Lili went to the flower beds where the spring flowers were showing off their colourful outfits. The sky was overcast, and the air damp and cold. She hoped to goodness the poor baby wasn't out here somewhere. Unlikely, but she'd better have a good search. Fanny might have placed her under a bush or a shrub.

She noticed curious eyes watching her from window seats in the dining room. It was the older couple from Norfolk, who were down for the Easter week. They must wonder what on earth she was doing, though the cooks did often come to snip herbs and collect vegetables from the kitchen garden.

As she approached the shed, tucked away on one side, a dread seized her. What if the poor little mite was inside, but... gone. The phrase *missing, presumed dead*, slammed into her mind. Missing, yes, but hopefully very much alive.

However, when she reached the shed, she realised there was a padlock on it. Of course: old Mr Hargreaves always locked his tools away now, as they'd once been stolen.

'You looking for something, miss?'

'Mr Hargreaves, we've, um... this might sound barely believable, but we've been sent to search for a baby.'

'A *baby*?' His face was a picture of confusion.

'Someone will explain later, probably when you come in for your morning break. But if you could keep that to yourself for now...'

He scratched his head, with its forest of grey hair. 'Do you need some help?'

'That would be really helpful, thank you.'

The pair of them searched under hedges, lifting and separating the branches and stems.

There was no baby here.

The pair of them met Mrs Leggett by the garden gate.

'You've had no luck either then,' said the housekeeper.

'No. Mr Hargreaves has been helping too.'

The housekeeper nodded. 'We'd better have a look around the front, just in case. The early risers must wonder what on earth we're doing.'

'I'll give you a hand,' said the gardener. 'I'll go left, you two go right, and we can search around the wall, just in case. We'll meet at the front.'

'Very well.'

They did a circuit of the outside wall of the hotel, then searched in the grounds at the front, but had no more luck. Standing by the back wall once more, overlooking the sea, Mrs Leggett did a sweep of the area with her eyes. 'I don't know where we'd go from here.'

'Nor do I. Probably should go back in to see if they've had any luck,' said Lili.

'You two go back in,' said Mr Hargreaves. 'I'll do a sweep of the common, just in case.'

The housekeeper nodded.

In the scullery, Annie was washing a frying pan. 'What's the latest news? Hetty told us what happened.'

'Then you know as much as we do, Miss Twine,' said Mrs Leggett. 'But I'd appreciate it if you or your sister could throw some boiling water over the... effluent, in the yard, and wash it down the drain.'

Annie grimaced. 'If we must.'

As they entered the staff corridor, Mrs Turnbull emerged from the storeroom, clutching a mewling baby covered in a blanket.

Lili ran forward. 'You found her?'

'She were wrapped up in this, in a cardboard box, fast asleep.'

Lili peeped over the blanket. The baby was white-blonde. Her eyes were narrowed, as if trying to work something out, and she was opening and closing her mouth as if trying to find milk. Mrs Leggett seemed reluctant to come any closer.

Helen emerged from the door of the stairs. 'Oh Bridget, where was she?'

'In the storeroom, madam.'

'And she's alive! Thank goodness. How did we not hear her crying, when she was so close?'

'Her little mewls are barely as loud as a kitten's, poor pet. No wonder we couldn't hear her above the noise of the kitchen and scullery.'

'That doesn't sound good. You must take her to Dr Ferngrove immediately. I'll be up in a moment.' When Bridget had gone, she added: 'I don't want my husband getting wind of this yet. He's planning on spending the morning in the office, so that's something. I need to work out what to do before he finds out, so I'm asking everyone to keep it to themselves.'

'I shall spread that message as much as I can,' said Mrs Leggett. 'And I will accompany you to see Mr Bygrove, should you desire support.'

'That's very kind, Imogen. I will let you know.'

'I'd better go and tell Mr Hargreaves to call off the search, as he was doing a sweep of the common,' said Lili. 'Then I should get to the dining room before it gets busy. I'll make sure any staff there who know keep quiet.'

'Thank you, Lili. My, what a day. And it's barely begun.'

Chapter Sixteen

'What is all this about, Helen? I have work to do.'

She wasn't sure what work he was doing, locked away in the office, but she let that go.

'And it's coming up to luncheon, when I was hoping to greet some of the guests coming in today. I hear that Lord and Lady Raynolt have booked, as has Sir William Mowbray, *and* Mr Rotherham, an important member of the local council. All are useful for keeping and expanding our clientele.' He looked up at her from the office desk, with that superior grin.

Helen had never been convinced that Douglas's *ambassadorial skills*, as he liked to call them, had garnered them much extra trade – but again, now was not the time to discuss that.

'By the way, I hear Miss Harvey won the afternoon tea in the raffle,' Douglas continued. 'She told me yesterday when I went for a walk. I thought the raffle a splendid idea to raise money.'

Yes and I bet you took the credit. 'I've also had some very positive comments,' said Helen. 'I did say people like to feel they are involved in doing something for the war effort. And the other raffle, for the tea treats, was very popular too.'

'However, there were a few complaints about the Easter activities.'

'Complaints? About what?'

'The noise of the children's egg hunt and the party in the ballroom. Those having afternoon tea thought it quite disruptive. It spoiled the occasion for a few people.'

'Who complained, exactly?'

'You don't need to worry about it. I sorted it out with my managerial talents. Now, what is it you have to say?'

He wasn't going to take this well. She'd rehearsed it in her head over and over, but it hadn't made it any the easier.

'We've had a bit of an incident in the hotel.'

He stood, his wheeled chair clanking into the metal filing cabinet. 'What's happened now? I hope you haven't called the police again without consulting me.'

'No, no, it's nothing like that. Please, Douglas, just sit down and hear me out.'

He did as she asked.

'One of the chambermaids, Fanny Bullen, had a baby last night.'

'*What!*' He was up again, both hands on the desk, leaning towards Helen. 'Kick her out. Kick her out now!'

'Keep your voice down, Douglas. We don't want the whole hotel to hear. I've tried to keep it quiet, just among staff for now. And we can't kick her out. Dr Ferngrove says she must stay in bed for a few days to recover, as she had a bad time.'

'Let her family take care of her. It's not our responsibility.'

'She has no family, as far as we're aware. We think she might have been abandoned at the workhouse in East Preston as a baby.'

'That's your answer then. Send her back to the workhouse. That's where her sort belongs.'

'That would be a terrible thing to do to a young woman.' Even if she had been the cause of quite a lot of trouble in the past couple of years. 'And imagine what people would say about this hotel if it got out. A house of loose morals, they'd likely call us. We've already had one pregnant maid, who had to marry the dairyman's son.'

'There you are. The father can take responsibility.'

'She won't say who he is. And we suspect he's away in the army.'

'Well, *I'm* not paying to keep the slut and her bastard. How can she work as a live-in with a baby?'

'Douglas, that is a terrible way to speak of her. She's a poor young woman who probably got taken advantage of.'

She wasn't so sure about that where Fanny was concerned. She didn't seem naïve, like Gertie had been, but it was better to put it like this.

'Miss Bolton will keep an eye on her as she recovers. Then Vera, having less childcare to do in the day with Dorothy and Arthur being at school, will look after her. We can't afford to lose any more staff and Fanny knows the job well.'

'*You* can organise it then.' He pointed his forefinger at her and narrowed his eyes. 'I don't want to have anything to do with it and if there are any negative consequences, I will dismiss her. And I don't want it costing me any extra money.'

'No, it won't cost *us* any extra money,' said Helen. Although there would be the doctor's bill to pay and eventually the baby would need feeding after she was weaned. Douglas didn't need to be reminded of any of this.

'If that's all, I'm busy now.' He sat back down to examine an accounts' sheet in front of him.

'You know, Douglas, anybody would think I was an employee here – and one you didn't like very much, rather than your wife.'

His eyes looked up, though he stayed in the same position. 'Then perhaps you'd like to act more like my wife and support my decisions. I am the *man* of the house.'

'You're hardly at home these days, always finding other places to be.'

'That's the nature of the business.' He was back to looking at the accounts' sheet.

'It might be nice if we could go out together one evening.'

'I haven't got time at the moment.'

'I need to go on the desk now. It will be busy for lunch today, so Edie is going to help in the restaurant.'

'Off you go then.'

She left, saddened by the conversation, but already planning a meeting with the staff later.

As it happened, with the hotel being so busy that Easter Monday, Helen didn't get to speak to the staff until the following day. So here she was, at five fifteen, post-afternoon tea and pre-dinner, updating a full dining room on the latest developments. Some were already getting the table ready for the early staff supper.

'Thank you for coming to this meeting. I'm sure most of you know what it's about and have probably heard some of the news from other staff. Fanny, much to everyone's surprise, had a baby girl yesterday.'

'How is she doing?' asked Annie.

'She was rather unwell to begin with, but she seems to be on the mend now, thanks to Dr Ferngrove. She's able to feed the baby, who appears to be healthy.'

'That's a blessing, seeing as she left it in the storeroom.'

'Let's not linger on that, Annie,' said Helen. 'We should be grateful they're both all right.'

'What's gonna happen when she's better?' said Annie's sister, Alice. 'She can't work with no baby and we heard Fanny ain't got no family.'

My, they had been chattering together. 'Since we have a live-in nursemaid here, in Vera, and Arthur is now at school, she will look after the baby. I also have my children's grown-out clothes, and their perambulator, in the loft, so she'll be well provided for.'

Lili put her hand up. 'Has Fanny said any more about the father?'

'Only that he's in the army now, and that the pregnancy hastened that.'

'What a so-and-so,' said Hetty.

'Well, the bairn might not have a daddy, but we can all be like aunties,' Bridget chuckled.

'It's not funny,' said Alice. 'Having a baby out of wedlock. It's a sin.'

'Aye, but you'd be surprised how common it is, pet. Even if some of the parents later marry. I bet at least one or two of you were conceived the other side of the blanket.'

'That aside,' said Helen, feeling the conversation had taken an awkward turn, 'I'm sure we can help the poor child have a decent life. Better than being in a workhouse, which is what Fanny feared and why she hid her away. We shouldn't be too quick to judge.'

'Reckon you're right there,' said the chef, old Will Fletcher.

Helen hadn't mentioned Fanny's own workhouse back-ground to anyone outside of those who'd overheard the young woman talking about it. And she wouldn't mention it now. If Fanny wanted to tell people, that was up to her.

'Has she decided on a name yet?' asked Lili.

'That was the other thing I wanted to tell you. Elsie. Elsie Francine.'

'Francine? That's a bit fancy, ain't it?' said Alice.

'It's actually Fanny's first name.' Helen had known this since she'd employed her, though she'd insisted on being called Fanny. By the surprised chatter, she clearly hadn't told many people.

'Did you know that, Gertie?' said Annie.

'No. I assumed she was a Frances.'

'I would implore you all to keep this little episode to yourselves, please. It doesn't really look good for the hotel, and we don't want to lose business over it.'

There were nods and words of agreement.

'Now, is there anything else before I end this meeting?'

'Nothing to do with Miss Bullen and the baby,' said Will Fletcher, holding up a newspaper, 'but I've just read that there's trouble on the home front now, with an uprising in Ireland.'

'Major Thomas mentioned it earlier,' said Lili.

'Wonder what Lorcan makes of it,' said Jack.

'Who's Lorcan?' said one of the newer chambermaids.

'He was an Irish porter here, 'til he enlisted,' said Jack. 'Was one of the first to go.'

'I'll tell you, if he shares his opinion with me in his next letter,' said Hetty.

'He's your sweetheart, is he?' said the chambermaid.

'No,' said Hetty crossly. 'But he wanted someone here to keep in touch with.'

'Sorry. Didn't mean to cause no offence.'

'Now, I believe some of you are on early supper and others have jobs to do, so I won't delay you,' said Helen.

She left the room, relieved that the task was over. She was sure the news would escape to those outside the hotel eventually, but hopefully, by the time that happened, it would be old news.

Chapter Seventeen

Lili was relieved, the following Friday, to have a gap between shifts in the afternoon. Having been on breakfasts, morning coffee, lunches and due on dinner later, she wasn't on afternoon tea.

It was a clear, sunny, surprisingly warm day for April, and she knew that Mr Janus's Pierrots were playing on a stage not far from the back wall of the hotel this afternoon. She adjusted her straw hat in the mirror that was on the wall of the staff corridor, glad to wear her new cotton skirt, even if it was a little shorter than she was comfortable with. But Edie had persuaded her it was fashionable and quite acceptable now to show a little bit of ankle. After all, most of the female guests did so these days.

Edie also had a gap in her shifts at the same time, so they'd agreed to go together.

'I'm looking forward to this,' said Edie, as they met outside the scullery entrance. 'With us not getting our half-days off this week.'

'I know it's Easter week, but I think it's been even busier than usual. And that was *without* all the drama with Fanny.'

'Indeed.'

'I went to see her this morning. And baby Elsie. She's very sweet. I do like babies.' The possibility of having any of her own seemed so far away to Lili that she felt sadness in her heart. 'Have you seen her yet?'

'I'm not sure my turning up to her bedroom to be sociable would be appreciated,' said Edie. 'It's not as if she has ever liked me. Especially since she was fond of Charlie.'

'I'm not sure she's ever liked any of us, not even Gertie. And with Charlie, and him being sent away, reckon she was just trying to get at you, I do. At least now we have an idea of why she might be so angry all the time.'

'Has she said any more about her time in the workhouse?'

'Not to me. Come on. Mr Janus's Pierrots will be starting soon.'

They left through the staff exit and followed the wall around until they spotted the tiny stage, with an upright piano next to it.

'I'm surprised Mr Bygrove has never moaned about the stage being close to the hotel and the noise it might cause,' said Edie. 'Apparently, he claimed to Helen that several guests had complained about the noise of the Easter egg hunt and the children's tea.'

'I bet they didn't really. Or one person mentioned it and he's making out there was more to it. He's just annoyed because it were a success and he didn't think of it. I've only heard guests say what a good idea it were.'

Edie looked around the common. On the other side of the fountain from them, there was a sea of striped deckchairs, leading up to the stage. Many were already occupied. 'Oh dear. It looks like we'll have to sit quite far back. Or stand.'

About halfway down, Lili spotted a familiar face at the end of one of the rows. 'Isn't that Miss Nye?'

'So it is.'

Julia spotted them and beckoned them over, standing up and pointing to the empty seats next to her.

Edie hugged her friend. 'Julia, how lovely to see you.'

'The feeling is mutual. I only came out on the off chance something was going on here, what with it being Easter week. And I came across this. Hello there, it's Lili, isn't it?'

'Hello Miss Nye. That's right.'

'Please, when we're not in the hotel, call me Julia.'

Lili would feel awkward with being so familiar, but she didn't want to offend her.

Julia shuffled along, allowing Edie and Lili to take the seats at the end. Edie sat next to her friend, leaving Lili with the end seat.

'One of the reasons I'm thrilled to see you is I have some news,' Julia said, more to Edie than to Lili.

'Good news, I hope,' said Edie.

'Very good news.' She pulled off her glove to reveal a solitaire diamond ring on the third finger of her left hand.

'You and DI Davis got engaged?'

'On Easter Sunday.'

'Congratulations, Julia.' Edie took her hands to give them a squeeze.

'Yes, congratulations.' Lili smiled. She was happy for Julia, but it was like another drop of sadness had fallen on her heart and spread around her body, like ink on blotting paper.

She must try to cheer up, after looking forward to coming out. And it should be good. Why was she feeling so down today? Maybe it was to do with Fanny having a baby. She'd cheer up once the entertainment started.

The show began and six of the Pierrots came to the front: two of them clutching mandolins, while one sat at the piano. Four of them were women, when before the war there had been only one among them. Mr Janus must have engaged more entertainers since last summer. They all sported white makeup and conical clown hats with pompoms. The men had on white silk pantaloons and loose silk blouses, with black pompoms down the front. The women were similarly dressed, only with white silk skirts.

They began by singing a rousing rendition of *Be My Little Baby Bumble Bee*, getting everyone in the mood. There was a mixture of funny, romantic and patriotic songs, and even an operatic song or two. They were excellent performers and the audience clapped loudly after each song.

'For our last song,' said one of the men playing a mandolin, 'We are going to sing something that is always appropriate here, in Littlehampton. So we want to hear everyone joining in, even if only for the chorus.'

Lili looked forward to having a singsong, hoping it would be something she liked.

The female singer started on her own, with just a few notes of the piano.

> *'Everyone delights to spend their summer's holiday, down*
> *beside the side of the silvery sea.'*

Oh no. It was the song she'd sung last summer at the charity concert, when Rhodri had turned up with his friends, and she'd heard... that Norman had gone missing.

A pool of emotion welled up inside her as the verse continued. *Norman. Rhodri.* Both were now gone for different reasons. She bit her bottom lip, breathing deeply, willing herself not to cry.

When the chorus began and everyone sang, '*Oh! I do like to be beside the seaside...*', Lili simply mouthed the words vaguely, hoping no one would realise what she was doing. She managed to keep her emotions in check, longing for the song to come to an end. The last line of the final chorus played and Lili sighed with relief.

But the singer decided to do an encore and the last chorus was sung again.

Finally, it came to an end. The Pierrots bowed and announced that their next performance would be in an hour. Lili wanted to go, to escape, to walk on the prom and feel the sea breeze on her face. The people around her got up from their seats, chatting excitedly.

'Are you all right, Lili?' Edie asked, as Julia chatted with someone in front of them.

Lili forced a smile. 'Of course I am.'

'It's just, the last song...'

'Yes, well... it did bring back that day, I can't deny it. But I'm all right.' The urge to cry had passed, but she still felt the sadness. And imagine how things would be if she saw Norman's sister, Florence, here, like last time. Hopefully not.

They stood and moved out of the seats. Julia joined them a few seconds later. 'I was thinking of having some tea at the Harbour Tea Rooms. Do you two fancy coming along?'

'I wouldn't mind,' said Edie. 'We've got to be back by five, but there's plenty of time. Lili?'

She'd rather have gone for the walk on the prom she'd been thinking about but didn't want to appear rude. 'Well, I... oh.'

'What's—' Edie started, then must have noticed who Lili had seen.

Walking towards them, looking equally surprised, was Rhodri Morgan. Lili's heart thumped in her chest and her stomach fluttered nervously.

'Lili. I'm so glad to have bumped into you,' he called, as he quickened his pace, still displaying a slight limp. My, she'd almost forgotten how handsome he was, with his shining black hair and his large brown eyes. She noticed several women looking at him appreciatively as he got closer.

'You two go on,' said Lili. 'I'll see you back at the hotel, Edie.'

The two women nodded and left, Julia looking curiously on. She wondered how Edie would explain it to her.

Rhodri stopped in front of her. 'Hello, Lili. I'm sorry, am I, um, keeping you from joining your friends?'

'Hello... Corporal.' She wasn't sure why she hadn't used his name, but it felt a little too familiar now, even though he'd used her name. 'No, I wasn't going to join my friends. They're going to the tearoom and I, well...' She looked towards the promenade. 'I wanted to go for a walk anyway.'

'We could, um, we could, you know, take a walk by the beach together. Only if you want, of course.'

'I guess so, as that's where I was going.'

They started off across the common, Rhodri with his hands linked behind his back, still limping.

'Were you at the Pierrot concert?' she asked.

'I was. I must have been sitting a few rows behind you. I came with my aunt and uncle, but Auntie Charlotte wanted to get back home. She's not been well.'

'I'm sorry to hear that.'

'Look…' He didn't continue for a few seconds. 'I apologise for not contacting you. Thought of it several times, I did. Then my aunt was very unwell over Christmas and has taken a long time to recover. My leave days were all spent with her.'

And Nurse Caffyn? No mention of her, but then, there never was.

'That's understandable. But, you know, I wish you'd written to explain.'

'I was going to speak to you at the end of that concert, in November, to apologise again, but when you turned away, I thought you didn't want to talk to me any more.'

She stopped abruptly and turned to face him. 'You must 'ave got the wrong idea. I was hoping to have a word too. I only turned away because I was ordered by Mr Bygrove to accompany a guest back to their room.'

'I see. I wish I'd realised.'

Now was the time to tackle the subject she'd been avoiding. Whether Nurse Caffyn was still around or not, and whether Rhodri was playing with the hearts of two women. She needed to know.

'Is your, um, sweetheart here? I presume you've been able to see her.'

He screwed up his face in puzzlement. 'My sweetheart? What sweetheart? What are you talking about?'

'Nurse Caffyn, I believe she was called.' Had she got this all wrong? She might be making an idiot of herself. And would it look like she had romantic designs on him? Her stomach squirmed.

'Why would you think she was my… sweetheart?'

Or was he trying to play her for a fool?

'I saw you with her, that time we had a walk up to the pier, back in September.'

Something unexpected happened. He put his head back and laughed. Lili wasn't sure how to take this. 'I remember it now! I bumped into her, that's all. She wanted to know how I was doing.'

'She took your arm!'

He looked sheepish and she wondered what was coming.

'Er, yes, she were a little… over-familiar, I suppose. I think she were, you know, maybe interested. In me.' He scratched the back of his neck. 'She asked me to write to her, but I never did. And you thought that we was… courting?' All this time?

'The thought had occurred to me.'

'I would have mentioned it if we had been. Look, I really 'aven't been able to spare the time, but you're right, I should have written to tell you about my aunt. But I were afraid you were so angry with me – for being such a silly fool, lurching at you like that. I only meant to kiss your cheek, but… it were a little forward of me. Well, especially if you thought I were courting.'

He stared at the grass, dejected. She shouldn't have been feeling like this, but a warm glow was growing inside her, one that tempted her to take his arm. *No*, she mustn't do that, especially after getting cross with him for being too forward.

'Look… I wasn't *that* angry, I s'pose' she said.

He looked up and smiled. 'That's a relief.' He stared at her for some moments, making her insides go a little… mushy.

'Shall we go for that walk?' She pointed to the promenade ahead.

His grin became broader. 'Yes, definitely.'

Once on the prom, walking towards the coastguard cottages, she said: 'Your limp seems better. You don't have the stick any more.'

'I don't. And yes, it is a little better.'

'Will you be in Shoreham for the duration of the war?'

'I… guess so.' He seemed disappointed by the prospect. 'How about you?'

'Nothing's really changed for me since I last saw you. Except I'm now head waitress in the restaurant and conservatory, but I occasionally get to go on the desk too. We've lost a couple of the young porters, a waiter and one of the desk clerks since conscription came in. Guests come and go.'

She wouldn't mention Fanny and the baby. Not yet. *Not yet!* What was she thinking? That she'd have the opportunity in the future? If only.

They dawdled along their route, chatting about things that had happened at work, about their families, about the visits to Cardiff and Barry Island they'd each made at different times. Reaching the Pepperpot lighthouse and the pier, they turned to walk by the river, down to Pier Road and past the fisherman's cottages. Lili glanced in the Harbour Tea Rooms as they walked by on the opposite side of the road, but she couldn't see inside well enough to spot Edie and Julia. She wondered if they'd noticed her.

As time passed, the conversation became easier, less stilted. She could have walked and chatted with him like this forever – or so it felt in that moment. But she knew she'd have to get back to the hotel at some point. They'd just reached the end of Pier Road, where it turned on to Surrey Street, in the town.

'Do you have the time?' she asked him.

He turned his hand to look at his wristwatch. 'Just coming up to half-past four.'

'I'd better be making my way back. I'll have to start getting the dining room ready for dinner soon.'

'I'll walk up with you. If you don't mind.'

'Don't you need to catch a train back to Shoreham soon?'

'Not today. I've got a couple of days leave, so I'm heading back tomorrow.'

'I don't mind you walking me back. But you're almost at your house now.'

'That's all right. I don't mind the walk. It's good exercise for my leg.'

They turned around, strolling a little faster. At the end of Pier Road, they took the more direct route down South Terrace instead of going back the beach way. There were some silences now, in between bits of conversation, but they were comfortable silences.

As the hotel loomed closer, Rhodri cleared his throat. 'I 'ope I can see you again, Lili. Not just by bumping into you by accident.'

'Then you can send me that letter like we originally decided, to tell me when you're in town again.'

A grin lit up his face, intensifying his good looks, giving her that weird feeling in her tummy again. 'I will do that.'

Reaching the hotel, she said: 'Well, here I am. Be sure to send that letter now.'

'I will. I definitely will.'

They both stood for a while, silent, looking at each other.

'I'd better go,' she said.

'Of course. Bye bye, Lili. I'll look forward to seeing you again soon.'

'And so will I. Bye bye, Rhodri.' She just stopped herself blowing him a kiss. How she wished he might have… But no, it was too soon. And it was broad daylight, and they were out in the open.

She walked backwards, watching him stroll down South Terrace. He turned at one point and, seeing her still looking, waved. She waved back and, having reached the left end of the front wall, took one last look at him. Sighing, she turned and headed to the staff gate.

How much happier she felt now, than when she'd left the hotel earlier. She was heartened by the thought that, with his limp, they'd never send him back to the Front.

Rhodri took one last look at Lili as she disappeared around the wall of the hotel. What a shame he hadn't written, just to apologise. They could have kept in contact, even if it had been difficult to get away to see her. He hoped so much that she really meant it about the letter. He hated the thought of sending one, only for it to be ignored.

It was such a shame he wasn't stationed a little closer, which would have helped with seeing his aunt too. But then, there wasn't an army training base any nearer. Besides, he had to go where he was told. And it could have been worse: he might have been stationed somewhere like Colchester or Aldershot. No, he'd been lucky to be so close to his home.

He carried on down South Terrace, with a smile on his face and a lightness in his heart.

Chapter Eighteen

Edie had greeted several guests as they'd sauntered through for afternoon tea, when Lolita Carmichael appeared in the foyer from the stairs. Edie assumed she was heading to the conservatory, but she came to the desk instead. She had looked rather a lost soul since Leslie had been conscripted.

'Good afternoon, Edith.'

'Good afternoon, Mrs Carmichael.'

'I was wondering whether you could telephone the Theatre Royal in Worthing for me and book a ticket for a performance there next week.'

'Of course.' Edie pulled a pad of paper and a pencil towards her to take details. 'What kind of time would you…?' Her last words were drowned out by two new guests coming through the front doors, fussing.

Edie looked up and her heart sank. What on earth were her sister-in-law and Clotilde Dubois doing here?

'Isn't that Lady Lucia Forsyth?' said Lolita, looking around.

'Lady Lucia Moreland now – but yes, it is.'

'Moreland?' Lolita swung around to face Edie. 'That's *your* surname.'

'She married my brother, Freddie.'

'Ah, Edie,' Lucia called, spotting her. 'She's on the desk, Clotilde. How fortunate. Good afternoon, Edie, we have come for tea,' she said, rather loudly, for no reason that Edie could make out. 'Well, if it isn't Lolita Foster. I haven't seen you in a while.'

'It's Lolita Carmichael now. My husband's Captain Clifford Carmichael.'

'Means nothing to me, I'm afraid,' Lucia turned back towards the desk. 'Now, Edie.'

'I'll return later about the theatre.' Lolita left the desk and headed to the stairs.

'Clotilde and I have come for afternoon tea,' said Lucia. 'And we were wondering if—'

'*Lucia*,' Edie hissed, losing patience. 'I was in the middle of dealing with another guest. It's very rude to interrupt.'

'It's only Lolita Foster. She was always rather a bore at social events, going on about herself.'

'Rather like you then,' said Edie, raising her eyes.

Clotilde laughed. 'You were a little impolite, *ma chérie*,' she said to Lucia, in her French accent.

'I'm sorry, but it was a *beastly* trip on the train, as I was unable to get any fuel for the motorcar today. Apparently, there's a shortage.'

'And has been for a while,' said Edie. 'Now, if you're here for afternoon tea, I will ask Gertrude to show you to the conservatory.'

'We were hoping you would be able to join us.'

'Lucia, I am on duty until five o'clock. I cannot just abandon my post. And I wouldn't be able to join you anyway, as a member of staff.'

Her sister-in-law sighed. 'I suppose not. What a bore.'

'Is there something in particular you wanted to speak to me about?'

'No no. I just wanted to see how you were.'

There was another fuss by the doors, and this time it was Lady Blackmore and her companion.

'Come along Cecelia, otherwise tea will be over.'

'I'm sorry, Lady Blackmore, I just caught my dress in the door.'

'You're so clumsy. But then, you always have been.'

Poor Cecelia, being harangued as usual.

'I'll tell you what,' Edie whispered to Lucia. 'I'll meet you at the fountain, at the back of the hotel, just after five. We can go for a walk and have a chat.'

'Very well. We will have afternoon tea and wait, shan't we, Clotilde?'

'I think, *ma chérie*, that you have already decided.'

'Lady Lucia Forsyth! We are honoured by your presence.' Bygrove reached the desk at the same time as Lady Blackmore, who seemed put out that he'd greeted another guest before her.

Where had he appeared from? He must have come out of the staff door without her realising.

'Miss Moore, *I* will deal with Lady Lucia Forsyth. How may we help you today, my lady?'

'Lady Blackmore—' Edie started, only to be waved away by the woman, who was more interested in the new guests.

'First of all, Mr, um...' said Lucia.

'Bygrove,' he said, his ingratiating smile becoming wider.

'First of all, Mr Bygrove, I am now Lady Lucia Moreland, married to the Honourable Frederick Moreland. You might remember, from the visit by Baron and Baroness Moreland, that Edie – the Honourable Edith Moreland – is my sister-in-law. I am quite content to be dealt with by her.'

Lady Blackmore looked sharply in Edie's direction, pulling her chin in to the point where it merged into her neck as she narrowed her eyes in disbelief. Edie felt like burying her head in her hands. What was the point of escaping your past if people kept popping up and reminding everyone, or informing them for the first time, of your privileged background? The only guest who'd known about her background was Major Thomas, and that was only because he'd been at the court when her name was called. He'd promised to keep it to himself.

'Yes, of course, of course,' Bygrove spluttered. He started walking backwards, performing a grovelling bow and looking thoroughly ridiculous.

'Gertrude,' Edie called, spotting her coming out of the lift. 'Please show Lady Moreland and Miss Dubois into the conservatory.'

Lucia took Clotilde's arm and followed the portress through the dining room.

'And how can we help you today, Lady Blackmore?' said Bygrove.

'You can't,' said her ladyship. 'We can find our own way to the conservatory.'

Bygrove followed them in nevertheless, no doubt on his way to spread his grovelling charm around the afternoon-tea guests. She shivered. How Helen put up with him she would never know.

So now Lady Blackmore knew her secret. She had no doubt it would get around the other regular guests, especially those from South Terrace.

Why had Lucia turned up like that and then, to make it worse, said such a thing in front of other guests? It wasn't like she was worried about her parents knowing where she was any more, or that the staff would find out as they already knew, but she preferred to keep her two lives separate. A nugget of annoyance gnawed away at her, and she only hoped she could keep a lid on it during her shift.

-

The common had few people on it when Edie got out just after five. Lucia and Clotilde were already by the fountain. Her irritation had been building during the afternoon, especially as the guests started to leave afternoon tea and regarded her with curious stares. Yes, Lady Blackmore had definitely been whispering it around the room.

'Ah, Edie, there you are. Shall we walk?'

'I'd rather not now, if you don't mind, as I'd like to get back for a cup of tea. I'm on the desk again later, so I can't stay long.'

'That's a shame.'

'How was your afternoon tea?'

'It was a little less lavish than I'd 'ave expected from such a luxurious 'otel,' said Clotilde, 'but still very good. I suppose that is the war. We 'ave started to notice shortages in our local shops.'

'I think it will get worse,' said Edie. 'The kitchen staff here do very well with what we can get hold of at the moment.'

'What a bother,' said Lucia. 'Though the local shops do seem willing to put a little extra away for those that can afford it.'

'That's hardly fair though, is it.' Edie felt even more cross now. 'And why, oh why, did you have to mention my title and who my parents are?'

'I thought everybody knew now?'

'The *staff* know, but the guests didn't. Now I suppose I'll have people asking questions and poking their noses in.'

'It might bring more custom to the place, with people knowing that someone *titled* is helping to run it.'

'I'm not helping to run it. I'm just an employee. Anyway, how are you two? I've heard from Freddie a few times.'

'We're as fine as one can be under such circumstances. Clotilde is now staying at the house, which has made things a lot better.' She took her lover's hand and smiled at her.

'Isn't that a little... insensitive. To Freddie. He's away, so you've moved your lover into the house?' She frowned, feeling the annoyance building once more.

'Don't look like that,' said Lucia. 'I know what you're thinking, but it is with Freddie's blessing.'

'Won't other people think it strange.'

'Of course not. We're two women, left alone, keeping each other company. And Clotilde is due to marry Percy when he's next on leave.'

'I thought you and Percy weren't keen on the idea.' She directed her comment at Clotilde.

'We weren't, but we both can see the merit of it. We can go to stay with Lucia and Freddie as friends and conduct our real relationships in private.'

'And what if something happens to one of them in the war?'

Lucia gasped and her eyes widened. 'You are not suggesting that we wish them... dead.'

That wasn't what Edie had meant but, now it had been mentioned, it would be advantageous for them. They'd be free and, in Clotilde's case, probably inherit a good deal of money from Percy. Lucia was already well-off.

'Oh no, that is not our plan.' Clotilde shook her head forcefully.

'It's not what I meant,' said Edie. 'I meant, if one of them is lost, the situation between you would be more... awkward.'

'Let us not anticipate such an 'orrible situation,' said Clotilde. 'I am very fond of Percy and would be most upset if anything 'appened to 'im.'

'I'm sorry, I didn't mean to upset you. Look, I need to get in. Why don't you enjoy a walk while you're here? The promenade is very pretty and usually has a lot going on. And the river is interesting.'

'Yes, a walk might do us good,' said Lucia. 'It would be nice to see a little more of you, though.'

'Then you should have written and we could have arranged to meet on one of my half-days off.'

'I might do that.'

Edie gave Lucia a quick hug. 'Keep in touch – but I'd rather you didn't come to the hotel.'

Clotilde took hold of Edie's hands. 'I am sorry if we 'ave made things awkward.'

Edie nodded. 'Cheerio then. See you sometime.'

'Anon anon!' Lucia called as Edie walked away.

–

'There you are,' said Lili, as Edie came into the staff dining room and squeezed in next to her. 'I thought you said you were on late tea break.'

'I had to have a word with my sister-in-law first. Honestly, I wish she hadn't just turned up. And then she mentioned in front of Lady Blackmore that I was the Honourable Edith Moorland.'

'That's what I was going to tell you. I'm afraid Lady Blackmore was full of it at afternoon tea, telling anyone who'd listen. Our regulars were quite surprised, as were some of the staying guests.'

'Yes, Lady Blackmore was having a field day!' said Phoebe, opposite. 'One of my customers asked if I knew about it, so I said, "Of course, we've all known for ages," like it was nothing special. Because we have.'

'Thank you, Phoebe. I'd rather it was treated as "nothing special". I'm surprised that my sister-in-law didn't have something to say about it though.'

'It was all done in whispers,' said Lili. 'I think Lady Lucia and Miss Dubois knew it was going on but chose to ignore it.'

'Bygrove came in today too, doing his usual strut around,' said Phoebe. 'Until the Major showed him his newspaper and the piece about how a second military act might be extended to married men. He soon left after that.'

'D'ya think Bygrove'll be conscripted?' said Gertie, half-smiling.

'I don't see why not,' said Lili. 'We all know Mrs Bygrove could run this hotel on her own. She has most of the ideas and does most of the work anyway.'

'It's a right shame,' said Mrs Turnbull, sitting at the end of the table in Mrs Leggett's absence, knitting a scarf. 'Mr Bygrove was a better manager at one time, if truth be told. And a better person. Reckon mixin' with all the fancy folk has gone to his head. It's a pity it's come to this.'

The conversation moved on as several smaller discussions started.

'I saw you had a letter today,' Edie said to Lili in an undertone. 'Did Rhodri write to you?'

'Not yet. It was from my mam. Family news and village gossip.'

'I'm sure he'll write soon.'

She grinned. 'Yes, I think he will.' The way he'd smiled at her the last time they'd met, she really believed he felt... something. 'And it'll be May in two days, my favourite month. It's getting warmer and lighter. So, life feels good at the moment.'

'I'm glad to hear it.' Edie smiled and winked.

Oh yes, life felt much better than it had for a long time.

Chapter Nineteen

Lili looked at the envelope that Mrs Leggett had just given to her at breakfast. It had a Shoreham postmark on it. She was glad the housekeeper hadn't commented on it, as she often did with different postmarks.

She didn't feel inclined to open it here – at the table, with prying eyes – even though no one was taking any notice and were either reading their own letters or eating breakfast. She popped the letter into her apron pocket and helped herself to some porridge. The excitement of receiving the letter had replaced her hunger, but she'd have to eat something or else she'd be sorry later.

Placing the ladle back in the pot, she made a decision. There was no point in waiting until she left breakfast to read the letter, as she'd have to get to her shift. And she was too excited to leave it until later.

She pulled the envelope from her apron and opened it nonchalantly, as if it were like any other letter. She scanned the lines quickly, praying it would be a suggested date to meet up, not a reason not to.

> *Dear Lili,*
>
> *How pleased I was to see you at the concert last Saturday. I have been able to secure Friday 26 May off, which I am rather pleased about as it is the day of the fair. Would you be able to get that afternoon off that week?*
>
> *Things are still busy here, what with conscription bringing more men into the army to train. I guess you are busy too, with it being the summer season.*

Hope you are well.
Yours sincerely,
Rhodri Morgan

She kept the desire to emit a little mew of pleasure under wraps and made sure her smile wasn't as wide as she wanted to make it.

Twenty-sixth of May. It was a popular day to have off, given the fair was in town, but if she went to Mrs Bygrove today, she might secure it. She really hoped so.

She ate the porridge as quickly as politely possible, then swallowed her cup of tea in one go. Now might be a good time to see Mrs Bygrove, who she knew to be in the office.

As she rose and stepped over the bench, Mrs Leggett said: 'Have you finished already? That's not much to go to work on.'

'I, um, need the WC.'

'Very well, off you go.'

Goodness, it was like being in the classroom, Lili mused. It was a little lie and she did so hate them, even white ones, but she was hardly going to tell all and sundry what she was really doing.

At the office door, down a small corridor off the main staff one, Lili knocked. With any luck, Mr Bygrove hadn't turned up in the meantime.

'Come in,' came Helen's voice.

Lili entered cautiously, relieved to find it was just the manageress there, sitting behind the desk.

'Mrs Bygrove, could I have a word, please.'

'Of course. Don't look so worried. Come and sit down. What's on your mind?'

Lili remained standing: she didn't intend on staying long. 'It's about my day off near the end of the month. I've had a letter from Corporal Morgan, who was in Belgrave House Hospital when we had the do for them.'

'Yes, I remember him. He was Welsh, wasn't he?'

'That's right, madam. He came originally from a nearby valley to mine. Well, Rhod— Corporal Morgan, was wondering if I could have Friday twenty-sixth of May as my afternoon off. He'll be in town on leave. I know it's the day of the fair, and I'm sure it's a popular day off but—'

'It's all right, Lili. No one else has requested it yet. Of course you can have it as your afternoon off.'

'I don't want the hotel to be short of staff nor nothing.'

'We won't be. When the fair is in town we're never as busy, as people – even our clientele – tend to patronise the cafes and hotels in the town.'

'Thank you, Mrs Bygrove. I much appreciate it. I think Corporal Morgan enjoys meeting with someone from his old country, see, so to speak.'

She wasn't sure why she felt the need to add that. Maybe so Mrs Bygrove didn't think she was courting.

Lili performed a little curtsy, such as she might to a guest, and left the room, her heart light. She had something to look forward to, at last.

–

It was the day of Lili's afternoon off. Butterflies had been dancing around her stomach all morning. She'd finished her shift and had got changed quickly, having already decided not to stop for any lunch but to head straight off. Rhodri had said he'd be wandering around the fair before their planned meeting at one o'clock, should she be able to arrive earlier.

The weather was sunny today, though a little on the cool side for the end of May. Nevertheless, she wore her new cotton skirt and a blouse that she'd bought from a jumble sale and sewn a broader collar onto.

As she opened the back door, from the scullery, she almost bumped into the post woman, about to knock with the second post.

'Afternoon, m'dear,' said the young woman in her blue serge uniform. 'There's a bundle for you today.'

'Thank you, Clarice.'

It made a change for Mrs Leggett not to get to them first.

She thought she'd better take them to the dining room, where some of the staff were on middle lunch. Even as she carried them there, she had a sudden fear that there would be a last-minute letter from Rhodri, saying he couldn't make it.

She shuffled quickly through the dozen or so letters, relieved there were none for her. However, there was one with Mr Bygrove's name on. It looked official. She wondered whether it could be a conscription order. Already? It had only become law in Great Britain yesterday: Mrs Norris had read it out in the paper at breakfast this morning.

As she entered the staff corridor, the manager was strutting down it, towards the kitchen.

'Mr Bygrove, sir, there's a letter for you.' She extracted the official-looking one and held it up.

He snatched it from her, about to turn, but changed his mind. 'Miss Probert, I might have to go out and need someone to take my shift on the desk. You look tidy enough.'

'I can't sir, sorry. I'm just heading out on my afternoon off.' Oh, why had she not just left the post with Annie in the scullery to sort out.

'And I'm giving you an order. You can have your day off another time.'

A burning defiance rose in her. He was *not* going to ruin her day off, not after what she'd been through the past few months. 'I'm sorry, sir, but I have already made an arrangement and I cannot let the person down.'

'Well, you'll have to *un*make the arrangement.'

'What's the problem here?' said Helen, coming down the corridor.

'I have just told Miss Probert that she'll have to take on my shift and have her day off another time, but she is answering me back! There is no room here for staff members who do not do as they are told.'

'Douglas, Miss Probert came to see me three weeks ago to secure this afternoon off. It's important. Lili, off you go.' Helen tipped her head towards the exit to emphasise her point.

'Here's the post, madam.' Lili handed the letters to Helen before walking swiftly away, just catching her say: 'And why can you not do your shift on the desk *this* time.'

Oh dear, she'd likely started a row between the two. Not that *that* was unusual – and it was his fault, after all. Where was Bygrove trying to get out to now, she wondered. He'd recently taken up bowls, so it could be that.

As she left, she thought about something else that Mrs Norris had read from the newspaper. There'd been an agreement signed for the transfer of British and German wounded and sick prisoners of war to Switzerland. At the back of her mind, she wondered whether Norman was a prisoner and that was why they hadn't found him.

She put the thought to one side. It wouldn't do to dwell on the matter. And she was meeting Rhodri now and didn't want to spoil his day by being maudlin. No, she was going to make the most of this time off.

–

Lili was nearing the end of Pier Road when she heard the sounds of the fair: the music, people shouting, the engines of the rides. A small shiver of delight went through her, followed by slight anxiety. What if she couldn't find Rhodri in the crowd? At least she still had the meeting place to go to at one o'clock – on the pavement outside the Littlehampton Motor Garage – if all else failed.

But she needn't have worried. He was standing by the merry-go-round, in his uniform, looking very smart.

'Rhodri, hello!'

He turned abruptly, smiling as soon as he spotted her, giving her stomach that funny melty feeling once more.

'You're early. That's good.'

'I said I might be. I'm so glad I found you quickly.'

'There's not so much here as there used to be, I'm afraid. It's the war, I guess.'

Lili stood next to him. 'Yes, Edie told me there wasn't as much when she came last year.'

'Have you been on one of these before?'

'Oh yes. I went on it last time I was at this fair, what, four years ago? And I used to go on the roundabouts at Barry Island.'

'Me too! Would you like to go on, when it stops?' He looked hopeful.

'Yes, I would. Edie went on one of these for the first time last year, would you believe?'

'How did she manage never to go on one before?'

'Well, you see, she's a bit posh, like, and her mother thought it beneath them.'

'I bet her mother's one of those what *thinks* she's posh, eh?' He chuckled.

'No, actually...' Oh dear, she should never have started down this track. But then, loads of people knew now, so what difference did it make? 'You see, Edie is the daughter of Baron and Baroness Moreland, what own a few timber yards in Sussex.'

'Really?' He took a step back and widened his eyes. 'I've heard of them timber yards. So, Edie must be...?'

'The Honourable Edith Moreland. But she hates people referring to her as that.'

'What on earth is she doing working at the hotel?'

'It's a long story. I'll tell you over afternoon tea. If we're still doing that.'

'Of course. Here, it's stopping. Let's get on.'

He paid the money and helped her onto one of the horses, then climbed on one himself. As it started, she giggled, enjoying the sensation of it going around. He laughed too. It seemed odd in a way, to be doing with Rhodri what Edie was doing with Charlie this time last year. And look at what had happened since? He was now in France. Even if he hadn't enlisted after initially falling out with Edie, he'd still be in the army now. Life was odd. It reminded her of something else, which she decided to mention when they got off.

The ride came to an end; Rhodri helped her down from the horse and they walked away.

'I've just remembered that when Edie and her sweetheart Charlie were here last year, there were women with white feathers. They gave one to Charlie and he got quite upset. Then they turned up at the hotel and bothered the guests having afternoon tea. There was quite a to-do and the police were called.'

'I remember Uncle Islwyn telling me about them. Sounded like they did more harm than good, even if they thought themselves patriotic.'

'What made you sign up then? You mentioned before that you went early on.'

'I went to one of them recruitment talks at The Empire Theatre. September 1914, it were. That were it, really. Auntie Charlotte and Uncle Islwyn were a bit upset, given they'd moved here to get me and my brother Glyn, and my uncle, away from the danger of the mines, but I felt I had a duty. Anyways, what would you like to do now?'

'Look, there's a coconut shy. I love those.'

'Come on then.'

Neither of them had any luck knocking over a coconut, but they'd laughed a lot at their failure and it felt good to Lili.

As they walked away to find something else, a Welsh voice behind them called 'Hello there, Rhodri. Are you enjoying the fair?'

'Auntie Charlotte!' he said. 'Are you sure you should be out?'

She did look a little pale and was limping worse than Rhodri.

'It's only down the road from us and I'm only out for a bit. I always enjoy the atmosphere, see, and I needed a bit of air.

Takes it out of you, it does, when you're stuck indoors. Hello there. You must be Rhodri's friend, Lili?'

'That's right. Nice to meet you, Mrs—'

'Hughes.'

'Nice to meet you, Mrs Hughes.'

They shook hands.

'Likewise. Enjoying the fair, are you?'

'It's a bit sparse compared to the last time I came, but it's still good.'

'Lili used to go to Barry Island, Auntie.'

'Such a lovely place for a day out, it is. I do miss it, even though I live by the sea now.' She laughed. 'The beach here is nice though, with lots to do. And you work at the Beach Hotel, I understand.'

'That's right.'

'Ooh, there's posh.'

'And a very nice place to work.' Apart from the presence of Mr Bygrove.

'I bet. Well, I'll let you two get on. I'll probably get 'ome now. But maybe you could come to our house for tea one day. We're just down there, on River Road.' She pointed past the White Hart Hotel.

'Yes, maybe I could,' said Lili, beaming.

'*Hwyl fawr*,' Auntie Charlotte called in farewell.

–

Lili and Rhodri went for afternoon tea at Read's Dining Rooms in Surrey Street, overlooking the fair as they ate. The sandwiches weren't quite up to the Beach Hotel's standard, and she suspected they'd started using some of this 'adulterated flour', as Mr Strong, the pastry chef at the hotel, had put it. The scones were smaller than theirs and the butter pats a little mean, but from what she'd heard, the Beach Hotel would have to start cutting more corners now too. The blackberry jam was not as sweet as it would normally be, maybe due to the sugar shortage.

She wouldn't say any of this to Rhodri though, who'd insisted on paying for the treat. And if he thought the same, he didn't mention it.

There had been several admiring glances in Rhodri's direction, and she wondered if he'd noticed.

'The women certainly seem to appreciate a man in uniform,' she whispered, teasing him, though she knew it would be more than just the outfit.

'In what way?' he said, tilting his head to one side.

'You must have noticed the ladies looking over at you.'

'I can't say I have,' he said, looking uneasy.

'Sorry, I didn't mean to embarrass you.' What had made her say such a stupid thing. 'But I think all the men in uniform get that reaction. I remember Charlie at the hotel saying the same when he came on leave at Christmas.'

'It seems a little... shallow a reason to rate a man.'

'I don't disagree,' she said quickly. 'It was just something I noticed.'

'I do seem to get more respect since I've been in uniform, that's for sure... Since we've both finished, I'll get the bill.'

'All right.' Oh dear, was he wanting to end the afternoon early? She really should have kept her gob shut, as her mam would have said. Perhaps he thought she was being a little shallow too.

Outside, back in Surrey Street, she anticipated Rhodri telling her he had to get back to his aunt now. The disappointment was overwhelming. She had enjoyed his company this afternoon even more than she'd thought she would. She didn't want it to end.

'So...'

Here it comes, she thought.

'How about a walk on Fisherman's Quay? We haven't looked at the fair there yet.'

Relief washed over her and she felt her body relax. Still a little more time in his presence.

'I'd like that.' They wandered down towards the river, between River Road and Pier Road, passing the Britannia Inn and on to the quay, but none of the fair was here this year.

'I guess the Admiralty taking over the harbour has meant they can't put anything here,' said Lili.

'Yes, that'll be it. Now there's a sight, though.'

As they stood, looking across the River Arun, a naval ship floated past with its dazzle camouflage.

'I've seen a few of them. They do look quite crazy.'

He chuckled. 'Like something from a circus... While I think of it, could you get the afternoon of Friday the ninth of June off? I got my next leave day off sorted out early like, so I could ask you in person, rather than write.'

'I'll have to check it with Mrs Bygrove, so I will have to write to confirm it.'

'That's all right. If you want to meet again, that is.'

'Yes. I'd like that.'

They smiled at each other for a few moments, until Lili got embarrassed and lowered her head, pushing an imaginary piece of hair behind her ear.

'Shall we go back down River Road and have a walk over the bridge?' he asked.

'All right.' She did look at him now, before they both turned and went back the way they'd come.

–

Lili entered the staff entrance in the side wall, humming *By The Light Of The Silvery Moon* to herself. She hadn't felt this happy since she'd been courting Norman. A very brief guilt ran through her, before she dismissed it. Why shouldn't she find happiness now? There was nothing she could do about Norman's sad fate.

She was wondering what was for supper when she entered the staff area via the scullery.

Alice Twine, standing at the sink, greeted her with: 'You were lucky to be out this afternoon.'

'Why's that?'

'There was a right to-do with Mr Bygrove. Seems he received a conscription order.'

'I did wonder if it were that when I took the letters from Clarice before I left,' said Lili. 'That were quick.'

'Guess they're desperate for men. He was shoutin' at his poor wife in the corridor about how he'd appeal as he was doin' necessary work. Then he went storming off saying something about seeing his solicitor.'

'Does he need a solicitor to appeal?'

Alice shrugged. 'No good asking me. Don't suppose it'll do any good anyway. Running an 'otel ain't necessary work.' She picked up a towel to dry her hands. 'Anyway, it's time for early supper, which I presume is what you're back for.'

'I certainly am. I'm on a dinner shift at six.'

They walked into the staff dining room together. Fanny was sitting at one end, breastfeeding her baby. 'Hello. You had a good day, Lili?'

Lili couldn't get over the change in the chambermaid since she'd recovered from the birth.

'I did, thank you. I had a look around the fair.' She certainly wasn't going to mention Rhodri.

'That's nice. I'll look forward to taking Elsie when she's old enough.'

'Hopefully, the war will have ended by then and they'll be more to the fair again. There's quite a lot less now.'

'That's a shame.' Fanny started humming a lullaby to the baby as she gently swayed.

A few more staff entered the room, ready for an early supper.

'I'm enjoying the daylight-saving hour that's just come in, I must say,' said Alice.

Fanny nodded. 'It's given me time to take Elsie out in the perambulator of an evening, after turning down the beds.'

'It was kind of Mrs Bygrove to lend you that,' said Mrs Leggett.

'I wonder if she kept it with the intention of 'aving more children,' said Fanny.

'That is not for *us* to ponder,' said the housekeeper, not unkindly. She had been much more tolerant of Fanny since the baby had been born, yet Lili would have expected her to be harsher.

It was strange to witness, but not an unwelcome change. She knew that, with the war, things were not good for people. But for her, at least for now, life seemed a little brighter.

–

Afternoon tea had been interesting for Lili today. The three artists – Hazel, Ebony and Marigold – were back, and Lili had caught snippets of their discussions on theatre and art trips in London. When Mrs Carmichael had appeared, they'd invited her to join them and Lili had been surprised to see the woman become engaged with the conversation, not sitting smoking cigarette after cigarette in her usual agitated way. Perhaps all she needed was some female friends.

Major Thomas came in part way through, brandishing a newspaper as he often did. With him was his retired army pal, a colonel from across the road on South Terrace.

'Good afternoon, Major,' Ebony called lightly, as Lili was putting down their teapot, jugs and sugar bowl.

'Good afternoon, ladies. Just been reading that the government has definitely decided to defer the Whitsun bank holidays on Sunday and Monday, until after July.'

'That's a shame for ordinary working people,' said Hazel.

Apart from hotel and restaurant workers such as me, thought Lili. Bank holidays might as well not exist for them.

'Indeed, indeed,' said the major. 'But they're wanting to keep necessary workers, such as those in the munitions factories, working. And the trains, which would carry large crowds of day-trippers, can be used to convey more soldiers and munitions to the places they are needed.'

'How glad I will be when this beastly war is over,' said Marigold.

'And I,' said Mrs Carmichael. 'For then dear Clifford can…'

Lili was glad to be finished and away from the table, so as not to hear yet another time about *dear Clifford*, who half the staff were convinced didn't even exist. She hadn't made her mind up either way on that one. As she went, she overheard a table of councillors earnestly discussing the news of Field Marshall Kitchener's ship being sunk by a mine off the coast of Scotland. His death had been a shock, and a common topic of discussion among the guests in the past couple of days.

In the kitchen, she waited for the cake stand for the artists' table to be ready. Mr Strong was just adding the last of the dainties. There were hazelnut meringue genoises, petits fours and fruit tarts. With its fat scones and enticing treats, it looked much more appealing than the one she and Rhodri had shared in Read's Dining Rooms. But the attraction there had been Rhodri's company.

She was so looking forward to seeing him tomorrow, on her day off. She wondered if he was feeling the same. Since he wasn't courting Nurse Caffyn as she'd suspected, both of them were now free. Perhaps, just perhaps… but she might be fooling herself. She had to admit – though she'd been reluctant for a long time to do so – that she had been struck by him the very first time she'd met him. She'd liked Norman the first time too, but it had been… different. More a, *ooh, he's nice* with Norman. With Rhodri, it had been more a… how could she describe it? More an *oh my goodness!* moment. It was as if she'd always known him, and she'd just been waiting to meet him. If she hadn't been courting Norman when she'd first met Rhodri, she would have undoubtedly encouraged him more.

'Are you with us, Lili?'

She came to. 'Sorry? Did you say something, Mr Strong?'

'I said that the stand is ready and you can take it.'

She looked at it and saw that it was. 'I'm so sorry. I was miles away.'

'So I could see,' he said with a chuckle.

She lifted the stand carefully and walked away. She must really keep her mind on the job, otherwise she'd end up dropping something and that would be terrible.

There'd be plenty of time later to daydream about tomorrow.

–

Lili was glad of the break when she got to early supper in the late afternoon. She was the last into the staff dining room and the talk was inevitably about the bank holiday, or rather the lack of it.

'I can't see it being good for the hotel,' said young Jack, the sous chef.

'It won't make no difference to us,' said Gertie, helping herself to boiled potatoes. 'As the rich'll have their bank 'oliday, even if the workers don't. And I know we're fully booked.'

'She's right,' said Lili. 'It's the poorer day-trippers what'll lose their day off. The cafes and entertainments on the beach what cater for them will suffer from lack of custom.'

'I have to agree,' said Mrs Leggett, perched on her chair at the end of the table. Lili and Edie always referred to it as her 'throne' in private. 'And that reminds me: a letter came for you in the late post, Miss Probert. It has a Welsh postmark, so probably from your family. It's on the dresser.' She pointed to the wall opposite the fireplace.

Typical of her to be having a nose, thought Lili, as she rose to collect the envelope.

She sat and had a few more mouthfuls of her meal before picking it off her lap. It was only then that she noticed that the writing was that of her oldest sister, Carys. She screwed her lips up to one side. What was she going to be complaining about now? She'd only ever sent a couple of letters and they were always full of moans about neighbours or other members of the family. It was that or her harping on about how Lili should be at home helping out with family, or married now. She was tempted to leave the letter until later, but she might as well get it over and done with.

But she hadn't got past the first line of it before she felt a weight on her chest. She could hardly breathe. Her mother, wrote Carys, had been gravely ill for the last week with shingles. Why hadn't they written when she first got it?

Shingles.

One of their aunts on their father's side had got that and died, not long before Lili left Dorcalon. A next-door-but-one neighbour, a fairly young woman, had died of it too.

'What's wrong, pet?' said Mrs Turnbull, sitting opposite her. 'You look upset.'

'It's my mam. She's gone and got the shingles.'

The chatter around the table dwindled and stopped, as the message was passed on.

'My gran got that,' said Gertie. 'But she got better.'

'Not everyone does,' said Lili, staring at the letter. 'My sister, Carys, says mam is gravely ill and that I should go home.'

'Then it sounds like you should, pet. Go and see Mrs Bygrove and tell her what's happened. I'm sure she'll let you have a few days off.'

'That is not for us to surmise,' said the housekeeper. 'She is at the front desk. I suppose you *could* have a peep around the door to see if she is busy. If she isn't, have a word with her.'

Lili rose, leaving three-quarters of her meal. 'Thank you, Mrs Leggett. And if anyone would like anything off my plate, please help yourself. I've lost my appetite.'

She found Helen alone at the desk, making some notes on a sheet of paper. She looked up. 'Hello Lili. Is everything all right?'

'Could I have a quick word, while it's quiet. I'll leave if someone comes to the desk.'

'You're very jumpy. What on earth is wrong?'

She told Helen about the letter and requested the days off. 'I know the hotel is fully booked, so I'll understand if—'

'Of course you must go. We have a bigger workforce now, what with the newer live-out staff, so some of them can fill shifts. And, what's more, I'm going to give you the train fare for—'

'Oh no, I couldn't—'

'I insist on it. But don't tell anybody about it.'

'That's so kind, Mrs Bygrove. Thank you.' She suddenly remembered. 'Oh, but I'm meant to be meeting Corporal Morgan tomorrow, in the afternoon, and I have no way of telling him about this.'

'Where and when are you supposed to be meeting?'

'At the side entrance of the hotel. One o'clock.'

'I'll go and tell him what has happened.'

'Thank you *so* much, madam.' She spotted a guest arrive through the front doors. 'I'd better get back.'

The relief of being able to go to her mother was mixed with the searing disappointment of not being able to see Rhodri tomorrow. But her mother came first. She could never forgive herself if Mam died and she hadn't been there. The relief and disappointment were replaced by a trickling chill down her back. She closed her eyes briefly.

Oh Lord, let my mother get well.

Chapter Twenty

Lili had left Littlehampton early that morning and was now on the last train she needed to catch to get home. It felt strange, passing towns, villages, mountains and valleys she'd not seen for years. She'd gone past Bargoed and New Tredegar stations, recognising the green hills and the clumps of woods as she approached Dorcalon.

As the train drew into the station, Lili, the only person left in her carriage now, shuffled up the seat, away from the window, waiting until the train stopped before she stood up. She picked up the carpet bag Edie had lent her and entered the corridor. The station guard must have spotted her, as he came running forward to open the door for her. She didn't recognise him, and at once felt both at home and yet somewhere strange. It was the oddest feeling.

She thanked the guard and started to walk away, looking around. The smell of the colliery hit her. She'd never noticed it, living here. Coming out on to the street now, she was at the bottom of Station Road. She looked up towards the grand edifice of the McKenzie Arms Hotel, as she used to consider it, before she left to work at the Beach Hotel.

As she started off up the hill, a young man came out of number four. It was somebody she'd been at school with. He squinted as she passed by, raising a hand in a half-hearted greeting, perhaps unsure whether it was her or not.

Reaching the crossroads, she stopped on the pavement and regarded the McKenzie Arms once more. It seemed quite small and shabby now, which made her sad. The whole place compared very unfavourably with the south coast, on the face of it. And yet there was a close community here, the like of which didn't seem to exist in the same way in Littlehampton.

She looked around at the lines of terrace houses and opposite the front of the hotel to the Jubilee Green gardens. There were a few people walking around, most of whom were taking no notice of her. She crossed over to the grocers, peeping in as she went past. She was glad to see Mrs Brace was still there, serving a customer. Reaching the corner, she smiled. The bookshop was on the other side of the street. It had been her favourite place in Dorcalon.

She crossed the road once more and was thrilled when Mr Schenck came out of the front door, which was right on the corner. He came to a sudden stop, eyes widening. 'Why, Miss Probert! It's been many a long year since I've seen you.'

'Hello Mr Schenck. My mam is ill, so I'm here to visit her.'

'Of course, of course. I heard she had the shingles.'

'Lili?' came a new voice.

'Someone else keen to greet you,' said Mr Schenck.

She looked around to see Anwen Rhys, who was two or three years younger, but had been in the choir with her.

'How nice to see you. It's been a while.' Anwen said this in Welsh, which threw Lili for a moment. Apart from the one sentence spoken to Rhodri, it had been a while since she'd spoken her mother tongue.

'Hello Anwen. How are you? I was so sorry to hear about your sister's death.'

'Yes, a terrible blow it were. And I'm sorry about your sister-in-law, Jane. Both had the consumption.'

Lili nodded and looked down, not knowing what else to say.

'Sorry about your mam's shingles, too,' said Anwen. 'Are you here to visit or are you back for good?'

The idea of the latter almost had Lili shuddering. As nostalgic as she felt coming back, she didn't think she could stay here too long.

'Just for a visit, to help look after Mam.'

'I'll leave you to get home then. It looks like you've only just arrived.' She pointed at the carpet bag.

'That's right. Well, cheerio then. Might see you at chapel.'

Lili carried on down James Street, past Carys's house, turning on to Bryn Street half-way down. A little way up, the turning for Lloyd Street was on the right. Her family home sat three doors in. She took a deep breath and made her way down the lane between the long back gardens of the James Street houses and the tiny front yards of the Lloyd Street homes.

As she reached number three, the door opened. Carys came out with a cloth. Whatever it was she was going to do, she stopped when she saw Lili.

'Ah, there you are, Liliwen. So, you've come 'ome then.' The way her sister said it, anybody would have thought she'd only been gone a few hours, and that she was cross for Lili for going out.

'I was back ten months ago, for Jane's funeral.'

'Not for a while before that though. That's a fancy bag. Huh, and a posh handbag. Better come in, then.'

Lili placed the carpet bag in the hall and went straight to the kitchen. She was pleased to see it hadn't changed. The dining table had a chaise longue down one side and there was a dresser in the corner. The stove in the fireplace had a kettle on, from which steam was starting to emerge.

On one of the two wooden armchairs, in front of the stove, sat her mother, Glenys, huddled in a blanket. She looked pale and was coughing but, other than that, didn't look too ill.

'Mam!' she ran to her, throwing her arms around her shoulders to hug her. 'How are you, Mam? Oh, why wasn't I told before? Carys said in her letter you'd had it a week already.'

'I didn't want to worry you. I didn't need you to come rushing home.'

Her other sister, Dilys, came through from the scullery. 'You're home then, are you Liliwen? About time.'

'I only got the letter yesterday,' said Lili, standing straight. 'Wait. Are you—'

'Pregnant? Yes. Coming up four months. I've not told no one till recently, after losing the last one, apart from Carys.'

Although Lili could understand Dilys's reluctance to share the news, she was her sister too. She felt sad that they'd grown so far apart.

'To answer your earlier question,' said Glenys, 'I've got a lot better the past few days. I did tell them not to fetch you back, as I wasn't that bad in the first place.'

'Oh, you were, Mam,' said Carys, who then moved closer to Lili. 'She's been so ill that she doesn't know what she's talking about. Now, we've both got our own jobs to do. I take in washing, see, and Dilys works in a shop in Rhymney, Monday to Thursday. And it's about time you came back from that holiday and did some work yourself.'

Lili concealed her rising temper, not wanting to upset her mother. 'It just so happens I work very hard in the hotel. Been doing several jobs there since the war started. Now I'm head—'

'Yes, yes, Mam has wasted no time telling us what you've become. Now you're here, you can make some tea. The kettle's nearly boiled.'

Her sisters sat at the table as if waiting to be served. It was like being back at the hotel, but with less appreciation.

'All right.' She went to the scullery to fetch the milk, but couldn't find any in the bucket of water they normally kept it in. 'Where's the milk?' she said, on her return.

'Morgan the Milk don't have much now, as it's getting harder to come by,' said Carys. 'Don't s'pose you 'ave those troubles in your fancy 'otel.'

Her sisters gave her a rundown of their mam's illness, of calling the doctor, of the days in bed, making it sound very grave. Glenys sat, unspeaking, pulling the blanket around her, looking alarmed. Really, her sisters should have discussed this with her later, when they were on their own.

'At least she's out of bed now.' Lili smiled at her mother.

'But for how long if she starts having to do things again?' said Dilys. 'And I can't see her going back to them jobs.'

Glenys slumped in the seat and her head lolled forward. 'I did like those jobs too. Got me out of the house they did, and I do need the money.'

'We can sort the necessary money out another way,' said Carys, leaving Lili wondering if they were all planning to contribute something.

The front door opened and two male voices were heard, one laughing. It was her brothers, Morys and Wyn, their wet hair suggesting they'd just had their baths.

'Oh, here she is,' said Wyn. 'Back from her holiday by the sea.'

Not again. Was this going to be a recurring comment? It had worn thin already.

'Make some more tea, Liliwen.' Carys was talking to her in the same way Mrs Leggett would. 'The kiddies'll be back from school soon, so make a nice big pot.'

'All right.'

Hopefully, Mam would make a good recovery in the next few days and she could get back to serving tea to people who were grateful. Mostly. For taking orders from her siblings would eventually drive her up the wall.

–

Rhodri was five minutes early turning up at the side wall of the Beach Hotel. His excitement had accelerated his pace, as he'd walked from his home in River Road.

They would go back to the town in a while, to meet his aunt for afternoon tea. He would rather have spent the time with Lili alone, but he had promised to take Auntie Charlotte so she could meet Lili properly. They'd have several hours afterwards to be on their own and it was a beautiful day. There was bound to be plenty happening on the common and promenade at that time. Or they could walk somewhere a little quieter, maybe along the beach to Rustington.

He was looking out, over the common, when he heard the gate in the wall creak open. His welcoming grin was ready.

But it wasn't Lili. It was the hotel manager's wife.

Thinking at first that she'd be heading out somewhere, he was surprised to hear her say, 'Corporal Morgan?'

'That's right.' Maybe she remembered him from one of the dos he'd attended at the hotel. He hoped it was all right to be waiting here for a member of staff.

'I have a message from Lili.'

His bubble of excitement popped. This must be some kind of brush-off. Perhaps they were getting closer than she was comfortable with, when she was still mourning Norman. Or might he have been found?

'She sends her sincere apologies for not being able to meet you today. I'm afraid she got a letter from home yesterday, to say her mother is very ill with shingles. I'm sure you'll understand that she needed to get home to see her.'

'Yes, of course.' Now he didn't know what to feel. Happy that Lili wasn't ending the friendship, but sad for her.

'How long will she be gone for, do you know?'

'I'm afraid not. I just told her to take the time off she needs.'

'I see. Well, thank you, Mrs Bygrove, isn't it?'

'That's right. You've been to a couple of the events here, haven't you?'

'I have. Thank you for letting me know about Lili. I don't suppose you have an address for her?'

'I have an address for her next of kin, which I would imagine is her mother's house. But I shouldn't give it to you without her permission.'

'No, of course not. Quite right. Would you then, when she returns, ask her to write to me? She has my address.'

'Of course, Corporal.'

'Thank you. Good day to you, madam.'

'Good day, Corporal.'

He'd taken a few steps away, his body heavy with disappointment, when Mrs Bygrove called his name.

He did an about turn. 'Yes, madam?'

'Is there a telephone number Lili could call you on? I understand that you work in the office at Shoreham camp.'

'Yes, there is a telephone that I'm actually in charge of. Hold on.' He took a notebook and small pencil out of the top pocket of his uniform jacket and wrote the number down. He tore out the sheet and took a few steps forward to hand it to her.

'I will ask her to telephone you when she returns.'

'Thank you, Mrs Bygrove.'

He walked away, upright like the soldier he was, though he felt like slumping and dragging his feet. At the back of his mind was a worrying niggle.

What if she doesn't come back?

–

An hour had gone past in her mother's kitchen, with her four older siblings relating what had occurred in the village in her absence. She knew most of it, as Mam kept her informed, but she listened as they passed their own judgements on it. The seven children belonging to her sisters sat at the table, some sharing chairs, being told to *shush!* every now and then when their own whisperings became loud enough to interrupt what the adults were saying.

Lili sat opposite her mother, in the other armchair, regarding her as people spoke. She didn't add much, but mostly stared ahead, smiling wanly at Lili every now and again.

'Is that the time?' said Carys, peering up at the clock on the mantelpiece. 'We'd better get back to our own houses. I've certainly got jobs there to do.'

The others each mumbled an agreement and rose.

'And now Liliwen is here, we won't have to have someone taking turns to be here all the time,' said Dilys.

'That will be all right for a few days,' said Lili. 'But I do need—'

'We can sort out anything you need later.'

'I suppose you've let Auntie Megan know about Mam?' She was surprised her aunt wasn't already here, organising things. She was good in a crisis.

Carys flicked her hand into the air. 'Yes, of course. But not 'eard a thing we 'aven't. Now, there's some ham and cheese, some bread and a coupla eggs in the larder cupboard. That'll be enough for meals for you and Mam the next coupla days. We'll fetch some rabbits from the butcher tomorrow and some nice veggies from the allotments here. They were set up by Anwen Rhys and—'

'Yes, I know. Mam told me.' She was fed up with having everything explained, as if she were a toddler.

'There's no need to snap. Anyway, you can make a nice roast with the rabbits and veggies, and we'll all be around on Sunday, after chapel, for dinner.'

'*All* of you?'

'Yes. Our four families. You'll have Sunday morning to prepare it. None of your fancy foods 'ere, I'm afraid.'

'What if I want to go to chapel? I haven't been for ages.'

'I don't suppose you do, working in the ungodly hotel. You're here to look after Mam. She can't get to chapel.'

Lili glanced over at her mother, who shrugged.

'Come on now.' Carys waved her hands at various members of the family to indicate they should go, shuffling them out to the scullery to go out the back way. She was the last to leave. 'Someone'll pop in tomorrow with the food and we'll see you Sunday. *Hwyl fawr!*'

Lili stared at the door to the scullery for a while after she heard the back door close. All four families, so that would include spouses and children. Carys and Harry had four children, Dilys and Huw had three, Morys one, while Wyn and Maisie had six. With her and Mam, that would be… twenty-three of them! That would require a lot of rabbit and veggies.

And room. She guessed the kiddies would sit at the table in the front room and they'd bring extra chairs, as was usual, but still. She'd forgotten how hectic these gatherings had been and there'd been fewer children then. And they had been a lot younger.

A sudden feeling of the walls closing in on her overwhelmed her.

'Are you all right, *cariad*? You look all worn out.'

'It's a long journey on the train.'

'I'm sorry about Carys and the others. They have rather put on you. But don't worry, it is only for a few days. And it'll be nice having you around for a bit.'

Lili felt guilty. She should have come home for a break long before now. The last time she'd been back, apart from for Jane's funeral, was for two days in 1913. How she wished her mother lived in Littlehampton, like Rhodri's aunt and uncle.

Rhodri. It would have been about four hours ago that Helen would have spoken to him. She only hoped he had understood.

Lili stood up. 'I'd better write to the manageress, Mrs Bygrove, and tell her I'll be about a week. Is the writing paper in the usual place.'

'That's right, *cariad*, in the top drawer in the front room. Then, when you've finished it, you can come and tell me a bit more about your lovely hotel.'

'Of course I will.'

She only hoped she *would* get back to it in a week.

–

Lili stirred the rabbit stew in her mam's largest pot. Yet more stew sat in the second-largest pot, on the stove next to it. After Carys had presented her with the skinned rabbits and vegetables yesterday, announcing once more that they'd make a 'lovely roast dinner', she'd panicked. How could she roast the rabbit, potatoes and veg, and have it all ready and hot at the same time for twenty-three of them? She felt an appreciation of what Mrs Norris and her staff went through every day.

But there were several of them in the large kitchen of the Beach Hotel, and several ovens and stoves. And room.

It was when Carys had left her to stare at the foodstuff on the table that the idea had occurred to her. A stew! It was something Mam had made a lot of when they'd been growing up. And there were still some herbs growing in the corner of the garden, even if the rest of it had gone to seed.

The potatoes, she'd decided, could still be roasted, and they were now crowded into two roasting tins in the oven.

'That smells lovely,' said Glenys, laying what knives, forks and spoons she owned on the table. 'I 'ope they remember the cutlery and crockery, as well as the chairs.' They heard the scullery door open. 'There they are.'

Carys was first through the kitchen door, carrying a sack bag. 'What are you doing, Mam! Sit down. Lili, you shouldn't have let Mam do anything.'

Glenys laid the last spoon down. 'She didn't. I did it myself.'

'Then she should have stopped you!'

The rest of the adults, along with both Dilys's and Wyn's two oldest children, all girls, came in with chairs and bags.

'Hello Carys, it's nice to see you too,' said Lili.

'And that's enough of your sarcasm. You might get away with that in that posh hotel, but you won't here.'

Lili felt like laughing. She could imagine what Mrs Leggett would have said to that. She greeted and hugged her four nieces. 'Where are the rest of the kiddies?'

'Playing in the garden until we get laid up,' said Carys.

The family got on with organising the rooms. Glenys sat back down, looking weary. Or was she fed up?

Lili gazed down at her four-year-old niece, Morys's daughter, who was standing next to her, looking up at the stove. Her face was sad.

'Hello Ffion. Why aren't you playing with your cousins?'

260

She shrugged. 'I like it in here.'

'Come and sit on my lap, *cariad*,' said Glenys. 'You don't want to get burnt on the stove.'

'All right, *Mamgu*.'

Ffion went towards her grandmother and was about to climb on her lap when Carys called: 'Don't sit on *Mamgu*! She's not well.'

Ffion put her leg down and leant against Glenys's arm instead.

Poor little mite. As if her slight weight, for she was small for four, was going to do Mam any harm.

'What on earth is this?' said Carys, hurrying towards her.

Lili's other siblings stopped and came over.

'It's rabbit stew, of course.'

'But I said a *roast*. It's Sunday, after all.'

'A roast would have been impractical, what with twenty-three of us.' Lili carried on stirring, hoping her sister wasn't going to keep on.

'Thought it would have been easy for you,' said Dilys, 'being in that fancy 'otel all these years.'

'Don't they do roasts there?' said Wyn.

'On Sundays, yes, but I don't work in the kitchen, do I. I'm a waitress and—'

'So you keep telling us.' Dilys raised her eyes heavenward.

'And it's got nothing to do with my skill. If there'd been only six of us eating, say, I could have done it.' Lili felt like being quite rude, but with Ffion standing there, she'd better keep her tone reasonable. Even if her siblings were being *un*reasonable.

'Should have done it at my house,' said Carys. 'I'm sure I could have managed it.'

I'm sure you couldn't have, thought Lili. 'Anyway, I have done roast potatoes.'

'Well, that's something,' Morys conceded. 'It smells good, at least.'

'Yes, it does,' said Glenys. 'And I'm sure it'll taste lovely.'

The other three siblings added nothing, simply walking away to continue getting the rooms ready.

Lili checked the roast potatoes again. Soft on the inside, and brown and crispy on the outside. Just right.

'I'd call the kiddies in and get them settled,' said Lili. 'Lunch is ready.' She felt proud of herself, despite their criticism.

'Lunch?' said Carys, frowning. 'We'll have none of your fancy words here, Liliwen Probert. Only the Merediths have *lunch* at this time of day. We have *dinner!*'

Lili sighed. It was going to be a long afternoon. 'Then, dinner is served.'

—

Lili had sat on the side of the table nearest the stove, with her mother on one side and Ffion on the other. Morys was on the other side of his daughter, sitting at one end of the table. The little girl had not wanted to sit at the children's table in the front room, holding on to her father when it was suggested. Both Dilys's and Wyn's wives had their youngest sons on their laps, despite Dilys's lap room being depleted by her pregnancy. Their husbands sat next to them, while Carys and her husband sat at the head of the table.

Wyn came through from the front room to sit next to Morys. 'Having a spat, they were, about which two was going to share a seat, but it's sorted now.'

'Shouldn't there be an adult in there with them?' said Glenys.

'They're fine, Mam. Carys's oldest two are in charge.'

Like mother, like children, thought Lili, glancing at Mam. By the look she gave back, she must have been thinking the same thing.

Ffion was silent for the first half of the meal. While there were two or three other conversations going on, one with Carys dominating, Lili leant over to speak to her.

'So, when do you start school then?'

'I dunno.'

'Are you looking forward to going?'

The little girl shrugged.

She'd hoped to engage her in conversation, so she wasn't sitting there looking so sad. Realising it was going to be a struggle, she was surprised when her niece piped up in a little voice: 'What's the house you live in like, Auntie Liliwen? Da says it's big. Is it like the Big House here?'

'Not really, *cariad*. It's much, *much* bigger. It's an 'otel, which means fancy people come to stay there for 'olidays. It's got lots and lots of rooms, with two big rooms for people to eat and drink. There's a big room called a ballroom for dancing too.' Not that there had been many actual balls held in recent years, especially since the war had begun. 'And it's by the beach.'

'Are the people there like Miss Elizabeth, and her mam and da?'

'Some of them are. Some are lords and ladies with fancy clothes.' She started to tell her about some of their guests, weaving stories around the funnier incidents that had happened.

Ffion, from looking very serious, started to smile and even giggled at Lili's impersonation of Lady Blackmore. Morys looked around, surprised at his daughter's reaction. He smiled. From what Mam had told her, both her brother and his daughter had been wretchedly unhappy the last year. Who could blame them, with Jane and the baby's demise? But she was heartened to be bringing a little cheer to them, particularly her niece.

She moved on to Mrs Carmichael's arrival. She altered the story to make the woman sound even posher and sillier. Major Thomas, meanwhile, became the hero of the hour, defending them all from Mrs Carmichael's nagging. She was just getting to the bit where Edie and Mrs Bygrove had arrived back, when she was halted by Carys barking her name.

'Liliwen! Ffion does not need her head filled with such frivolous tales. They're not for a child's ears.'

Lili was about to open her mouth to speak, when Morys got in first. 'Actually, there's nothing untoward in the stories. Quite amusing, they are. And Ffion is enjoying them, so let her, eh?'

Carys's eyes widened in surprise and she tipped her upper body back a little. She regarded her husband, as if waiting for him to stick up for her, but instead he said: 'Aye, well, it's good to see her cheerful. And you, Morys.'

Adding nothing, Carys turned to Dilys and her husband to complain about her neighbour.

–

After everyone had finished – while the women were clearing the tables and the men lit cigarettes and pipes at the kitchen table to chat – the children went into the garden to play once more. Lili noticed Ffion hanging around just outside the scullery door, in the yard, looking up the long, sloping garden as her cousins played catch.

Lily stepped outside. 'Why don't you join them, *cariad*?'

'They did ask, but I said I were tired.'

'But you're not really?'

'They're all brothers and sisters, and I'm on my own.'

Lili felt herself tearing up. Poor little mite, feeling like she didn't belong. She hunkered down and held Ffion's hand. 'You're not on your own, *cariad*. They're all your cousins and are just as good as brothers and sisters. You don't see Betris and Iola saying they can't play together 'cos they're not sisters, do you? Or Dai and Teilo, 'cos they're not brothers.' She pointed to those she'd named.

'No. 'S'pose not.'

'I know you were looking forward to having a brother or sister and was sad when baby Emily died. And I know you miss your mam. But you have got a big family of people who all love you, Ffion. You don't feel happy now, doing things, I know that. But you will slowly feel better. And it will help to play with the other children.'

'Come on, Ffion,' called Dilys's daughter, Lynn, who was the same age as her. She held out her hand.

'See? She wants you to play.'

Ffion said nothing for a moment, looking up the garden at her cousins. Then she turned her head and smiled at Lili. 'All right.'

She ran up to join Lynn, who took her hand before they skipped together to join the others.

'Thank you,' said Morys, who Lili found standing in the doorway when she stood back up. 'I've been worried about how solitary she'd become. Used to love playing with the other kiddies, she did.'

'It's bound to take a while, after what happened.'

'Yes.'

Morys looked down at his feet. Lili wondered if he was thinking about himself. Would he ever find someone else and remarry?

'Anyway, Carys and Dilys are brewing a pot.'

'Lovely. I could do with a cuppa tea.' She followed him in.

—

Lili's family had finally left, coming up to four o'clock, bearing the chairs they'd brought. Carys had been the last to leave, calling gaily: 'We'll come and pick our crockery and cutlery up at six thirty, by which time they'll hopefully have been washed up.' Sure enough, it was all piled up on the table in the scullery. Standing in the middle of the room, looking at it, Lili groaned quietly.

She had better get it done, otherwise she'd never hear the end of it if they turned up to collect their bits and they were still dirty.

'I'll help you with that,' said Glenys, coming into the room with her cup and saucer.

'No you won't, Mam. I'll be fine.'

'I can manage, you know.'

Lili could just imagine what her siblings would have to say if any of them popped back and caught their mother helping.

'It's all right. It's been a hectic day for you, having everyone here. You have a sit down and read that book that Dilys brought you from the library.'

'All right, if you're sure.'

'I am.'

With having to boil the kettle four times to get all the washing-up done, and having to dry things on the draining board several times to fit the next lot of washing-up on, she was on the job for nearly an hour.

As she was drying her hands, Glenys popped her head around the door. 'Good, you've finished. That took a while. It's sunny out. Why don't you take a walk? Used to like doing that, you did, when you lived here.'

Yes, she'd always loved walking on the hillside and by the stream. What if she passed one of her siblings' houses and they told her off for leaving Mam, though? She could plot a route that avoided their houses completely, so that's what she'd do.

'I think I will, Mam, if you'll be all right for an hour or so?'

'Course I will. Off you go now.'

'Why don't you come with me? You haven't been out for a while.'

'No, I'm enjoying my book.'

Lili went to fetch her hat and jacket for, although it was sunny, the air wasn't as warm as it might have been for June.

She left through the back garden, taking the path between the back of the Lloyd Street houses and the allotment on Edward Street. At the end, she walked down the path that skirted the houses at the end of the village, heading towards the Nantygalon stream.

Reaching it, she took a deep breath. Freedom. She was out of the four walls and not being nagged by anyone. She walked along the path, shaded by the abundant trees, listening to the stream as it sang its watery tune. At times like these, it felt good to be back. It was a treat. Like seeing Mam and speaking in her own tongue without someone making some silly comment. She appreciated it more because she knew she wasn't staying forever.

No. She'd be gone soon enough.

Chapter Twenty-One

Edie entered the Harbour Tea Rooms and spotted her friend, already sitting at a window table, overlooking the river.

'Good morning, Julia.'

'Good morning.' She smiled as Edie took a seat, but it didn't reach her eyes. 'How are you, today?'

'I can't complain. Lili, however, had to leave yesterday morning to spend a few days in Wales. Her mother has shingles.'

'Oh dear, poor thing. Shingles can be nasty. And sometimes fatal, of course.'

'Let's hope not on this occasion.'

Edie and Julia chatted about minor things that had happened at the hotel and in school, as they perused the menu.

'There don't seem to be the cakes there used to be on here,' said Julia.

'I'm not surprised. We're starting to have trouble getting the ingredients we need at the hotel. I think I'll have a fruit bun.'

'Me too.'

They ordered their coffee and buns, and both sat staring at the river for a while, watching a fisherman mend a net, standing among the rowing boats.

'Are you all right, Julia? You seem a little... out of sorts.'

'There is something I want—'

'Ah, it *is* you. I thought it was.'

They looked up to find Lolita Carmichael standing close by. 'I've been sitting over there.' She pointed to a table in the opposite corner. 'I thought I ought to get out a bit more, see the town, instead of having all my meals in the hotel. I hope you don't mind.'

'Of course not. It's a good idea,' Edie agreed. 'Especially now it's summer.'

'Quite. And dear Clifford would want me to. Anyway, must go and pay. I'm taking the omnibus to Arundel to visit the park. Ta ta.' She glided to the counter.

When she was out of earshot, Julia said: 'Is she a guest at the hotel?'

'That's Lolita Carmichael, who I told you about.'

'Oh, *that's* her.'

'I'm surprised she didn't mention that Clifford is a captain.'

Mrs Carmichael, meanwhile, was flirting with the owner, showing off a bit of her Italian.

Once she'd left the tearoom, Edie said: 'You were about to tell me something.'

'It might take me a while, as speaking of it makes me want to... to cry.'

Edie took her hand. 'Oh Julia, what's wrong?'

'It's Philip... He's... he's been... conscripted.'

'But he's a detective inspector, a policeman... how can they conscript him?'

'They reckon he'll make a good officer and they are short of them.'

That was because they'd been killed, thought Edie. 'But we still need police here. How will law and order be maintained?'

'I've no idea. I don't suppose they'll conscript them all.'

'He should appeal.'

'I've already suggested it, but he says he won't.' Julia's eyes teared up. 'I just can't, can't bear the thought of it... Philip, out there.'

Edie squeezed her hand gently. 'I know.'

'Of course you do. I'm being selfish. Charlie and your brother are already out there.'

'Philip will have to go through training first, which is about six months. Charlie's was longer. So, who knows...'

'What, the war might be over by then? I hope with all my heart it is, not just for Philip's sake, but I can't see how it will be... Here's the waitress with the coffee. Let's speak of something else.'

After the coffee pot and jugs had been placed down, Edie said: 'It's not a completely different subject, but Mr Bygrove has been called to a tribunal next Wednesday.'

'He's not still trying to claim he has a necessary job, surely?'

'Yes, he is. I can't see him getting away with it, though I have noticed in the newspaper reports that some are granted an exemption for a certain time. I suppose to put other arrangements in place.'

'If he does succeed, I shall be most annoyed, given they're sending Philip away.'

'You won't be the only one, believe me.' Edie didn't expand on her meaning and, hopefully, Julia would just think she meant generally. She didn't want to voice the wish of many of the staff to see the back of Bygrove.

They'd know next Wednesday, one way or the other.

–

It had seemed like a long journey to Chichester in the Sunbeam Cabriolet that morning, Helen reflected, as they sat in the foyer waiting for Douglas's turn with the tribunal. The town was only twelve miles away, yet her husband's constant barking of instructions at her during the journey, telling her what she should say at the tribunal if asked anything, had tired her out by the time they'd reached their destination.

'Now, don't forget what I said, Helen.'

'Very well, Douglas.'

'I don't suppose they will bother asking you anything, though. It will be quite clear that I do work of national importance.'

270

'I don't know why you didn't bring our solicitor along, instead of me. He would have represented you.'

'I don't need to spend money on him when it's a cut-and-dried case.'

Then why was he going on and on about it?

A small elderly man appeared in the corridor from the nearest door, calling, 'Douglas Jonathan Bygrove'.

Helen and Douglas followed the usher to a nearby room. Inside, a table was set out at which three men in smart suits sat. There was also a line of chairs a few yards in front of the table. Douglas sat in the middle and indicated that Helen should sit at the end.

'Stand up, Mr Bygrove,' said the man in the middle, who was perhaps in his late-fifties, with copious grey hair and a handlebar moustache. On his nose were perched a pair of round glasses. 'I'm Mr Stephenson, the chairman of this tribunal.'

Douglas stood, making himself as tall as he could, putting on that superior expression. He wasn't going to impress anybody with that, thought Helen.

'You claim on your exemption application, Mr Bygrove, that you are the manager of a hotel in Littlehampton and do vital work for the war effort. How so?'

'Not just any hotel, but the *premier* hotel in Littlehampton. And one of the best on the south coast. We have politicians and government officials who come to stay at the hotel. It is important for me to run the place properly and thereby provide a service that will help keep up their morale, for they do important jobs.'

They'd had a few members of parliament and a number from the House of Lords visit the hotel, that was true, but it wasn't as if they were there regularly. By government officials, he was presumably including the councillors they sometimes had in for a meal or coffee.

'But why does that make *you* important, in particular?'

Douglas pulled his mouth into that odd expression he often used when people questioned his wisdom. 'I'm the *manager*.

271

Without me, the whole place would fall apart. I'm the beating *heart* of the place.'

'Really?' The chairman widened his eyes and peered over the top of his glasses.

Helen noticed the other two members of the tribunal smiling. The *heart* of the place? If her own heart had gone missing that often, she'd be dead by now.

'Is there any other compelling evidence you'd like to present?'

'On top of the important work of keeping up the morale of vital members of our country, I run a lot of charity events to raise money for the local hospitals and troops. And I've already provided the army with about twenty men. We now must run the place mainly with *women*.' He lifted his eyes heavenward as if the very idea was ridiculous. 'I am the only man left who isn't either in their dotage or a boy too young to fight.'

'I see. What do you mean by *in their dotage*?'

'Over sixty.'

'So, you consider someone over sixty to be in their dotage?' He regarded his colleagues.

Too late, he realised that, by saying such a thing, he was insulting the very panel he was trying to impress.

'I just mean, they're not in a position to run the hotel – being specialists in their own field, but not of managing.'

'There are plenty of young women though, including your wife, who is, I believe, manageress?'

Douglas gave her a disdainful glare before replying. 'My wife does work in the hotel, but she is not the *manageress*.'

'That's interesting, because many of your own staff refer to her as that.'

'Which staff?' Douglas almost barked. 'When was anyone talking to my staff?'

'That I cannot tell you, as we necessarily need to make enquiries of people without them being harassed into giving a pre-arranged story.'

Helen was herself surprised about this, as no one had reported talking to an official. Perhaps they were instructed not to.

'Mrs Bygrove?'

She stood, feeling anxious. Despite Douglas's instructions to her, she didn't really expect to be asked anything. 'Yes, Mr Stephenson?'

'The charity work your husband spoke of. Could you tell us about it?'

'We've held a few events, particularly at Christmas and Easter. A concert, a reception for wounded soldiers, raffles and a tea for children. That sort of thing. The money has all gone to charities, either to help a hospital or send items abroad.'

'And your husband has been involved in these?'

'He has been most supportive.'

'Well, that may be, but according to what is written here, it sounds like you, and members of your staff, have been the ones to organise these events and do the work. It was the opinion of at least two members of staff that your husband merely took the credit.'

'I, um… well, his contacts do help us get the numbers up.' Helen didn't know what else to say. She should deny the chairman's claim, and say they were his ideas and that he did lots of work. But they weren't and he hadn't. She couldn't make herself sound like she was complicit in some lie.

'In fact,' Mr Stephenson continued, 'it sounds, from what staff have told our official, that you are more than capable of running the hotel yourself. And I believe it was your family's money that bought it?'

How had they found that out? Only Edie at the hotel knew. 'Yes, that is the case, but my husband is the owner.'

'I'm most surprised about that,' said the man on the chairman's left. 'Women have been allowed to own property for quite a few years now. It's not always wise to have only your husband's name on what is essentially *your* property.'

273

That, coming from a man, thought Helen. Clearly, an enlightened one. Edie had said the same thing to her though, when she'd confessed her own privileged background.

She risked looking sideways at Douglas. By the clenched fist and his stiff manner, he was not at all pleased with how this was going.

'And, to be honest, none of us can see that running a hotel is of any national importance. Unless you're putting up officers there. Are you?'

Douglas jumped in: 'We do have officers coming in for meals.'

'They can go anywhere for meals, Mr Bygrove,' the chairman said with a sigh. 'It sounds like you have a very proficient workforce and a wife who has a lot of respect from them, not to mention skill in running the place in your absence.'

'But, but—'

'You have one week to get everything in order. Then you must report to the Shoreham-by-Sea camp to train. Your organisational skills might be useful and you may be considered for training as a corporal – maybe, eventually, a sergeant.'

God help the soldiers, thought Helen.

'Dismissed.'

'But I'm doing important work,' said Douglas. 'I can't just—'

'*Dismissed!*'

'Please come this way,' said the usher.

Douglas marched ahead, overtaking the usher, vacating the room swiftly. He kept on walking, out of the building and down the road, where he'd parked the motorcar. This was not going to be a pleasant journey home.

–

They were outside of Chichester, on the road that headed towards Bognor, before he deigned to speak to her, although she'd asked him several times if he was all right. He was driving a little faster than the twenty-miles-an-hour speed limit; his expression set hard.

'What the hell was that?' he shrieked, finally. She jumped.

'What, Douglas? I didn't see anything.' She looked around the countryside.

'Not on the road, you stupid mare!'

'Douglas! Don't speak to me like that.'

'You made it sound like *you* run everything and that I'm manager only in name.'

'No I didn't. They only asked me about the charity events.'

'Which *you* apparently run whereas *I* just take the credit.'

'I didn't say that. Someone else did.'

'And I bet you know who... When did an official come talking to the staff?'

'I honestly have no idea. It was as much a surprise to me as it was to you.'

'Bloody liar.'

From being upset, she felt her temper rising. She'd suspected he wouldn't win the appeal, but she hadn't anticipated it being blamed on her.

'Do not call me a liar. I am *not* a liar.'

'You didn't tell them how much work I put into the hotel.'

'Because you *don't*, Douglas. You have been more and more absent the past few months, with your so-called activities as an *ambassador* for the hotel.'

'Did you brief the staff on what to say to the official?'

Stay calm. There was no point in them both becoming irate. 'I have told you already, Douglas, that I had no idea about any official.'

'If I find out who's been telling lies to the tribunal, they'll be out on their ear. That's if I don't thrash them first.'

'And that would just land you in gaol.'

'Better that than fighting in a muddy field.'

Would Douglas do something like that, break the law so he would end up in gaol, not in the army? She was feeling she knew the real him less and less. Perhaps she could try reasoning with him?

'I hear Detective Inspector Davis has been called up. If he isn't considered in a position to be exempt, I don't know why you would be. You surely realised it was a vain hope, appealing against the enlistment?'

'No, it was not a vain hope. It wouldn't have been if you'd just agreed with everything I'd said.'

'They had clearly already made their minds up, Douglas. Nothing either you or I could have said would have changed their minds. I've read a lot of the reported tribunal cases in the newspapers, and retail and hotel jobs are just not considered important enough.'

'We'll have to beg to differ,' he snarled.

He said not another word for the rest of the journey.

–

It was five past six when Edie saw Helen and Bygrove return through the front doors, into the foyer. She could tell, even from the desk, that all was not well. Bygrove looked like he'd swallowed sour milk. Helen was smiling, but she'd seen that strained expression on her face before. The tribunal couldn't have gone his way.

She really shouldn't feel so pleased, but she was. Oh, she was.

Helen headed to the desk, while Bygrove marched to the side of the foyer and entered the door to the staff area.

'How have things been going, Edie?' asked Helen.

'Fine. It's been busy, but everyone has coped admirably.'

'I knew you all would. Thank you for standing in as temporary manageress.'

'I didn't really have to do much. How did the tribunal go?'

'Much as I expected.' Helen said, wearily.

'He lost then?'

'Yes, of course. And, somehow, it's all my fault. They asked me about the charity events and Douglas thinks I made it sound like I did all the work.'

'Well, you did,' said Edie.

'But I didn't mean it to sound like that. It appears they sent an official to talk secretly to staff, who told them that *I* did most of the work in the hotel.'

'Sorry, but, once again, you do.'

'Are you aware of anyone asking questions of the staff?'

'I can't say I am.'

Helen seemed to be considering something. 'Edie, you didn't mention to anyone about the money for the hotel coming from my family, did you?'

'Goodness, no. Did that come up?'

'It did. I don't know who else knows about it.' She paused for a second. 'I'm sorry Edie, I didn't mean to accuse you of anything. You're one of the people I trust the most. I'm just surprised the tribunal knew.'

'When did your mother die?'

'In 1912. Why?'

'She was living here, wasn't she? Some of the present staff were here then. Might she have mentioned it to any of them?'

'I suppose it's possible. Mrs Leggett, Mrs Turnbull and Mrs Norris were here, among others.'

'It could have been anyone then, really. Maybe even that someone else was told something or found out another way.'

The grandfather clock struck six. 'Shouldn't Mr Watkins be here to take over from you?' said Helen.

'He did say yesterday that he might be a little late, as he'd be coming back from Lancing on the train. His mother seems to have rallied somewhat from her decline in January.'

'So I gather. I'll take over until he arrives. Your shift has ended now. You get off to supper. You're doing a stint in the restaurant later.'

'Are you sure? You look exhausted.'

'I need something to do to take my mind off the whole beastly business. And I want to avoid Douglas for a while. Goodness knows what kind of mood he'll be in for the next week. And after he's gone, well, I will be in charge, and the prospect of that responsibility, frankly, is quite alarming.' Her eyes widened as she stared into the distance.

Edie felt so sorry for Helen, but she needed to bolster her confidence, even if it meant being a little blunt. 'But you are already in charge a lot of the time, even when he isn't off at one of his activities. If anything, it might even be easier. He doesn't always make the best decisions, especially recently, and often creates more work than necessary. I'm sorry if that sounds harsh, but looking at it from my point of view, that's what I see.'

'Between you and me, Edie, I know you're right. But somehow, the idea of being *officially* in charge is, terrifying.'

Edie placed her hand on Helen's forearm. 'We'll all be here to support you, Helen, you know that.'

Helen gave her a wide smile. 'Thank you. You're a marvellous workforce, and I do appreciate you all.' She took a deep breath in, as if gathering courage. 'Now, when Mr Watkins arrives, I might take the children for a walk by the beach.' She took off her jacket and unpinned her hat, then handed them to Edie. 'Would you take these with you, please?'

'Of course.'

In the staff corridor, Edie hung Helen's jacket and hat on one of the coat pegs there, before entering the dining room. Staff from the early supper shift were still finishing off their puddings.

'Come on, you lot,' said Annie, sweeping in with a pile of cutlery in her hand. 'I've been told to lay up for middle supper.'

'Give us a chance, our supper time's not over yet,' said Gertie, before shoving a last spoonful of spotted dick and custard into her mouth.

Annie was about to say something else when they heard a door in the corridor slam.

'Who's banging doors?' said Hetty, the head stillroom maid. 'Someone was doing it five minutes ago too.'

She'd barely finished when the door to the dining room was slammed towards the wall and Mr Bygrove entered. It knocked into Annie, who dropped the cutlery. It clattered to the floor.

'Here, what the—' she started.

'Who has been telling lies to the authorities?' Bygrove hollered to the room.

The people around the table looked from one to the other. Edie realised only she knew what he was talking about but said nothing.

He stamped along the floor to the table, pushing bowls out of the way, some unfinished, causing a clatter. One bowl rolled off the other side of the table and smashed to the floor.

Mrs Leggett stormed into the room. 'What on *earth* is… oh, Mr Bygrove.'

'I want to know who's been speaking to the tribunal officials about me.' He thumped his fist on the table, making the crockery jump. Hetty let out a little scream.

'What do you mean?' The housekeeper said this curtly, not bothering to use his name or add, *sir*.

'At the tribunal, they said they'd spoken to some staff at the hotel and that they'd said it was my wife who really ran the place.' He held up a forefinger, jabbing it into the air. 'If I find out who's been speaking to them, they'll wish they'd never been born.'

'You can't come in here making threats like that,' said Mrs Leggett. 'For all you know, they made it up.'

'Of course they didn't. And don't talk back to me. There might be a staff shortage, but don't think that means you're safe from being replaced.'

Mrs Leggett's expression in reply said *I'd like to see you try.* Was she being so bold because he'd be going soon? He hadn't mentioned how the tribunal had gone, but his words and actions said it all.

He swooped out, with a parting threat. 'When the war's over and I'm back, I'll replace the lot of you.'

There was silence until they heard the office door slam in the distance.

'Well, looks like he lost the tribunal,' said Annie.

Gertie stood to gather the scattered bowls. 'Bloody good riddance.'

'Miss Green...' the housekeeper started, and Edie anticipated the portress getting a telling off. 'For once, I agree with you. Come on, let's clear this mess up before the next supper sitting gets here.'

Edie went to fetch the dustpan and brush, with a sense of relief. Bygrove was one problem that at least might be solved. For a time.

Chapter Twenty-Two

Nine days she'd been here now, thought Lili, as she dried up the breakfast things in the small scullery. It was Sunday and her mother was keen to go to the chapel today. She hadn't been allowed to take her there last week, but none of her siblings had mentioned it this time. And at least she didn't have to do a huge Sunday dinner for them all today. It had made her glad that she didn't work in the kitchen at the hotel.

She thought about the letter that Mrs Bygrove had sent her, in reply to hers. Rhodri had left a telephone number for her to ring when she returned, so he must have been understanding. The thought of it gave her a little flutter of hope. Her mother already seemed better. It shouldn't be too long before she could get back to Littlehampton. And she did so hate letting Mrs Bygrove down when she'd been so good to her.

She dried her hands and went back to the kitchen, looking for her mother.

'Mam?'

'I'm in the hall.'

Lili found her, pinning what passed for her Sunday best hat on, in front of the hanging mirror. She already had a jacket on.

'You still want to go, then?' said Lili.

'Yes. With your help, I'll be perfectly all right walking that short distance.'

'It's almost at the other end of the village.'

Her mother gave her an indulgent grin. 'A very small village. Look, I fancy a walk, see.'

'But you are still 'obbling.'

'Only because I spent a few days in bed and haven't been allowed out to walk around. My legs are out of practice, see, that's all.'

'You're probably right. I'll get my jacket and hat.'

Ten minutes later, they'd made it down to James Street, plodding along slowly. Lili had her arm through her mother's. They'd picked up the pace a little from when they'd first set out. Perhaps this was something she could do with Mam every day – a little walk around the village, maybe along the stream – to get her back to normal again.

She was pondering this when she heard a front door slam behind them.

'Where d'you think you're going?'

Carys had soon caught them up and her face was red with fury.

'Looking out the window, I was, and there you were. Good job I was looking, as who knows what damage you might have done.'

'I want to go to chapel,' said Mam. 'I know I can do it.'

'And I know you can't. Liliwen, what on earth did you think you were up to?'

'Giving Mam a little exercise. It's what she needs. And going to chapel would do her good – lift her spirits.'

'Aye, it would,' her mother agreed.

'I know better what she needs,' Carys barked, ignoring their mother. 'And what she needs is to go home.'

Carys grabbed hold of her mother's other arm and yanked her away from Lili.

'Carys, be careful!'

'You're the one wants to be careful.'

'You get along to chapel, *cariad*. No point us both going home.' After perking up a bit, as she'd done earlier, her mother now looked even more disheartened.

'Aye, that's right, you go,' said Carys. 'I'll stay at home with Mam and look after her. And you'd better pray to the Lord,

282

while you're there, to make you a better daughter. Come on, Mam.'

Lili watched them walk away for a while, wondering if she should go after them and say she'd take Mam home. But a little niggle of annoyance told her to carry on to chapel. It was like her sister was trying to make prisoners of the pair of them.

Past the green, and halfway down Gabriel Street, the chapel loomed into view with its pointed roof and five first-floor windows. Lili climbed up the steps, a couple of other members of the congregation looking at her curiously.

Inside, she was amazed at the number of greetings she received. Many were from people she'd been to school with.

And there was Miss Elizabeth, the daughter of the mine manager, whose house she used to clean. She'd always been a kindly soul.

'Good morning, Liliwen. How lovely to see you. Anwen told me you were back in the village.'

'Only for a bit, while my mam gets better, Miss Elizabeth.'

'Ah, of course. She's had shingles. I hope she gets better soon. And how is your life in Sussex going? I hear you're working at a very stylish hotel by the sea. It sounds lovely, from what your mother has told me.'

'It's very smart. We're just minutes from the beach and there's loads going on in the summer. I started as a chambermaid, but I'm now head waitress in the restaurant.' She felt proud of her achievement, even though it wouldn't have happened without the war and the men enlisting.

'Well done. They clearly value you.'

'The manageress does. She's very good to her staff. Not so much the manager, who's a bit... strict and unappreciative.' That was one way to put it. 'We've lost most of the men to enlistment and conscription. And now the manager might have to go.' She wondered what was happening about that.

'Did you hear that a few of the young men here ran away to enlist. They were underaged,' said Elizabeth.

'No, I didn't.' She'd been mostly shut up in the house, with her family bringing around the food they needed. She had hardly spoken to anyone. 'That must be a worry for their families.'

'It is. It's not as if they'd even have to go when they're older, working in the mines.'

'True.' She was glad that her brothers didn't have to go. And if Rhodri hadn't moved from Senghenydd, he wouldn't have got the bullet wound. But then, they'd never have met.

'Liliwen?'

It was Dilys calling her from a few rows back, where she was sitting with her husband.

'There's my sister. I'd better go,' said Lili.

'I'm glad I got to speak to you. If I don't see you again, have a good journey back.'

'Thank you, Miss Elizabeth.'

'What on earth are you doing here? And where's Carys?' said Dilys as Lili approached.

'She's staying with Mam so I can come to chapel.' She didn't need to know the whole story.

'Ah here's her family.'

Carys's husband, Harry, came charging over with the four children. 'You lot get to Sunday School now.' The children skipped off towards another door. 'What the heck did you think you were doing, Liliwen?'

'What's happened?' said Dilys.

'This silly girl was only bringing your mother to chapel. Luckily, Carys caught them, on the street, and took her home.'

'Oh, Liliwen, that's not what you said.'

'Mam is fine. She was walking all right. You can't keep her locked up for the rest of her life.'

'She is *not* all right,' said Dilys. 'We know better than you, 'cos we're the ones what have been here. Now Pastor Richards is coming, so you get in the pew behind.'

Lili sat in the seat she was directed to, as she always had.

After chapel, Lili had it decided for her that she should go straight home and not stop for tea. Dilys and Wyn went with her, surrounding her, saying little. Did they think she was going to run away if they didn't accompany her? She had to admit, it would have been tempting.

'Here you are then,' said Carys, when they entered the house around the back, into the scullery. 'I'm just doing a bit of cleaning for Mam. You'd think you could have done a bit more, Liliwen. After all, you're a chambermaid, so it's what you do.'

'It's what I used to do. I'm head waitress now, in the restaurant.' She already knew this.

'Until the men come home, then you'll be back to chambermaid. Anyway, that's neither here nor there any more. Close the door, Wyn. I've put Mam to bed for a nap.'

'She doesn't need naps in the day now.'

'You hush, Liliwen, for you clearly know nothing. In future, you are *not* to take her out, you understand?'

'I can't say I do. Wouldn't it be better for her to get some fresh air and build up her strength with a bit of a walk?'

'No, it would not.' Carys looked at the other two siblings, who nodded in agreement. 'Now, we can't keep providing money, but Mam can't do her jobs. She's been cleaning at the Workmen's Institute, the bookshop and the chapel. They've been very good and kept the jobs open for her while she's been ill, 'cos she's a good worker. Since cleaning is what you did, both here and at that hotel, you can take over her jobs.'

'But I 'ave a job, at the hotel.'

'What, you'd leave Mam to suffer alone? We've all got proper jobs and families. We can't keep sparing the time to look after her.'

'You're so selfish, Liliwen,' said Wyn. 'But that's what comes of being the youngest. You were spoiled by Mam and Da.'

'Your first duty is to your family,' said Dilys. 'It's not like you've got an 'usband and kiddies to look after.'

'That's right,' said Wyn. 'You're the obvious person to look after Mam.'

What could she do? She couldn't just leave Mam to fend for herself. Maybe they were right about her not being well. It would be just like her mother to be putting on a brave face and pretending things were better than they were.

'Good, that's settled,' said Carys, without waiting to hear a response from Lili. 'Now, we've all got families to get back to. One of us'll pop in during the week. I'll go and sort out you taking over the jobs from Mam.'

'But who'll look after Mam while I'm working?'

'She'll be all right for the few hours you're out cleaning. It's not like the three jobs add up to a full week. Now, make sure you have some dinner ready for Mam when she wakes up. Come on, you lot.'

The three siblings left the scullery and soon Lili was alone. Her life had just exploded, the broken pieces of it lying around her. What about her lovely job? What about her friends at the hotel? And what about Rhodri? Perhaps this was punishment. She shouldn't have been walking out with him on the rebound like that. Not that it could exactly be called 'walking out', but she was sure that was where it was heading. Oh, but she'd be sorry not to see him again. She pictured his lovely face: the kind, dark eyes and the smiling full lips. Should she write to him? And to Mrs Bygrove? Not now she couldn't. She'd leave it a few days.

Hadn't she told Edie she'd been thinking of going home? But that was before. And she'd never really meant it. She'd be a cleaner for evermore now, and she had so liked waitressing in the posh dining room and conservatory. And standing in occasionally as desk clerk. She'd become more important. And now... this. But she couldn't just leave Mam to fend for herself, not after all Mam had done for her during her young life.

She looked around the dull scullery, desperate for a lick of paint. It was a small community, a small world, in which she was only a tiny dot who nobody listened to.

286

Lili leant her hands on the edge of the sink and lowered her head. She wanted to cry. She'd lost Norman. Not that anyone had asked how she was feeling about that now. She supposed it was because no one here had met him, so maybe he didn't seem real. Now she'd lost Rhodri too, her job, her friends, her... what had Edie called it? Self-esteem. That was it.

About to give in to the internal pain, she heard something. It was the sound of sobbing, but it wasn't coming from her, but the next room.

She pulled herself together and walked to the door, pushing it open gently to see her mother, sitting at the table, crying.

'Mam, I thought you were in bed. What's wrong?'

'Ca... Carys put me to bed when we got back, but I didn't want to go.'

Lili pulled out a dining chair and sat next to her. 'How long have you been in here?'

'Long enough to hear Carys say I can't do them jobs no more. I thought I was getting better, but maybe she's right. But I don't want to keep you from your nice job.' She sobbed a little more and Lili took her hand. 'I wish Megan were here. She's always known what to do. It's strange she never replied to Carys's letter. That's not like her at all. I hope she's not ill too.'

Her mother was right: that wasn't like Auntie Megan, Mam's older sister. She was only in Pengam, about eight miles down the Rhymney Valley. She could have got here easily on the train. And not even to reply? Something was amiss.

'I'll write to her later and make sure the letter gets off early tomorrow. You get comfortable, Mam, and I'll make us some lunch. I mean, dinner.'

Dinner. She'd got used to dinner being in the evening for posh people.

There was so much else she'd have to get used to again.

Chapter Twenty-Three

Helen had ensured as many staff members as possible were lined up in the corridor of the staff area. Since it was between breakfast and morning coffee, that was most of them. The chambermaids, who would normally be cleaning rooms at this time, had been asked to take a brief break. Douglas had insisted on it. He claimed he was going to give them a lecture on keeping up appearances while he was away. Only Edie on the desk and the two live-out porters had been spared the ordeal.

They were all waiting for him now, with Mrs Leggett at one end, looking bored, and Gertie at the other, fiddling with her fingernails.

Finally, he deigned to honour them with his presence, as he came out of the door to the stairs with his suitcase. Helen had watched him packing it earlier and was sure he was taking more than he needed.

For a brief moment, he looked unsure. She fancied she spied the man he'd been, in their early days together. The thought was fleeting.

He put the case down and stood in front of the middle of the line. 'Right, you lot, listen up.' He walked up and down, glaring at each staff member in turn as he passed them. 'I'm off now to serve my country.' He lifted his chin and sniffed. 'While I'm away, my wife will step in. You will need to help her as much as you can.'

Helen noticed both Mrs Turnbull and Fanny raise their eyes heavenward. Luckily, he'd walked past them so he didn't notice.

'I need you all to work extra hard in my absence, since I won't be here to do what I normally do.'

This time, Mrs Leggett raised her eyes, unseen by him once more.

'I will receive regular reports from my wife on how you are all doing. She will seek my advice while I'm away. Be sure that if I hear of any laziness or bad work from any of you, I shall advise my wife to sack you. Be warned, I will still be in charge even though I won't be here. That is all. Back to your jobs.' He flicked his hands to disperse them.

Dorothy and Arthur, who had been kept back from school for part of the morning, had been waiting in the staff dining room with their nursemaid, Vera. They now came running out to Douglas, to cling to his waist.

'Daddy, we wish you didn't have to go,' said Dorothy.

'When will you be back, Daddy?' Arthur asked, sadly.

'When the war's over.'

'You'll probably come back on leave at some point,' Helen reminded him.

'Yes, yes, of course.' He pushed the children away. 'Anyway, Daddy must go. And you've got to get to school.'

That was it? No hugs or kisses? He'd been so delighted by the children's arrivals when they were born. Now it was as if he couldn't wait to be shot of them. She breathed in deeply, stalling the tears she longed to shed.

Vera put a hand on each of their shoulders and knelt. 'Wave to Daddy now.' After a little wave each, she said: 'Come on, let's get you ready for school.'

'The motorcar has been brought around from the garage, so it's ready,' said Helen to her husband. 'I presume you know what time train you're catching.'

'Train? I'm not catching a train. We're driving to Shoreham.'

'But that will mean using more petrol and I might need it for business reasons. There is a shortage.'

He walked towards the exit to the foyer. 'I'm sure with you being *so* good at managing things, you will find a way. Isn't that what some of the staff told that tribunal?'

'Shouldn't we take the staff exit?'

'No. I want the guests to see what a splendid fellow I am, doing my bit for the nation.'

There was no one in the foyer, apart from staff, when he got there. He looked rather frustrated.

When they reached the motorcar, outside on the road, Douglas said: 'Anyway, if we drive all the way, people will see my motorcar and realise how well off I am. They'll see I should be a corporal, or a sergeant, not some lowly private.'

'I think you have to work your way up to those ranks.'

'Nonsense. If anything, they should make me a commissioned officer.'

He really was getting carried away with it all, but she couldn't be bothered to contradict him any more.

'This journey's going to take a while. I should leave someone in charge,' she said.

'Go on then, but don't be long.'

He got into the driver's seat.

'I thought I was driving, Douglas.'

'I've changed my mind. It will look better if I drive myself there. You will, of course, drive back.'

She shook her head as she hurried back inside, going to the desk, which was now free of guests.

'Edie, we're taking the motorcar to Shoreham-by-Sea, so I might be a while. I'm sorry about this, but I'll have to leave you in charge again.'

'That's all right. Have a good trip.'

On the way back, maybe, thought Helen as she left.

—

In Shoreham-by-Sea, Douglas got lost, not knowing where the actual camp was. They drove into High Street, where they stopped for Helen to ask for directions. They soon found it after that, to the north of the town.

Douglas stopped outside the barrier, where two guards were stationed. One of them came forward.

'Excuse me, old chap,' said Douglas. 'Could you let us in?'

The guard looked the Sunbeam Cabriolet over. 'Have you an appointment with one of the officers?'

'In a manner of speaking. I was told to report here today.'

'You're one of the new conscripts?' The guard looked puzzled.

'That's right, my man.'

'That's corporal to you, mate. You can't bring the car in. And you'll have to say goodbye here to your... wife? You'll go in by foot. Alone.'

'How intolerable,' Douglas said, opening the door.

This was not a good start. Putting on airs and graces, especially ones he didn't really possess, and to people above him in rank, wasn't going to make him any friends.

He pulled the suitcase from the backseat. Helen got out of the car her side and came around. 'Goodbye for now, Douglas. I hope the training goes well.'

He didn't reply to her. Instead, he walked away, saying to the guard: 'So, which way is it?'

'Hold on mate, not so fast. I have to check your name first.'

No kiss for her either, even just on the cheek? Or a hug?

Helen had decided to wait there until he'd walked out of sight, before getting back into the car – just in case he came back to say goodbye. However, the other guard stepped forward.

'Could you move that along please, madam, in case we need to get some vehicles in.'

'Yes, of course. Sorry. Could you tell me how to get back to the main bridge please?'

After taking note of his directions, she took one last look at Douglas as he spoke to the first guard. He wasn't going to wave, or call goodbye now, of that she was sure. She got back into the motorcar, pumped the lever up and down, and fiddled with the dials before starting the car and driving away.

What she expected to feel was disappointment that her husband still blamed her for his predicament. What she actually felt was a sense of peace. Relief washed through her body. That she felt like this, in turn, made her feel guilty.

Nevertheless, she was determined to enjoy the freedom, at least for the duration of the journey.

There were a few decisions she needed to make and the journey back, by herself, was the perfect time to think about them. She was now in charge of the hotel. *Her* hotel.

In charge. Could she really do this, all by herself?

She had no choice. And the first thing she needed to do when she got back was to speak to Edie.

–

Helen had been back at the hotel a few hours when she entered the dining room. She'd called a meeting for late in the evening, when the dinner service would be over and most of the live-ins – and some of the live-outs too – could attend.

She wasn't sure why she was nervous, having had many such meetings with the staff. But that had been as the manager's wife. Not even officially as manageress.

In the staff corridor, she could already hear chatter from the staff dining room. She stepped in, leaving the door open in case there were any late comers.

'Please, carry on helping yourself to tea and biscuits. I'll try to make this as brief as possible, as I know some of you need to finish up and others want to get home.'

'I presume you dropped Mr Bygrove off and everything was fine?' said Mrs Leggett.

'Yes, fine. First of all, as I'm now acting manager, I have appointed Edie as under-manageress.'

There were a few 'oohs', but there seemed to be no objection. She looked in the housekeeper's direction but saw that she was nodding in agreement. Good. She didn't want any upsets between staff members.

'I have also decided to have the tennis courts dug up and have them planted with vegetables. I know my husband would be horrified, but food will only get in shorter and shorter supply. It is necessary.'

'It's an excellent idea,' said Mrs Leggett.

'Mr Hargreaves has already told me he has some competent friends with allotments who would be happy to earn a bit of money, so they could help the existing gardening staff get it started.'

Now to tackle the problem she'd been pondering since Douglas's tribunal. She hadn't wanted to mention it before, but she had to know who had said what.

'There is another matter to discuss. I want to say, first of all, that I am not annoyed, and I am not here to reprimand anyone. I found out, at the tribunal, that an official was sent to speak to members of staff about my husband's role here. I'm aware of some of the things said. I'm not condemning anyone, for you had to speak what you thought was the truth. I understand that.'

There was a brief pause. Then Gertie spoke, putting up her hand from where she was standing by the fireplace. 'I'm sorry, Mrs Bygrove. But the man what spoke to me told me I wasn't to tell no one he'd been. You've been running the hotel more than Bygrove, I mean, Mr Bygrove has, as he was always disappearing or shut in his office. So, I had to tell the truth.'

'Me too,' said Phoebe. 'I told him how you'd organised all the charity events and that Mr Bygrove was often out.'

'I see,' said Helen. 'Well, it is the truth, as you've said. And, to be honest, I don't think it would have made any difference. They just didn't consider hotel managing as a job of national importance. So please, do not feel bad about it.'

'I'm afraid I might have mentioned that the business really belonged to you,' said Mrs Leggett. 'That is, it was bought with your inheritance. I know that because your mother, God rest her soul, told me.'

Helen was taken aback. So were much of the staff, by their reactions. But *their* surprise would be for a different reason. Edie had suggested that the information might have come from one of the staff who'd been here while her mother was still alive, so she'd been right.

'So, it's really *your* hotel?' Gertie asked.

'Yes, I suppose it is. Though it is in my husband's name. But, when he returns after the war, I would prefer it if people made no mention of it. And please, this information is not to leave this room… Now, I'll let you get on. Thank you for your time and patience.'

She left the room and headed straight to the stairs. A good night's sleep was what she needed, for what she considered her new start tomorrow.

Chapter Twenty-Four

It had been two days since Lili had sent the letter to Auntie Megan. That morning she'd been cleaning in the Workmen's Institute. It was a different kind of cleaning to that she'd done in the hotel, with its fancy rooms and bed-making, or even in the Big House, when she'd worked there. Here, the job consisted of washing down surfaces and sweeping the floors in more utilitarian rooms used for gatherings. Even the large, tiered meeting room – which often hosted talks, plays and operettas – was plain and simple.

She thought about Auntie Megan as she cleaned, wondering whether she'd received the letter yet. If so, and she wrote back, a letter might arrive by Friday.

Her shift had finished at noon, allowing her to get back and make Mam some dinner. At one o'clock, she headed to the chapel to do a couple of hours there.

When she arrived back at ten past three, her mother was still in one of the armchairs by the stove, reading the newspaper Lili had brought for her.

'Are you comfortable there, Mam? Or would you like me to help you upstairs for a nap?'

'No, I'm quite comfortable. And I've told you before – I'm not a baby, so I don't need no nap.'

'Sorry, I know that. I'm just trying to make sure you're all right.'

Her mother took hold of her arm. 'I know you are, *cariad*. I'm sorry to be a bit short with you. It's just… you going out to do the jobs I liked doing, it's—'

'I know, Mam. I'm sure I'd feel the same.' She *did* feel the same. It wouldn't be long before her job at the hotel would be taken by someone else. Phoebe would probably become head waitress permanently. The thought depressed her.

'Miss Elizabeth popped around to see me about an hour ago.'

'That was kind of her.'

'She brought me those flowers.' She pointed to the jug on the dresser, in which sat some white foxgloves. 'They're from the Big House's garden. She mostly grows veggies in it now, but she still has some flowers.'

'How pretty.'

She was about to take a better look when she heard the back door in the scullery open, then close. She stifled the moan she wanted to voice. She was fed up with her sisters barging in whenever they felt like it to bark instructions and criticisms. Which one of them was it this time? She pulled open the ajar door.

'Auntie Megan!' There she was, with her fine silvery hair pulled into a bun on the top of her head. She had on her favourite green shawl.

'In the flesh.' Her aunt placed a couple of sack bags on the scullery floor and strode into the kitchen.

'I got your letter this morning, Liliwen. Glenys, what on earth is going on and why wasn't I told before?'

'Carys said she wrote to you when Mam was first ill.'

'I've had the shingles,' said Glenys. 'Dr Roberts diagnosed it twenty-ninth of May, but I'd had a rash on one side of my chest for a few days before. And a headache.'

'I didn't receive no letter. Twenty-ninth of May? But that was well over three weeks ago. How are you now?'

'The rash has mostly gone – just a few red patches left – and I thought I was feeling a lot better quite early on. But Carys and the others told me that it was probably a bit of delirium, and that Dr Roberts said I was *really* ill and needed to have a long period of recuperation.'

'You don't look particularly ill.'

Lili was about to argue about that, but she realised her aunt was right. Mam might look thoroughly depressed all the time, but she wasn't pale and sickly looking.

Megan looked at Lili. 'How long have you been here?'

'Since the ninth. So… twelve days.'

'What's happened about your job in Sussex?'

'I've, um, well…'

'Tell me the story from the beginning. While you're at it, I'll get the kettle on and make us a nice cup of tea.'

Glenys told her bit of the story first, then Lili joined in when they reached the point of her arrival. While waiting for the kettle to boil, Megan folded her arms across her chest, nodding and shaking her head, asking the odd question.

When they got to the end, the kettle on the stove was starting to boil, so she lifted it off and put it on the hearth. 'That'll have to wait. I'm popping out for a bit. I'll be back soon.'

'You're not going to get Carys or Dilys, are you?' Lili called as her aunt headed for the door to the hall.

'I certainly am not.'

'What on earth is she up to?' said Glenys after her sister had left.

'I dunno, but let's make this tea anyway. I'm parched, I am. We can make a fresh pot when she gets back, if she takes a while.'

Ten minutes later – as Lili and her mother sat opposite each other by the stove, sipping tea – they heard people coming through the back door.

'That's not just Megan,' said Glenys.

Sure enough, Lili's aunt came into the kitchen with a man in a suit: Dr Roberts.

'I went to the hospital to ask the doctor about your shingles.'

'Hello Mrs Probert. Nice to see you again, Liliwen. I understand your siblings got you to come home by claiming that your mother was seriously unwell.'

'That's right. Sent me a letter, they did.'

'I'm not at all sure why. I came to see your mother a couple of days before your arrival and found her recovering very well. It was only a very mild bout of shingles. Didn't I tell you that, Mrs Probert?'

'You did, doctor. But my children said you were only saying that so as not to scare me, and that I was in a poor way and would take a long time to recover.'

He pulled a face as if to say, *Really?* 'Well, that is not what I told Carys. In fact, I told her you were recovering quickly and ought to start going for little walks. Your heart is strong as an ox. I certainly don't see why you're still housebound.'

Lili felt relieved and angry all at once. Had her siblings exaggerated everything, just to get her back to Dorcalon?

'However, let me have another look at you while I'm here.' He turned to Lili and Megan. 'If you wouldn't mind.'

'We'll be in the scullery,' said Lili.

They'd been in there a couple of minutes when the back door flew open. In rushed Carys.

'It is you. The children said they thought they'd seen you walking along the street.'

'Aye, it's me,' said Megan. 'And I'd like to know what the devil you've been up to, not letting me know.'

Carys glanced at Lili, then said: 'I sent a letter. It must have got lost in the post.'

'Rubbish.'

'Where's Mam?' Carys hurried towards the kitchen, but Megan caught hold of her. 'Dr Roberts is in there, examining her. You'll have to wait.'

'What is *he* doing here? We already know what's wrong with her.'

'Which is nothing now, according to him. She was making a good recovery before Lili even got here. All that stuff about her being really ill is downright nonsense.'

'Why are you here now?'

'Because Liliwen had the good sense to write to me.'

Carys glared at Lili. 'You did *what*?'

'I thought it odd that Auntie Megan hadn't replied to your letter, or come to see Mam, so I wrote to her.'

'I didn't give you permission to—'

'Carys, I'm an adult. I don't need your permission to do anything.'

The door from the kitchen opened and Dr Roberts entered. 'All right, ladies, there's no need to argue.' He looked at Carys. 'I hear you've been insisting your mother stays in and have claimed she can't do anything. That is not what I told you and your siblings. I've just examined her. She has, like I said, made a very good recovery. She should be at least a bit active now. I really can't understand why you told your sister that your mother was on her last legs.'

'I do,' said Megan. 'Jealous, the lot of them are, of Lili's new life in Sussex. Always complaining about her absence they are when I come to visit. Particularly you, Carys. This was just a way of getting her back home.'

'No, it wasn't,' said Carys, but she blushed as she said it.

'Yes, it was. You should be ashamed of yourself, or yourselves, as the four of you all had a hand in it. Though I wouldn't mind betting you played the biggest part. Always jealous of her leaving, you were.'

'You need to sort this out among yourselves,' said Dr Roberts. 'But my advice is to get her on her feet and doing small jobs. She'll soon get back to work if you do. Good day to you all.'

When the doctor had left, Megan said: 'What I've got to say, I'm going to say in front of your mother. Come on.'

Carys and Lili followed her into the kitchen, where she sat opposite her sister.

'Right, I should have done this when your father died, already being a widow myself. Much more practical it'll be.'

'What's that?' said Lili.

299

'As long as your mam agrees, I'll move in.' Megan regarded her sister. 'I can do your jobs until you're on your feet. Then I'll find some jobs of my own. And we could take in a lodger or two since there'll be a spare room. I'll arrange to move my things in the next few days and sort out my old tenancy.'

Glenys stared at the fire, her eyes slightly narrowed, as if thinking. She looked up at Megan. 'Yes, it's a splendid idea. We'll both have company and keeping one house between the two of us, instead of having separate homes, will be much more practical. You're right: we should have done it before.'

Carys crossed her arms and let out a loud breath of impatience.

'Liliwen can go back to her job in Sussex,' said Megan, 'and continue to regale us with all her adventures in her letters.' Her face became serious as she said: 'It's just a shame you lost your young man, Norman.'

'It is,' said Lili, deciding not to say anything about Rhodri yet. 'Though it's been a while now and I have come to terms with it.'

'It's a shame you're not a bit closer, like Cardiff or Swansea, as you might have met a nice Welsh boy. But there it is.' Her mother smiled sadly.

Lili couldn't help but see the irony in the situation. If only she could tell Mam that she hadn't even needed to be in Wales to meet a nice Welsh boy.

'So, you'll catch an early train back tomorrow and we'll all chip in for your ticket,' said Megan.

'I don't see why we should have—' Carys started.

'It's fine,' Lili interrupted. 'Mrs Bygrove gave me the money for the return ticket too.'

'There's generous,' said Megan.

'She is that,' said Lili. 'Very generous. Now, shall we make some more tea?'

'I'm going to fetch Dilys,' said Carys. 'And Morys and Wyn should be back and washed by now. They need to know about this.' She swivelled on one foot to face the scullery and marched out.

'Oh dear,' said Glenys, when her eldest daughter had gone.

'There's no *oh dear* about it,' said Megan. 'They were all thoroughly badly behaved, making up things about you being at death's door just to get Liliwen home. I shall give them a good telling-off when they arrive, mark my words.'

Lili had no doubt she would, and it wouldn't be a pretty scene. Despite that, she felt lighter in spirit than she had before the doctor had arrived. It was the relief of knowing she could go back to the hotel. And see Rhodri. She'd write him a letter tonight, when Mam and Auntie Megan had gone to bed, and post it on her way to the station tomorrow.

'Right, tea.'

Chapter Twenty-Five

As Lili walked out of Littlehampton station she stopped just outside the main door. In the courtyard, in front of the station building, were a couple of the small horse-drawn carriages, known as horse buses, waiting for passengers needing a ride to various parts of the town. But they were for those who could afford them.

She yawned. The long journey and several changes of train had been tiring, but her elation at being back here was enough to propel her through the town and on towards South Terrace.

Reaching the hotel, she stood on the opposite side of the road, studying it. The clock above the hotel's public house, on the left of the hotel, showed it had just gone half-three. It was good to be back, especially after all the trouble her siblings had caused. Despite her mother's supposed ill health, she might have enjoyed the trip back home had they not made it so hard for her.

When she entered the scullery at the hotel, she was greeted with, 'Lili, you're back!'

'Hello, Annie. Yes, I'm back. I don't suppose you know where Mrs Bygrove is?'

'No, sorry. You're back in time for the afternoon tea break though.'

Lili laughed. 'I'm not sure I've earned it.'

She carried the carpet bag into the corridor and placed it by the wall, before entering the dining room.

'Hello Lili!' said Gertie, the only person facing her. 'I didn't know you were back today.'

The others at the table – including Mrs Turnbull and Fanny, who had Elsie on her lap, asleep – turned to look at her.

'Neither did I until yesterday.'

'You'll never guess what,' said Gertie. 'Bygrove did have to join the army. He's now in Shoreham at the camp.'

'Really? Good heavens.'

'Aye. He went yesterday,' said Mrs Turnbull.

'After giving us a right talking to,' said Gertie.

'Well, that's…'

'Good news, that's what it is.' Gertie nodded enthusiastically.

'I think we all agree.' Mrs Turnbull stood up. 'Come and sit down, pet. It's lovely to have you back. You must be worn out after your journey. I'll pour you a cup of tea. Edie is under-manageress now, by the way.'

Lili plonked down on the end of the bench. 'My, a lot has happened while I've been away.'

'How's your mother, pet?'

'Recovering very well.' She wasn't going to go through the whole charade. She'd save that for Edie, later. And explain a little to Mrs Bygrove, just so she didn't think she'd been dodging work.

'We've missed you here, pet.'

Mrs Bygrove walked through the door, humming to herself. She stopped and her eyes lit up when she spotted Lili. 'How marvellous! You're back! I wish you had let me know, then I could have picked you up in the motorcar.'

'I'm sorry I couldn't write to tell you, but it wasn't decided until yesterday afternoon. I hope I haven't let you down too much.'

'Of course you haven't. I'm just glad to see you back. I do hope your mother is quite well now?'

'She will be soon. My aunt's come to look after her.'

'Splendid.'

Lili looked around, not knowing whether to ask the question she desperately wanted to know the answer to, with others around. She decided on: 'You said in your letter that you had something for me?'

'Yes, I have.' She indicated for Lili to follow her out to the corridor. 'I went to meet Corporal Morgan as arranged, as you know, and he gave me the number of the office telephone where he works. It might be an idea to ring him as soon as possible, to reassure him you are all right. And to arrange to meet him, of course.'

'But I've been away nearly two weeks. I can't be taking more time off.'

'Never mind that. You can have your half-day off next week as usual, for I know you'll work hard the rest of the time. You always do.'

Lili was touched that she had such confidence in her. 'Thank you so much, Mrs Bygrove. I will work all the harder. I'm so sorry for being away longer than I intended. My family were rather... difficult. In fact, I was on the verge of writing to say I wouldn't be back. I was lucky Auntie Megan came to the rescue.'

'My, you sound like you've had a time of it. But you're back now, so you can put those troubles behind you.'

'Thank you, Mrs Bygrove. I really appreciate your support.'

'You're welcome, Lili. Why don't you ring Corporal Morgan now, from my office?'

'Are you sure?' Lili felt a shiver of excitement at the idea of speaking to Rhodri.

'Yes. The sooner the better. Come on.' Helen led her to the office and picked up a piece of paper from the bottom of the tray there, handing it to Lili. 'You know how to use the telephone, so I'll leave you to it.'

When Helen had left, she picked up the receiver and placed the wide end of it to her ear. She put the paper on the desk and stared at it. What if Rhodri wasn't in his office now and somebody else replied?

She'd never know unless she tried. She got through to the operator and gave her Rhodri's number. Then she waited, her heart thumping in her chest. *Please let him be there.*

At last, she heard Rhodri's Welsh voice.

'Hello?'

'Hello Rhodri, it's Lili Probert.'

'Lili?' She could hear the surprise from the other end of the line. 'I'm so happy to hear your voice. Are you back in Littlehampton?'

'Yes, yes, I'm back. I was wondering if we could reorganise that meeting we were supposed to 'ave?'

She awaited his reply, holding her breath, then smiled when he gave her his answer.

—

Lili had to wait nine days before she could meet Rhodri, due to his rota. Her anticipation had grown with each day. By the time she reached the bottom of Pier Road on the Saturday, she was so excited, yet nervous, that she felt quite lightheaded. She stopped outside of a fruiterer to catch her breath, gazing through the window at its produce.

She wasn't only meeting Rhodri, but having afternoon tea first with Mrs Hughes, Rhodri's Auntie Charlotte. They were taking her to Read's Dining Rooms, as they had planned before. How she wished she could have Rhodri to herself, but this arrangement would only be for an hour or so. Besides, it would be nice to meet her properly.

Right, come on now. She turned decidedly and set off with determination, rounding the corner between Pier Road and Surrey Street. She saw straight away that they had already arrived and were standing outside Read's, chatting. Mrs Hughes spotted her first, nudging Rhodri and holding up a hand to wave. He turned his head, a wide smile appearing immediately that he spotted her.

She was afraid for one moment that her knees would give way. *That's just silly*, she told herself, ploughing onwards. But the sensation his presence caused was a mixture of exhilaration and fear. She wasn't frightened of *him*, but of herself, doing or saying something daft, of putting him off her. And, if she were honest, a little frightened of her growing feelings for him.

'Lovely to meet you again,' said Mrs Hughes, coming forward and clutching Lili's hands. 'I hear you've been back in the old country.'

'That's right. My mother had the shingles, but she's all better now.'

'So Rhodri was telling me. I've been looking forward to this and to spending some time with you. Not been in here before, I haven't. Always seemed a little posh. But then, it probably isn't so posh to you, working in that lovely hotel.'

'I don't get to have afternoon tea in the conservatory there, though.'

Mrs Hughes chuckled. 'No, I don't suppose you do. Sorry, I haven't given you a chance to say hello to Rhodri.'

'Good afternoon, Rhodri.' She so wanted to take his hands, as his aunt had hers, but it didn't seem quite proper. Not yet.

'Good afternoon, Lili. Or should I say *Prynhawn da*, as I'm guessing you've been speaking Welsh the past coupla weeks.'

'Mostly, yes. It took a while to get used to it again, I must admit.'

Rhodri opened the door to let the two women in. The table had been booked, so they were soon accommodated beside the first-floor window, overlooking the shops on the opposite side of the street.

'I suppose you don't have anyone at the hotel you can speak Welsh with,' said Mrs Hughes, once they'd sat down and been presented with menus. 'Whereas we speak it at home. Not in public though. People look at you funny when you speak it outdoors. I was out with my husband, Islwyn, in the town one day and we were talking in Welsh. Beginning of the war, it

306

were, and someone actually accused us of speaking German. As if it sounds anything like it!'

'I guess people are suspicious of any "foreign" language at the moment,' said Rhodri. 'Not that Welsh is a foreign language, of course.'

'It might as well be to some people,' said his aunt.

Lili recalled an incident at the hotel at the beginning of the war. 'We used to have a German waiter, called Günther. Naturalised, he were, and not a threat to no one. But one of the guests reported him and, because he hadn't got around to registering, they took him away to an internment camp, in Berkshire.'

'Such a shame,' said Rhodri, 'but I suppose they have to err on the side of caution. Do you know how he is now?'

'Yes. He's being well treated. He writes to Phoebe, the other live-in waitress. I think they were maybe a bit romantically attached.' Nobody had ever been quite sure about it and Phoebe wouldn't say either way.

'It's not been easy for any of the German businesses in the country,' said Mrs Hughes. 'I read about them anti-German riots in London last year, where shops were smashed up and their belongings stolen. Frightful really, for us so-called civilised British to act in such a cruel way. I can't imagine many Germans will be welcomed back when the war finally ends.'

It made Lili wonder about Günther, whether he'd come back to the hotel after the war.

'Well, this *is* nice.' Mrs Hughes looked around the room.

'It is,' Rhodri agreed. 'But the afternoon tea Lili and I had last time maybe wasn't up to the same standard as the first time I came.'

The first time? He hadn't mentioned that before. She wondered who he might have come with and whether it was a woman.

'I can't say I'm surprised,' said Mrs Hughes. 'Savings must be made now. Maybe, after the war, we'll come back again.'

All three of them? That was supposing she and Rhodri would still be… what? Friends? Or developed into something else. Did his aunt think there was already something between them? She wondered now what he'd told her.

'It'll be tea and scones for me,' said Mrs Hughes. 'I don't think I could manage a big tea.'

Lili had only had a small early lunch so that she'd have room for this. So, she was relieved when Rhodri said: 'Well I could, so I'm having the whole afternoon tea.'

'Then I will too,' she said.

–

After the tea, Rhodri and Lili walked his aunt home, along the remainder of Surrey Street and down River Road. They passed the flint and brick warehouses on the left and domestic buildings on the right, the bigger and posher ones being closer to Surrey Street. His aunt's small terraced house was near the other end, not far from the swing bridge.

'*Hwyl fawr*, Lili. Hope to meet you again soon.'

'Me too. *Hwyl fawr*, Mrs Hughes.'

When his aunt had let herself in and closed the door behind her, Rhodri smiled and said: 'How about a walk across the bridge and on the other side of the river towards West Beach? Despite living on this side of town, I haven't walked over there for a while.'

'Neither have I. It would be nice to visit that beach. It's so different to the one this side. So yes, I'd like that.'

As they headed towards the bridge, Lili remembered something that Edie had told her. The first time Charlie had kissed her was when they'd taken a walk over to West Beach. After going to the fair with Rhodri, it was like she was repeating their romance.

You should be so lucky!

There was a flutter in her stomach as she thought about it. Rhodri, kissing her.

308

Edie and Charlie's walk had been in the winter though, if she recalled correctly, when hardly anyone would have been on that beach. Now, it would be quite busy and not very private.

What a wayward piece she was. And how likely was it to happen for her the same way? But she did so like the idea of his lips on hers. Or even for him to hold her in his arms. There it was again, the flutter. She gave a little involuntary shiver.

'Are you cold?' said Rhodri, concerned. 'It's not as warm as it could be for July and a bit cloudy.' He looked up at the sky.

'No, I'm fine. Just enjoying my day out, back in Little-hampton.'

'You're not missing the Valleys then? It must have been nice to get home for a bit.'

'It would have been.'

'If your mother hadn't been ill? Of course. Sorry.'

'No, not that. It turned out, you see, that she wasn't as ill as my brothers and sisters had made out.'

'Why did they tell you she was then?'

'It's a bit of a story.'

'You've got time to tell it to me. If you want to, that is.'

'I suppose I have. And I would like to.'

They'd reached the bridge by now and started to cross on one side, avoiding a couple of motorcars and a horse and cart. She started with the letter she'd received from Carys and told him the whole sorry tale as they turned left to walk down the other side of the river, on a path past the shipbuilding yard and the timber docks.

By the time they'd reached the other side of them – and again had a view of the river and the warehouses on the other side – she'd finished. The tide was out, creating a wide river beach of sand.

'That certainly was a story and one I'm glad had a happy ending. Would you have minded a lot, if you'd had to stay?'

'Yes, I would. As much as I love my family and have an affection for the place where I grew up, I've been happy here.'

'Me too. And I enjoyed my work at Dando.' He looked right, over the golf course that was now visible. 'Looks like there are quite a few golfers out today.'

'Our manager used to play there.'

'Used to?'

'I didn't tell you, did I? He was conscripted. He left the day before I got back. He tried to appeal, on the grounds of doing work of national importance.'

Rhodri laughed. 'Sorry. You probably think me very rude. But I'm not sure how—'

'It's all right. I quite agree. He's a pompous piece is Mr Bygrove. It's not as if he did much work at all. Especially recently. Mrs Bygrove did a lot more. She's now the manageress and much happier we all are for it.'

'Where has he gone to train?'

'That's the thing, see. He's gone to Shoreham, to your camp. Douglas Bygrove, he's called.'

'Can't say I've come across him yet.'

'Lucky you.'

Passing the ferry landing stage, Lili saw that a boat had just arrived and passengers were getting off. Some would be arriving to play golf, by the looks of the way they were dressed. There were women, too, and a couple of small children, who had most likely come to spend some hours on the beach. She'd only been on the ferry once, enjoying the walk over the bridge and along the path more. Since the war had begun, she'd done the walk a couple of times. She'd have passed Rhodri's house and not even been aware he existed.

'Watch out!' Rhodri clutched her hand and pulled her to one side of the path as a cyclist came rushing by.

'He wasn't going to stop for us, was he?'

'Didn't look like it.'

They went back to the middle of the path, but Rhodri didn't let go of her hand. Perhaps she should pull hers away. But she couldn't. It felt too nice: warm and comforting, like being wrapped up in a blanket in cold weather, even though the sun was shining down on them from a blue sky.

They both went quiet, enjoying the view as they strolled along, or limped, in Rhodri's case, though it was nowhere near as pronounced as when she'd first met him. The women and children who'd got off the ferry to go to West Beach overtook them, chatting and laughing as they went, the kiddies skipping along. She was content for her and Rhodri to take their time.

They were passing the large lifeboat house – which lay on the opposite side from the windmill and Casino Theatre – when Rhodri spoke again.

'Do you mind walking on the sand, with your dress and shoes?'

'Not at all. Love walking on the beach, I do.'

'Good. I like walking in the dunes here. Hope that won't be too hard for you.' He looked down at her Oxford shoes.

'I'll manage. I have before. Will, um, you be all right?'

'You mean with my limp?'

'Sorry, I didn't mean to offend you.'

'You haven't.' He smiled at her. 'I can manage fine. But it's nice that you're concerned.'

Disconcerted by his gaze, she looked away, into the distance across the sea.

The path became sandier as they approached the river's mouth. The smell of the briny sea began to tickle Lili's nose and she breathed in deeply. She'd come to appreciate it all over again since she'd returned from her village.

The beach on this side of the river started quite a way further out than the one on the eastern side. She looked back and across at it as they strolled, spotting the hotel in the distance.

'It's quite something, even from here, isn't it?' he said.

'The hotel? Yes. Even from here.'

Reaching the beach proper, she looked at its pale-yellow expanse. Still holding hands, they turned right to walk on the lower layer. There were a lot of people here today, some sitting on blankets enjoying the sun, some picnicking.

There were people in the sea too. She pointed at them. 'Brr. Rather them than me. I've been in the sea in July. It still won't have warmed up that much yet.'

'You've been swimming here?'

'No. In Barry Island, as a child. I've paddled over on the other beach. Only in the evenings though, when there aren't many people around.'

'I used to go swimming a lot on the east beach here, the summer before the war. It is warmer in August and September.'

She tried to picture him in a costume, exposing his lower legs and his forearms, feeling ashamed of her wilful imagination.

They walked down towards the water, which was far out on an ebbing tide. Reaching the damp sand, they stopped to look out to sea. Lili turned her head, concentrating, trying to catch a sound she thought she'd heard. It was a kind of rumble that got slightly louder every now and again.

'Is that the sea I can hear, or something else?'

He listened for a while. 'It's not the sea. It's far too calm. I think that it might be artillery, on the other side of the Channel.'

'Would we be able to hear that from here?'

'If there was enough heavy artillery.'

'That means that there's a battle raging somewhere.'

'Or more,' he said, in a whisper.

They stood for a while, listening. She was convinced he was right and that what they were hearing were large guns being fired. It unsettled her. It was weird, standing here, people all around her enjoying themselves. But over the water, not many miles away, men were fighting and dying. It didn't feel right.

Rhodri's brow was creased as he looked out to sea. It might be the sun shining in his eyes. Or maybe he was thinking of his brother, Glyn, out there somewhere, and his fellow soldiers from the battalion he'd been in before being shot. Then he stirred. 'Shall we take a walk up into the dunes?'

'Yes. I'd like that.'

As they trudged up, he let go of her hand and she was disappointed. The dunes had sandy pathways through mounds on which marron grass was growing. Her feet sank into the soft sand as she made her way up. Even he struggled in his flat army shoes, though his limp couldn't have helped. When they reached the top, she looked around, northwards, over the golf course, towards the warehouses on the river's edge, beyond that to the countryside and onwards to the South Downs. Rhodri, meanwhile, stared out to sea. She turned to do the same, realising they could still hear the rumble of distant guns.

'Let's walk further down,' he said.

They wound their way around the marron grass mounds, spotting the back of the bathing huts as they went. He took her hand once more and she smiled to herself. She could feel that some of the sand had sneaked into her shoes, but she didn't care. The crowds on the beach lessened as they walked and, eventually, part way down the dunes, there was no one. He stopped and faced her, taking both her hands in his.

'Lili, I've been wanting to ask you, but I don't know if I dare.'

'Ask me what, Rhodri?'

'Please, tell me I'm out of order, if you consider me to be.'

'By doing what? You are simply holding my hands.'

'But I would like more, but only if you feel the same. And, and... I know this might not be the right thing to do, or the right time, what with Norman having gone and it's only been, what? Under a year, hasn't it?'

'Ten months.'

'Yes, ten months. And I did tell myself I would wait a year, but...'

He looked at their hands, his expression troubled. She wanted to see him smile, to make him happy. And she so wished he'd get to the point.

'I don't know if you'll think me too forward.'

'Oh Rhodri!' She leant forward, pulling herself up on tiptoes, and kissed him on the cheek. 'I think more likely you are backward at coming forward.'

He chuckled, going slightly pink, then leant down towards her face. He stopped just short. Her breath hitched and she felt confused, her senses tingling at his closeness. Finally, he moved in and placed his lips on hers. He was tentative at first, their mouths barely moving. It was almost unbearable; she wanted to press herself against him and hold him tightly. Slowly, the pressure of his mouth on hers increased and the kiss became more insistent. She'd never felt such desire before, not even for Norman. That had been more of a sweet love, almost childish; this was something much fiercer.

When he pulled away, he still looked uncertain of himself. 'Are you sure it's all right, for me to kiss you?'

'I wouldn't let you if it wasn't.'

'Do you mind if we sit down, as my leg is aching slightly. Or would that make your clothes too sandy?'

'I can brush any sand off.'

They sat next to each other, close, hidden by grass but just able to spy the sea. He put his arm around her waist and she leant against his shoulder, feeling the two corporal's stripes on his sleeve against her cheek.

A tiny fleck of guilt flicked through her mind as she thought of Norman. Had he not been lost in the war, she wouldn't be here with Rhodri. But that was fate. She couldn't live forever in the past.

After some moments, Rhodri twisted around and lifted her chin.

'You are very beautiful, Liliwen Probert.'

'Liliwen now, is it? I think I 'ad enough of that from my family. My siblings always seem to use it as a reprimand.'

'Lili it is, then.'

'And I have to say, Rhodri Morgan, that you are *very* hand-some.'

He leant forward to give her a peck on the lips, before taking her in his arms and kissing her again.

So once more, like Edie and Charlie, the first kiss had taken place on West Beach. But there the likeness in the relationships would hopefully end. Charlie had headed to war a while after. Rhodri had already been and his injury meant he wouldn't have to go again. For that she was relieved and grateful.

-

Lili had been serving breakfast in the hotel dining room, which had been unusually busy for a Monday, with several tables of outside guests. She was still feeling the exhilaration of her outing with Rhodri, two days before.

By the time the staff had cleared up after breakfast and got the room in order, she was ready for her morning break, humming *On Moonlight Bay* as she entered the dining room.

'You've been very chirpy the past couple of days, pet,' said Mrs Turnbull, as Lili sat down.

'She's got a sweetheart, ain't she,' said Gertie.

'Is that right?' said the storekeeper.

'I saw her, walking back with him to the hotel on Friday. Just been running a message, I had, and there she was with one of them corporals what came to the party for the wounded soldiers last year, and then to the concert – the one what had been shot in the leg. And he was limping, so I'm sure it was him.'

Lili had wanted to keep it to herself for now, especially since Hetty and Annie were also sitting there. But there was no point lying about it. They'd been holding hands on the way back to the hotel and Gertie would have noticed that.

'Corporal Morgan and I have only just started walking out. That's all.'

'Good luck to you, pet. Has he been discharged now, what with the leg wound?'

'He was in uniform,' said Gertie.

'Let the girl speak for herself.'

315

'He's still in the army, doing clerical work at the Shoreham camp.'

'Hope he doesn't have to deal with Bygrove,' said Hetty. There was a murmur of agreement.

'He said he hadn't come across him yet.'

Mrs Leggett entered the room, brandishing a newspaper. Lili didn't want her getting wind of her romance. When she'd found out about Norman, she'd given Lili a lecture about concentrating on work. She didn't want another talking to. She shook her head at Gertie to indicate that she should keep quiet now. Gertie, in return, placed her forefinger over her mouth to show she understood.

'Oh dear, oh dear, oh dear,' said the housekeeper as she sat in her chair at the end.

'What's ailing you, Imogen?' said Mrs Turnbull.

'I've just been reading the newspaper. I really should avoid the war news. There seems to be a lot going on around what they call the Somme. They make it sound like our troops are gaining ground, but that's not to say we're not losing a lot of men in the process. I get the impression the men from here might be in that area, from letters some of you receive.'

'The South Downs battalions are now part of the 39th Division,' said Hetty. 'Does it mention them?'

'It rarely mentions which allied battalions are involved. And not all the men from here are in the South Downs, especially the ones who went early.'

'Only Lorcan and Jasper aren't,' said Hetty, referring to the two porters who'd been the first to enlist. 'But they're still in France.'

Lili was glad that Edie wasn't in the room to hear Mrs Leggett's thoughts. She didn't need another reason to be worried about Charlie or her brother.

'We'll likely get more letters from some of them soon, then we'll be reassured that they're all right,' said Hetty.

'Except if they aren't,' said Mrs Leggett. She rose and left the room once more.

'Well, that's cheered me up for my next shift,' said Gertie, picking up her cup, 'what with having three brothers in them battalions.'

Lili was once more thankful that Rhodri was serving his country at home. It would be another seventeen days until she saw him again. She'd been counting them down since their last meeting. She prayed that they passed by quickly.

Chapter Twenty-Six

They'd been busy in the hotel the past three weeks, yet the time had still dragged for Lili. At last, the day was almost here when she'd see her... sweetheart. She still couldn't quite believe that she was able to call him that, but what else was he? Tomorrow afternoon, that's when she'd see him again. The anticipation was almost too much. Several times she'd had to tell herself to calm down, especially when she wasn't occupied with serving guests.

She was on her afternoon break now and staring into her tea, picturing Rhodri's dark eyes and that dimple in his chin she adored. There was a conversation going on between Edie, Phoebe and Hetty that Lili hadn't heard a word of, so absorbed was she by her internal world.

'Oh dear, that's another hotel loss to the war and not even a man this time,' said Mrs Bygrove as she walked into the room with Mrs Turnbull, snapping Lili out of her fantasy.

'Who's left now?' said Edie.

'The bookkeeper, Amanda Lovelock. She's decided to become a WPC.'

'A policewoman?' Hetty scrunched up her nose. 'She's far too mousy to command any respect.'

'Be that as it may, I had better advertise for an accounts person,' said Helen. 'It was the post you originally applied for, Edie. But you have taken on rather a lot recently, since becoming under-manageress.'

'Lili's wonderful at sums,' said Edie. 'You should see her adding up the bills. She's so quick at calculations.'

'That's a bit different to doing accounting,' said Lili.

Helen held her chin. 'Maybe you could help out a bit with the day-to-day accounts, just until we get someone? You are very proficient and popular in the restaurant, so I wouldn't want to remove you from there permanently. I'd show you how to do it and, of course, it would be a bit of extra money for you.'

Extra money. That was always useful, to save for the future. A future she now had some hope of.

'All right. But only until you get someone else.'

'Thank you, Lili. That will get me out of a temporary spot.'

Helen turned to the others at the table as Mrs Turnbull took a seat. 'We've not had a head chambermaid for a while, not since Lili became a waitress. But Fanny, you've effectively been doing the job, guiding the live-outs, some of whom were frankly clueless when they first started. And you've managed that with a baby to care for.'

'It helps that Vera looks after Elsie when I'm working. Which I'm most grateful for.'

Lili had seen a big change in Fanny since Elsie had been born. It was as if she'd grown up. It was still rather surprising to hear her speak like this though, politely and with appreciation. She kept wondering when the 'real' Fanny might re-emerge.

'Since you've been doing the job, you should have the title,' said Helen. 'And the little extra wage that goes with it.'

'Oh,' said Fanny, her mouth and eyes opening wide in surprise. 'Really?'

'Of course.'

'Thank you. I did point out to Mr Bygrove that I were doing the job, but he said I couldn't be promoted because I didn't deserve it.' She looked glum.

'You should have come to me.'

Fanny nodded. It was followed by a sniff, as she got her handkerchief out and blew her nose. Had she come over all emotional? There was a first time for everything!

'My, how things have changed,' said Mrs Turnbull. 'For the better, what with you being manageress, Helen, and Edie next

319

in charge, and so many of the women stepping up in the men's absence.'

She didn't mention Mr Bygrove being gone, but Lili was sure most of them would be thinking this was one of those improvements.

'Things might be better for us,' said Edie, 'but the reports in the newspapers don't make it sound good for the men fighting in the Battle of the Somme, as they're calling it. I haven't heard from my brother or his friend, and none of us have heard from any of those who used to work here since it began.'

Edie would be thinking primarily of her Charlie, but plenty of the men from the hotel were in France and might be involved. There was the desk clerk, Stuart Coulter, along with the porters, Lorcan Foley, James Wood, Alan Drew, Jasper Jupp and the twins, Stanley and Leslie Morris. There were the waiters, Peter Smith and Anton Martin. Then there were the chefs, Alex Tuppen and Mrs Norris's son, Joseph. And that wasn't counting the live-out staff, including gardeners and other part-time young men they'd employed to do various jobs around the place.

'I'm sure they're much too busy to think of writing at the moment,' said Mrs Turnbull.

'I wish we could do more to help them.' Edie frowned and placed her head in one hand.

'*They also serve who only stand and wait*, to quote Mr Milton,' said the storekeeper.

Edie heaved out a sigh as she stood. She started to walk towards the door.

'Are you all right, Edie,' Lili called.

'I'll be fine. Don't worry. I just need a moment.'

'Oh dear, poor Edie,' said Helen, once she'd gone. 'I do wonder, sometimes, if this war will ever end.'

'Perhaps now Mr Lloyd George is secretary of state for war, things will be managed better,' said Lili.

'What, because he's Welsh?' said Mrs Turnbull.

'No I didn't mean—'

'Don't looked so worried, pet. I'm only pulling your leg. I hope you're right.'

'I'd better get that advert for a bookkeeper out,' said Helen, leaving the room.

Hetty passed the plate of digestives around once more, as Lili said: 'We had Miss Harvey in for luncheon today, you know, the tennis friend of Bygrove's, who has the guest house on Selborne Place. She was with a couple of other women and I heard her complaining loudly about the tennis courts being dug up. "It wouldn't have happened in Douglas's time," she kept saying, in that irritating high-pitched, put-on posh voice of hers.'

They all laughed. 'You imitate her very well,' said Phoebe. 'And that's not the first time she's moaned about it. She was in for afternoon tea last week and was saying the same thing. I'm sure she means for us to hear.'

'I bet she's written to Bygrove to tell him too,' said Fanny.

Phoebe nodded. 'I'm convinced she has a crush on him.'

They all pulled faces and displayed their own distaste at the idea.

'If he were my husband, I'd let her have 'im,' said Mrs Turnbull, and they all laughed again.

Chapter Twenty-Seven

The day of meeting Rhodri had arrived.

It was sunnier and warmer than on their last outing, without even the slightest hint of a cloud in the sky. Lili decided to wear one of only two cotton summer dresses she owned. It was the prettiest item of clothing she possessed and she hadn't yet worn it in his company. It was a few years old, but she'd taken up the hem slightly to fit in with the latest fashion. She'd spent some time on her hair, pinning it up in a neat chignon, as Edie had shown her. She wanted to look her very best, to stun him, the way he did her.

She was meeting him today at the bottom of Pier Road. They planned to go up to the picture house to see *The Prince and the Pauper*, showing along with a Keystone comedy. She was looking forward to sitting in the dark with him, the opportunity to be so close once more giving her a tingle when she thought about it. Maybe, if they sat in the back row, and there was no one else nearby, he might kiss her again. The thought made her breathless.

As she passed the sawmills on Pier Road, she was overwhelmed by a certainty. She was in love with Rhodri. At first, the thought made her giddy. She stopped for a moment to gather her thoughts. Love. Yes, she loved him. It was at once wonderful and terrifying, as so many of her thoughts involving him were.

But how many hours had she spent in his company, if she added them all up? Probably more than some couples. And it didn't matter. If she were honest with herself, it had been love at first sight. Or, it would have been, had she not still been involved with Norman.

But did he feel the same way about her?

On Surrey Street, she spotted Rhodri looking in the cycle agent's shop. That sensation of love washed over her once more.

'You looking for a new bicycle?' she quipped.

'Hello, Lili.' He took her hand and kissed it. 'I might do, after the war. My old cycle's seen better days, but it don't matter right now.'

'There was one old bicycle in our family, when I were a child, but after it being handed down through my four older siblings it weren't much good by the time it got to me. So, I never really learned to cycle properly.'

'That's a shame. After the war, I'll let you have a go on mine.'

'That's a deal.'

She took his arm and they crossed over to the other pavement. After the war... So he was intending on this being a long-term relationship, not just a short romance. Why did she keep doubting it?

As they turned on to the High Street, towards the railway station, Rhodri stopped to look in the bookseller's shop window. It was then she heard her name being called.

She twisted round to find Florence running across the road towards her.

'Lili, how fortunate. I was going to head to the hotel later to see if I could speak to you.'

Rhodri turned around as Florence caught them up. She gave him a quick once-over. 'Oh, you're out with your friend.'

'Why did you want to speak to me?'

'Have you heard the news?'

'What news?' said Lili.

'Such good news! So he hasn't written to you?'

Lili was confused at first as to what this could be. Then a feeling of dread overwhelmed her, followed by guilt. If this meant what she thought it did...

323

'Norman's alive!' Florence jumped a little on the spot, clapping her hands.

Of course that was good news. But why did it have to be revealed now, when she'd just moved on? Why not before she'd made a new commitment, or much later, when she and Rhodri had become properly established?

'Are you sure?' This felt unreal, like the dreams she'd had in the early days of his disappearance. 'But, how? Where has he been all this time?'

'He was injured and ended up with the French somehow. He had a head injury and was in a coma for a while. Then had a bit of amnesia. It took him a long time to recover. Then there was a clerical mix up. That's what Norman said in his letter. It's wonderful news though, isn't it?'

'Why yes, of course.'

'I can tell it's a shock for you.'

'Y—yes, it is rather. Norman didn't write to tell me.'

'I thought he might have done. Maybe he could only write one letter.'

'He didn't say in his letter to you?'

'No. But I'm sure he'll write soon. I'll keep you up to date anyway. If I can't get to speak to you at the hotel, I'll leave a note. I'll let you know when he's returning, in case he hasn't written.'

'All right. Thank you.'

'So, it's your day off?' She glanced at Rhodri again, who remained near the shop window, with his back to them. 'Are you doing anything nice?'

'Going to see *The Prince and the Pauper* at the Electric Picture Palace.'

'I hear it's very good. I've got to go for my shift at the chemist now. Enjoy your afternoon.'

'Th—thank you.'

'My, that's a bit of a surprise,' said Rhodri, turning fully around now Florence had left. His expression was neutral.

'Surprise. More like a shock. Come on, let's get to the picture house before the film starts.'

She took his arm, but he wasn't very responsive. Neither of them spoke as they walked on to Terminus Road, where the picture house sat almost opposite the station.

'Can I buy the tickets this time?' she asked.

'No, you're all right.'

She was disappointed when he headed for a middle row, not the back, but then, it was quite busy. No chance of canoodling. But maybe now would not be the time, after the news of Norman's return. What on earth would she say to him? She ought to write: to tell him what had happened, that she'd met someone else. If only she'd got an address from Florence. But maybe he was somewhere temporary at this moment in time.

The whole issue rather marred the afternoon's programme for her, as she pondered what exactly she should do.

-

At the end of the last film, Lili and Rhodri swiftly exited the picture house. She was relieved, wishing to find somewhere quiet where she could talk things over with him. He'd not held her hand during the films. He could be feeling guilty that he'd taken a fellow soldier's girl, especially when Norman had been through such a lot. She needed to reassure him.

They stepped outside, moving along a little so as not to get in the way of the other patrons leaving the building.

'I'm pleased for you, Lili, that Norman is alive. I know you missed him so. I do hope you'll be happy.'

'I… well, I—'

'I've decided to spend the rest of the afternoon with Auntie Charlotte. And Uncle Islwyn should be home soon.' He pointed up Terminus Road to where it turned on to River Road in the distance.

'I see. You don't want to talk about this?'

'What is there to talk about? Your sweetheart is coming home. I always knew there could be a chance of that, since they never found his body.'

'I suppose I used to think so. But I thought it couldn't be possible now.'

'See, miracles do happen. Goodbye, Lili. It's been nice knowing you.' He did an about-turn, like the soldier he was, and marched off down the road.

She wanted to stop him going, to run after him and call his name. But poor Norman. He'd been through a lot. Was that what Rhodri was thinking too? That she couldn't let him down? And, if she did, would Rhodri think less of her and not want to be with her any more anyway? Or maybe being with her wasn't what he wanted after all and he was using Norman's return as a reason to end the relationship. He had done the deed rather swiftly, not asking her what she wanted. And he'd had three weeks to think about their relationship since their last meeting. But he'd been so affectionate when they'd first met up today. Or had that just been her perception?

She continued to watch him as his form became smaller, walking into the distance.

'Oh Rhodri,' she whispered.

When Norman came home, she'd feel the same way about him again. How could she not? Poor Norman. What she'd prayed for all those first months had now come true. And she should be so happy.

Not in the mood to spend the rest of her free hours alone, she walked towards Surrey Street. She'd be better off going back to the hotel. The urge to cry was tempered by a gathering numbness. What she'd tell the others once she got back, she had no idea.

–

So, it was over?

And it had barely got going. Rhodri was tempted several times to turn and look at Lili, but he might have changed his mind and gone running back. She probably wasn't even there any more, having instead walked away, just like he had.

Captain Deeprose had said, in general conversation, that it wasn't a good time to start a romantic liaison in these days of uncertainty. He hadn't known that Rhodri was meeting Lili on his leave days. He'd been talking about a sergeant who'd started walking out with a young woman in Shoreham. He'd been late on duty a couple of times because of it.

The captain was probably right. And far be it for him to deprive a fellow soldier of his sweetheart, especially if he'd been through the wringer, as this Norman seemed to have been. It wasn't the decent thing to do. He knew what he'd have felt like had he gone missing only to come back to find his sweetheart had moved on.

So yes, it was over.

—

Lili's intention on getting back to the hotel was to join whatever break was happening, likely the last afternoon tea break, and to sit quietly with a drink and listen to the chatter. To escape her own troubles. She had so much to take in, but she didn't want to think about it just now. If anyone asked how the afternoon had gone, she'd just give them a vague answer about the films at the picture house being enjoyable. And they would have been, had things not turned out the way they had. If they wondered at her being back earlier than she'd said, she had a ready excuse about Rhodri needing to spend time with his aunt and uncle.

She'd say nothing of the situation until later and then only to Edie.

But when she got back to the hotel, it was clear something was up. She could hear the crying before she even got to the dining room. Mrs Leggett lamenting: 'It's terrible, just terrible.'

She pushed the door open to see it was Annie and Alice Twine at the table, sobbing. Gertie and Jack opposite looked like they were in shock.

Mrs Norris was perched on the edge of the bench, wiping her eyes with her apron. 'He was a good worker, was Alex. Had great potential. This damned bloody war! I just hope my Joseph is safe.'

Mrs Leggett was standing next to Edie, who was holding a letter in her hands.

'What on earth has happened?' Lili asked.

'Oh Lili!' Edie hurried towards her. 'I've had a letter from Charlie. He says Alex Tuppen, James Wood and Anton Martin… they… they were killed in a battle. Just before the Somme campaign started.'

'Who are they?' said one of the live-out waitresses.

'Alex was second chef, James was a porter and Anton a waiter,' said Gertie, her face pale.

'That's just… just *awful*.' With her emotions already fragile, Lili's tears came quickly. 'The Somme battles started three weeks ago though, didn't they?'

'He's only just found out,' said Edie. 'They were in the 3rd South Down battalion, whereas Charlie's in the 1st. The 13th and 11th they call them now. He's not said a lot else, but I suppose he's not allowed to.'

Could this day get any worse? Norman being alive should have been the very opposite to Edie's news, yet it had caused her such… complications. She sat at the table, next to Alice, and cried along with them.

—

It had been well over three weeks since Lili had heard about Norman from Florence. News of the demise of Alex, James and Anton had spread around the staff quickly, and then around the regular guests who remembered James and Anton in particular.

It hadn't been until three days after this news that Lili had confided her situation to Edie. A couple of days after that she'd told Mrs Bygrove. She'd been aware of the pair of them keeping an eye on her since then. Both had asked, maybe a few more times than was necessary, whether Lili was feeling all right. She guessed they were only trying to look after her, as they were the other staff members who felt the loss of their fellow workers.

This week, being under-manageress now, Edie had organised it so she and Lili could have the afternoon off together. They were going to the Electric Picture Palace to see *The Battle of the Somme*, recently filmed on the battlefields.

'I'm not entirely sure of the wisdom of this,' said Edie, as the two of them got ready in their bedroom. 'Yet, I really do want to see what it's like out there, for Charlie, Freddie and Daniel. And for the rest of the men. I think it's the least we can do.'

'I know what you mean. We can never know what it's like to be in it, but at least it gives us some idea. It will certainly help me appreciate what Norman has been through, when I finally see him.'

'I can't understand why he hasn't already written to you. And you've heard nothing more from Florence?'

'Not a thing. I had thought of calling by their house last week, on my day off, but... I don't know, I didn't have the courage to.'

'But you've met his family before.'

'Only a couple of times though.'

Edie was fiddling with her hat, standing in front of the square mirror she'd bought recently for the top of their drawers. 'Lili, I wonder...'

What was coming now? Something, by the tone of her voice.

'Do you think you're doing the right thing, giving up Rhodri? You seemed, well, very fond of him. And I thought you'd recovered from Norman's disappearance. You're not being too hasty, are you?'

'I have thought about this.' She'd done little else in her spare time. 'Heartbroken, I was, when Norman enlisted. More so when he went missing. Yes, time had healed that, but when he comes back I will feel the same about him again. Why wouldn't I, since I felt it the first time?'

'I don't know. When you've talked of Rhodri to me, you've always had more of a... sparkle – that's the only way I can think of putting it – than you did when you spoke of Norman.'

'Oh, that's nonsense,' said Lili, shaking her head. 'Of course I didn't. What does that even mean – a *sparkle*?'

'I don't know. You know best how you feel, of course.'

She wasn't at all sure she did, but she wouldn't admit that. 'Are you ready then?'

'Yes, I'm ready.'

Their walk to the Electric Picture Palace brought back her last meeting with Rhodri. She wished the film had been showing at the Empire on Church Street instead. Outside the picture house there was a queue. Lili felt a moment's hesitation when she wondered whether to tell Edie that she'd changed her mind. But no, she'd feel guilty doing that. As she and Edie had said, the least they could do was see what it was like for the men. The queue started moving and it wasn't long before they'd entered the building.

There was no turning back now.

–

The Battle of the Somme had been a harrowing hour and a quarter. Lili was glad of the fresh air and sunlight when they emerged back on Terminus Road.

'I'm still glad I saw it,' said Edie, beside her, 'but I wouldn't want to see it again. What a terrible place a battlefield is. And what a place to be living, month-in, month-out, year-in, year-out. And that was filmed in summer. Can you imagine what it would be like in winter?'

'My thoughts, too,' said a woman standing near them. 'My poor Walter. And to think what we saw was all real, none of it acted.'

'Come on lovey, you could do with a cuppa tea,' said the woman with her, putting an arm through hers.

'I could do with a trip down High Street, to look in Freeman, Hardy and Willis for a new pair of shoes,' said Edie. 'If that's all right with you?'

'Yes. A bit of window shopping might take my mind off what we've just seen, for a while at least.'

'Indeed. I thought the film would help me understand more what Charlie and my brother are going through. Now I'm just more worried.'

They dawdled down High Street, glancing in the windows as they went, talking every now and then of how there seemed to be even less in the shops now than there had been a few months back. The rest of the time they were silent. Lili assumed that Edie, like her, was reflecting on what they'd seen in the film.

'It can't be easy for the shopkeepers,' said Lili.

'No. We're fortunate that the richer members of society can still afford to come to the hotel. Though – with the continuing presence of the U-boats around the coast, and a struggle to grow and produce all the food we need – I do wonder how long it will be before the hotel is struggling too.'

The thought depressed Lili even more. If the hotel went bankrupt, or even if it was just struggling, jobs would be lost and she'd do, what exactly? Marry Norman and be a housewife? It's what she had wanted. But she wanted to work too, even if only part-time, like some of the married live-out staff they had. For many it was necessary, now that their husbands were away fighting.

They were standing outside Townsends Bazaar at the other end of High Street, looking at the china in the window, when Edie said: 'Isn't that Florence Stubbs, coming out of the chemist?'

Lili looked at the shop opposite. 'Yes, it is. She must have just finished a shift.'

'Why not ask her if they've heard from Norman again.'

But before Lili had the chance to get her attention, Florence had seen her and had crossed the road. She glanced around, looking awkward, before saying: 'Hello Lili. I went to the hotel this morning, but the desk clerk there said you were on a shift and I couldn't speak to you.'

'That would be Mr Watkins,' said Lili. 'He didn't tell me anything.'

'I thought not. He didn't seem pleased for me to be there and told me not to come in the foyer again.'

'I'm sorry about that, Florence. He's a bit of a snob, I'm afraid. You have news for me then?'

Norman's sister looked around the area again, her brow creased.

'Is there a problem?' said Lili. 'Is Norman still all right?'

'He's... he's changed, Lili. I don't know if it was the knock on the head. Or the war. It's just that, well, oh dear...'

'Isn't that him, coming down East Street?' said Edie, leaning sideways.

Lili looked around. Sure enough, there he was. But he wasn't alone.

Walking next to him, with her arm through his, was a young woman. A very pretty woman.

'Oh dear,' said Florence. 'I told Norman he should write to you and tell you himself. But he didn't seem to think it was necessary.'

'What's going on?' said Lili.

Norman spotted them, looking a little surprised at first. He spoke to the woman, then the two of them crossed the road diagonally to reach Lili and the others.

'Hello Lili,' Norman called. 'Fancy seeing you here. Hello Edie. We meet again.'

'And who is this?' said Lili, indicating the woman, who was beaming.

'Let me introduce you to Meline. She was working in the French hospital where I ended up. She nursed me back to health after I came out of my coma.'

'And before, *mon cher*,' said Meline. 'But you do not, 'ow you say, *souviendrais*.'

'Remember,' said Norman. 'See, picked up a bit of the lingo while I was there.' He grinned.

'I'm sorry if I seem rude,' said Lili. 'But I really don't quite understand. *Who*, exactly, are you?'

'I am 'is wife. We were married last week.'

'Yep. We arrived in Blighty yesterday. My family weren't 'alf surprised.'

'Excuse me!' said Lili. 'When you left, you were *my* sweetheart. You never broke it off. When you went missing, presumed dead, I was… *devastated*. And you didn't have the decency to write to me and tell me you didn't want to court me any more?'

Meline's eyes widened and her mouth hung open, as she regarded Norman. 'What is zees, Norman? You never told me.'

'I do think you are rather out of order,' said Edie, glaring at him.

'There, I told you,' said Florence, crossing her arms as she regarded her brother.

'What? It's been a year,' said Norman. 'I thought you'd have forgotten me long ago. To be honest, I could barely remember our relationship when I awoke. And it were love at first sight with Meline.' He turned his head sideways and a silly grin appeared. She squeezed his arm affectionately, but her half-hearted smile didn't reach her eyes, which were narrowed in uncertainty.

'That is not an acceptable explanation! You have acted like, like… a *rotter*!' Lili's volume rose during the sentence, ending on a shouted last word, garnering odd stares from people nearby.

She turned her head to look at Meline. 'I hope he treats you with more consideration.'

Lili twisted around and stormed off, catching only a glimpse of Edie giving Norman a piece of her mind. She raced around the corner and up Beach Road, having no idea where she was heading. The hotel would be quick to get back to from here, but she couldn't face it yet. She'd reached the tiny public garden with the fountain, close to where six roads met, before stopping to take a breath. Her head was swimming with all that had happened during the past few weeks. She'd given Rhodri up – and for what? For something she hadn't even wanted. And Norman hadn't given a fig about her.

She'd been there a few minutes when Edie caught her up.

'Would you prefer to go back to the hotel?'

'No,' said Lili, still shaken by what had just happened. 'I want to go to the tearoom on Pier Road, as we planned. Then I'd like to go for a walk to shake off the awful scenes in the film and Norman's *very* bad behaviour.'

'I think it's time to forget Norman.'

'I couldn't agree more. I should have been as inconsiderate as him in the first place.'

'You don't mean that, Lili. That's not the kind of person you are.'

'No, because I have respect for people. Norman clearly doesn't. I wish I'd seen that side of him before. It's so different to the way Rhodri behaved. He tried to do the decent thing.'

'You know what I was saying earlier, about whether it was the right thing to give up Rhodri.'

'You were right. I feel so much more for him than I did for Norman. I did from the moment I saw him. I know that sounds daft, but it was like, I dunno, like I'd been waiting for him all my life.'

'That doesn't sound daft. You need to contact him.'

'But it were him what broke it off.'

'Only because he thought you and Norman wanted to be together. It turns out that neither of you do.'

'But what if Rhodri were using Norman's return as an excuse.'

'Does Rhodri's behaviour towards you up to that point suggest as much?'

'No.'

'Then the only way you can find out is to contact him and tell him. Ask Helen if you can use the telephone again. I'm sure she'll let you.'

Lili nodded. To contact Rhodri was what she wanted. More than anything else.

Chapter Twenty-Eight

Dinner time for the guests was due to start in under an hour by the time Lili and Edie returned to the hotel. Lili wasn't working in the restaurant until later in the evening, but Edie was due to take over from Helen at the desk in the foyer at six o'clock.

When they entered the staff area, Edie said: 'Why don't we go and see Helen now and you can ask her if you can use the telephone.'

'I don't know. Would she mind me coming through to the foyer?'

'You've worked on the desk in that skirt and blouse before, so I don't see why not.'

Lili wasn't sure, but she nodded anyhow. 'All right. The sooner I sort it out the better, I s'pose.'

On entering the foyer, they noticed a man in an army uniform marching towards the desk, where Helen was smiling to greet him. He must be a captain by the three metal star buttons on the cuff of his sleeve.

'Good afternoon, sir,' said Helen. 'How may I help you?'

'Good afternoon, madam. I am Captain Carmichael and I believe my wife, Lolita Carmichael, is staying here.'

Edie and Lili glanced at each other, widening their eyes, as they waited to one side of the desk. So, he really did exist!

'That's right, Captain. In fact, I believe she is still sitting in the conservatory, if you'd like someone to show you through?'

'Yes, yes I would. Thank you.'

'I'll see if I can find out where the porters have got to.'

'It's all right, Mrs Bygrove, I will show the Captain through,' said Edie, stepping forward. 'This way, sir.'

As they entered the dining room, Lili went to the desk. Since there was no one else around, this was her opportunity.

'Lili, what can I do for you?'

'Well, it's a bit of a story, but you see, Norman's now back in Littlehampton. We saw him today.'

'So you'd like some time off to spend with him before he returns? If he returns?'

'No, no, that's not it.'

At this moment, Edie came hurrying back into the foyer. 'Come and hear this!'

'You go,' Helen told Lili. 'I'd better stay on the desk.'

Lili followed Edie back, where they stood by the door into the conservatory, listening.

'I'm sorry, so sorry, Lolita,' said Captain Carmichael. 'I know you think I acted inappropriately. And I will apologise a thousand times, if it helps. You were right: I was taken by Miss Beauchamp's charms, but I honestly didn't start any kind of affair with her. You must believe me.'

'Then why, Clifford, did you enlist after you were found out?'

'Because you told me to leave and never come back. And, being a former soldier, the sensible thing to do was to join the fray.'

'I heard you'd joined one of the South Downs battalions and taken your previous rank of Captain.'

'Yes. I thought, without you, I might as well dedicate my life to this country. My sister told me you came here a year ago. Why are you still here when you have our lovely house in Kemptown.'

'In which your sister still lives. Without you there, it didn't feel like my house any more. And she is not much company – always in her rooms, reading or sewing. Always slightly disapproving of me. I was lonely and there are always people here to talk to. Socialising in Brighton did not make up for it. And I didn't know if other people there knew what had happened. I missed you, despite what you did.'

'But I *didn't* do it. Oh, you must believe me, my darling.'

Lili and Edie risked peeping around a little more and saw him going down on one knee.

'Oh, I do, Clifford. I do.'

'Then come back to Kemptown, Lolita. I'm on leave until Sunday.'

'I will Clifford. I will.'

They stood and fell into an embrace. Edie crossed her arms over her chest and smiled, then indicated with her head that they should leave. 'I guess we'd better get Lolita's bill ready.'

On entering the foyer, Helen waved them over. She looked excited about something.

'Edie, Gertie's just told me that Charlie is here, in the dining room. He's on leave for a few days.'

'Oh my, he never wrote to tell me,' said Edie. 'But I'm on desk duty soon.'

'No. Go and talk to him. I'll stay on the desk. You can do my later shift as a swap.'

'Are you sure?'

'Yes, I'm sure.'

'Thank you.'

As Edie headed to the staff area, Helen said: 'You were telling me about Norman.'

'Yes. He's married someone else—'

'He's *what*?'

'And, to be honest, I'd rather be with Rhodri, so I'm not sad, and it's good that he's alive and...' She was rambling. 'To get to the point, I'd like, if I could, to ring Rhodri to tell him.'

'Of course you can. I've been wondering, since you told me, whether you were doing the right thing in letting Corporal Morgan go. You're welcome to use the telephone in the office.

Go now. You've got next Tuesday off, haven't you? The sooner you see him, the better.'

'I have, but it depends whether he can get that day off too.'

'We might be able to swap things around, if he can't.'

'Thank you, Mrs Bygrove.' She was about to head off when she remembered something. 'By the way, I think Mrs Carmichael will be wanting her final bill.'

'It's about time,' said Helen.

–

It took a while for the operator to get a reply from Rhodri's telephone, but finally she was put through.

'Corporal Morgan speaking.'

'Rhodri, it's Lili. I 'aven't wanted to be with Norman for quite a while now. I've wanted to be with you. Him being back wouldn't have made any difference to that. But if it's that you'd already decided you didn't want to be with me, I'll understand but—'

'Whoa, whoa, Lili. Slow down. I didn't walk away when we last met because I didn't want to be with you. I just thought it was fair for me to free you, so you could be with Norman. I thought I'd spare you the ordeal of being afraid to hurt me.'

'No, it's not like that at all.'

'It's all right, Lili. You can tell me when we meet up.'

'You will meet me, then?'

'Of course I will. I didn't want to give you up.'

'I've got next Tuesday off, if you can make it.'

'I haven't had a day's leave since I last saw you, so I'm sure I can arrange it. And I am looking after the rota at the moment. Unless I ring the hotel and leave a message saying otherwise, shall we say one o'clock, somewhere?'

'By the swing bridge.'

'By the swing bridge it is. I'd better go. The sergeant's just coming in. Cheerio, *fy annwyl*, Lili.'

'Cheerio, Rhodri.' She put the receiver back on the hook. The rest of the story would have to wait until next week.

Fy annwyl, Lili. My darling Lili. She liked him calling her that. She liked it a lot.

–

Several staff members were in their dining room for middle supper when Lili arrived, relieved and happy to have arranged a meeting with Rhodri. But as she entered, she could tell the mood was sombre, despite Edie being reunited with her sweetheart.

'Charlie's just started to tell us about the battle Alex, James and Anton were killed in,' said Jack, his head in his hands as he leant his elbows on the table.

'Battle of the Boar's Head, it was,' said Charlie, who was staring down at his hands. His voice was flat.

'So, what happened?' said Jack. 'There's not been anything much about it in the newspapers.'

'Nah, there wouldn't be. It all went horribly wrong. Our commanding officer, Colonel Grisewood knew it would. He told the Divisional Commander and someone overheard, so it got back to us eventually. It were some foolhardy plan to make the three South Downs battalions a diversion, to make the Germans think we was making that area the main offensive, instead of the Somme.'

'Are you supposed to be telling us this?' said Mrs Leggett, in her seat at the end.

'Don't bleedin' care either way. Done up like kippers, we was. We started training for the offensive, behind the lines. Only had days when we should have had weeks. And they also changed the plan. Us in the 11th were meant to take the lead. The 12th were on our right and the 13th in reserve. After Grisewood complained that he wasn't sacrificing his men, they swapped us with the 13th, so *they* led.'

'So that's why James, Alex and Anton were killed,' said Edie.

'Not just them. The 13th was more or less wiped out with the deaths and casualties. There was a hidden dyke in no man's land that made crossing difficult and they ended up in hand-to-hand combat with the enemy. Brutal it was. They couldn't send in reinforcements 'cos it was so bad. Majority of the officers were killed or wounded and the NCOs had to lead then. Finally, the battalions were driven back, but only after hundreds of men were killed. They reckon a thousand or so were wounded or taken prisoner.'

Jack let out a long whistle. 'How many men were in those battalions?'

'About four-and-a-half-thousand.'

'So, if they'd sent the 11th in first, as they'd planned, *your* battalion would have been the one wiped out,' said Edie, her hand on Charlie's shoulder.

'Yes.' His head went down, almost on his chest. 'We didn't get away scot-free either though.'

'Oh Charlie.' Edie put her arms around him now.

He lifted his head once more and regarded those there. 'Lowther's Lambs is what they nicknamed us – on account of the battalions being formed by Lieutenant Colonel Lowther – but lambs to the slaughter we was.'

'Charlie, I don't suppose you know if Freddie and his friend Daniel are all right?'

He took Edie's hand and looked up at her. 'I don't, sorry. It's been such chaos the past coupla weeks, with loads of men sent home on leave while they sort things out. I only know that Joseph, Alan and Peter from here are all right. Dunno about our lot in the 12th neither.'

'So there could be more casualties,' said Jack. 'It doesn't bear thinking about. At least we know Leslie, Stanley and Stuart are all right, since they're still training. Wish I could get out there and help out.' His mouth went down at the corners.

'Nah, ya don't. It's bleedin' awful. And you're doing your bit with the Voluntary Training Corps. If Britain's ever invaded, it'll need men like you to defend it.'

'I'm glad you're all right, Charlie,' said Lili. 'When are you due back to your battalion?'

'Next Monday. Lord knows what we'll all be going back to. And it'll take a while for some of the wounded to rejoin, if some of them ever do. Reckon we'll be in the back lines for a while. I hear Norman's alive. He was in the 13th, wasn't he?'

'That's right. He was lucky, in a way, to have been lost for a while.' She didn't really want to talk about that here, but she'd have to tell people eventually and now was as good a time as any. 'He's back on leave in Littlehampton now. Brought a French wife back with him.'

There were gasps of surprise around the room.

'It's fine,' said Lili. 'I have a new sweetheart, anyway, having believed Norman dead for so long.' *Fy annwyl.* She kept hearing Rhodri's voice in her head speaking the endearment to her.

Edie whispered something to Charlie and, after he nodded, she said: 'We're going for a walk.'

Lili took Charlie's place at the table after the pair had left. She wanted to feel happy. She *was* happy about her and Rhodri. And, despite how selfish he'd been, she was glad Norman had survived. But it always seemed that with some happiness came an equal dose of sadness with this war.

At least she was seeing Rhodri next Tuesday. She'd concentrate on looking forward to that.

Chapter Twenty-Nine

Lili was early the following Tuesday, hurrying as she had to their meeting place, filled with eager anticipation. She stood in the middle of the swing bridge now, awaiting Rhodri's arrival. The sky was blue, the air was warm, and she was filled with a contentment she hoped would last forever. She stood and watched as a steamship trudged downriver towards the mouth. How she missed the old regal sailing ships, of which there were fewer now than there had been when she'd arrived in Littlehampton in 1911.

Appearing around the bend, in the distance, was a naval vessel, one of the blue, grey and white camouflaged ships. She'd have to move off the bridge for they'd be opening it soon for the ship to go through. As she crossed over the road, towards the Steam Packet public house, she spotted Rhodri walking up River Road.

She waved and ran towards him, her heart thumping. 'Hello Rhodri. I had to come off the bridge as there's a ship coming.'

'Lili.' He caught hold of her hands. 'I was so happy to get your phone call. Are you sure about this?'

'Oh yes, absolutely sure. I know you were trying to do the right thing and so was I, but I've so much to tell you.'

'And I you.' He looked worried for a moment. 'I'm sorry that I went off in a hurry after the pictures. I'd been thinking about it all the way through the films and it just seemed like the decent thing to do. I should have talked to you... found out whether you really wanted to be with him.'

'I thought I was doing the right thing too,' she said. 'But a lot has happened, and I realised I really had got over him. And I found out the most extraordinary thing.'

'Look, why don't we go and get some refreshments, and you can tell me the story. There's a nice tearoom at the end of the High Street, next to the Cypress Hotel. I had a heck of a journey on the train today and it was packed with soldiers on leave.'

'I'd like that.' They started walking towards Surrey Street. 'A lot of the Sussex battalions are coming on leave after the Battle of the Boar's Head. Charlie, from the hotel, went back yesterday, but we've had a few who worked in the hotel before enlisting who've been on leave and come to see us during the week.'

'I gathered that something has happened out there and that those battalions are out of service. The men I saw all looked very down at heart. They didn't seem inclined to say much.'

It seemed Rhodri didn't know as much as she did. Charlie had asked them, when he and Edie had returned from their walk, to keep what he'd said to themselves, so she couldn't tell him what she knew.

As they passed Rhodri's house, the door opened and his Aunt Charlotte stepped out. 'Ooh, I didn't expect to see you here. I assumed you'd be going for a walk on the other side of the riverbank.'

'The bridge was about to open,' said Lili.

'Where are you heading?'

'To the High Street,' said Rhodri.

'I'll walk up to Groom's with you as I need some groceries. If that's all right.'

'Of course.' What Lili wanted to tell Rhodri would have to wait until they were alone again.

On the bit of the High Street that met with the top of Surrey Street, Auntie Charlotte bid them farewell and entered Groom's. They were about to walk away when Lili saw a familiar face come out of the shop.

No, surely not again! It was like she couldn't escape the Stubbs family.

'Lili?' said Norman's mother.

'Hello, Mrs Stubbs, I'm so sorry, but I'm in a hurry.' Not that she was, but this could only be embarrassing.

'That's all right, me too.' Despite saying that, she lingered in the doorway.

'Is that Norman's mother?' Rhodri whispered.

'Yes.'

'We've finished here, Mum. Come on, let's go,' came a voice behind the older woman.

Mrs Stubbs came backwards out of the shop once more, followed by Norman, in uniform, and Meline.

'Oh no,' said Lili, about to walk away.

'What's up?' said Rhodri, clutching hold of her hand.

'Oh, it's you, is it?' said Norman.

'Is that Norman?' said Rhodri.

'Yep, I'm Norman. And who the devil are you?' He marched up and must have noticed Rhodri's chevrons. 'Sir.'

'I'm Corporal Rhodri Morgan, soldier. I heard you'd gone missing. Good to know that you were found.'

'So, you have a sweetheart?' said Norman, ignoring Rhodri's comment.

'Yes, yes I do.' Lili felt defiant, yet knew she had to keep calm. This wasn't how she'd wanted Rhodri to find out, but there was nothing she could do about it now.

'Then why were you so cross with me for getting married?'

'Getting *married*?' said Rhodri.

Meline came forward. 'Why bother, *mon cher*, it not matter now.'

'Yes, it does matter, for who knows if he might do the same to you one day.' Lili knew this was a little cruel, but she was angry at Meline too, even though it wasn't really her fault. 'I was cross because *he* didn't even have the decency to write and tell me what had happened, and we'd been courting for nearly a year before he went missing. And I split up with Rhodri when I found out he were alive, because it were only right.'

'Were you courting with Norman though?' said Meline. 'He says you were… exaggerating.'

'I certainly was not exaggerating!'

'Norman, you said you only were, 'ow you say, walking out, sometimes,' said Meline.

'We saw each other whenever we could. I met his family at Christmas. We wrote to each other. He treated me as if we were courting.'

'Wouldn't call it courting,' said Norman, in a sulk, like he was a young lad. 'It was only for the four months before I enlisted.'

'You were courting,' said Mrs Stubbs. 'That's what you told me.'

'Mum!'

'You shouldn't have lied about it, Norman. You should tell the truth and shame the devil.'

Norman at least had the decency to go red with embarrassment.

'You were out of order, son. Florence and I did tell you that. You should at least apologise.'

'Come on, Norman,' said Meline, pulling him away. 'We go.' They marched away, her saying something rapidly in French.

'I'm sorry about what happened,' said Mrs Stubbs, head tipped to one side.

'It's not your fault,' said Lili. She took Rhodri's arm. 'Let's get ourselves that cup of tea.'

They'd walked a few steps when he brought them to a halt. 'Can we go back to the river? Let's walk down to Fisherman's Quay.'

'All… right.'

He walked a little ahead, leading the way down Surrey Street and on to Pier Road, before they turned on to the quay. They said nothing as they walked.

Rhodri strode past the Britannia Inn, the pebbles crunching beneath his feet, until he reached a space between the lobster pots and the rowing boats close to the warehouses. There were no fishermen here currently. She stopped next to him.

'You found out he was married?' Rhodri was frowning.

'Yes. I found out the day I telephoned you. We came across him in the town. I wanted to tell you then, but you had to go because of your sergeant coming into the office.'

'Really. So it wasn't that, having found out he was married, you wanted to get your own back on him?'

'Oh, Rhodri, no. His marriage was neither here nor there. Only that he'd been a coward and hadn't written to tell me.'

'Or that I'm just your fallback sweetheart?'

'No.'

'Then why carry on being mad with him? Why not be glad? He's alive and you don't have to be with him.'

'I told you: because he was selfish.'

'Then you *were* getting your own back. Did you know he'd be here today?'

'Of course I didn't. When I saw his mother, I was trying to get away quickly, remember?'

A few men came out of the Britannia, chatting. Rhodri moved a little closer to one of the warehouses, behind a horse-less cart. She followed him.

'Rhodri, I'd already grown very fond of you. You weren't second best or picked on the rebound. That day Florence told me Norman was back, I didn't know what to think. I assumed that you and I would talk about it after the pictures, but when you finished our day out early, I thought, well, maybe it was a convenient way of dropping me.'

'Lili, that was the last thing on my mind. The very last.' His head drooped and he shook it.

'Look, Rhodri, it's going to take a lot for me to tell you this, but… well, I think I fell in love with you that very first time I saw you, at the do for the wounded soldiers.'

347

'You did?' He straightened himself and stood in front of her.

'Yes. I know it sounds stupid and I felt so guilty, since Norman hadn't even gone missing then. So, I put it out of my mind. Or I tried to, but then it—'

He placed his forefingers on her lips to still her words. 'Lili, I felt the same the moment I saw you too. It was love at first sight. And such deep, searing love. I've never felt like this about any woman. But... to be honest, Lili, it's not just the thing with Norman.'

Oh no, what was coming now?

'I suppose I was using the situation as an excuse to spare you.' He looked away again. 'So maybe, when you rang, I shouldn't have agreed to meet. It was selfish of me.'

'I don't understand.' She felt her breathing hitching. She didn't want to cry in front of him, so she bit back the tears that were already stinging her eyes. 'I thought you were keen to meet up today. And you've just said you love me.'

'I was keen to meet up. I still am. And I do love you, I really do. But I have something to tell you.'

'Then tell me.'

'I'm... I'm going back to the Front.'

The tears now fell. She put her hands to her face. 'But... but you're still limping,' she sobbed.

He put his arms around her shoulders. 'Lili, don't cry. I'm not going to fight. There's a clerical role at one of the HQs near the front. I applied for it because I need to get back to doing something more useful.'

'But isn't it... useful, training new recruits?'

'Yes, of course. But I need to be more... involved.'

'It'll be more dangerous at HQ.'

'Of course, but that's the point. Someone's got to do it.' He pressed his forehead against hers. 'Do you still want to be my sweetheart after that news? It's up to you.'

'I'm sad. More than sad, that you're going back, but I do... see, I do love you. So of course I still want to be your sweet-heart.'

'And maybe, when the war is over, we could, we could… be more than just sweethearts? We could… be together forever.'

'Yes. I'd like that, Rhodri, I really, really would.'

Rhodri moved his head and looked around. The quay was quiet. He lifted her chin and kissed her lips, softly at first, then more insistently.

When they parted, he said: 'I love you so much, my Lili of the Valley. But I'll be off in the next fortnight, so this will probably be our last trip out for a while.'

'Then we'd better make the most of it,' said Lili, and they kissed once more.

A letter from Francesca

Thank you to all the readers who've sent lovely messages since the publication of *A New Start at the Beach Hotel*, the first in the series.

This time it was the turn of chambermaid Lili Probert to have her story told. Lili hailed from Wales, from a village I called 'Dorcalon', based on Abertwyssyg in Monmouthshire. Those of you who've read the Wartime in the Valleys series will recognise it as the setting of those books. I enjoyed revisiting the village with Lili once more, if only for a short while.

This era was a time of great change for women. With many of the men away fighting in World War One, women were given opportunities to take on jobs with more responsibility. And so it was with Lili. But the downside was that many women were missing their husbands and sweethearts, and Lili was no different.

This was also a time when people started to move away from the towns and villages their families had lived in for generations, to find new work and a better life. Lili chose to work a long way from home and from the rest of her family, in a time when you couldn't just whizz down the M4 in a car for a visit. Being so far from home, separated from her large family, had its drawbacks, as Lili would find out.

Like me, some of my readers from Littlehampton who remember the real Beach Hotel, sitting proudly on the common, regret its demise. It's been a pleasure being able to give it a new lease of life.

Do book in for another stay by the seaside early next year, when the staff and guests of the Beach Hotel will be back for another adventure.

If you'd like to contact me to discuss the novels, or discover more about them, I'd love to chat to you on social media here:

Facebook: www.facebook.com/FrancescaCapaldiAuthor/
Twitter: @FCapaldiBurgess
Website and blog: www.francesca-capaldi.co.uk/

Best wishes
Francesca xx

Acknowledgments

A big thank you to Keshini Naidoo, at Hera Books as always, and to the editors whose skills I appreciate.

Grateful thanks to the Library of Scotland for its fantastic archive of OS maps, which has been invaluable in researching the layout of Littlehampton and other towns in the 1910s. Also, to the Ancestry website for providing the 1911 census.